The
FLEDGLING

An Ursula Nordstrom Book

The
FLEDGLING

JANE LANGTON

HARPER & ROW, PUBLISHERS

NEW YORK

Cambridge
Hagerstown
Philadelphia
San Francisco

London
Mexico City
São Paulo
Sydney

1817

For Chris

Library of Congress Cataloging in Publication Data
Langton, Jane.
    The fledgling.

    Ill. by Erik Blegvad.
    "An Ursula Nordstrom book."
    SUMMARY: Georgie's fondest hope, to be able to fly, is fleetingly fulfilled when she is befriended by a Canada goose.
    [1. Canada goose—Fiction.   2. Flight—Fiction. 3. Fantasy]   I. Blegvad, Erik.   II. Title.
PZ7.L2717F   1980   [Fic]   79-2008
ISBN 0-06-023678-7
ISBN 0-06-023679-5 lib. bdg.

I think that no experience which I have today comes up to . . . the experiences of my boyhood. . . . Nature developed as I developed, and grew up with me. . . . In youth, before I lost any of my senses, I can remember that I was all alive. . . . This earth was the most glorious musical instrument, and I was audience to its strains. . . . The morning and the evening were sweet to me, and I led a life aloof from the society of men.

In Wildness is the preservation of the World.

HENRY THOREAU

CONTENTS

vii

CONTENTS

CONTENTS

THE PRESENT

The old goose found the present at Walden Pond.

The flock had flown all day, and all the night before, and all the day before that, migrating from their summer breeding grounds at Hudson Bay. Tired and hungry, they dropped to the still evening surface of the pond, splashing down in great foaming sprays of water, squawking at the tops of their lungs, *a-WARK, a-WARK!* Then, drifting silently like a majestic fleet of ships, they moved in the direction of the southern shore.

All but the old goose. Turning away, he paddled by himself to a sheltered cove on the other side of the pond, heading for a place he remembered from years gone by, a place where acorns were scattered thickly on the ground.

And then he saw the present.

It was bobbing in the shallows, floating in the water, bumping the alder stems, nudged by empty beer cans, brushed by downy pinfeathers that had scudded across the pond.

It was a bright object, moving up and down in the small lapping waves, glowing by itself in the dusky air.

The old goose had never seen anything like it. Journeying south, year after year, gazing down at the landscape streaming away below him, he had sometimes seen the Atlantic Ocean alight with glowing sea creatures. But they were not like this.

Carefully the old goose picked the thing up in his beak and carried it ashore. Then, waddling slowly up the steep wooded slope, he found the place he remembered, where ten stone posts stood erect in a shadowy clearing.

The thing was a present.

Something solemn and compelling in the air of the quiet clearing seemed to speak to him, to tell him that. It was a present, and he must give it to someone.

The old goose shuffled with his webbed feet in the dry leaves beside one of the stone posts, making a hollow place like a nest. Dropping the present into it, he covered the glowing surface with another thick layer of leaves. Then he waddled slowly back to the water, turning the matter over in his mind.

He must give the present to someone. Not just anybody. Oh, no! It was too good for just anybody. He must give it to someone who would understand how precious it was. Someone who would take good care of it. But who? That was the question.

GEORGIE

Georgie was reading a book on the landing of the front-hall stairs. The window on the landing was open. She looked up to see the wind tossing the branches of the big tree outside.

If one leaf touches another leaf, thought Georgie, it doesn't make any noise at all. But when all the leaves touch each other, the tree whispers all over.

Then she saw the big birds in the sky. They were flying over the tree, making a loud noise, *a-WARK, a-WARK!*

Oh, swans! thought Georgie.

She jumped up and watched the swans fly in a ragged line over the house. They were not white like swans in a book. They were white and gray and black. They were flying so low over the tree Georgie could hear the sound of the air flowing through their feathers. It made a soft noise, *sssh, sssh, sssh.*

If only I could fly like that, thought Georgie. If only I could do it again.

Because she had done it. She had. She knew she had. She had waked up in the middle of the night. She had jumped down the stairs in two great floating bounds.

Unless it was only a dream.

Georgie turned around on the landing and

looked at the twelve stairs falling steeply to the downstairs hall. Below her the bronze lady stood on the newel-post, gazing as usual out the front door, holding her light fixture in one upraised hand. Her light was turned off. The hall was dark.

Only the white marble head of Henry Thoreau glimmered in the watery gloom. Henry was a statue in the curve of the stairs, a carved bust on a tall stand. Everything else in the front hall was nearly invisible in the murky shade of the downstairs, but through the oval glass of the door Georgie could see a piece of the front yard.

The sun was shining brilliantly on the green grass beyond the porch, and on scraps of long legs and big feet and shorts and skirts and blue jeans. Georgie's mother and Uncle Freddy were teaching a Saturday morning class in the front yard. Teachers and students were sitting in a circle on the grass. It was Uncle Freddy's school. Georgie's mother and Uncle Freddy had a school, right here in the house, and in the front yard and the backyard, and sometimes they even held classes way up in the branches of the apple tree. It was a college, really, with a funny name: The Concord College of Transcendental Knowledge.

This year they were studying a book by Henry Thoreau, who had lived in Concord, Massachusetts, down the road at Walden Pond, a long time ago.

Uncle Freddy liked to pretend Mr. Thoreau

wasn't dead. He called him Henry, as if he were an old friend.

"Nice morning, Henry," he would say to the white marble bust in the hall, or "Henry, old man, listen to this," and then Henry would gaze wisely at the wall with his unblinking marble eyes as if he were listening with his stony ears and wondering and thinking it all over in his mind.

Georgie stood on the landing and listened. From the kitchen she could hear a murmur of voices and a clatter of dishes. Eddy and Eleanor were bumping around in the kitchen, having a snack.

She put her feet side by side on the top step. Then she took something out of her pocket and looked at it. It was a milkweed pod from the meadow across the street. Downy seedlings were puffing out of the pod. Georgie pulled one free, tossed it over her head, and blew it high. The milkweed seedling twirled, then wafted sideways like a fluffy parasol. Georgie took a deep breath and blew it down the stairs. Lightly it drifted halfway down, and then it was caught by a little draft from the crack around the front door. Up it went again. At last it floated against Henry Thoreau's marble ear and clung there.

I can do that too. Georgie put the milkweed pod back in the pocket of her red overalls. I know I can. Two big jumps. Just floating. I did it before. I think I did. I can do it again.

Georgie clenched her fists. I've got to. I've got to.

In the kitchen Eddy and Eleanor heard the *thumpity-bump* and the thin squeal.

"Oh, no," said Eddy, jumping up, "it's Georgie! There she goes again!"

"Oh, poor Georgie!" Eleanor ran out into the hall after Eddy. "Georgie, not again!"

Georgie lay in a heap at the bottom of the stairs, a jumble of red overalls and skinny arms and legs. Whimpering, she looked up at the two big faces bending over her with the light from the front door fuzzing around their hair. "Honestly, Georgie," said Eleanor. Gently she picked up Georgie and sat down with her on the bottom step. Georgie pressed her face against Eleanor's sweater. "Now, promise me, Georgie dear," said Eleanor, "you won't ever do it again."

"You crazy little kid," said Eddy. "You know you can't fly downstairs. I told you that the last time. Next time you'll break your neck. Nobody can fly downstairs. Jump, maybe—sure, you can jump. But you can't fly."

Eddy and Eleanor were much older than Georgie. They were like a king and queen, towering and majestic and kind. It was true that they shouted at each other sometimes, and even punched back and forth, or shrieked and slapped, but they were always nice to Georgie. "Look," said Eddy, "I'll show you how to jump, Georgie. Just move over. Come on, get out of my way."

"Don't push," said Eleanor testily, but she hitched over on the bottom step and squeezed up against the newel-post, while Eddy demonstrated exactly how far it was possible to jump down the stairs. His final mighty leap was a tremendous plunge from halfway to the second floor. Eddy thundered down with an enormous crash that shook the bust of Henry Thoreau. Then he staggered to his feet, breathing heavily. "Just try it a few at a time, you see, Georgie. Work your way up. But don't try it from the top. You couldn't ever jump from the top of the stairs. Well, maybe after years of practice, sure. But not now."

Eleanor was scornful. "Oh, Eddy, Georgie doesn't want to jump down the stairs. Look, Georgie, I'll show you something better than jumping. Something that feels like flying, it really does. Are you all right now?"

Carefully Eleanor set Georgie on her feet, and then she stood up too. "Watch this, Georgie." For a moment Eleanor stood erect, scowling at the thick dark air, and then she ran forward and made a mighty spring. In midair she whirled around, her orange pigtail flying, and then she came down hard at the other side of the dim, hollow hall, facing the other way. Breathing heavily, she grinned at Georgie, feeling pleased with herself. "There, you see, Georgie? Didn't that look like flying? It feels like flying, it really does." I should have gone on with those ballet lessons, thought Eleanor. I could be dancing before the whole world right now, instead of just my kid brother and my little stepcousin who may be going crazy. "When you flew downstairs, that wasn't real at all, Georgie. It was just a dream. I mean, come on now, Georgie, really."

Georgie stared at Eleanor and waited a minute. (Georgie often waited a minute before she said anything.) "Well, I guess so," she said. "Well, maybe." But she didn't really think it had been a dream. It had been so bright! It had felt so lovely! She had flown! Like the swans!

The jumping and dancing lessons were over. Georgie went out on the front porch. "I'm all right now," she said, shutting the door behind her. Then she opened it again and put her head back inside. "Thank you," said Georgie.

Eddy shook his head and grinned at Eleanor. "What a crazy little kid." Then he looked up quickly. There was a noise in the sky. "Listen, you hear that? It's geese, Canada geese!"

A-WARK, a-WARK! High over the town of Concord the great flock of sixty geese was banking and turning, flying back from Walden Pond to feed on the marsh grasses of the Great Meadows. Their wings pumped strongly. They made a waving pattern like an arrow in the balmy September sky. From wing to laboring wing they passed the creamy air, gabbling to each other in their hoarse strident talk.

Go DOWN! go DOWN! go WHERE? go THERE? where, WHERE? here, HERE? no, THERE! there, THERE! come DOWN! down, DOWN! right HERE? yes, HERE! down, DOWN! come DOWN! right DOWN! Far below them lay the town of Concord, its rooftops barely visible under the puffy green and yellow trees, the streets running straight and black, the rivers looping in round curves, flashing back the image of the racing sun.

The largest bird of all flapped heavily at the end of the line. No longer was the old goose flying with his mate, guiding another young family of excited half-grown fledglings from the blue northern lake where the goslings had been born. His mate had died long ago. He was a lone bird, old but mighty in wingspread, an outsider, traveling with a busy, clamoring flock of younger geese—mothers and fathers and children, sisters and brothers, cousins and uncles and aunts.

Now the old goose slowed the rhythmical beat of his wings and lowered his long black neck to stare down at the roofs of the houses running away below him. One house was different from the rest, odd and tall, with a tower at one side. Straining his bulging eyes, he saw a circle of men and women sitting in the front yard. Their heads were lowered. They were looking down.

A small red person was standing on the front porch, looking up.

For an instant the old goose wavered in his

flight, staring down at the small red spot. But then the circle of people in the front yard looked up too. They became a ring of white faces, gazing back at him, jumping to their feet, pointing upward. The old goose summoned the powerful muscles that flexed and stretched his wings, and caught up with the rest of the flock as it began its long gliding descent—down, down to the sheet of blue water and the sedgy marsh grass of the Great Meadows.

And all along Walden Street and Main Street and Monument Square, all the way down Monument Street to the North Bridge, people ran to the windows and looked up and smiled, pleased by the racket and the sight of the strong pumping wings against the sky.

"It sounds like fall," they said to each other. "When the geese come back, you know it must be fall."

WANTING THINGS

Fifteen students went back and forth to college classes in the big house at No. 40 Walden Street, but only five people lived there all the time:

1. Frederick Hall was the founder and president of The Concord College of Transcendental Knowledge. Concord College was the best place in Massachusetts—no, in all New England—no, no, more than that, it was the best place in the entire United States—oh, no, no, that's not enough, it was the best place in the whole wide world!—to learn about the wise men who had lived in Concord a hundred years ago, Henry Thoreau and Ralph Waldo Emerson and all their poet-friends and fellow thinkers.

Uncle Freddy was also the guardian of his orphaned niece and nephew,

2. Eleanor Hall, 14, and

3. Edward Hall, 12.

4. Alexandra Dorian Hall was not only the wife of Frederick Hall, she was his colleague and fellow professor. Before marrying Uncle Freddy she had been a student in

his school, a widow with a little girl. The
little girl was

5. Georgie Dorian. Georgie was eight years
old, but she looked much younger—six, or
even five—she was so small and skinny.

Of course, if you counted the animals that lived
at No. 40 Walden Street, the list could go on and on:

6. cat,
7. cat,
8. cat,
9. cat,
10. cat, and
11. cat.

And then there were the pieces of statuary
standing around the house. They were almost like
members of the family:

12. The white marble bust standing in the
front hall was Uncle Freddy's "Henry." In
real life Henry Thoreau had lived in a small
house at Walden Pond with all nature at his
doorstep, and he had written a book about
it, called *Walden or, Life in the Woods.* Of all
the books in the world, *Walden* was Uncle
Freddy's favorite.
13. "Waldo" (for Ralph Waldo Emerson)
was Henry's friend. He stood at one side of

the fireplace in the parlor.

14. "Louisa" (for Louisa May Alcott) stood on the other side of the fireplace. (Eleanor had once tried to marry Louisa's bust to Henry's, but Uncle Freddy had plunged in on the tender scene and forbidden the union.)

15. Last of all was the bronze woman standing on the newel-post of the staircase in the front hall, holding up her lamp like the Statue of Liberty.

There, that was it, the whole list of residents at No. 40 Walden Street. It was a long and confusing list. But under the high peaked roof and within the swollen porches of the house, the five human inhabitants felt like an ordinary family.

Ordinary? Uncle Freddy sometimes wondered if it was ordinary for Eddy and Eleanor to yell at each other so much, to be so often at each other's throats. Again and again he was shocked by the fury that shook the house. And then Aunt Alex would say, "It's just a phase. Don't worry, Fred dear. I'm sure they're just going through some sort of phase."

But now it was Aunt Alex's turn to worry. She was anxious about Georgie. Was something the matter with Georgie? Once again she had tried to fly down the front-hall stairs. It was the third time. It was a miracle that she had not yet been hurt. Aunt Alex sat at the table in the parlor, grading papers with Uncle Freddy, trying to focus her attention on Arthur Hathaway's first assignment of the college year. But all she could think about was her daughter Georgie.

On the other side of the table Uncle Freddy looked up at her and beamed. "My dear, you must read this paper of Millicent O'Toole's. I am truly pleased."

"You know, Fred dear," said Aunt Alex, staring through the gap in the parlor curtain at the stairway in the front hall, "she thinks she can fly. She really does."

"Millicent O'Toole?" Uncle Freddy was astounded.

"Oh, no, not Millicent O'Toole." Aunt Alex laughed. "Georgie."

"Oh, Georgie, yes, of course." Uncle Freddy put Millicent's paper down, and then he too looked through the gap in the parlor curtain. The pale bust of Henry Thoreau gazed back at him like the old and valued friend he was. "Poor Georgie," said Uncle Freddy. "She is too young to know the limits of human possibility. For Georgie, anything is possible! She lives entirely in the pure ideal. And, after all, why should we not have been born with wings?" Uncle Freddy crowed like a cock, *AR-AR-AROOOO!* Flapping his elbows, he thumped up and down in his chair like a giant bird. "It's too bad! What a terrible cosmic mistake!"

"But she wasn't born with wings," said Aunt

Alex, looking at him steadily. "And I'm really so afraid she may hurt herself. She's so certain. She really *believes* she can fly. It's because she *wants* to so badly. *Wanting* has turned into *believing*."

"Wanting?" said Uncle Freddy. "But look at Eddy. Do you know what Eddy wants? All the rocket models in the sporting goods store. He told me that. He wants them all. He's going to buy them one at a time and bring them home and sit up in his room, hour after hour, week in, week out, gluing them all together. That's what Eddy wants. What, I ask you, is going to happen to the boy's homework? And as for Eleanor, merciful heavens, when it comes to wanting things, there's no end to the things that Eleanor wants."

"But that's different. That's the way most children want things. But Georgie—" Aunt Alex hunched up her shoulders with worry. "Don't you remember when she wanted to learn to read? It was a passion with her. You remember—it wasn't just picture books. She was lugging that giant dictionary around with her. She *had* to read, she just *had* to. And she was only four years old! Well, that's the way it is now. She wants to fly. And she'll go on wanting it and hungering for it and jumping off the top of the stairs until she breaks every bone in her body before she gives up. She doesn't give *up*. That's the trouble. And this time no one can help her. How can anyone teach the poor child to fly?"

Uncle Freddy looked dreamily at his wife. "But

maybe she's right. Perhaps she really can learn to fly. After all, the child is hardly more than a wisp of thistledown. I sometimes wonder myself why the wind doesn't just pick her up and blow her away."

"She *is* awfully small and spindly for her age," muttered Aunt Alex. "You know the way she just picks at her meals. She eats like a bird."

"Well, perhaps the birds will teach her how to fly." Uncle Freddy exchanged a long, piercing glance through the parlor curtain with the bust of Henry Thoreau. "After all, my dear, you know what Henry said. The birds, he said, bore messages that were important to his life. *The sparrow cheeps to the great design of the universe!* That's what he said. The only reason we don't understand their language, he said, is because we are not one with nature. But Georgie is. Just look at Georgie!"

For once Aunt Alex wasn't interested in Henry Thoreau. "Eleanor thinks Georgie spends too much time by herself. She thinks Georgie should have playmates. Eleanor thinks—"

"Eleanor thinks!" Uncle Freddy jumped up and began striding back and forth on the worn parlor carpet. "Eleanor thinks too much. Eleanor doesn't understand. Georgie has a great many friends already. The birds, I tell you. The squirrels. The flowers and the trees. She is a child of nature, like Henry. Have you seen her little house in the bushes? It reminds me of Henry's, that famous little house that used to stand on the shore of Walden Pond.

Like Henry, she is basking on the bosom of Mother Nature! That's Georgie. Let her alone!"

Aunt Alex's grave face lighted up with one of her rare smiles. "Oh, Fred dear, that's what I said. That's what I told Eleanor. I said she should let her alone." But then Aunt Alex's face fell. "I wish she would forget about flying. I just wish she would."

THE BUSH HOUSE

A tangle of bushes grew around the place where the old summerhouse had stood. The summerhouse was gone, but there was still an empty place in the middle of the bushes. Long wiry stems of forsythia arched over it like a lattice roof.

It was Georgie's bush house. After school Georgie crawled into it, carrying her doll under one arm. She sat down cross-legged in a nest of leaves with the doll in her lap. Dappled sunlight fell on her face in flecks and splotches. It poured in round nickels and dimes on the sleeves of her jacket. The jacket was Eddy's. That is, it had once been Eddy's. With lordly generosity Eddy had handed it down to Georgie. The denim of the jacket was heavy like armor. Sitting in Eddy's jacket now, swallowed up in it, Georgie felt stiffened with some of Eddy's bold courage.

She listened. There were bird noises in the sky, light chips of sound far away, small sharp scissorings and snippings. They sounded high and thin, like the air. Another bird sang in the apple tree: *Pe-ter! Pe-ter! Pe-ter! Pretty-Pretty-Pretty!* He flew from the apple tree, jostled one of the arching stems over Georgie's head, landed on her shoulder! and flew away.

Georgie sucked in her breath. She sat very still. Would the bird come back? But he was gone.

She turned her head. Beside her cheek a smooth brown ball was stuck to a twig. Georgie put her ear against it and listened. She knew the ball was crawling with tiny bugs. But she could hear nothing but the cawing of a crow high overhead. A distant hum of traffic was the sound of cars and trucks on Route 2. A throb in the sky was a plane.

Georgie looked down. A green inchworm was crawling up her knee. She watched the worm inch his way over her doll and start a long journey up the sleeve of her jacket. She sat very still while he crawled up her neck and cheek. The inchworm tickled. Georgie giggled, but she didn't budge.

Georgie's doll was called Dollabella. Uncle Freddy had made Dollabella from an ear of Indian corn. He had scraped off the dried kernels and set them aside for the birds, and then, impulsively, he had pulled some of the husks back down around the empty ear. "Look, Georgie," he had said, "doesn't it look like a person? See, the corn husks are a cloak and the silk is her hair."

Georgie had clapped her hands and taken the ear of corn to her heart and named it Dollabella. She had wrapped Dollabella in oak leaves tied with a ribbon. "Now, isn't she pretty, Uncle Freddy?"

"Indeed she is. A little woman of character."

And it was true. The poor doll had no face, but she had a quiet, friendly personality all the same, altogether different from the flouncy chic of the rest of Georgie's dolls.

It was time to get to work. Georgie swept the floor of the bush house clean of last year's leaves, and spread fresh green ones flat for a tablecloth. Then she set the table with a collection of precious things from the pocket of Eddy's jacket.

Three yellow elm leaves, here and here and here. They were the plates.

Blades of grass in a heap on one of the plates. That was the salad.

Milky stones from the beach. Vanilla puddings.

Dried winged seeds from the maple tree. Cookies and crackers.

Acorn caps and tiny twigs. Teacups and spoons.

A burr basket stuffed with small flower heads from the wild asters that grew on the other side of the road. The centerpiece.

Georgie picked up an acorn cap and stirred the air in it with a twig. "Would you like some tea, Dollabella?"

"Thank you," squeaked Dollabella, "I don't mind if I do."

Georgie tipped the cup against Dollabella's face at the place where the mouth would have been if Dollabella had had a mouth. Then she picked up her own cup, threw her head back, drank her cup of air-tea to the dregs, smacked her lips, and smiled at Dollabella. "Isn't the tea delicious? How about a cookie, Dollabella?"

There was a rustling in the bushes. It was Eleanor, on hands and knees. "Oh, Georgie," she said, "what a nice tea party. May I come too?"

Georgie smiled broadly in invitation, and Eleanor crawled into the bush house and sat down beside her on the nest of leaves. Eleanor had just had a bath. Her hair was wet. She was hot and clean, with wrinkled fingers. Damp pinkness steamed from Eleanor and filled Georgie's bush house. "Why don't you invite some of your friends over, Georgie?" said Eleanor. "You know, from school. They could bring their dolls too."

Georgie waited a minute. "Well, all right," she said. But she didn't know if she would or not.

Eleanor was satisfied. "Oh, look at that," she said, picking up one of the maple seeds. "Those funny things from the maple trees. Look, Georgie, you know what you can do with these?" Eleanor pulled apart the seed and fastened it to the bridge of her nose. The dry wing of the seed stuck straight up. "See? It's like a rhinoceros horn. Isn't that great?"

Georgie picked up another winged seed, pulled

it apart, and fastened it to her nose. "It feels funny," she said, giggling at Eleanor.

"Oh, wow," said Eleanor, "here's something else. A grass flute. Wait till you hear this." She picked up a thick blade of grass from the plate of salad and stretched it carefully between her two thumbs. Then she blew on it. The grass made a soft hooting noise, like music.

"Oh!" said Georgie. She was enchanted. She tried it too.

Nothing happened.

"No, look, Georgie. You have to stretch it really tight."

Georgie tried again. This time a thin flutelike noise came from the grass. Georgie was thrilled.

The bushes thrashed. Georgie and Eleanor looked up, startled. A huge shaggy head was ramming through the leafy gateway to Georgie's bush house. It was Eddy's enormous friend, Oliver Winslow.

Eleanor was outraged. She fell forward on her hands and knees and shouted at Oliver. "Oh, no, you don't, Oliver Winslow. You get right out of here. Come on, get out right now."

"Well, well," boomed Oliver, grinning hugely, "what have we got here?"

Eleanor punched him in the shoulder. Then she leaned all her weight against him and shoved. "Go on, Oliver, you big dumb—just get out. This is private, strictly private."

But Oliver was colossal. He brushed Eleanor aside like a feather and bashed his way into the tea party. Lumbering on his tremendous knees, he crawled right over the tea table and sat down on Dollabella.

"Oh, no," said Georgie. She pounded Oliver with her skinny fists. "Oh, move over, oh, please, please."

Obligingly Oliver butted Eleanor out of his way and moved over. "Where'th my dolly?" demanded Oliver. "I want thum tea for my dolly."

Eleanor's face was bright red. Her hair was beginning to spring away from her head in fluffy orange tangles. She pummeled Oliver. "Out, out! Come on, just get right out!"

"No, wait," said Oliver, laughing, fending her off with one arm. "I've got a song. Wait till you hear. It's a nice song for the dollies' tea party."

"Oh, shut up, Oliver, you just shut up!"

Shrinking into her corner of the bush house, Georgie put Dollabella behind her back while Oliver held Eleanor's flailing fists at arm's length and bellowed his song.

Great green gobs of greasy, grimy gopher guts,
Mutilated monkey meat,
Little birdies' dirty feet,
Chopped-up chunks of little wormies' dirty teeth,
All in a bowl of blood!
All in a bowl of blood!

All in a bowl of blood!
That's my mother's newest tasty recipe,
All in a bowl of blood!

"Oh, Oliver, *stop.* You're absolutely *repulsive.*
That's just *disgusting.*" Eleanor punched and
shoved. Oliver began crawling heavily out the door-
way on his knees, doubled over with laughter. In a
wild scramble the two of them tumbled out of Georgie's house. The bushes snapped back.

Georgie stood up and peered over the arching
branches and watched Oliver pound down the cement walk to the street, roaring *All in a bowl of blood!*

Eleanor was rushing the other way, hurrying up
the porch steps, going indoors. Her face was
flushed. She was grinning!

Georgie was amazed. She sank back down into
her house and looked at the remains of her tea
party.

The burr basket was gone, fastened to Oliver
Winslow's pants. The leaf dishes were tumbled
every which way. Georgie sighed and got to work,
cleaning up. But she could find only one piece of
vanilla pudding, a single acorn teacup, and a couple
of maple seed crackers. Not a single blade of grass.
Georgie picked up what was left of the tea party,
stored it in the pocket of her jacket, and crawled out
of her bush house with Dollabella.

There was plenty of grass outside the house.
Where the bushes ended, the lawn began. It was

patchy and weedy and in need of cutting. Georgie put down Dollabella and plucked a long blade of grass. Then she stood up, arranged the blade of grass carefully between her thumbs, and blew. The grass trembled and issued its fragile sound, like a little horn, *hoot, hoot.*

And then, to Georgie's delight, there was an answering noise in the sky. She looked up. She had heard that noise before. It was the swans! They had come back! They were flying over the house! Their necks were stretched forward, long and black, their beating wings were gray, the sunlight on their chins and tails was a blinding white. They were shouting, *a-WARK, a-WARK!* Georgie counted them, one, two, three, four, five, six, seven, eight . . . she lost count. There were too many, a long undulating flapping row, flying in the direction of Walden Pond.

The last swan was the biggest. He was looking down at Georgie. He was! He was looking right down! And now he was slowing the beat of his wings; he was turning, tipping, dropping. Georgie gazed up at him and threw up her hand. Oh, swan, come down!

But there was a sudden commotion in the house. Uncle Freddy burst out on the front porch, shouting, "Geese, geese!" He stood on the porch staring up at the sky. "Oh, noble birds, welcome! I bid you welcome!"

Georgie's swan seemed to balk. He flapped his wings uncertainly, circling, and then he began to lift again, squawking, flapping strongly until he was high in the sky once more, then higher and higher, until he seemed as high as the racing clouds. In an instant he had vanished from her sight over the tops of the trees next door.

But Uncle Freddy continued to rant, quoting Henry Thoreau at the top of his lungs. *"Great birds that carry the mail of the seasons, welcome! In your wildness is the preservation of the world!"* When he dropped his arms at last, Georgie looked up at him dolefully.

"He was coming down," said Georgie. "The swan was coming down right here in our yard."

"Not swans, Georgie dear. Those were geese. Canada geese. They're flying south, you see. Stopping over in Concord on their way south." Looking down from the porch at Georgie's pinched face, Uncle Freddy suddenly felt clumsy. Somehow or other he had blundered. Flushed with his own foolishness, he didn't know what to say.

A car went by in the street. Another car. A motorcycle. Then nothing more. Everybody else in the world might have disappeared forever. "Well, I'll go in now, Georgie dear," said Uncle Freddy awkwardly. "My goodness, all at once it looks like rain."

Uncle Freddy opened the screen door and went inside. Then Georgie said, "Oh!" and bent down to pick up something from the grass. It was a feather. A grayish-white feather, fluffy at one end, smooth and shining at the other. It had fallen from the swan.

GEORGIE TRIES AGAIN

At suppertime it began to rain. The sky thickened with clouds like inkblots, and then raindrops began pelting down, drumming on the cement walk and the roof of the porch and the slanting wooden doors over the cellar stairs. There were rumblings of thunder. The dishes clicked and rattled on the shelves. Four cats meowed at the back door. Georgie opened the door, and the cats came streaking in, soaking wet.

Uncle Freddy was talking about the house next door. It had been sold, and the new owner had moved in. "I called on our new neighbor this afternoon," said Uncle Freddy.

"Who is it?" said Eleanor and Edward together, looking up eagerly from their dessert.

"Madeline Prawn."

"Miss Prawn?" They were horrified. "Oh, no, not Miss Prawn!" There were groans of dismay.

"Miss Prawn," repeated Uncle Freddy dismally. "Miss Madeline Prawn."

Miss Prawn was not popular with anybody at No. 40 Walden Street. She was the personal secretary of Mr. Ralph Alonzo Preek, the president of the Thoreau Street Bank. Mr. Preek wasn't anybody's favorite fellow citizen either.

Uncle Freddy tried to make the best of things. "Miss Prawn was out in her front yard today, digging up the grass. I think she's making a flower bed. Maybe it will be nice to look out the window at Miss Prawn's flowers."

"Oh, no, ugh, ugh," said Eddy. "Not if we have to look at Miss Prawn at the same time. I hope she digs a hole all the way to China and falls through."

Eleanor cackled and scraped up the last of her applesauce. "Down the hole with Miss Prawn!"

Georgie's applesauce was untouched. She gripped her spoon tightly, then put it down, and looked at her mother. "What do the swans do in the rain?" she said.

"Swans?" said her mother.

"Geese," explained Uncle Freddy, smiling at Georgie. "She means geese. Canada geese."

"Oh, geese, of course," said Aunt Alex. "Why, they're fine in the rain, Georgie dear. They're water birds, after all. Don't forget that."

"They've got this oil on their feathers, Georgie," said Eddy. "Goose grease."

"No, no," said Uncle Freddy. "Goose grease is when you have roast goose, and the fat collects in the pan, and then . . ." Uncle Freddy stopped and looked at Georgie. "Or then again maybe you don't. You wouldn't have roast goose unless it was the hunting season. I mean, right now it would be against the law to shoot a goose."

He was making it worse and worse. Georgie put

one spidery hand on his sleeve. "Do people shoot them? Do they really?"

"I'm afraid so," said Uncle Freddy sorrowfully. "But only during the hunting season. And the hunting season doesn't last long. But I agree with you, Georgie dear. Those noble birds! What a terrible thing!"

After supper the sky cleared. The air was fresh. The leaves were moist and dripping. A thin mist hung low between the trees. Faraway houses were dim. Trees loomed hugely in the fog.

Georgie came out on the porch after sunset, carrying Dollabella. The air was thick with dusk. It looked heavy and solid in layers of shadow. Thick enough to hold me up, thought Georgie, like the water in Walden Pond.

She put Dollabella down on the floor of the porch and felt in her pocket for the feather of the swan. No, no, it wasn't a swan. It was a goose. It was a goose's feather. Georgie stood on the top step of the porch stairs and tossed the feather over her head. The feather twirled airily and landed far away on the front walk. Then Georgie bent her knees and spread her arms to the side and jumped lightly off the porch. She came down beside the feather. She picked it up. Then she turned around and looked back at the porch. Had she lifted a little? It had felt nice.

Inside the house in the parlor Eleanor was making a dress. She was crouched over the sewing machine, driving her yellow cloth through it. The sewing machine felt like a motorcycle, and she was hunched over the handlebars, as the belt-driven wheel whirled and the motor buzzed and whined. Her foot pressed down on the button that lay beneath the table on the floor, then lifted and pressed down again. Start, *bzzzzzzzzzzzzzzzz*, stop, click the lever up, whip the cloth around, flick the lever down, start again, *bzzzzzzzzzzzzzzzz*. The yellow cloth was bright with orange splotches.

Eddy was doing his homework at the table. The homework was boring. It was only the second week of school, but he was tired of school already. In class he would slump down in his chair with his eyes half shut, trying to be invisible, but already his Social Studies teacher had learned to look sharply past everybody else and say, "Edward, what do *you* think?"

Eddy lifted his eyes from his homework and gazed dreamily out the window. Then he jerked up in his chair and stared. "Hey, Eleanor, did you see that?"

Eleanor didn't hear. Her dress was whizzing through the machine. The grinding of the motor pounded in her head. She didn't look up.

Eddy got out of his chair and parted the parlor curtain. The hall was dark. He put out his hand and felt the smooth round marble head of Henry Thoreau. Georgie was coming in the front door, noiselessly, like a moth in the gloom.

"Say, listen here, Georgie," said Eddy, "didn't I see you just now—"

"Oh, Eddy, look," said Georgie. She was holding something up for him to see. "I made Dollabella a new dress. See? It's ferns. It's all made of ferns."

"Oh," said Eddy, "Dollabella. Well, well. Good old Dollabella. Hurray for Dollabella."

Eddy dropped the curtain and went back to his homework. He must have been mistaken. He couldn't have seen what he thought he saw. That Georgie. She certainly was a nutty little kid.

THE EXPEDITION

Next morning before dawn the geese flapped up from the marshy water of the Great Meadows. In a frenzy of splashing and hoarse calling, they flew over the town and headed south in the direction of Walden Pond.

Uncle Freddy and Aunt Alex lifted their heads as the flock darted over the house, crying, *wake-UP, wake-UP!* Uncle Freddy smiled sleepily and murmured aloud, *"A clanking chain. A clanking chain drawn through the air."* (It was something Henry had said.) Aunt Alex smiled too, and then they both put their heads down and went back to sleep.

Eleanor half woke too at the sound of the geese. Groaning, she turned over and fell asleep again.

Eddy was a sound sleeper. He never woke up at all.

Only Georgie came fully awake as the geese flew over the house. Jumping out of bed, she ran to the window. And then she saw him. She saw her swan. Her own special swan. He was bigger than the rest, like a king or a prince. A swan prince! The Swan Prince was flying at the end of the flock. They were winging low over the housetops, their long necks stretched forward. Only the Swan Prince was looking down. Could he see her at the window? She watched him fly away with the others. He was trailing a little behind them, looking back.

Georgie stared at the empty sky. Where were they going? She thought about it for a minute, and then she knew. They were flying toward Route 2. Maybe they were heading for Walden Pond. Walden Pond was just down the road. She could go there. She would! She would walk to Walden Pond! She would walk there and be back before school!

Georgie turned to the rocking chair where her clothes were folded in a neat pile. She felt keen and fresh and wide awake. She pulled off her pajamas and got dressed in a clean jersey and yesterday's red overalls. Then she stopped and looked at her shoes and socks. Eddy's green rubber boots were in the coat closet downstairs. The boots would be better for an expedition. They would be too big, but she would wear lots of socks. Georgie pulled on three pairs of socks. Then she put her pajamas under her pillow and made her bed and laid Dollabella in the middle of the pillow. Padding softly downstairs in the silent house, she tiptoed into the kitchen to make herself a picnic breakfast. Carefully and quietly, pulling out the drawers slowly, setting things down on the counter softly, Georgie made a peanut-butter-and-grape-jelly sandwich, wrapped it in a paper napkin, and stuffed it into the bib pocket of her overalls. She put a ripe banana in one of the side pockets. Then she put away the peanut-butter jar and the jelly and left the sticky knife in the sink. One of the cats was meowing and rubbing against her leg. Georgie gave it a saucer of milk. Then she went to the coat closet under the front-hall stairs and opened the door. She pulled the string hanging down from the bulb. Light flooded the thick coats and the tumble of boots. The closet smelled of warm rubber and moth flakes and woolen cloth. Georgie put on Eddy's jacket. Then she found his big green boots. She sat down on the hall carpet and pulled them on. They were much too big, but the three layers of socks filled up some of the extra room, and they felt fine. Georgie stood up and walked to the front door, lifting up the big boots and putting them down as softly as she could. At the door she stopped. She was thinking of her mother. Her mother would be coming into her bedroom later on to wake her up for school.

Georgie crept back into the kitchen. Eddy's notebook was lying on the kitchen table. Georgie took a piece of paper out of it and wrote a note:

HAVE GONE TO FIND SWANS.

A moment later, closing the front door gently, Georgie remembered that they weren't swans, they were geese. It didn't matter. She didn't go back to fix it. She walked to the top of the porch steps and paused. Should she jump? No, her boots were too heavy for jumping. Softly Georgie walked down the three steps to the cement walk in front of the house and looked at the enormous star hanging low over the pink place where the sun was waiting to come up.

Georgie had figured it out. She knew what stars were. They were pinholes in the sky, letting the white fire shine through. This star's pinhole must be very large, the star was so bright.

It was a windy morning. Across the Mill Brook meadow Georgie could see the old elm trees on Lexington Road lifting the trailing ends of their branches and letting them go again. A brisk breeze was whipping down Walden Street.

She would take the shortcut. Georgie clumped past her bush house, past the laundry line, and started to walk through the yard of the house next door. Then she stopped short. She had forgotten that the house was no longer empty. It had been sold, and the new owner had moved in. The new owner was right there in her front yard, down on her hands and knees before dawn with a trowel in her hand, looking up sharply at Georgie.

It was Miss Prawn, Miss Madeline Prawn.

MADELINE PRAWN

Two things were more important than anything else in the world to Madeline Prawn:

1. Hard work
2. The finer things of life

Hard work was something Miss Prawn knew how to do. There was boundless energy in her thin, nervous frame. At the bank she worked very hard indeed, bustling from Mr. Preek's desk to her own, typing up letters and mortgage agreements and loans, running her bony finger down columns of figures, popping documents in and out of her tidy, well-organized files.

At home she worked even harder. In exactly two days Miss Prawn had rearranged all the furniture in her new house until it looked just right. She had pushed and pulled at chairs and sofas, shoving them here and there with all the strength in her stringy arms and wiry legs. She had banged up nails for pictures. She had dusted the pantry shelves and unpacked all her dishes and stacked them on the shelves.

So much for the hard-working part of Miss Prawn's daily life. The finer things were more spiritual. They were bits of sentimental poetry and albums of dark old pictures and folders of art songs spread out on the piano. They were

THE REVERIES OF MADELINE PRAWN

—a notebook with a padded silk cover. The pages of the notebook had once been blank, but now they were covered with inspirational thoughts. Sometimes Miss Prawn rummaged through books of sermons and poetry to find things to copy down. Sometimes she thought up her own. But *The Reveries of Madeline Prawn* was part of her hard-working life as well, because it was full of lists of things to be done *today*. She would consult her list and run from one thing to the next, hurrying back to the book on her desk to check off each item with a dashing stroke of the pen. Oh, the day was too short to get everything done! Miss Prawn got up early, terribly early, ridiculously early, to squeeze more accomplishments into every passing day.

This morning the first item on her list was

Plant Flowers

So Miss Prawn was planting flowers.

The flowers were white roses. She had bought them in the dime store the day before. They were all exactly alike, long stiff sprays with green plastic stems and white plastic blossoms.

It was five o'clock in the morning. The sky was still gray, only a little rosy at one side. The grass was wet. Nothing daunted, Miss Prawn put on her galoshes, took down her garden fork and iron rake from their new hooks on the wall of her garage, stuck a trowel in her pocket, and attacked the front yard.

She had already marked out a rectangle in the lawn. Now Miss Prawn forked out clods of wet grass and broke up the dirt underneath. Then she smoothed the dirt with the rake. At last she got down on her knees and began planting her plastic flowers with the trowel.

The child from the house next door gave her a turn.

Miss Prawn dropped her trowel. "Go away, little girl," she said.

Georgie was struck dumb. Her face flushed with embarrassment. Her feet were stuck to the ground.

Miss Prawn shook her head in irritation and picked up her trowel. "Oh, dear, now I suppose I've hurt your feelings. But look here, it's nothing against you personally. It's just that I don't like children. I mean, it's just part of my personality. Everybody has their own personal tastes. Some people don't like olives. Or fish. It's just the way they are. I myself don't happen to care for children. I mean, it's really not your fault."

Georgie nodded without a word and melted away into her own front yard. A moment later she was running down Walden Street with the wind at her back.

THE KIND INTERFERENCE OF MR. PREEK

It seemed sensible to Georgie, what Miss Prawn had said. People liked things and they didn't like things. Miss Prawn didn't like children. She, Georgie, was a child. She would try not to offend Miss Prawn. From now on she would stay out of Miss Prawn's sight as well as she could.

Georgie clumped in her rubber boots past the police station and the row of young maple trees that grew beside the road. The leafy heads of the trees were rumpled in the wind. The field across from the police station was full of enormous cabbages. Packing boxes for the cabbages were stacked beside the road. Georgie half ran and half blew past the maple trees and the cabbages and the cabbage boxes. Then she slowed down as the flat road began to go uphill beyond the high school. Sturdily Georgie walked up the hill. At last she came to Route 2. The traffic light hanging over the highway was red. There were no cars coming in either direction, because it was too early for the morning rush of cars to Boston. But Georgie waited patiently for the light to turn green, and then she galloped across the wide four-lane highway and stalked along the road beside the woods on the other side.

As she walked, she listened to her boots. Each

boot made two noises at every step, one when the foot inside the boot came down, and another when the rubber toe came down. *Ka-bump, ka-bump, ka-bump, ka-bump.* Georgie strode along firmly. She wasn't tired. There wasn't enough flesh on her light bones to weigh her down. She felt she could tramp onward steadfastly forever.

But perhaps she should stop for a snack. The smell of the peanut-butter sandwich in the bib pocket of her overalls was making her hungry. She would save the sandwich, but perhaps she could eat her banana right now. Georgie sat down on the dusty grass beside the road and peeled the banana and ate it slowly. Then she stuffed the peel in her pocket and reached out idly for a fat blade of grass. Putting it between her thumbs, she blew on it. *Hoot, hoot* went the grass.

A dog barked. Was it a dog? Georgie looked up. No, no, it was the swans. Not swans, geese! They were coming back! They must be flying back from Walden Pond. Flying away! Oh, oh, she had missed them!

Georgie flung up her arms to say, *Wait, wait.*

A-WARK, a-WARK! hooted the geese, flapping over Georgie's head, over the pine trees in the woods. And then, once again, the last goose in the flock fell back and veered away and dropped out of the sky toward Georgie. He was coming, he was coming again! It was the Goose Prince!

Georgie's lifted face shone in the flat rays of the

rising sun. Once again the great bird hovered over her, looking down at her with his round black eyes, making some sort of warble in his throat. She could see the delicate white edgings and the soft shadings of the gray feathers on his breast. She could feel the breath of his flapping wings on her forehead!

But then the goose was startled once again. A car was squealing its brakes beside Georgie, jerking to a stop, and the driver was beeping his horn in loud blasts.

Georgie's goose flew away. He flew straight up over the trees and disappeared, racing after the rest of the flock in the direction of Nine Acre Corner.

Georgie's face twisted with disappointment. She dropped her arms and turned to look at the car. A man was jumping out, running up to her.

"Are you all right, little girl?" He was bending down, the round gray mass of his face filling all the world.

Georgie stared up at him dumbly, tears running down her cheeks.

"That big duck, he was attacking you, didn't you see? It's a good thing I came along and had the presence of mind to honk my horn. A fine thing, when a little child isn't safe on the streets of Concord. I just wish I had a gun."

"No, no," sobbed Georgie.

"Just get in my car now, honey, and I'll take you home." The man still towered over Georgie. His hat and coat were made of fuzzy fur. The fur was shiny with tiny glittering fibers. His face was so close Georgie could see the black coarse lopped hairs on his chin. His cheeks were like the whitish-gray clay she made from flour and salt.

Georgie didn't want to get in his car. She shook her head and backed away. But the man put his arm around her shoulders and bundled her into the back seat.

"You're Fred Hall's little stepdaughter, isn't that right?" he said. "I thought so. I must say, I'm surprised Fred would let his little girl run around all over the place, crossing a big highway all by herself at this hour in the morning. Mind your own business, I always say, but just the same I'm a little surprised."

The man was Mr. Preek. Georgie had seen him in his bank on Thoreau Street. She was afraid of him. She huddled in the back seat and looked at the plump creases on the back of his neck as he zoomed his car across Route 2. Then she looked away from Mr. Preek and stared blankly out the window.

Ralph Preek would have been astonished to know that Georgie was afraid of him. Unlike his secretary, Madeline Prawn, Mr. Preek loved children. Well-behaved children. Polite, well-brought-up children. Chubby children with pink cheeks and golden hair. *I am the sort of man who loves children,* Mr. Preek often said to himself. And whenever his customers brought their children into his bank, he would open the gate that separated his desk from the windows of the tellers and stroll up to the children, beaming, and pat their heads and hand them lollipops. Some of the children would say thank you. They were the good children. Others would stop up their mouths with the lollipops and stare back at him sullenly. They were the bad ones. And then Mr. Preek's generosity would turn sour, and he would go back to his desk in silent scorn.

Now, looking in the rearview mirror at the small child in the back seat of his car, he felt the same disdain rising in his breast. The child was pitiful, a poor specimen, all skin and bone and lank pale hair. Just look at the way she was staring out the window with her lower lip hanging slack! She was probably stupid. You could always tell. She might even be retarded. It would serve Fred Hall right to have a backward child. The man was infuriating. Fascinating and infuriating at the same time. Oh, everybody always thought he was so clever, keeping a school! Calling it a *college*! When it was just a bunch of ragged tatterdemalions hanging around Fred Hall's front porch, pretending to be *graduate students.* As if that big ugly house on Walden Street were an accredited university. Which it wasn't. Oh, it made Mr. Preek so mad. And the place wasn't even solvent. The school wasn't making any money. As Fred Hall's personal banker, Ralph Preek knew that solid fact better than anyone else. And then, of course, as if the poor fool hadn't been in deep enough trouble already, Fred had gone and burdened himself with a family. He had married that widow-woman with the retarded child. Oh, the mess some people made of their lives!

Mr. Preek pulled his car up in front of Georgie's house and got out. He could have saved time by dropping the child on the sidewalk and driving away. But he wanted credit where credit was due. Shrewdly he suspected that Georgie might say nothing to her family about the kind man who had saved her life. Squeezing her delicate fingers tightly in his fat hand, he walked her up to the front porch and rang the bell.

But Eddy was just opening the door. Eddy was on his way to school with his knapsack on his back. Eddy took one look and shouted over his shoulder, "Here she is. Georgie's back."

Aunt Alex came running, her face flooded with relief. "Oh, Georgie dear," she said, "thank goodness." Then she recovered herself and smiled her ordinary motherly smile. "Did you find the swans?"

Georgie shook her head miserably. Tugging her hand free from Mr. Preek's grasp, she slipped in the door. The gloomy depths of the front hall swallowed her up.

Aunt Alex and Eddy were left alone with the bulky object on the front porch.

Mr. Preek was feeling neglected. "I just wanted to be sure, Mrs. Hall, that the child was all right. I mean, the poor little thing had such a scare out there on the road."

"A scare?" Aunt Alex put her hand to her mouth. "Georgie? Was it a car?"

"No, no, not a car. A duck. A giant duck attacked her from the sky."

"A *duck*?" said Eddy in disbelief.

"It attacked her?" Aunt Alex stared at Mr. Preek, and then she smiled. "Oh, surely not."

"I was there," said Mr. Preek. "I saw the whole thing." He frowned through the door at the white bust beside the stairs. The bust gazed back at him solemnly, and for a moment Mr. Preek was transfixed and almost forgot where he was. Then he blinked and shifted his eyes to the threadbare fringe of the parlor curtain. "I tell you, Mrs. Hall, I saw it with my own eyes. I was a witness. If I hadn't come along at that very moment and honked my horn, the bird would have knocked her down. Or snatched her up into the sky and carried her away. You hear about such things. But fortunately, by a stroke of luck, I just happened to be passing by. Quick as a wink, I knew what to do, and I honked my horn. It flew away. It was a whole flock. There were several hundred giant ducks."

"Giant ducks!" Eddy giggled. He edged around Mr. Preek and clattered down the porch steps.

"Well, I don't know," murmured Aunt Alex vaguely, staring past Mr. Preek, turning to watch Eddy jog around the corner onto Everett Street.

Mr. Preek was shocked. The woman wasn't taking the matter seriously! "Does Fred own a gun?" he said. "Look here, I'm going to get a gun myself. We can't have little children attacked on the streets of our own hometown. Something's got to be done."

"Oh, but you shouldn't," said Aunt Alex, putting out her hand. "Oh, I don't think—"

But Mr. Preek was turning away. He was lifting his puffy hand in farewell. "Oh, it's nothing at all, Mrs. Hall. Don't thank me."

Aunt Alex closed the door softly. "I didn't," she said.

THE GEORGIE PROTECTION SOCIETY

"Now, Georgie dear," said Uncle Freddy, "what's all this about a giant duck?"

Supper was over. Uncle Freddy and Eddy were doing the dishes. Uncle Freddy was washing the pots and pans, Eddy was drying the silverware, chucking forks into a drawer. Eleanor and Aunt Alex and Georgie were doing a puzzle on the kitchen table. The puzzle was a picture of the Bay of Naples, with a volcano erupting in one corner. Most of the pieces were the same color, blue water or blue sky.

"It wasn't a giant duck," said Georgie. "It was a swan. Oh, no! I mean a goose." Then Georgie jumped up from the kitchen table and ran to the window. A moth was fluttering up and down the window screen. "It was the Goose Prince," said Georgie. "He wants to be my friend." The screen came up with a jerk. The moth darted into the kitchen and began thumping its soft body against the shade of the lamp hanging over the table.

Aunt Alex stirred the pieces of the puzzle in the box. "A prince? A goose prince? He wasn't going to hurt you, was he, Georgie?"

"Oh, no." Georgie was shocked. She slammed down the screen. "You know what?" Plumping herself down at the table again, Georgie beamed at her mother. "I think he wants to teach me how to fly."

"Oh, Georgie, there you go again." Eleanor looked meaningfully at Eddy.

Eddy hurled the dish towel at the towel rack and rolled his eyes at Eleanor. "Oh, come on now, Georgie," he said, sitting down beside Eleanor, jabbing her in the ribs with his elbow.

"Ouch," said Eleanor, jabbing him back. But she knew what his elbow meant. He was reminding her of their new agreement, their secret pact. Eleanor and Eddy had organized a new club, the Georgie Protection Society. It had a membership of two. Its whole purpose was to help Georgie, because the poor little kid didn't seem to be able to help herself. The Georgie Protection Society would keep her from doing queer things. It would help her grow up to be all right. Normal, like other people. Not crazy and a little bit weird.

"Flying again, eh?" said Eddy, giving Georgie a friendly poke. "What a crazy little kid!"

Georgie smiled at Eddy and said nothing. Then she hooked together two blue puzzle pieces, and two more.

Eddy watched the puzzle fall swiftly into place under Georgie's clever fingers. It was funny the way she made him feel. She was only his stepcousin, after all, but for some reason he wanted to do things for her. He didn't know why. He certainly didn't feel that way about his sister Eleanor. Eleanor could take care of herself—altogether too well! Being the brother of Eleanor meant you had to be on your guard all the time, and grab the best half of something before Eleanor grabbed it herself. But it was different with Georgie. Georgie didn't know how to grab. She just took whatever was left over. She didn't stick up for herself at all. And now she seemed to be in some kind of funny trouble. So they had decided to do something. They didn't know what. They were going to keep their eyes and ears open. They would wait and see.

Uncle Freddy was sitting down at the table, completing the family circle. "So it's flying again, is that it, Georgie dear?" he said. "Are you sure, dear heart, that you really want to fly? Don't you think it is happiness enough to walk freely on the ground?"

Georgie smiled back confidently at Uncle Freddy. "Oh, but I already know how to fly. I mean, I think I do. I mean, I think I can a little bit." Georgie's face blanched. Her mouth turned blue around the edges. The moth battered itself weakly against the lampshade, and then it fell to the table and keeled over on its back. Georgie was transfixed by doubt. Could she fly or couldn't she? Deftly she reached out and tipped the moth right side up, and then she rose from the table and slipped out into the hall.

Eleanor shook her head as the door closed softly behind Georgie. "You know what Georgie needs? A friend. She should have friends her own age to play with. She needs to get her mind off flying." Eleanor scowled at Aunt Alex. "I'll tell you what I'll do. I'll ask somebody over myself. You know that little girl who lives right around the corner on Laurel Street? Dorothea Broom?"

Eddy recoiled in horror. "Oh, no, not Dorothea. Georgie doesn't want to play with creepy little Dorothea Broom."

"Now, look," said Eleanor. "Think about it. What if Georgie decides to fly off the roof?" Staring fiercely at Eddy, Eleanor pounded her fist on the table. The puzzle jumped and came apart. One of the cats leaped off Aunt Alex's lap and skittered across the floor. And then Eleanor stopped, frightened by her own question, remembering John Green. John Green had fallen off the roof a couple of years ago. It had been terrible. Horrible. He had recovered at last, but the whole thing had been ghastly. Absolutely ghastly.

Eddy winced and closed his eyes. Eddy remembered John Green better than anybody. How could he ever forget? "Well, all right. Go ahead and invite somebody over. But not Dorothea. Not gruesome little goody-goody Dorothea Broom."

"Now, listen, Eleanor dear," said Aunt Alex, "don't do anything yet. Just be patient. Not yet. Just wait."

The bronze figure on the newel-post was lighting up the front hall, just as usual, casting a warm radiance over the stair carpet and the white bust of

Henry Thoreau and the faded wallpaper and the picture of the clipper ship over the piano.

Georgie hesitated beside the white bust of Henry in the curve of the stairs. If he were alive, would he like children? Yes, decided Georgie, he would. And anyway, he *was* alive, even though he didn't get down off his tall stand and move around like other people. He was awake inside his marble whiteness. He was listening. He could hear what went on around him, Georgie was sure of that. She turned away, then glanced back at him quickly, trying to catch him off guard, hoping to see him yawn or blink or turn his head to look at her. But he was still gazing straight ahead at the wall in front of him.

Georgie went up close to Henry and stared into his marble eyes. They were wonderful eyes, so real! In the middle of each eye a ring had been carved, and in the center of the ring there was a deep hole. Henry's eyes looked big and sparkling and alive. Georgie moved closer still, until her nose was brushing Henry's, until his eyes melted away and gazed vaguely right through her, right through her own eyes and her own brain and out the back of her head and through the wall of the house and through the walls of all the other houses. Uncle Freddy said Henry was looking all the way across fields and highway and woods, all the way to Walden Pond and the stone posts where his house used to be. The question that was on Georgie's mind spilled over, and she murmured, "Henry, do you think I can fly?"

Then she backed away, and Henry's eyes came into focus again. He looked amiable and friendly. *Yes,* he seemed to be saying. *Yes, Georgie, you certainly can.*

Georgie turned away and stalked to the front door. But what if she had only dreamed it? And that big jump yesterday from the front porch, what if that was all it was, a big jump and nothing more, like Eddy's huge crashing leap from the front-hall stairs?

Putting an anxious hand on the knob of the front door, Georgie went out on the porch. She stood at the top of the steps and stared down at the cement walk in front of her.

In the kitchen they were still talking about Georgie.

"She's such a sober little person," said Uncle Freddy, shaking his head. "When she gets an idea into her little noggin . . ."

"I know," said Aunt Alex, looking at him solemnly. "She holds fast."

MISS PRAWN
BEHOLDS A MIRACLE

In the house next door, Madeline Prawn was sitting at her desk, feeling cozily surrounded by her things. Her front room was chockful of furniture and ornaments, lumped and puffed and cluttered around Miss Prawn in a padded kind of cushiony order. Flat things were fancy with doilies and cloths and shawls. Round things were fluffy with crocheted covers and embroidered scarves. The tufted chairs and overstuffed sofas were mounded with pillows. The tables were crowded with pictures and knickknacks. Gold jars of gilded cattails and ostrich plumes stood here and there. On the mantel squatted an immense purple pincushion stabbed with antique hat pins. And in front of the window an enormous fern on a wicker stand blocked out the soft light of evening.

But it didn't block it out altogether. Around the edges of the fern Miss Prawn had Seen Something.

She had been watering the fern. She had stood staring out the window for a moment with the watering can in her hand, and then she had put it down and darted to her writing desk.

Miss Prawn's book of reveries was lying open on the desk. At the top of the page was her inspirational quotation for the day:

You must wake and call me early, call
me early, mother dear. . . .
ALFRED, LORD TENNYSON

Under the quotation was a reminder to do something the next day:

Tomorrow: dig a shrub border along the property line. Plant sharp things, spiny things, thorny things. The children next door don't seem to know where their yard ends and mine begins.

>   *1. Dagger plant?*
>   *2. Sword bush?*
>   *3. Roses with giant thorns?*

If this barrier fails to keep them out, I will be forced to speak to their parents (or guardians, or whatever mixed-up relations those people are to each other). I'll simply explain that I really don't care for children.

But now Miss Prawn had lost interest in her book of reveries. She pushed it aside with trembling fingers and snatched up her pen and began driving it wildly across a clean sheet of paper. She was writing a letter to her employer, Mr. Ralph Preek, president of the Thoreau Street Bank.

Dear Ralph,

I write in haste about a matter of supreme importance. Since my telephone has not yet been connected,

I will send this by special messenger.

I have just witnessed a miracle. Oh Ralph, it is vouchsafed to few of us to behold such things!

The child next door is a SAINT.

Either that, or she is a visitor from FAIRY-LAND.

Believe me, Ralph, cross my heart and hope to die. Far be it from me to let a fib or the tiniest little white lie cross my lips. THIS IS THE NAKED TRUTH.

A moment ago I happened to glance out the window, and I tell you, Ralph, I nearly fell to the floor in a swoon. She was FLYING. She had climbed up on the railing of the front porch (this is Fred Hall's youngest, that skinny little stepdaughter), and then she jumped, and believe me, Ralph, I hope to die, she went up in the air as high as the roof and then came down easy and landed on the grass. It was a genuine bona fide guaranteed miracle, and think of it, Ralph, it was vouchsafed to me, Madeline Prawn, to stand here and behold it. I swear this is the truth. What have I done, I said to myself, to deserve this blessing. Oh, unknown to us in our humbleness, Ralph, I said to myself, how our inner goodness works in mysterious ways on the Almighty Deep.

Of course on the other hand perhaps she is a fairy moon-child. You must know, Ralph, I mean it is a well-known fact that fairies come at the full of the moon and kidnap a newborn babe and leave one of their own in its place and then one day at the full of the moon the moon-child flies away to join the fairies and is gone forever. That is a fact. A scientific fact. You see them every now and again, you know, Ralph. These weird children. Odd little creatures. Peculiar. And I must say this little girl next door really fills the bill. She is certainly strange. You know what I mean. Big eyes, skinny little toothpick legs. Hair without any color to it. Skin like blue milk. That kind of child. And oh, Ralph, doesn't it make your blood boil to think that somewhere out there in fairyland there may be a healthy pink-cheeked darling lost to the world forever because of this little GNOME?

So you see, Ralph, we must get together and talk. There are things that might be done. Who knows where such a piece of good fortune might lead? Having been vouchsafed the witnessing of this miracle, I have a responsibility to myself and what's more, dear Ralph, just think of it, TO THE WORLD AT LARGE.

I am thinking, for instance (just to get the ball rolling), of filling small bottles with water and having them blessed by the young saint. We could offer them for sale. A healing elixir.

This is the sort of thing you do with saints.

Or we could even consider a more practical enterprise like renting out parking lots from which the child's ascents might be observed. The possibilities are ENDLESS.

> *Breathlessly,*
> *Madeline*

Miss Prawn put down her pen and read her letter over. Astonished by the force of her own words, she felt suddenly very pious and very rich. It felt wonderful to be both of those things at the same time. Miss Prawn stuck the letter in an envelope and scrawled on the outside *RUSH RUSH: Deliver at once to Mr. Ralph Preek.* Then she hurried out of doors with the letter in her hand, crossed Laurel Street, and knocked on the door of the first house.

A little girl opened the door and looked up at Miss Prawn.

Miss Prawn inspected the little girl with sharp attention. Now, if it had been at all possible for Miss Prawn to like children, she might have become fond of this one, because the child looked the way children were *supposed* to look, plump and pink with a rosebud mouth and yellow curly hair.

"How would you like to earn a quarter, Dorothea?" said Miss Prawn.

DOROTHEA
BRINGS THE WORD

Ralph Preek was dozing in front of his TV set after supper when he was awakened by the barking of dogs in his front yard. He rushed to the window. Two half-grown German shepherds were bounding through his perennial border, trampling his prize chrysanthemums.

Mr. Preek threw up the sash and shouted at the dogs, but they went right on frisking among his flowers, knocking the giant blossoms this way and that, snapping the tall stems. He rushed outside, remembering, too late, his resolve to buy a gun. A duck gun! It would come in handy for emergencies like this. A little spray of buckshot, and these dogs would never come back. They would have learned their lesson. "Get out," he shouted at the top of his lungs. "Get out, out, out!"

The dogs stopped tumbling over each other in his flower bed and looked at him in surprise. Then they lunged the whole length of the chrysanthemum border, barking, and raced away up the street. Mr. Preek ran after them, gasping, and then he slowed down and stopped, to look at the little girl who was marching up the sidewalk.

It was a nice little girl in a pretty dress. Her hair was yellow. Her cheeks were chubby. Why, it was little Dorothea Broom. Mr. Preek had often given Dorothea a lollipop when she came into the bank with her mother. She had always said thank you so nicely! Mr. Preek's anger cooled. How he loved little children!

Dorothea walked straight up to him and stopped. "This is for you," she said, holding up an envelope. "From Miss Prawn."

"Why, thank you, dear child." Mr. Preek took the letter. Dorothea's chubby cheeks grew chubbier. And then she curtsied. She did! She curtsied like a lady-in-waiting at the Court of St. James's!

Mr. Preek was stunned. He gave Dorothea a dollar. Then he went inside and read Miss Prawn's letter and sat down at the kitchen table to write a reply. Dorothea waited outside, pressing her nose against the screen door.

My dear Madeline, [wrote Mr. Preek]

There are no such things as miracles. The child is in the power of a very large duck. Only this morning I beheld a similar event. I believe it is an example of that peculiar attraction by which beasts of the lower orders exert dominion over other creatures in mysterious ways. You are familiar, I am sure, with the cobra, which can freeze its victim into immobility by some sort of powerful hypnotism. And you must have heard of animal magnetism. Surely these forces explain this phenomenon. The duck simply PULLED the child into the air. This morning I drove it away before it could snatch her up in its claws or draw her up from the ground by the force of magnetic attraction. She is a very small child, you will remember, almost weightless, compared to the immense size and wingspread of the giant bird. The creature is a menace to hearth and home and must be destroyed.

Do nothing till you hear from me.

Yours truly,
Ralph

Then Mr. Preek wrote Miss Prawn's name on the envelope and handed the letter to Dorothea Broom.

Dorothea smiled again.

Why, the child had dimples! A delicious pair of dimples, one in the middle of each chubby pink cheek! Mr. Preek gave Dorothea another dollar.

AT LAST

It was bedtime. Georgie put on her pajamas, pulled back the covers of her bed, laid Dollabella on the pillow, and climbed in beside her. Then she adjusted the blankets carefully so that they came up only as far as Dollabella's chin (or as far as the place where Dollabella's chin would have been, if Dollabella had had a chin). Then Georgie turned off the light beside the bed and lay back on her pillow and stared up at the dark, smiling.

Her smile stretched from the closet on one side of the room to the window on the other, she was so glad.

She had flown. There was no doubt at all. She had drifted up to the top of the house, and then she had floated to the ground, coming to rest on the grass in the front yard like a feather or a piece of milkweed down. . . .

So when the Goose Prince came for her, Georgie was ready.

His gentle hooting woke her before dawn. The sound was like a blade of grass trembling between her thumbs. Georgie cocked her head up from the pillow, instantly alert, her body tense with listening. *Tap-tap.* He was tapping lightly with his beak against the glass.

Eagerly Georgie slipped out of bed and pattered across the floor.

The Goose Prince was standing on the porch roof, his long neck erect, the narrow crescent moon cocked behind his head. Soon the sky would be glimmering with morning.

Georgie lifted the window. The sash slid easily to the top. She could feel herself beaming, pieces of happiness flying off her face to the quiet trees and the sleeping houses and the empty road. "Oh, hello there," whispered Georgie.

The Goose Prince was a little comical, seen close up. His long beak was like a big nose, and his two round eyes bulged a little away from his head. His webbed feet turned in like a pigeon's. He spoke, and it was like a flute talking. His voice was a little husky, like the note of the blade of grass.

"Would you like to fly around the pond?" said the Goose Prince.

"Oh, yes!" Georgie climbed out the window and stood on the roof of the porch, gripping the shingles with her bare feet, shivering a little in the night air. Then she turned quickly around, reached back through the window, and pulled Eddy's jacket from the back of the rocking chair.

The Goose Prince stood stock-still, waiting for her. He was smiling. His beak didn't turn up at the corners like the smile of a person, but Georgie could tell that he was pleased. Perhaps he was as glad as she was—and that was very glad! Now he was turning around awkwardly and bending down. Georgie climbed on his back. It was cushiony and soft, but there was a hard feeling of strong muscles beneath the feathers. At first Georgie sat upright with her legs folded under her. But that didn't feel right. The Goose Prince waited patiently while she tried lying forward and tucking her head into the space between the base of his throat and his left wing.

There, that was better. Georgie locked her thin arms gently around his chest. Now her knees fitted perfectly behind his wings.

The Goose Prince curved his neck and looked back at her kindly. "Are you all right now?" he said.

"I'm fine," said Georgie.

"Well, then, hold on tight," said the Goose Prince.

And then he took off. Clumsily he slithered down the sloping shingles and sprang off the edge of the roof, flapping heavily over the bushes. Georgie could feel the brave cry choking in his throat as the great buckets of his wings caught the air and hurled it downward. His body was rocking up, up, up, flapping and rising. Georgie rocked with it and clung with all her might. They were lifting, lifting, straight up over the house to the top of the chimney. For a moment they were poised over the steep intersecting roofs of Georgie's house, and she could look down past the house next door and see the white flowers in Miss Prawn's front yard.

"Oh!" said Georgie. Miss Prawn had finished

her flowery message. Her plastic rose garden said

WELCOME TO CONCORD

But now Miss Prawn's house and Georgie's house were tipping backward as the Goose Prince stretched his long black neck and began flying in the direction of the highway. Lying on his back, Georgie could feel the rapid thump of her excited heart against the flexing pull of his wings. Together they were like a single engine throbbing smoothly through the air.

She was filled with delight. The wind blew her hair streaming away from her face, it rippled the hems of her pajamas, and it breathed cool on her bare feet as she lay like a feather between the churning wings, looking down at the houses rushing away below her. Walden Street was a long gray ribbon, turning and bending on its way to Route 2. She could see the flat top of the police station, she could see Laurel Street, she could see Dorothea's house. It looked as small as a dollhouse. And the people inside would be tiny too, Mr. Broom and Mrs. Broom and Mary Jane and Dorothea. They would be like dolls, with perfect little fingers and toes. Rushing high over the house on the back of the Goose Prince, Georgie felt as if she could reach down with her giant hands and take off the roof of the house and pick up Dorothea and say, "Okay now, Dorothea, time to get up," and prop her in a kitchen chair like a doll.

The houses were gone. The Goose Prince was flying on steadily over the cabbage fields. The air blowing in Georgie's face had risen cool and moist from the boggy place in the woods. It smelled of cabbages growing in wet earth. It was spicy with the scent of a hundred thousand leaves in the Town Forest. And there was a musky smell too, from a fox that still lived in the forest. (Georgie didn't know about the fox. She only knew the air smelled fresh and a little wild.)

The flight didn't last long. Already the Goose Prince was descending in a long glide over the highway toward Walden Pond. Already she could see the tops of the pine trees in the woods around the water. And then at the last minute, Georgie glanced back over her shoulder at the town of Concord. Her hair was blowing over her face, the buildings were half hidden by the puffy trees, but Georgie thought she saw for just a second the dark windows of her own house visible above the trees, far away. The whole house is asleep, thought Georgie. They are all asleep, breathing sigh, sigh, and their breath blows the curtains in the windows, and the curtains are floating out white, and my mother and Uncle Freddy are in there sound asleep, and they don't know I'm flying! flying! up here in the sky!

"Oh, bring her back safe," murmured Aunt Alex, standing behind the curtain, gazing at the small moving spot that was Georgie flying in front of the crescent moon.

EDDY KEEPS HIS
EYES AND EARS OPEN

On weekdays the Thoreau Street Bank closed its doors promptly at three in the afternoon. Usually Ralph Preek stayed at his desk working diligently until five o'clock, but today he slipped out with the last of his customers and made his way to Macone's Sporting Goods Store on Lowell Road.

Mr. Preek was entirely unaware of Georgie's miraculous flight before dawn on the back of the Goose Prince, but the enormous bird and the little girl were both very much on his mind.

"What can I do for you?" said the man behind the counter, spreading his hands wide on the glass case of jackknives and fishing lures and looking at Mr. Preek. There was only one other customer in the store, a redheaded boy examining a shelf of model rockets and airplanes.

"I would like to purchase a gun," said Mr. Preek.

"What kind of gun do you want?"

"Something large and powerful. For large waterfowl. Giant ducks." Clearing his throat, Mr. Preek introduced himself. (His name ought to mean something, after all: *Ralph Alonzo Preek, the president of the Thoreau Street Bank.*)

The eyes of the man behind the counter failed to blink with recognition. "Ducks?" he said. "Oh, you don't want anything too powerful if you're going duck hunting. This one here would be about right. Twelve-gauge. Pump-action. Three shots and you load again."

"Hmmmm," said Mr. Preek. He took the gun and fiddled with the trigger. "Looks kind of feeble to me. I tell you, this bird is gigantic. Dangerous. Attacking little children on the streets of Concord."

"Attacking children? Oh, you must mean somebody's barnyard Toulouse goose. I had a flock once myself. They sometimes run out and peck at strangers."

The redheaded boy put a long narrow box on the counter. *Assemble your own PHOSPHORESCENT MOON ROCKET X-100,* said the label on the box. "I'll take this one," said the boy.

"No, no," said Mr. Preek, "this is a wild bird, I tell you. It descends from the air and snatches little children. I saw it with my own eyes."

"Is that so?" The man behind the counter looked doubtfully at Mr. Preek. Then he rang up the boy's money in the cash register and put the rocket model in a paper bag. "Well, I don't know. Anyway, that's the kind of gun you want if you're going after any kind of ducks or geese. Have you got a license? And you can't shoot anything now, you know that? The season doesn't begin for a couple of weeks."

"A couple of weeks?" Mr. Preek was indignant. "But the matter is urgent. I'll speak to the selectmen."

"Not the selectmen. That wouldn't do any good. You'll have to go to the State House in Boston. It's a Massachusetts state law."

"The governor then. I'll go straight to the governor."

"Well, lots of luck. You want this gun or not?"

"I'll take it," said Ralph Preek.

The boy left the store with his paper bag and started home. Along the road beside the supermarket, the September sunlight struck the shiny leaves of the pokeweed bushes, bouncing off them as from so many glittering mirrors. But Eddy saw nothing but the black pavement in front of him and his own advancing feet.

Mr. Preek was buying a duck gun. Because of Georgie. Mr. Preek was trying to protect Georgie from the attack of a giant duck. But it wasn't a duck, it was a Canada goose. It was Georgie's goose, the one that wanted to be her friend. But of course Georgie was crazy. The goose didn't want to be Georgie's friend. It was just an ordinary goose in a great big flock of Canada geese. It had just happened to come down near the place where Georgie was. Crazy little old Georgie. She needed protecting, all right, and that was a fact. But not by Mr. Preek. The Georgie Protection Society could take care of Georgie perfectly well, without any outside help from big fat bossy men with guns, like Mr. Ralph Preek.

Eddy turned in at the gate of No. 40 Walden Street and started up the steps of the front porch, calling, "Georgie, hey, Georgie." Then he had to step aside, because people were pouring out the door, Millicent O'Toole and Arthur Hathaway and all the rest. They all said hello to Eddy and ambled down the porch steps, laughing and talking. Classes were over for the day. They were all going home.

"Here I am, Eddy," said Georgie. She wasn't in the house. She was standing up in the bushes, smiling up at Eddy through arching boughs of forsythia.

"Oh, there you are, Georgie." Eddy ran down the steps and crawled into the bushes and squatted down beside her. "Listen here, Georgie, I want to know what that goose was like. I mean, what did he *really* do? You know, that big goose you saw yesterday morning."

Georgie smiled down at Dollabella. Carefully she picked up a maple leaf heaped with blades of grass and red berries from the hedge in front of the house. "Here, Eddy, have some lettuce and tomato salad?"

"Gee, thanks." Eddy took a berry and squished it between his fingers.

Georgie stirred her air-tea in its acorn cup with a twig and took a sip. She couldn't stop smiling. In the hour before dawn the Goose Prince had carried her three times around Walden Pond, skimming the tops of the pine trees, and then he had brought her safely home, secretly, silently. In plenty of time for breakfast. In plenty of time for school. It had been wonderful, a dream come true, a dream that was real. Georgie looked at Eddy. She didn't know what to say. It wouldn't be right to lie, not to Eddy. But it was all right anyway—Eddy was talking about yesterday morning, when Mr. Preek had frightened the Goose Prince away—not about today.

"He was nice. He was coming down. Over there by the woods. By the highway. It was right between the woods and the highway."

"But he wasn't coming down just to see *you*?"

"To see me?" Georgie paused and thought it over. "Well, yes, he was. He was really nice! And then that man honked his horn, and the Goose Prince—I mean, the goose—flew away."

"He was just coming down, that's all, and then he flew away? Well, where did Mr. Preek get the idea he was dangerous? I saw him just now, Mr. Preek, I mean. He was buying—"

And then it was Eddy's turn to hold something back. He stood up. "Say, Georgie, you want to see something? Come on inside. I've got a new plastic model to put together. It's a moon rocket. It glows in the dark. Come on, I'll show you."

"It glows in the dark? It *does*?" Georgie couldn't believe it.

But in the stuffy narrow space behind the coats in the closet under the stairs, the hundreds of little plastic pieces of Eddy's rocket ship glowed softly in the velvet dark, an eerie luminous green. "Isn't that great?" said Eddy.

"Wow," breathed Georgie.

"Wait till I put the whole thing together," said Eddy.

The doorbell rang. Eddy fumbled through the coats, opened the closet door, and went out into the front hall.

Georgie looked timidly out of the closet.

It was Miss Prawn, Miss Madeline Prawn, the new neighbor who didn't like children. Quickly Georgie ducked back into the closet.

But Miss Prawn had seen Georgie. Hungrily she looked past Eddy at the closet door. Miss Prawn was carrying two big empty plastic jugs. She was smiling and smiling and showing her teeth. "Might I have some water, young man? My faucets have stopped working."

MISS PRAWN
AND THE SAINTLY CHILD

"Your faucets have stopped working?" Eddy was surprised. "That's funny."

"I know," said Miss Prawn. "But they did. They stopped. Not a drop from a single faucet in the house." She cocked her head sideways and stared past Eddy at the closet door, grinning and grinning. It looked like hard work to Eddy, the way she was stretching her face in spasmodic jerks, then stretching it some more, trying to pull her mouth sideways from its customary pursed-up spot in the middle of her face.

"Maybe you should call a plumber," he said slowly, standing smack in the middle of the doorway.

"Well, of course, of course, of course, I'll call a plumber!" Miss Prawn frowned at Eddy. Then she remembered, and showed her teeth again. "But in the meantime, if I could just fill up my jugs at your kitchen sink?"

Eddy couldn't think of any reason why not. He stood aside and led the way to the kitchen. As they passed the closet door Miss Prawn's greedy eyes flashed in at Georgie. Georgie winced and turned away and pressed up against the coats. She could hear water splashing in the kitchen, going *glug-glug*

into the jugs. Quickly she slipped out of the closet
and hurried through the velvet curtain and hid herself in the parlor. (Georgie was just trying to be
polite. Now Miss Prawn wouldn't have to look at
her. Miss Prawn, who didn't like children.)

But a moment later Miss Prawn sought her out.
She poked her head through the parlor curtain and
stared at Georgie. Her teeth glittered roguishly. "I
saw you." She chuckled. "I saw you last night on the
front porch."

Georgie jerked guiltily. Miss Prawn always
made her feel she had done something bad.

"I saw you jump off the front porch and fly way
up in the air."

"Oh." Georgie looked around for a way to escape, but Miss Prawn was blocking the only door.

Then Miss Prawn disappeared for an instant.
When she came back through the parlor curtain she
was carrying her two jugs. They were heavy with
water. She thumped them on the floor. She was still
beaming. "Here, dear," said Miss Prawn, pulling a
piece of paper out of her pocket, "just read this out
loud."

Georgie looked at the piece of paper. She
rocked back and forth on her toes. She glanced shyly
up at Miss Prawn and whispered, "I don't understand it."

Miss Prawn was amazed. She took the paper
back and read it aloud to Georgie. "It says, *OFFI-
CIAL DOCUMENT: I have blessed this water.* Now, sign

it, dear. Just sign your name right here underneath."

Georgie looked vaguely at Miss Prawn's shoes. They were sharp-pointed shoes with fringed flaps and shoelaces and holes pricked all over the toes. Georgie pulled her chin down into her shirt and sucked the edge of her collar. Slowly she shook her head from side to side.

Miss Prawn poked something at her. "Just take this pen and sign it, I tell you, right down here at the bottom."

Georgie turned her head and gazed out the window. Fluffy pieces of milkweed were floating across the porch, drifting through the moon-shaped opening in the lattice, blowing upward and out of sight. In the meadow across the street the sun glistened on the tall stems of amber-colored grass. Georgie dropped her eyes and whispered, "No."

Miss Prawn stared at her, opening her mouth in astonishment. Why, the child couldn't write. That was the trouble. She couldn't read and she couldn't even write her own name. She must be stupid. It was pitiful. Miss Prawn thought it over shrewdly and guessed the reason why.

She was a fairy, that was it. Fairies couldn't read or write. That was a well-known fact. And just look at her. The child was certainly a fairy. (Miss Prawn narrowed her eyes and studied Georgie closely.) There were blue shadows under her eyes, and her face had a sort of skim-milk look to it. And her hair wasn't yellow or brown or any particular color. The child's hair had no more color to it than the water in the jugs. She *must* be a moon-child.

Miss Prawn gave up. She stopped smiling. Her face sagged into its usual expression of smelling something slightly unpleasant. She took an envelope out of her pocket and handed it to Georgie. "Give this to your mother, will you?" she said sharply. Then she turned on her heel and plunged through the curtain.

"Oh, wait," said Georgie, "you forgot your water." Hefting the jugs off the floor, Georgie dragged them out into the hall.

But Miss Prawn looked back at the jugs in contempt. "Never mind," she said. Marching out the front door, she yanked it shut behind her with a bang.

It was a shame about the water, thought Miss Prawn. It would have been like selling expensive perfume, only better. Think of it! Some kinds of perfume cost twenty-five dollars an ounce! And wouldn't the healing water from the Holy Well of the Saintly Child have been far more precious than the most precious and expensive perfume? Well, it had been an attractive idea. It was too bad. One hated to give it up.

The child *must* be a fairy. The evidence was all on that side.

But then again, it was still possible that she was a saint. One was caught on the horns of a dilemma.

What if she *were* a saint, after all? An illiterate, igno-
rant, rather stupid saint? One didn't want to be
overly respectful to a mere moon-child, but on the
other hand (having been vouchsafed the witnessing
of a genuine miracle!) one dared not be anything
but nice, terribly nice, in case the poor little waif
turned out to be a genuine holy bona fide saint after
all.

Miss Prawn walked through her own front yard,
gazing absentmindedly at the white roses that said
WELCOME TO CONCORD in her garden of plastic
flowers. She would make up her mind later on. For
the present she would walk a careful line between
worship on the one hand and outrage on the other.

With fairies and saints and weird abnormal
creatures like that, you really had to watch your step.

TARGET PRACTICE

At the bottom of South America there is a place of terrible heavy seas, where two oceans meet. Gathering in moving masses of water thousands of miles away, sweeping up from the South Pole in the Pacific, rolling southward from the equator in the Atlantic, opposing waves meet at last in a tremendous smash and crash of thundering crosscurrents at the tip of Cape Horn.

And yet until their climactic meeting they are nothing more than ordinary waves with schools of fish sporting in them and seabirds flying over them, ordinary waves in peaceful seas.

There can be waves like that in small inland towns far from the ocean shore. Here and now in the town of Concord, Massachusetts, in the continent of North America, there were two such waves. Georgie and the Goose Prince were one. Ralph Alonzo Preek of the Thoreau Street Bank was the other.

On the way home from Macone's Sporting Goods Store, Mr. Preek had stopped at the Concord Library to pick up a book on the hunting of waterfowl. Now in the privacy of his own living room he took his new gun out of its box and inspected it. He oiled it and wiped it clean. He read the manual from cover to cover. Then he sat down in a comfortable chair and read aloud to himself the chapter on target exercises in his library book.

The chapter advised him to pick up his gun every now and then and point it at things at random, at the face of the clock or a picture on the wall.

> *. . . Now close your left eye and sight along the barrel with the right. You'll probably find you are pointing a bit over, under, or to one side or the other. Correct the hold and try again—and again and again. Before long you'll be on target every time.*

Mr. Preek looked around the room. Over the mantel hung a photograph of Henry Thoreau. That would do nicely for a target. Whipping his gun up to his shoulder, he pointed it at the picture. Then, squinting one eye, he sighted along the barrel. Right on the nose! Henry Thoreau's big nose was right in the middle of the gunsight! Pretty good for a beginner.

Grinning to himself, Mr. Preek put the gun down, picked up the book, and flipped to another chapter. Now the author was describing an exciting moment on a frozen lake during a hunting expedition with a friend.

> *. . . The geese bore down on me, one slightly ahead of the other, flying straight and true at the height of about forty*

yards. . . . I came to my knees and poured three loads from my pump into the nearest broad white breast. In one motion I laid my gun on the ice and grabbed Ollie's. As I brought it up I saw the first bird falling, so I rammed the two loads into the other. As the last charge thumped into him, his wings folded and the two birds crashed down almost together. . . .

I'll bet I could do that, thought Mr. Preek. I could learn how. I'll be ready by the time the duck hunting season begins. I'll practice hard.

Impulsively he snatched up his gun and aimed it once again at the picture of Henry Thoreau. This time Henry's left eye was smack in the middle of the gunsight.

The eye looked gravely back at him.

Ralph Preek blinked. Then he lowered his gun and muttered aloud, "Well, you know how it is, old man. No offense."

THE CUDGEL
OF FRIENDSHIP

Aunt Alex's afternoon seminar was over. The class had been conducted in the backyard right next to the laundry line, and the sun-washed smell of the flapping shirts and billowing sheets had blown over Millicent O'Toole and Arthur Hathaway and all the rest of them, bringing a fresh homey flavor to the morning's discussion of Henry Thoreau's life at Walden Pond.

Now they were opening their lunch bags under the apple tree. Arthur was strumming his guitar. Aunt Alex picked up her books and hurried into the house by the back door.

In the kitchen she found Georgie hopping around on one foot. Georgie stopped hopping and took something out of the bib pocket of her overalls. "This is from Miss Prawn," she said.

"Miss Prawn?" Taking the letter between finger and thumb, Aunt Alex held it at arm's length for a minute, and then she opened it thoughtfully.

Dear Mrs. Hall, [said the letter]

   Far be it from me to shrink from performing my duty especially where a neighbor is concerned, because you see, Mrs. Hall, it is vouchsafed to some of us to be presented once in a lifetime with the opportu-

nity to grant sometimes on occasion a little friendly advice and warning. In the nature of which I hereby undertake to impart the same out of a feeling of neighborly responsibility, taking up the cudgel of friendship, as it were. We go this way but once, I said to myself, and far be it from me not to interfere when I see calamity and doom and disaster coming down the pike. Speaking strictly as a neighbor, I now feel it incumbent on me to pass along to you certain pieces of information that have come my way as I have traveled along the highway of life, namely that certain things are apt to eventuate at the full of the moon. I do not wish to alarm you, but it is a well-known scientific fact. Your daughter may have been left on your doorstep by the fairies at the full of the moon. If so, then she may likewise be taken BACK by those selfsame fairies at the full of the moon. Therefore watch out. Be on your guard. At the full of the moon keep the child locked up. Don't say I didn't warn you. WATCH OUT WHEN THE MOON IS FULL.

> *Yours faithfully in days of trouble and strife, as well as in happier times,*
>
> > *Madeline Prawn*

> *So I'll travel along*
> *With a friend and a song.*
> > ***WILFRID WILSON GIBSON***

And the song, from beginning to end,
I found in the heart of a friend.
HENRY WADSWORTH LONGFELLOW

Let me live in my house by the side of the road
And be a friend of man.
SAM WALTER FOSS

Aunt Alex looked up from her letter. Georgie was gazing at her solemnly. Aunt Alex laughed.

"What does she say?" said Georgie.

"Oh, nothing," said Aunt Alex. "Just a lot of silly foolishness." Then, *rrrriiiipppp*, Georgie's mother tore Miss Prawn's letter in two and threw it in the wastebasket.

A PRESENT
FROM GEORGIE

That night the old moon was gone and the new moon wasn't born yet, so there was no moon at all. When the Goose Prince hooted softly at Georgie from the roof of the porch, there were only stars around him, sparkling through their pinholes in the blue-black sky. Joyfully Georgie hopped out of bed, snatched up Eddy's jacket, jerked it over her pajamas, threw up the window, and leaned forward into the cool night air to say hello.

Immediately the Goose Prince bent his long neck down to her in kindly greeting.

They were beak to nose. For a moment Georgie wondered if she should kiss the Goose Prince. If she kissed him, would he turn into a real prince? But she was too shy. And, besides, she didn't want him to change into something else. He was very beautiful just the way he was.

Nimbly she clambered out the window and lay down on his back. Then the Goose Prince began working his wings, shifting his weight, churring softly in his throat. The next moment he was scrabbling down the roof with his webbed feet, beating his wings in hollow fannings, struggling upward into the air over the dew-laden grass and the dim tangle of Georgie's bush house and the dark shape

of Uncle Freddy's car in the driveway and—
what were those ghostly things dangling in the backyard?—the laundry, the bedspreads and the shirts
and sheets, hanging wet and slack on the line. Tossing from side to side as the Goose Prince heaved
himself aloft, Georgie hung on tight, and then at last
the Goose Prince stretched his neck forward and
settled into a steady horizontal flight. They were
high over Miss Prawn's garden of plastic flowers,
they were high over the dim houses, with sky above
them and sky below them, and no sound but the soft
buffeting of the Goose Prince's wings, gathering the
air and hurling it behind him, gathering and hurling
it again. Tucked close and safe on his back with her
cheek pressed into the hollow between his neck and
his left wing, Georgie felt the night air flow by her
in running streams. Now they were over the fields,
and over the highway, and over the woods, and already, looking down, Georgie could see the pond
opening beneath them, flat and black below a milky
film of fog.

The Goose Prince was coming down. He was
going to land in the water! No longer was he choking back his hoarse cry. He was in full voice, shouting to the whole dark world of the night, "A-WARK,
a-WARK!" He was braking his flight, bellying out
his wings to slow his descent, rearing backward,
dropping his black feet, catching at the water, running across it, splashing great sprays of spume to

left and right. For a moment they skimmed upright across the surface like horse and rider, and then the Goose Prince sank down and settled on the water, bobbing like a cork. "Oh!" Georgie gave a small stifled cry, and pulled up her toes, shocked by the touch of the cold water. Then she let her legs fall again, and soon the water was no longer cold. Silently and serenely the Goose Prince began paddling toward the shore, moving like a ship, like a feathery galleon, stern high, bow low. Majestically he cruised northward until his breast nudged the reedy shore. Georgie could feel his feet touch bottom. Slowly the Goose Prince waded through a bristling growth of pickerelweed and gained the solid bank and climbed up on the trampled path to stand at his full height on dry ground.

Quickly Georgie hopped off his back, and then she stood respectfully at one side, wringing the water from her pajama legs, waiting to see what he would do next. The Goose Prince was waggling his tail, flapping his wings, spraying droplets of water all around, like a dog shaking itself after a swim. Then he poked his head at his back and nipped his tail feathers savagely.

Georgie waited. She looked around. They had come down in a little cove. They were standing on a curving shore. Below them the pond lay still, the mist above it thinning and vanishing. The whole luminous sky was still. Most of the stars had gone out. It was nearly dawn. Only one big star hung over the treetops, glistening, not twinkling at all. It was the same star Georgie had seen on the morning when she had set out to find the Goose Prince. Now it looked down at her enormously, one great ray falling from far away, a million miles! right into her eye. There wasn't the slightest breeze in the branches of the pine trees, only the liquid lapping of the water where they had come ashore, slapping around the stems of the bushes that grew in the water.

The Goose Prince looked kindly at Georgie. "Shall we walk up the hill?" he said.

It wasn't a big hill. Just a wide steep path up the sloping ground between the trees. They walked side by side. And then they came to a place Georgie knew.

Uncle Freddy had often brought her here. There were granite posts and a wooden sign. The posts were only gray shapes in the gray gloom of the woods, but Georgie went up to one of them and felt its stony surface. Henry Thoreau had lived here once, that was what the sign said. He had lived in a small house on the shore of Walden Pond, here where the posts were, a long time ago. Georgie smiled. If Uncle Freddy were here, he would tell her how Henry had made friends with a field mouse, how he had pulled a woodchuck out of its hole by the tail, how fishes had swum into his hand in the water, and snakes had coiled themselves around his legs. But Uncle Freddy wasn't here. Georgie said nothing.

The Goose Prince was looking at her, standing regally in the shadows, his dark neck erect. Then he yawned, stretching his bill hugely, and looked at Georgie sleepily. "Do you mind if I take a short nap?" he said.

Georgie was surprised. "Oh, no," she said. "I don't mind." Then she watched as the Goose Prince lowered himself to the ground and tucked his head into the middle of his back and closed his eyes. Sitting down beside a clump of fern, she waited for him to wake up. She didn't feel tired at all. And in a few minutes the Goose Prince lifted his head, shook himself, stood up again, and walked over to Georgie.

It made her smile, to see the way he walked. He was waddling slightly, pointing his toes in, holding his head high. But even in the dim morning light she could feel how solemn he was, and she stopped smiling.

"I want to give you something," said the Goose Prince, stopping in front of Georgie. "There's a present. I want to give you a present."

"A present?" said Georgie, startled.

Absentmindedly the Goose Prince turned and stared at the light patches of pond gleaming between the dark trunks of the trees. For a moment he seemed to have forgotten Georgie. But then he came out of his reverie and looked at her again. His face was swollen into fat bumps at either side, to show that he was smiling. "Wait," he said. "Later on. Not now."

"All right," said Georgie. But she wondered about the present. What could it be? She couldn't think of anything. And anyway what could be more wonderful than what she had already been given? Then Georgie had a guilty thought. She was suddenly overcome with the feeling that it was *she* who should be giving the present. *She* should be giving something to *him*. Oh, if only she had something to give him! Georgie put her hands in the pockets of Eddy's jacket, to feel if there was something there, pennies, or an apple, or—what would he like?— dried kernels of corn. But there was nothing in the pockets, only the withered leftovers from Dollabella's last tea party.

But then Georgie's fingers closed on a blade of grass. She pulled it out and stretched it between her two thumbs to make a grass flute. "Listen!" she said. And then she blew.

The grass made its familiar trembling hoot. Georgie blew again. *Hoot, hoot.*

The Goose Prince opened his beak with astonishment.

Georgie blew once more on her small green flute. *Hoot, hoot. Hoot, hoot.*

The narrow face of the Goose Prince was bulging at the sides. He was beaming. "Well!" he said, "isn't that nice!"

Georgie held the blade of grass out to him on the palm of her hand. "Would you like to have it?" she said.

The Goose Prince looked at the blade of grass. Delicately he picked it up in his bill. For a minute Georgie thought he was going to eat it, but instead he lowered his head and rustled with his webbed feet in a heap of dead leaves beside one of the granite posts. He was tucking the blade of grass under the leaves. He was lifting his head. "Thank you," he said to Georgie, the fat places on each side of his head bulging more than ever. "Now are you ready?"

"Ready?" said Georgie. "Ready for what?"

But it was the very thing that was brimming in her heart. He taught her how to fly.

FLYYYYYYYYYY!

They took off from the pond. The ascent was not like their clumsy upward struggles from the roof of the porch at home. This time the Goose Prince made a rush forward through the water, his wings flapping, his beak open in a loud triumphant shout, *"A-WARK, a-WARK!"* At once he was aloft, with a rain of crystal drops falling from his webbed feet and streaming backward from Georgie's soaked pajama legs as they rose higher and higher over the pond. Georgie hung on tight, feeling the cold rush of air on her wet legs. Now the Goose Prince was flapping strongly over the southern shore, turning in a wide arc. Then Georgie gasped. They were not alone. There was a flock of geese below them in the water, a whole flock. They were clustered along the shore with their drowsing heads tucked into their backs, fast asleep.

"A-WARK, a-WARK!" As the Goose Prince shouted above them, Georgie could see heads popping up in a flurry of beating wings. She could hear a chorus of shocked croakings. *What's that? What's that? Who's there?* But then they recognized one of their own, and the wings stopped fanning. The heads sank once more into the downy backs. They all went back to sleep.

High above the slumbering flock the Goose Prince swam smoothly once again through the thick river of air. His wings were moving easily, sending pulses of the cool fragrant morning over Georgie's smiling face, lifting the lank wisps of her fine hair, blowing it backward. Below them the pine trees flung up their dark arms, as if they were point-ing at Georgie—*Oh, look! Look at Georgie!* And then the Goose Prince turned his head on his long neck and gazed back at her, the dawn light shining through his bulging eyes. "Now," he said, "try it now."

At the top of the sky, clinging to him with her fingers knotted together around his throat, Georgie looked back at him, trying to understand, whisper-ing, "Try what?"

"*Flyyyyyyyyyyyy,*" said the Goose Prince. On the moving air the word flowed on and on, not dying away. Georgie was filled with longing. But she was afraid. She held on, wrapping her fingers together more tightly, shutting her eyes and pressing her cheek against the soft feathers of his neck. Not now. She couldn't do it now. Not yet.

"Just slip off and glide," said the Goose Prince. "You'll see. The wind is just right. It will hold you, if you try it now." And then he warbled it again in his soft fluting voice, "*Flyyyyyyyyyyyy.*"

For a moment longer Georgie kept her shoul-ders stiff and her arms pressed close against him. But then she opened her eyes and commanded all her muscles to go limp. Letting go, she slid down the feathery slope of his back until she felt something nudge at her from below. It was a pillow of air, lifting her, holding her steadily and firmly like the palm of a supporting hand. Then at last all the stringy little muscles in Georgie's body loosened. Spreading her arms, she floated on the column of air. Beside her, the Goose Prince floated too, watching her, his hovering wingtips brushing her fingers. Together they drifted, wheeling down and down in slowly descending circles, broad and wide, around and around the pond. Georgie wanted to say, "Oh, look, look at me!" but whenever she opened her mouth, the wind filled it. They were floating, soaring, skimming like sea gulls, like hawks, like swallows. Above them there was nothing but crystal air, and below them—and then for the first time Georgie looked down, and at once she was frightened. The emptiness below her was an immense gulf of nothingness. There was only the steely surface of the gray pond, far down, flat like metal, and the dark bristle of the trees poking up around it. Georgie gave a strangled cry, and dropped one arm.

Instantly she was falling, spinning over and over, plummeting straight down. But only for an instant. With a tremendous jerk and a terrible pinching pain in her left arm, she was snatched out of her plunging fall. The Goose Prince was dragging her through the air, his wings thundering, struggling to hold her aloft. And soon he was lowering her gently to the ground on the nearest shore.

Georgie lay on the stony path for a moment, trying not to cry, and then she stood up, trembling, rubbing her arm. "I'm sorry," she said.

But the Goose Prince was gallant. "Oh, it's *quite* all right," he said. "I hope I didn't hurt you?"

"No, no," said Georgie. "Could we try again?"

"Try again? Are you sure?" The Goose Prince cocked his head at her, and she couldn't help laughing. In his tender concern he looked for a minute more like her mother than like the splendid prince he really was.

"Oh, yes!"

They tried again. Once more the Goose Prince paddled out into the water, once more they took off in a rush of beating wings, once more he lifted Georgie high over the pond. And once again Georgie let go. This time when she clenched her teeth and slid off the back of the Goose Prince, she was careful not to look down. This time she lay perfectly still on the cushion of air. Keeping her arms spread wide, she circled like the Goose Prince as he rested beside her on the same sturdy ridge of warm vapor rising from the pond. She was safe now, perfectly safe. Watching her companion out of the corner of her eye, Georgie obediently copied his slightest motion. Whenever he adjusted the curve of his pinions to change the direction of his flight, Georgie bent her elbows too, and followed his lead. When the wind rocked him, and he spread the tips of his wings to let it flow through the gaps between his feathers, it rocked Georgie too, and she opened her fingers. Glide, glide, float and glide, lift and soar! Oh, how far she could see! All the way to Boston! There it was, the city of Boston, a cluster of dark towers against the sunrise, and there were the shadowy mountains, still blue with night, far away on the other side!

Proudly the Goose Prince flew beside Georgie, wingtip to fingertip, his head bent on his long neck to watch her. The sunlight was shining redly on his belly with the same streaking ray that warmed her own face. And then, at last, Georgie dared to cock her head and look down. She saw Route 2, there at the place where it turned the corner, and, look! there was the train! It was rattling along the shore of the pond on its toy track, shaking from side to side. Now the sun had risen far enough to shine on the trees around the pond. The tops of the trees were pink. For an instant the sun flashed back into Georgie's eyes from the window of a car in the parking lot, making her blink. But she banked and turned, following the lead of the Goose Prince, lifting her head to gaze once again over the whole broad landscape from horizon to horizon, feeling the sleeves of her jacket fill with air, listening to the legs of her pajamas flap like the laundry at home on a breezy day.

She was free. Georgie exulted. At last she was

free as air. With the Goose Prince she could fly everywhere, all over the world. There were no fences to keep them out. So this was the way birds felt! They could fly to China and France and Africa! To Africa, where there were lions and elephants! She could fly to the elephants' jungle! She could see monkeys, leaping in the trees!

Sitting in his car in the parking lot at Walden Pond, Ralph Preek gazed up at the giant birds circling in the sky. He was nearsighted. He couldn't see the birds clearly, but he knew that there were two of them, and that one of them was bigger than the other. Idly he picked up the gun that lay beside him on the front seat and pointed it upward, trying to follow the bigger of the two birds with the sights along the barrel. It was just for practice. Of course he wouldn't fire a shot until an instant after midnight on the first morning of the hunting season. But it was too bad to be forced to wait because of a stupid law. Ah, well, the first day of the hunting season was only a little more than two weeks off. He would bide his time. No one would ever be able to say that Ralph Preek was anything but a law-abiding man. Mr. Preek didn't know it, but there was another Massachusetts state law against firing a gun at waterfowl after sundown. And there was still another against the use of firearms at Walden Pond at any time of the day, all year round. Smiling to himself in his ignorance, Mr. Preek put his gun down beside him on the seat of the car, revved the engine softly, and backed the car out of the parking lot.

His time would come. Only two weeks from Saturday. He could wait.

TINY SPRINGS
AND LITTLE WHEELS

Back in her bed at home Georgie had hardly closed her eyes before it was time to get up again. But she wasn't tired. She woke up and got dressed and went downstairs even before her mother came to wake her up for school. Flying half the night didn't make Georgie tired. Flying was like resting. Resting on a bed of air.

In the empty kitchen the cornflakes rattled noisily out of the box. Two cats were curled in a patch of slanting morning sunlight. Heat was beginning to collect in the kitchen. It would be a hot day for the middle of September. Three or four flies were droning around the ceiling, hovering, crisscrossing, their buzzes mounting at different harsh pitches. One of the flies landed on the table and walked toward Georgie's bowl of cornflakes. Then it stopped and rubbed its hands together. Georgie put her cheek down on the table and looked at the fly's big eyes. "Hello, there," whispered Georgie. "You know what? You're not the only one who can fly."

"Drat those flies." It was Uncle Freddy, coming into the kitchen in his red bathrobe, reaching for the flyswatter. "They're coming in from out of doors. They know the weather is going to turn cold." Uncle

Freddy brandished the flyswatter around the room. Then he saw the fly on the table. "Don't move," he said to Georgie, poising the flyswatter over the fly.

Georgie sat up quickly and clapped her hands. The fly flew away.

Uncle Freddy gasped and stared after it. Then he laughed, and hung the flyswatter back on its nail on the wall. "Oh, fly, live forever," cried Uncle Freddy. "May your children and grandchildren populate the earth, a hundred thousand strong!"

Georgie's mother came running into the kitchen, her face drawn and pale, her dressing gown buttoned the wrong way. When she saw Georgie, she stopped and sat down hard at the table. Then she reached over quickly and patted Georgie's cheek.

Eddy was next. He came in sleepily, wearing only his pajama bottoms, opened the bread box, dropped two pieces of bread into the toaster, sat down at the table, and yawned hugely.

Eleanor was last. She strolled into the kitchen with her French book in her hand and plumped herself down at the table. Eleanor was dressed to the teeth for school. Everything was blue. Her skirt was blue. So was her shirt. There were pieces of blue yarn in her red hair. She opened her French book and hung over it, cramming for a test, murmuring French verbs to herself while the TV flickered on the windowsill, muttering its pale green morning news.

Idly Georgie dipped her spoon in the milk at the bottom of her bowl and scooped up a last mouthful of soggy cornflakes. Then she glanced up at her mother and Uncle Freddy and Eddy and Eleanor.

They didn't know. They didn't know she could fly. They could see her cheeks going up and down, they could see the trickle of milk leaking out of one side of her mouth, but they couldn't see what she was thinking. Georgie wiped her mouth and watched Uncle Freddy pour cream into his coffee. The cream swirled in curling patterns in the top of the cup. Uncle Freddy looked back at Georgie and smiled at her—but Uncle Freddy couldn't see the Goose Prince inside her head, floating beside her over Walden Pond, he couldn't see the ground spreading below them to the edge of the world. He could see only the outside of her, not the inside. Of course if she were to pull up her sleeve, then Uncle Freddy would be able to see the black-and-blue mark on her left arm, where the Goose Prince had caught her when she was falling out of the sky—the sore place ached a little, but Georgie didn't rub it. Her arm lay still in her lap.

It was because people had thick smooth outsides like the walls of houses. When you walked past houses in the street, you couldn't see the people inside. And it was like Uncle Freddy's wristwatch. Uncle Freddy had opened it up for Georgie, to show her how it worked. The inside was full of tiny springs and little wheels going back and forth and back and forth. Secretly. Quietly. There inside the watch where nobody could see. Like Eleanor. Just look at Eleanor! Eleanor had her book open on the table, and her hair was orange and her shirt was blue and she was glancing up at Georgie out of the corner of her eye. Eleanor was thinking something secret too, and Georgie didn't know what it was. Inside Eleanor's head the little springs and wheels were going back and forth and back and forth. Quietly. Secretly. Inside where nobody could see.

I wish I knew what's the matter with Georgie, thought Eleanor, looking back down at her French book.

j'aime	nous aimons
tu aimes	vous aimez
il aime, elle aime	ils aiment

said the French book. Eleanor turned the French words into English under her breath.

I love	we love
you love	you love
he loves, she loves	they love

Something was the matter with Georgie. Oh, whatever would happen to her? What if she grew up a little bit weird and peculiar? That would be terrible! Eleanor stared down at her book, but her attention was drifting away to other kitchens in other parts of the town of Concord. What did Robert Toby eat for breakfast? And Arthur Hathaway?

There was a small explosion. Eddy's toast popped out of the toaster. The two pieces were just right, warm but still soft. Eddy buttered them, then folded one piece over on itself and took a bite out of the middle. The middle bite was always delicious. The middle bite was the best bite. The middle bite was The Bite. Eddy chewed The Bite and looked at Georgie. She was sitting quietly, staring into her empty bowl. Her mouth was open. If you didn't know any better you would think she was a dumb little kid, thought Eddy. But she wasn't. Georgie had learned to read the dictionary when she was only four. Eddy felt a noble impulse of brotherly generosity. "Hey, Georgie," he said, holding out his second slice of toast, "you want a piece?"

Georgie smiled at him and shook her head. Then she hopped out of her chair and squatted down on the floor to pet one of the cats.

"Oh, well, then," said Eddy. He folded the piece of toast over and took The Bite.

Aunt Alex watched Georgie stroke Aphrodite's whiskers and scratch behind her ears. Georgie's mother felt heavy and tired. She didn't know what to think about Georgie. She didn't know what to do. Georgie had flown away twice in the middle of the night. She had come back twice, safe and sound. But what if—?

Aunt Alex held her knife in the air over her soft-boiled egg and stared at the shining blade. What if he came again to take Georgie away? What if he kept on coming? Should she let Georgie go?

Aunt Alex gave Georgie a flashing glance. Then she looked back at her knife and tapped the eggshell firmly. The egg cracked neatly into two parts.

Yes, she should. She would let her go. It was a precious thing. She mustn't be afraid. She wouldn't say a word. Oh, Georgie—Aunt Alex gazed at her daughter and worried silently—what do you see in the air in front of you? Not the cat, not the side of the stove with the drips coming down? What is it, Georgie?

But Georgie was jumping up now and running to the window. *A-WARK, a-WARK!* Another flock of Canada geese was flying over the house. Uncle Freddy got up too and went to the window and stood beside Georgie, gazing upward at the geese, who were flapping in a ragged line through the warm September sky.

Georgie was a little wild thing, too, like the geese, thought Uncle Freddy. She knew something he didn't know. Or something he had forgotten. Something too young and wild for him to remember. Oh, he'd give anything to remember!

The flock had set off from Walden in the direction of Bateman's Pond, but now they began wheeling in a great arc over the town, heading southwest.

The young gander who was in the lead was climbing higher and higher in the sky, gabbling noisily, giving directions. Obediently the flock flapped after him, shouting a chorus of frantic questioning and noisy understanding and consent. Soon they all stopped shouting and flew silently together, passing along a wave of air from wing to powerful wing. They were determined. They were earnestly resolved. They were ready to fly all day. This was not to be another short flight from pond to river, from marshy meadow to stubble field. In the minds of the full-grown geese an image of the day's destination was fixed and clear. It was a blue pond farther south, a small body of water surrounded by rocky pastures. And at the end of another day's journey still farther to the south and west they would look for a particular quiet harbor where a long wooden dock stretched out into the water. They would rest there and then fly on, farther and farther to the south. The entire flock of sixty geese was on the move again.

And this morning they were not alone. Other flocks of migrating waterfowl were streaming south over the town of Concord. The whole Atlantic flyway was noisy with ducks and geese. Commuters at the crossing of Walden Street and Route 2 could look up from their cars and see a small nervous family of buffleheads darting overhead. And far away against the vastness of the morning sky another squawking, undulating line was an enormous flock of Canadas from Newfoundland. The great flock of sixty Canada geese that had dallied so long in the mild September air, resting and feeding in Concord's ponds and rivers and fields, was only part of a great movement of other geese, and of brants and mallards and mergansers and blue-winged teal and every other kind of migrating waterfowl, rising from shiny spots of water all along the coast of New England in their hundreds and thousands, to carry on the long journey to their wintering grounds in the south.

Sixty geese? No, sixty minus one. As the flock soared high over Walden Pond, and higher still over Sandy Pond in Lincoln, and higher and higher and higher until the Atlantic Ocean rose in a flat blue line on the horizon to the southeast, the largest bird in the flock dipped one wing and turned in a wide arc and flew back to the water meadows of the Concord River. Silently he dropped to the surface of the river and splashed down, skimming across the choppy water with his wings spread wide, folding them at last and rocking up and down, then paddling slowly to dabble in the shallows in Fair Haven Bay, and duck his head to feed on patches of submerged grass around the island near the western shore.

The Goose Prince was staying on alone.

FLEDGLING NO LONGER

The moon had come back into the sky. It was growing bigger and bigger. It had been just a sliver at first, a crescent hanging in the evening sky like a fragile ornament just after sunset. But now it was large and lopsided, bigger than half, smaller than full. Night after night the vague shadowy eyes of the moon looked in at Georgie's window, and gazed and gazed at her until she woke up and lifted her head and looked back at it face to face. Then Georgie would lie awake, flat on her back in bed, waiting and waiting. She had taken to going to bed in her clothes. Her overalls and sweater were hot under the covers. She would push back the blankets and lie quietly, expectantly, until the Goose Prince would tap gently on the window, and then she would hop eagerly out of bed and pull on Eddy's jacket and push up the window softly and climb out.

Night after night the air was crisp and clear. There were no clouds. There was no rain. Night after night Georgie and the Goose Prince flew up and away, over the laundry line, over the garage, over Miss Prawn's plastic garden, over the cabbages, over the high school, over the highway, over the woods. Night after night they glided down at last and splashed on the dark surface of Walden, with

the foam rising in sparkling fountains on either side
and the moonlight rocking in shattered pieces on
the broken mirror of the pond.

And then Georgie would tuck her feet up high,
because the water was *cold* now, *freezing cold*, and
they would paddle to the shore of Henry's cove,
sailing grandly away from the new flock of geese
that lay sleeping on the other side of the pond.
Often the new geese would wake up to cluck at the
intruder who was making a midnight commotion (so
late, it was *shocking*)—and then they would nestle
their sleepy heads down once again in their drowsy
feathers and go back to sleep.

The short walk up the hill to the place of the
granite posts had become a nightly ritual. Every
night Georgie and the Goose Prince climbed the
steep slope side by side. Every night, as the moon
grew bigger and bigger, and as the leaves of the oak
trees parted from their stems one by one and fell to
the ground, the splashes of light on the deep rustling floor of the woods grew wider and brighter.
And every night the snagged trunks of the pine trees
threw out their evergreen arms over the rest of the
thin forest. And every half hour the train went rack-
eting along the western shore of the pond in the
middle of the night, breaking the quiet of the shadowy woods with its whining rattle and its flashing
windows and the dying hum in the rails after it had
vanished around the curving track.

Sitting among fallen pine needles and oak

leaves, waiting for the Goose Prince to finish his nightly nap, Georgie often listened for the train. And there were other noises, birds murmuring in their sleep, the almost inaudible cracklings and patterings of the small creatures that lived in the underbrush. Waiting patiently, Georgie would listen to everything. Sometimes when the wind was right she could hear the bell of the First Parish Church strike the hour. Most of the time there was no sound at all. In the daytime it was different. In the daytime everything rushed this way and that way, and there was loud talking and yelling, and cars honking and trucks booming along Route 2, and overhead in the sky the sun hurling down bold sheets of yellow. But at night everything just lay still and breathed quietly, as if it were thinking. The moon looked down at everything, but it never made a sound. It kept its secrets. It never told.

Sometimes it was the rattle of the train that woke the Goose Prince from his nap. Georgie would see him start awake, jerking his head up from the soft pillow of his back, and then he would stand and *streeeeeeetch* his wings and open his black beak in a wide comfortable *yaaaaaaaawn*, and preen himself, and then he would waddle over to Georgie, his cheeks bulging in his friendly, beaming smile.

And then would come the time for talking. Not that they ever talked very much. Georgie had never been a great talker, and the Goose Prince himself was a bird of few words. Often instead of talking

Georgie would pull something out of the pocket of her denim jacket, some new treasure, and give it to the Goose Prince—another blade of grass for making music or one of the white stones that were Dollabella's puddings. One evening the Goose Prince dipped his bill courteously in an acorn cap and took a sip of air-tea. The next night he stood patiently while Georgie fastened a winged maple seed to his forehead, and then he waddled comically a few steps from side to side, wagging his short tail, to make Georgie laugh. The Goose Prince seemed grateful for everything Georgie brought him. His cheeks would puff out to show his delight. Graciously he would admire it, whatever it was, and then he would tuck it carefully away under a dense pile of leaves beside one of the granite posts.

And then they would fly. It wasn't flying really. It was a kind of elegant slow falling from the very top of the sky. The Goose Prince would carry Georgie high over the pond until it was only a small irregular patch of light far below them, until the world was spread out wide all around and Georgie could see flashing beacons and lighted tankers far out to sea. And then she would slip off and drift downward in long gliding flights, floating on the wind, buoyed by feathery streamers of air.

The air had become Georgie's element. She had taught herself to plunge, to roll and dip and soar. She had caught the knack of a clever assortment of airy acrobatic tricks that were beyond the skill of the Goose Prince himself. Strong as he was, he was heavy in the air, while Georgie was light, only a bit of tossed silk. But of course Georgie couldn't come down on the water by herself. At the bottom of her long slow circling falls she still needed the strong back of the Goose Prince. She would feel him come up beneath her sturdily, until she was settled firmly once again on his back, and then he would carry her up and away, over the trees and over the highway and over the fields and safely home. Every night, as the moon grew bolder . . .

RALPH PREEK
TRACKS HIS PREY

Mr. Preek was doing research. Research in the field, that was what he called it. He was studying the habits of Canada geese. He had learned to his surprise that the bird he was tracking was not a giant duck after all, but a Canada goose, a single bird, a very large and particular Canada goose. It had become the object of his waking and sleeping dreams.

Sometimes Mr. Preek drove down the dirt road into the Great Meadows beside the Concord River to watch the migrating waterfowl feed in the open marshes. But of course he knew perfectly well that this sort of expedition was a waste of time. The Great Meadows was a wildlife refuge. You couldn't shoot anything there.

Sandy Pond was a better place, Sandy Pond in Lincoln. Mr. Preek often crouched in the woods near the spot where the little island rose out of the water near the shore, and watched the geese take off and land. And sometimes after his working day at the bank was over, late in the afternoon, he would drive to Nine Acre Corner, where he had once seen an enormous flock of geese feeding on a new growth of winter rye in a farmer's field.

A field! A farmer's field! A field would be the very best place for a sharp shot from his new gun to bring the big bird down! A field where the geese were ruining a cash crop, interfering with the livelihood of some good Concord farmer! But the trouble was, Mr. Preek never saw his own very particular Canada goose at Nine Acre Corner, or in the Great Meadows, or around the island in Sandy Pond.

Only at Walden. Like clockwork every night the bird turned up at Walden Pond. It was one of a pair. The other bird was small, but the big one was the largest bird Ralph Preek had ever seen. The two birds came and went every night from the cove on the northern shore of the pond. Watching them night after night from his car in the parking lot, he had worked out a plan. He knew what to do. On the first day of the hunting season he would find himself a blind in the bushes there, a hiding place, and await his chance.

The first day of the hunting season would also be the day of the full moon. That was a piece of luck. Even in the dead of night there would be plenty of light. He would bring down the bird at the full of the moon.

Bring down the bird—Mr. Preek didn't think to himself in words like *killing* and *murder*. He didn't say to himself, *It is all right to kill things.* He simply thought what most hunters think, that nature itself kills things, that hunting is only a part of the balance of nature. If you didn't kill things there would soon be too many things. They would multiply and multiply, and feed on other things, and before long they would overrun the earth. Like locusts! Think of locusts, darkening the sky! Consuming entire counties of growing crops and moving on and gobbling every single leaf in their terrible jaws!

ELEANOR
HAS A BIRTHDAY

If she didn't get going in five minutes she would be late for school. But it was her birthday, and Eleanor was determined to finish her new dress and wear it in honor of the day. The sewing machine droned *BUZZzzzUZZzzzUZZZ* as Eleanor pressed the button on the floor with her foot. Hunched over the machine, she overstitched the last corner of the neck edging. There. That was it. She was all done. Briskly Eleanor pulled up the lever, leaned forward, bit the threads, and pulled her dress free. She shook it smooth. Then she ran swiftly upstairs to her own room, jerked off her bathrobe, slipped the dress over her head, and twirled in front of the mirror. The dress floated free, then wrapped itself around her legs and floated free again. It was a yellow dress, with a dashing pattern of orange spots and splotches. The splotches matched her orange hair. Eleanor was pleased. She had a new-clothes feeling of happiness. She felt fresh and smart, jaunty and trim, tall and willowy and supple. Snatching up her books, she ran out the door, dodging Uncle Freddy's students, who were coming up the walk. With her hair flying and her skirt flowing out behind her, Eleanor plunged romantically past an admiring

Arthur Hathaway. Arthur turned around and whistled.

Aunt Alex had plans for Eleanor's birthday too, but in the middle of her last afternoon class she suddenly sniffed the air, rushed for the kitchen, jerked the cake pans out of the oven, and dropped them *bang, bang* on the drainboard of the sink. It was a little too late. The two layers were dry and thin and black on the bottom. But an hour later Eleanor's birthday cake was a triumph, a spectacular example of the art of the amateur cake decorator. Aunt Alex had whipped up three batches of lumpy frosting, and then she had lathered the two lopsided layers with the white batch, and now Eddy and Georgie were squirting frosting decorations all over the outside with the yellow batch and the green batch.

Georgie used the little flat-nosed nozzle on the pastry tube to make clusters of green leaves on the top of the cake (you push and squeeze, then flick the nozzle up). Eddy draped yellow swags around the side with the fancy little star-shaped gadget (you have to keep moving and squeezing, both at the same time). Aunt Alex had manufactured a dozen globby roses the night before on little squares of wax paper. Now she took them out of the refrigerator and slid one of them on a cluster of Georgie's leaves.

"Oh, no," said Aunt Alex, stepping back to look. "It won't do. It's too much."

"No, it's not," said Eddy. "You can't have too much frosting on a cake."

"It reminds me of Miss Prawn's front yard," said Aunt Alex. Reluctantly she stuck the rest of her vulgar roses all over the rim of the cake.

Then Georgie screwed a new nozzle on her pastry tube, knelt on the kitchen stool, gripped her sides tightly with her elbows, sucked in her lower lip, and wrote *Eleanor* across the middle of the cake in a flowing hand.

The front door slammed. Georgie paused with her pastry tube in the air. Eddy stopped running his finger around the bowl of green frosting. Aunt Alex looked up from the blackened cake pans in the sink. Exposed in plain sight on the table was Eleanor's birthday cake, gorgeous with thick smudgy frosting, encrusted with shapeless roses and sprawling leaves, heavy with drooping swags, crowned with Eleanor's name in yellow sugar.

Eleanor burst into the kitchen. She threw open the door and stood staring at the three of them. "A giraffe," shouted Eleanor. "My dress, it makes me look like a giraffe."

They gaped at her.

"My dress. It's Robert Toby. He says I look like a giraffe. He does. That's what he says." Eleanor's eyes were glittering. Her hair was wild, all tumbled to one side.

"Oh, well." Aunt Alex dismissed Robert Toby

with a wave of her hand. "He just likes to tease you, isn't that it?"

"*Oh*, no, he doesn't." Eleanor slapped her books down on the table. The cake bounced. "Not Robert Toby. He's so *sincere*. I mean, he *really* says what he really *thinks*. He says I look like a— And after I slaved! You saw me slave! Didn't I slave, Aunt Alex? I wore my fingers to the bone! Eleven *buttonholes*." Eleanor stared vaguely at the cake. She clawed at her hair. "I'll never wear this dress again. I'll die before I'll wear it again!"

"He's crazy, that Robert Toby," said Eddy slyly. "You don't look like a giraffe. Why would anybody say that? You look like an ostrich. A sick ostrich with the chicken pox."

Eleanor shrieked and threw herself at her little brother and slapped him twice.

Aunt Alex opened her mouth to say, *Stop it at once,* then thought better of it. Eddy was shouting. Eleanor whirled out of the room, tearing at her new dress, ripping at the buttons in the buttonholes. Buttons popped off and bounced on the floor. She slammed the kitchen door. Then Eddy whammed the door open again, *crash* against the wall, and yelled after her, "Some people just can't stand the truth about themselves, that's all that's the matter with them." Then Eddy stamped out too and slammed the door. There was an awful *screeeeeeech* from one of the cats. "Oh, sorry," said Eddy. He picked up the cat and slammed the door again with a final *crash.*

Aunt Alex and Georgie were left alone in the kitchen. The silence throbbed.

Georgie didn't understand what was the matter with Eleanor. Her dress was pretty! Sort of spotted and pretty and bright yellow. The spots were like the spots on an animal's back, like the spots on the cats, or the dog down the street—or a giraffe! Really pretty.

Aunt Alex sighed. Reaching down with one long arm, she picked up a button from the floor. Georgie got down on hands and knees, poked her narrow hand under the refrigerator and brought out another.

"Thank you, Georgie dear." Georgie's mother put the buttons in her apron pocket and looked helplessly at the cake. The top layer had slid a little sideways. She nudged it back in place. Silently she handed Georgie one of the bowls of leftover frosting and a spoon. Georgie scraped frosting from the bowl and sucked the spoon. Aunt Alex began cleaning up the sticky table.

How different they are, thought Aunt Alex, Eleanor and Georgie. Altogether different. And it isn't just that Georgie is younger. Georgie is different from Eleanor all the way through, from the inside out. Why, look at her, right now. She doesn't even know that she exists. She's just eyes and ears, that's all she is, just looking and listening. She doesn't think about herself at all. The world outside her rushes into her, and that's what she becomes. She doesn't think to herself, "This is me, Georgie." Instead she pulses with the sunrise and the rain and the geese flying over the house. She's in them, not outside them. She's more like a bird or a flower than a girl named Georgie. Whereas, Eleanor! Oh, Eleanor! Just look at Eleanor! Eleanor is all Eleanor! And everything outside Eleanor becomes Eleanor too—sisters, brothers, uncles, aunts! She sucks us all in! There isn't anything else but Eleanor in all the world!

The kitchen door opened. It was Eleanor. She had changed her clothes. She was wearing a pair of blue jeans and a shirt with a large red slice of watermelon printed on the front. Her hair poured hotly over her shoulders. Her face was red from crying. "My cake," moaned Eleanor. "Just look at my cake. It's beautiful, really beautiful. Oh, Aunt Alex, I'm sorry."

Eleanor collapsed against Aunt Alex and howled.

MISS PRAWN
LEANS IN AGAIN

Eleanor's birthday was the same day as the full moon. Eleanor didn't notice that the moon was full. Georgie did. So did Miss Prawn.

And therefore Miss Prawn was leaning in again, secretly, pressing against the people in the neighboring house as she had so often done before, making a new claim. It wasn't because she liked them. Oh, no! No, indeed! In fact, Miss Prawn found nothing but fault with all of them, all five of them, big and small. And yet somehow she couldn't leave them alone. She had even moved herself into the house next door, bag and baggage, just so that she could be even more outraged by the tomfool things they could be trusted to keep right on doing. It was horrifying and fascinating, somehow, just to see what those people would think of next.

Uncle Freddy couldn't understand it. What did the woman want? Why did she go right on poking in her nose? Aunt Alex knew why. One day when Uncle Freddy was protesting a new Prawnish assault, yet another rap on the glass, some further pressure from next door, Aunt Alex had explained it to him fiercely. "It's your *goodness* that attracts her, that's what it is. She can't stand it. She has to poke it and prod it and pinch it and squeeze it and try as hard as she can to squash it entirely. Only she can't. And it drives her mad."

Eleanor's birthday cake was delicious. There was so much frosting on the outside, nobody paid any attention to the compacted dryness of the inside.

After the cake came the presents. One present was a lamp from Eddy and Georgie. Eddy had made it at school. It was a pump lamp, like an old-fashioned pump in the backyard. When you pumped the handle, the light turned on. Georgie had bought a lampshade in the dime store and decorated it with red maple leaves. She had ironed the leaves between pieces of waxed paper and stuck them on the shade.

Eleanor unwrapped the lamp and squealed with delight. Eddy plugged it in. The light shone through the red leaves. "Wow," cried Eleanor, "just look at those leaves." Georgie giggled with pleasure. Then Eleanor opened the rest of her presents, and there were more rapturous squeals and ecstatic screams. The kitchen was loud with Eleanor's noise.

Suddenly Georgie felt hot. She had eaten too much cake. She said, "Excuse me," and slipped out of the kitchen. In the front hall the lady on the newel-post towered over her. The lady's lamp was turned off, because the sky outside had only just turned dark, but moonlight slanted through the oval window in the front door and spread a thin ray over the marble ear of Henry Thoreau.

Georgie looked at Henry's ear. She wanted to whisper in it, to tell Henry about the pond and the flocks of geese on the water, and the Goose Prince, and flying, and how nice it was at Walden in the middle of the night, did he remember? But then she was attracted by the brilliant moonlight on the knobby pillars and crisscross lattice of the front porch, and she went outdoors.

The porch was cool, dazzling with the splendor of the full moon, which was rising pale and calm over the Mill Brook meadow. The moon looked as big and round as the porch light.

Georgie leaned against the railing and stared at the moon. Why did it come up later every night? She thought about it and felt her fat stomach. The moon was heavier, that was it. It got rounder and rounder every night, and heavier and heavier, and so it came up slower and slower.

There were bubbles of paint on the porch railing. In the moonlight Georgie could see them clearly. She dented one with her finger. Then she took hold of one of the pillars and pulled herself up until she was standing on the railing with one arm twined around the pillar. Dreamily she stared over the meadow at the moon. Then she let go of the pillar, spread her arms wide, and bent her knees, intending to spring lazily over the bushes and drift down into the front yard,

"*STOP.*"

Something was rising out of the bushes with a shriek.

Georgie squealed, and her easy jump collapsed in midair. She fell. A stiff broken wand of hydrangea raked her side.

It was Madeline Prawn, standing up skinny and tall in the middle of the bushes. "Oh, no, you don't," gasped Miss Prawn, "not this time." Jerking Georgie to her feet, she clung to her and thrashed about in the bushes, confused by the brilliant contrasts of light and shade. At last she crashed her way out of the bushy tangle and dragged Georgie up on the porch and barged into the dark front hall and fumbled for the light switch, hallooing for Frederick and Alexandra Hall.

Everyone came running. "I warned you," cried Miss Prawn, staring around in savage triumph at the circle of shocked faces, "I warned you about the full moon. The child was taking off. She was flying away. She was going home to the fairies. Didn't I tell you to watch out? You can't say I didn't warn you!"

"Merciful heavens," said Uncle Freddy, "my dear Miss Prawn, whatever do you mean? Let go of the child at once!"

But Miss Prawn hung on. The more Georgie squirmed, the tighter was Miss Prawn's grip. The time had come for the Georgie Protection Society to spring into action. With one accord Eddy and Eleanor flung themselves on Madeline Prawn.

It was three against one. Four feverish bodies

wrestled in the dark, while Uncle Freddy and Aunt Alex stood on the sidelines, dazed and shaken by the vibration, knocked against by tussling arms and legs. Georgie yanked and struggled, trying to jerk herself free, Eddy clutched Georgie around the waist, trying to drag her away, Eleanor wrenched at Miss Prawn's two hands, prying up her fingers one at a time, and Miss Prawn kicked out blindly and uttered muffled cries. At last Eleanor sank her teeth into Miss Prawn's thumb. (It wasn't the first time. Miss Prawn had felt the imprint of Eleanor's teeth before.) Now she shrieked and let go of Georgie. Georgie ran to her mother, and Eddy and Eleanor backed away, breathing hard.

It was all over. Aunt Alex stared at Miss Prawn, her eyes blazing. (Aunt Alex didn't get angry very often.) "Just what *is* it you are trying to say, Miss Prawn?"

"The moon," said Miss Prawn again, panting, rubbing her shin where Eddy had kicked it, sucking her thumb. "I've told you and told you. Don't you remember what I said?" She closed her eyes and groaned. "Oh, why do I care what happens to the lot of you? Why, oh, why, should I be my brother's keeper? Why should I bother with my neighbor's welfare? But it's just the way I was born. I can't help it. A natural-born instinct for doing good and help-ing others. Now listen. It's a time of danger, the full of the moon. Disaster. I mean, it's a well-known scientific fact."

The five of them were staring back at her, Frederick and Alexandra Hall and their three impossible children. No, there were six, counting the metal woman on the staircase. No, seven! There were seven! The seventh was the grim stony visage of the bust of Henry Thoreau. Seven pairs of eyes were boring into Miss Prawn. Hatefully. Accusingly. Ungratefully.

Miss Prawn's lip trembled. She was only trying to help. To do her duty as a neighbor and friend. After all, it was *she* who had been vouchsafed . . . After all, far be it from *her* . . . Oh, it wasn't fair. It just wasn't fair at all!

Uncle Freddy felt sorry for Miss Prawn. He took charge. With perfect courtesy he began pouring oil on troubled waters. Stepping forward, he took her by the arm. "On the contrary, my dear Miss Prawn, in my opinion the monthly appearance of the full moon is a time of great good fortune." Smoothly he guided her out onto the porch and down the steps to the front walk. "You have only to study the nocturnal wanderings of our good Henry Thoreau, Miss Prawn, during the summer of 1851. Have you ever happened to glance at his journal for that year? Oh, you should! You really should!" They were out the front gate. They were gliding along the sidewalk and up the path to Miss Prawn's house. "I'm sure, Miss Prawn, you too would find it a record of blessing and joy." Uncle Freddy deposited Miss Prawn on her own front stoop. "What a glorious history it is, indeed, of the passage of the full summer moon over the rivers and fields of the town of Concord! Good night, my dear Miss Prawn!"

Miss Prawn was dizzy. For a moment she hardly knew where she was. But then, as Uncle Freddy ran up the steps of the porch next door, she took a deep breath and recovered some of her senses. Turning to the vague dark shape of the neighboring house with its porches swimming in moonlight, she called out, "Keep an eye on her! Don't say I didn't warn you!"

Aunt Alex opened the door for Uncle Freddy and watched him lean over the porch railing and toss a final salute to Miss Prawn. "It's very kind of you, Madeline, but I assure you, we can look after Georgie ourselves."

But can we? worried Aunt Alex in the middle of the night, lying wide awake beside a sleeping Uncle Freddy, listening to the rushing beat of the great wings and the quiet scrape of Georgie's window sliding upward. Filled with dread, she sat up and caught a last glimpse of Georgie clinging to the goose's back, lifting from the porch, vanishing into the night. Would she come back? Of course she would, of course, of course. She had come back many times before. There was really no need to worry.

The room was chill. Aunt Alex shivered and lay down again and stared up at the dark ceiling. Beside her, Uncle Freddy had turned over on his back. He was snoring gently. But Uncle Freddy's snoring wasn't the sort of noise that would break the silence, the kind of silence that muffled Aunt Alex now, a silence that fell like motes of dust around her from every side of the shadowy room, that drifted over her like blowing snow, piling its nothingness around her, covering her over, burying her, mounding above her in soft layers to the ceiling.

There was only one sound in the world that could cut through that mortal stillness: the sound of Georgie coming back, the scrabbling noise of the great webbed feet on the porch roof, the scraping of the window in its frame, the light spring of the bed in the next room.

Aunt Alex lay in bed with her jaw tightly set and her fingers clenched, while the silence weighed down on her face. How much longer could she bear it?

MR. PREEK
TAKES DEADLY AIM

"A-WARK, a-WARK!" The Goose Prince skimmed low above the surface of the pond where the reflection of the moon lay in a broad column of moving light. Far away on the other side Georgie could see heads jerking up among the sleeping flock, and here and there a scandalized flapping of wings. A mild scolding crackle drifted across the water. Then the spray dashed up around her and the moonlight broke into a thousand pieces. The water wallowed and slopped. Then it smoothed, and the moon was again a single rippling column. Serenely, with the bluff prow of his breast parting the water, hardly disturbing the liquid surface at all, the Goose Prince sailed to the shore of Henry's cove.

On the steep slope to the clearing in the woods the moon shone bald and bright through the open branches of the trees. Georgie walked up the hill beside the Goose Prince with her hand resting lightly on his back. Then she settled down on the leafy floor of the clearing while he took his nap. When he woke up, she took a fresh blade of grass out of her pocket and played him a tune. It was only a succession of hoarse breathy notes, but they vibrated on the still air with a haunting excitement like that of his own hooting cry, and she could see that the Goose Prince was pleased. With his usual regal courtesy he picked up Georgie's blade of grass in his beak and tucked it carefully under his pile of leaves. "Shall we go for a spin?" he said politely, bending his neck forward in the kindly gesture Georgie knew so well.

"Oh, yes, of course." Impulsively, without meaning to, without thinking about it at all, Georgie put her arms around his neck, kissed him smartly on the end of his beak, and stepped back, smiling.

The Goose Prince didn't turn into a man. He merely stood there, beaming at Georgie, his cheeks bulging in the funny way that meant he was smiling too. And then, not saying anything, because they never really needed to say anything to each other, they walked side by side, true friends and loving companions, down to the shore of the pond.

A moment later they were side by side in common possession of the air, drenched in moonlight, gliding in lofty circles over the pond.

Georgie saw the car in the parking lot. For an instant the moon glanced into her eye from the slanting windshield. But she barely noticed it. The car had been parked there many times before.

It was only when the smooth billows of creamy air had carried her around and around over the pond and down and down, closer and closer to the water—it was only when the Goose Prince had dropped below her, ready to lift her up at last and carry her home—it was only then that Georgie saw anything out of the ordinary.

The wind had freshened from the north. *Bong, bong, bong*—the midnight bell in the steeple of the First Parish Church was ringing clearly over the water. On the last stroke Georgie caught a glimpse of something glittering in the bushes along the shore. There was a metallic gleam on a long straight shaft. Something blue and shining was lifting, following the dropping arc of the Goose Prince.

Instantly Georgie woke up from her floating suspended dream. In one brilliant flash of understanding she knew what was happening. She knew what to do. Violently Georgie hurled herself downward, plunging between the Goose Prince and the puff of white smoke, shielding him from the great exploding noise that shattered all the world.

Down she fell, straight down into the shallows, while a thousand birds rose together from the other side of the pond, shouting, *DANGER, DANGER, DANGER.*

The warning was too late. With a despairing cry, the Goose Prince plummeted after Georgie, grasped her jacket in his bill, and dragged her out of the water and up on the shore. Then, swollen to twice his size, he made a rush at the clumsy man who was blundering out of the underbrush.

Georgie saw the furious assault. Sitting up and holding her bleeding arm, she watched the Goose

Prince stretch out his long neck and throw himself at his enemy, his beak open wide in a terrifying HHHHHHIIIIIIIIIIISSSSSSSSSSSSSSSSSSSSSSSSS, his thundering wings beating like the plunging hooves of a rearing horse.

The startled man dropped his gun, threw up his arms to protect his face, turned, stumbled away in the direction of the road, fell over a log, struggled to his feet and staggered forward, beating frantically through the bushes, until suddenly he found himself submerged up to his waist, cursing, in the cold slime of a swampy backwater.

And there the Goose Prince abandoned him. Turning away, he flew swiftly back to Georgie, hooting his dismay and grief.

But Georgie was already helping herself. "I think I'm all right," she said feebly. She had pulled up handfuls of leaves and pine needles. She was stuffing them into her sleeve to soak up the blood that was seeping from the upper part of her arm.

Trembling, the Goose Prince stooped low beside her. "Can you climb on?" he said. Reaching out with her good arm, Georgie struggled weakly up on his back and drooped her head into the hollow place between feathery wing and neck. Then she wrapped her good arm around his breast and gripped the wrist of the other with her good hand.

"Are you all right now?" said the Goose Prince, looking back at her, his great eye at once both fierce and sad. "Can you hold on?"

"Oh, yes," whispered Georgie. "I'm all right. Really I am."

Desperately the Goose Prince ran forward, headlong, trampling the hard-beaten dirt of the path and springing into the air, lifting his precious freight straight up over the trees, bearing her steadily home. Low over the highway, low over the high school, low over the cabbage fields he carried her, until they were circling at last directly over the house with the domed tower and the high peaked roof. This time the Goose Prince sank gently to the window that was next to Georgie's. Then he rattled frantically against the glass with his bill and beat against it with his wings, hooting, "*A-WARK, a-WARK!*"

In an instant the window was thrown open, and Georgie was tumbling through it into her mother's arms. And Uncle Freddy was leaping out of bed, his hair in a frowze. Together Aunt Alex and Uncle Freddy lowered Georgie to the warm bed, and Uncle Freddy pulled up the blankets around her and Aunt Alex ran to the phone to call the doctor.

Only Georgie, lying on the bed with her head lifted up from the pillow, only Georgie saw the Goose Prince peer in at her anxiously, his head craned to one side. Only Georgie saw him fly up from the porch, a heaving black shape, blurred at the edges against the sky. Only Georgie saw the blank window after he was gone. Beyond it the lavish moonlight had washed the sky clear of stars.

There was only the window itself, its rectilinear moldings raked by the light of the round moon, which stood now at the very zenith of the heavens, broad and majestic and wide and altogether full. There was only the window and the tremulous disordered curtain, caught between upper sash and lower, bellying out and flapping like the sail of an abandoned vessel.

"Good-bye, good-bye," whispered Georgie, bursting into feeble tears.

THE HUMILIATION
OF MR. PREEK

Ralph Preek was furious, humiliated, disappointed. He had failed. He had shot down a Canada goose, but it had been only the smaller of the two, and an odd sort of bird—silhouetted against the moonlight, it had looked distinctly queer. What was worse, he had failed to bag his catch and bring it home. And, worst of all, instead of destroying the bird that was a menace to hearth and home and to the safety of little children, he himself had almost been killed by the bird instead!

Mr. Preek stayed home from the bank and nursed his wounds and sulked. There were savage bites on his arms, on the back of his neck, on his back. The bird was a killer. This time there was no mistake.

But for some reason Mr. Preek's grudge had become entirely personal. He didn't want to bring anyone else into it. He would look so ridiculous— that was the trouble—getting beaten up by a stupid bird!

"It was dogs," he said, lying naked on the doctor's examining table, wincing as the doctor dabbed at him with disinfectant. "Savage dogs. They've been tearing up my flower bed. I was only trying to chase them away, and then look what they did, they attacked me."

"Funny sort of dogs," mused the doctor. "It looks more like somebody came at you with a can opener or a corkscrew." The doctor chuckled. "Are you sure it wasn't just a barroom brawl?"

"Oh, no, of course not. Don't be absurd. It was dogs, huge beasts with enormous, foaming jaws and colossal teeth and eyes like dinner plates. It's a mercy I got away alive. Oh, ow!"

"Foaming jaws? Were they really foaming at the mouth? Say, you'd better report those animals to the police. Look here, I'm going to have to start you on rabies shots, just in case."

"Shots?" said Ralph Preek. "No, no, I was mistaken. They weren't foaming at the mouth, after all. No, no."

"Well, we better be absolutely sure. Turn over." The doctor dabbed more disinfectant on a shrinking part of Mr. Preek, poised his needle mercilessly over it, and stabbed.

AUNT ALEX
TAKES NO CHANCES

The Georgie Protection Society had failed too.

"I'll bet it was that man in the store. Mr. Preek. That guy in the bank." Eddy pounded his fist on the kitchen table. "It was him, wasn't it, Georgie? The man with the gun? You know, the one who brought you home the other day?"

Georgie was sitting at the table, her arm in a sling, opening her mouth like an infant bird while Eleanor fed her spoonfuls of cornflakes. She swallowed a mouthful and shook her head at Eddy to say she didn't know.

Eleanor was envious. "Gee, Georgie," she said, dipping up another spoonful, "I wish a big goose would take me flying in the sky at night. Was it really wonderful?" In the back of Eleanor's head there was a dim memory of times when she too had been swept up into the air, dreamlike times that had been called into being by the diamond in the window of the little room in the attic, or the swing in the vanished summerhouse, or the stereoscope under Eddy's bed, times when they had been summoned by the handsome woman on the staircase, or by Prince Krishna, their uncle who lived in India. There had been all sorts of adventures, and some of them had been high-flying and far away, hadn't they, high and very far? But she had never flown by herself, had she? She had never been as lucky as that? Or had she? It was all beginning to run together in the back of Eleanor's mind, and the things that had probably really happened were confused with the things that probably hadn't. And every day everything in her whole past life—the real things and the imaginary things—was being pushed farther and farther back, because going to high school was so enormous, so vast! so different from all of Eleanor's life before. The milling crowds in the hall between classes, all those jostling elbows and swollen shoulders and bosoms, all those enormous hands and feet, they pushed and thumped and shoved at Eleanor's childhood, until there was no room anymore for anything but *now*, right *now*, a hurrying rushing *now* that was *just incredibly thrilling* or *absolutely rotten and just disgusting*, this heaving present moment, right *now*.

Georgie looked back at Eleanor and sucked the spoon. Had it been wonderful, Eleanor wanted to know, flying with the Goose Prince? Oh, how could she tell it? Georgie didn't know what to say. She wiped her mouth silently and shook her head at the next spoonful.

"Well, okay, Georgie. No more, then? Well, okay." Briskly Eleanor put down the bowl of cornflakes and bounded out of her chair and snatched up her coat and books and hoisted the strap of her pocketbook over her shoulder and ran out the front door, hurrying away to school.

Within a week Georgie was feeding herself. She was mending quickly. The wound had healed. The pellets had missed the biggest blood vessels in her arm. They had missed the bone. There was only a bandage now, held on with adhesive tape, to show that anything had happened at all. Georgie, too, could go back to school.

But not alone. Aunt Alex had decreed that Georgie was never to be left alone again. Aunt Alex was taking no more chances with a kidnapping Canada goose, no matter how good his intentions, no matter how noble a bird he might be, and gentle and splendid and kind.

And therefore the Georgie Protection Society was back at work, keeping her under guard. Eddy was to walk her to school in the morning and back again in the afternoon. Eleanor was to keep her company at home when Aunt Alex was out shopping or whenever she was busy with a class.

Miss Prawn had been right about Georgie. That was the trouble. In some terrible mistaken interfering way, she had been right after all. And therefore Aunt Alex and Uncle Freddy and the Georgie Protection Society were working full time, taking Miss Prawn's advice at last.

The first thing was the moving of Georgie's

bed. Eddy and Uncle Freddy took it apart and carried it across the hall and jammed it into the space between Eleanor's dresser and her desk. Georgie's bed was right under Eleanor's window, but that was all right. There was no porch roof below Eleanor's window. The window looked out over the other side of the yard into Miss Prawn's garden with its tiresome message in plastic flowers. The message was still plain. It still said *WELCOME TO CONCORD.* The white plastic petals of the roses never faded. The green plastic leaves never withered and fell.

"I'm sorry about the view, Georgie," said Eleanor, making the bed for Georgie, tucking in the tufted bedspread.

"Oh, that's all right," said Georgie. She smoothed the spread over the pillow, then turned her head and listened. There was a *bang-bang*ing noise across the hall. "What's Uncle Freddy doing?"

Eleanor avoided Georgie's eyes. "I don't know. Hey, Georgie, where's Dollabella? Oh, there she is. Let's put Dollabella on your pillow. There you go, Dollabella, old girl. Now, see, Georgie? Doesn't she look nice?"

But Georgie wasn't listening. She was walking stiff-legged across the hall. In her old bedroom she found Uncle Freddy hammering nails into the window frame. When Georgie came in, he stopped hammering and looked at her guiltily. "I'm just nailing the window shut to keep it tight until spring comes again. Your room is a little drafty, you see, Georgie."

Georgie nodded silently, and stood watching him, clasping her upper lip with her teeth, rocking back and forth on her heels.

Uncle Freddy hammered in another nail. Then he put the hammer down and turned around. "No, no, it isn't drafty in here at all." Picking up the hammer, he pounded in another nail with a great shivering of the window frame and rattling of the glass. Then he looked at Georgie helplessly and shook his head.

"It's okay," said Georgie. "No, really, I don't mind." And it was okay. It didn't matter. Because it was true—the Goose Prince really mustn't come again. Not now. It was too dangerous. He mustn't come until the end of the month. Georgie had found out about the hunting season. She had asked Eddy, and Eddy had asked Oliver Winslow. Oliver had a gun. Oliver even had a hunting license. He liked to pop away at bottles and tin cans and squirrels and passing birds and any other innocent thing that dove in front of him across his line of sight. So Oliver knew about the hunting season. He told Eddy, and Eddy told Georgie. The season would be over in less than three weeks. Until then the Goose Prince must stay away. He must hide. Because they were after him! It wasn't just that big fat man with the red face. It was all those other men. There were lots of them. They all had guns. They were everywhere! They were shooting everywhere!

Eleanor woke up suddenly and sat up in bed. Georgie was screaming.

"Georgie, Georgie, stop it." Eleanor jumped out of bed and crossed the room and shook Georgie. The room was gray with feeble dawn light. "You're just having a nightmare. It's all right."

Georgie stopped screaming. She sat bolt upright and stared out the window. "Listen," said Georgie. "I heard something."

Eleanor lifted her head and listened. There was a faint cracking sound far away out of doors.

"Don't you hear it?" Georgie grasped Eleanor's wrist. "It's guns. They're shooting over there somewhere."

"Guns?" The cracking sound came again. "Oh, is that what it is?" said Eleanor. "Well, maybe you're right. But the geese have all flown south, I'll bet." She patted Georgie's hunched shoulder. Georgie's arms were rigid in their sockets. "Your goose has gone away," soothed Eleanor. "You know that."

"But they shouldn't do it," said Georgie. "Those hunters. They shouldn't. They shouldn't."

Then Georgie lay down and allowed herself to be tucked in again, and Eleanor slipped back under her own covers and lay down on her side facing the wall. Poor old Georgie. She took things so hard. All she could think about was that big goose. She needed something to take her mind off her troubles. She needed friends to play with, that was it. If Georgie just had somebody to play with, she wouldn't brood about things so much.

Eleanor closed her eyes and vowed to do something about it. She would find a playmate for Georgie, right away, this very morning before school. She would call up Dorothea Broom before school.

Across the narrow bedroom Georgie lay on her back with her small bones straight and flat under the covers, her stringy sinews pulled up tense and tight, her eyes wide open, staring at the ceiling, listening to the *crackety-crack* of the guns in the faraway woods.

A PLAYMATE
FOR GEORGIE

Walking Georgie home from school on Monday afternoon was like dragging a ball and chain. She kept hanging back. Eddy had to keep turning around and egging her on. "Come *on*, Georgie."

Home at last, climbing the steps to the front porch, Eddy breathed a sigh of relief. His guard duty was over. Georgie was idling through the front gate. A moment later Eddy was upstairs in his own room looking at the complicated control-room section of his rocket model. Pieces were spread out all over his desk. He was ready to get to work.

Georgie was alone outdoors.

Slowly she climbed the three steps of the front porch. Then she turned around to look back at the front yard.

There had been a frost in the night. The marigolds along the fence had turned black. Georgie shivered in her puffy winter jacket. The jacket was last year's, too small for her now. Her bare wrists hung out of the sleeves. She held her arms out in front of her and looked at them. Then she bent her knees to jump down over the three steps to the walk below.

Something stopped her. Georgie hesitated and dropped her arms. The air over the wooden steps looked thinned out by the cold, too thin to hold her up, too thin to let her drift down lightly the way she had done before. Georgie decided not to jump after all. She turned away and opened the front door and stepped into the front hall.

Her mother was running toward the door, her face pale in the pitch darkness of the front hall. She was calling something to Eddy. ". . . not to be left alone!"

"It's okay," said Georgie. "Here I am."

Aunt Alex stopped and pressed her hand on her blouse. "Oh, there you are, Georgie dear. My goodness." Then she kissed Georgie lightly, followed her into the kitchen, and watched her hang up her jacket by the back door.

Eleanor was beating eggs in a bowl, whirring the electric mixer at top speed. Looking up, Eleanor exchanged a flick of a glance with Aunt Alex. Then she turned off the mixer. "Oh, say, Georgie, don't you think you should run upstairs and change your clothes? Dorothea's coming over. Dorothea Broom."

"She *is*?" Georgie was flabbergasted. "Dorothea *Broom*? She's coming over? Right *now*?"

"For tea, you see, Georgie," said Eleanor quickly, scooping up the eggshells and dumping them into the sink. "We just thought it would be nice for you to have a friend over."

Aunt Alex put on an apron. She felt heavy-footed and blundering. "Her mother is coming too," said Aunt Alex. "They're both coming. Oh, Eleanor, we haven't got a lemon. You're supposed to have a lemon, all cut up into slices, very thin."

Georgie was still staring at Eleanor, her mouth open in horror. But Eleanor was slapping down cookie tins. "Here, Georgie," she said recklessly, "hand me that flour sifter, will you? And you really ought to go up and change your clothes. Those good old red overalls of yours are way too small for you now. Look, they're halfway up your legs."

Georgie looked down at herself in dismay. Then she stumped reluctantly upstairs after Eleanor and stood stock-still while Eleanor held bits and pieces of her own clothes up against her, and pulled open drawers, and poked in her closet.

"Here's a funny one, Georgie. My watermelon shirt. It shrank in the wash. I bet it would fit you just right. See? It's only a little bit too big."

Georgie put on the watermelon shirt. She put on an old skirt of Eleanor's. The skirt drooped and sagged. "You're certainly not getting any fatter," said Eleanor. "Just taller. Here, we'll cinch it in around the waist with a belt."

Georgie looked at herself in the mirror while Eleanor pushed and pulled at her and beamed at her over her shoulder. "I think I look like celery," mumbled Georgie.

"Celery?" said Eleanor. "You mean watermelon."

"No, celery," said Georgie. She meant she was

long and stringy and thin like a piece of celery. In the mirror her arms hung out of the shirt, blue-white and dangling. Her hair and face were pale like blanched celery.

"Oh, celery," said Eleanor. "Oh, I see what you mean. Well, so do I. We're a couple of long skinny pieces of celery."

Dorothea Broom, on the other hand, was a choice piece of fruit, a succulent peach or a plump grape or a ripe cherry. Dorothea leaned back against her mother's knees in the parlor, while Georgie slumped round-shouldered in a chair on the other side of the room with her feet flat on the floor. (Georgie's feet had never touched the floor in that chair before.)

Mrs. Broom was smiling proudly, patting Dorothea's hair, winding curls around her finger, smoothing Dorothea's dress.

Eleanor gazed at Dorothea.

So did Aunt Alex.

Dorothea's pleased face collected all their looks. Her chubby cheeks absorbed them. She smiled her rosy smile.

Only Georgie didn't look at Dorothea. Georgie looked vaguely at the air in front of her. Driven into a corner in the same room with Dorothea, Georgie looked spindly and pale.

Dorothea had brought her doll. It was a big pink plastic doll with fluffy hair. Its mouth was open in a cooing *O*. "Show Georgina how your doll works, Dorothea," said Mrs. Broom.

Dorothea put her doll on the floor. The doll walked a few stiff steps, then toppled over. Dorothea picked it up. "Listen to this," she said. She pulled a string in the doll's back.

"My name is Bubbles!" said the doll. "I blow bubbles! I love you!"

"She blows bubbles?" said Eleanor. "Does she really?"

"Yes," said Dorothea. "Of course you have to put a bubble pack inside."

"Say, Georgie," said Eleanor, "why don't you go upstairs and get one of your dolls too? You know, show Dorothea."

Georgie's wan face brightened. She ran out of the room and came back a moment later with Dollabella.

"Oh, no, not that one, Georgie," said Eleanor, clapping her forehead. But then she laughed. She laughed too hard. She gasped, "I'll get the cookies," and sprang out of her chair.

Aunt Alex stuck up for Dollabella. "Actually, Georgie," she said loyally, "I like Dollabella best myself."

Dorothea was shocked. She stared at Dollabella. "Is that a doll?"

Mrs. Broom explained. "Oh, Dorothea, it's a terribly *interesting* kind of doll. Made out of a corncob, I think." Mrs. Broom lifted Dorothea into her lap. "Perhaps, Dorothea, someday soon you might give Georgina one of your older dolls to play with. Wouldn't that be a nice thing to do for your new friend?"

Aunt Alex looked out the window and mumbled something under her breath.

Georgie shook her head and hugged Dollabella to her chest.

Dorothea spoke up firmly. "No," she said, "it wouldn't."

Mrs. Broom untied Dorothea's sash and tied it again in a bow. "Why, Dorothea, I'm surprised."

"More cookies, anybody?" said Eleanor, heroically passing the plate. (It was hopeless. The tea party was a flop. She should have known. The whole thing was a big mistake. All that trouble, making the cookies and vacuuming the rug!) "Here, Georgie, have another cookie." Eleanor poked Georgie's watermelon shirt in a friendly way.

Aunt Alex had never been good at small talk. The only thing she wanted to say was "I'm sorry, Georgie." Instead she said, "Georgie dear, why don't you and Dorothea play outdoors for a little while?"

Georgie brightened, and looked at Dorothea. Dorothea hesitated, then slid slowly off her mother's lap.

"Put on your new coat, Dorothea," said Mrs. Broom, "and don't get it dirty, will you, dear?"

"What have you got to play with out here?" said

Dorothea, staring around doubtfully on the front porch.

Georgie looked dumbly at Dorothea. What did she have to play with? Then she beamed. "Something wonderful! I'll show you!"

Something wonderful? Dorothea hurried eagerly after Georgie, almost stepping on Georgie's heels with her shiny shoes. But at the entrance to the bush house she paused and hung back while Georgie scrambled inside on all fours. Bending down with her hands on her chubby knees, Dorothea stared inside. "I don't think I want to go in there," she said.

Georgie was holding the branches aside. She watched with surprise as the top half of Dorothea disappeared. Now she could see only Dorothea's white socks and shiny shoes waiting stolidly at the door of the bush house.

For a moment longer Georgie kneeled within her house and looked out. Beyond Dorothea's legs she could see the Mill Brook meadow. There were swamp maples growing beside the brook, their small leaves red as fire. And below the ridge the long stumpy branches of the dying elm tree were in full majesty of leaf, arching their yellow chains far out over Lexington Road. Somewhere a cricket was rasping one leg against another. The sun was spattering through the forsythia boughs. It was lovely and private in Georgie's bush house. If only she could stay there! If only Dorothea would go back to her mother and leave her alone!

But Georgie knew she had to be a good sport. She had to try to give Dorothea a good time.

She crawled out of the bush house and stood up beside Dorothea. Little pieces of leaves clung to her puffy jacket. Her knees were dirty. There was a twig in her hair.

"Let's watch TV, okay?" said Dorothea, gazing at Georgie.

"Well, okay," said Georgie, not looking at Dorothea.

MISS PRAWN
KEEPS HER EYES PEELED

On the last day of the hunting season Miss Prawn rose at five A.M., just as usual. She was merely following her weekly schedule, which called for cleaning the living room at five o'clock every Saturday morning.

It was no small task, there were so many surfaces to rush at with the dustcloth—all the little tables and dressers and the gold jars and the knick-knacks and the bric-a-brac. The antique hat pins must be removed from the pincushion one by one and dusted and polished and stuck back in. The doilies and dresser scarves had to be washed and starched. Of course it was impossible to clean the ostrich feathers, but at least they could be shaken out and combed. And every one of the pillows and bolsters and sofa cushions must be plumped and fluffed into a high marshmallowy mound. Last but not least there was the enormous fern in the window to be dabbed at with a wet dishrag, frond by frond.

It was while Miss Prawn was jabbing her dustcloth into the woven pattern of the wicker fern stand that a thought struck her. She put down her dustcloth, sank into the chair in front of her desk, opened her book of reveries, and wrote in a flowing hand across the top of a clean page,

*This morning my thoughts hover like the
fluttering wings of a butterfly.*

Oh, wasn't that good! Miss Prawn read the passage over and smiled with justifiable pride. After all, it wasn't everyone in the town of Concord who was forwarding the cause of Art and Literature this early on a Saturday morning! She paused, waiting for a new burst of inspiration, poising her pen over the page, her gaze fixed dreamily out the window on the house next door.

And then, once again, Miss Prawn saw something that startled her, something that straightened her back with determination, giving direction to her life and meaning to her day. Clapping shut her book of reveries, she snatched up a piece of letter paper and began writing a note to her employer. She would seal it, mark it *PERSONAL,* and send it by special messenger (that chubby little Dorothea Broom across the street). Miss Prawn had become addicted to writing notes. It was much more exciting than telephoning.

Dear Ralph, [scribbled Miss Prawn]

I am sorry to say that I have beheld no further miraculous flights by the child in the house next door. She was ill for a while, I understand, and has only recently emerged from the sickroom. But I write now in haste to inform you that a Foreign Party is threat-

ening her in some way. Something WITH WINGS is in the neighborhood. I catch glimpses of it from time to time, a SHAPE hovering in the sky at dusk, a wing flapping over the roof at the first glimmering of dawn. Considering its size, I would judge it to be either a small angel or a rather important and distinguished fairy.

Note: Tonight the moon will be full. I will keep a sharp eye out for trouble. I will stand true. You can rely on me.

Be strong! Be strong! We are not here to play!
    MALTBIE D. BABCOCK, 1901

Awake, my soul! stretch every nerve,
    And press with vigour on. . . .
      PHILLIP DODDRIDGE, 1755

Speak, and behold! we answer!
Command, and we obey!
    JOHN HAYNES HOLMES, 1913

      (Keep your eyes peeled, Ralph)
      As ever,
      Madeline

TOO BIG FOR FLYING

Uncle Freddy was trying to clear the front yard of leaves before suppertime. The springy bamboo rake vibrated in his hands. The leaves flew before it into a pile. It was only six o'clock, but the sun had already set and red shreds of clouds were rushing across the western sky. It was cold. Uncle Freddy shivered in his thin coat. Then he noticed Miss Prawn in the yard next door, and he leaned across the sharp spears of her yucca plants to say hello. "Good heavens, Madeline," he said, "you're not digging up those flowers of yours? Well, I suppose you're only being sensible. It will be winter soon, and they *would* look out of place, blossoming in the middle of a snow bank."

Miss Prawn had been down on her knees. But now she sat up and looked at Uncle Freddy in surprise. "Digging them up? Oh, no, I'm not digging them up. I'm just grubbing out the weeds. That's why I chose plastic flowers in the first place. They never fade. In rain or snow, hail or sleet, they will still say *WELCOME TO CONCORD*, proclaiming our hospitality to the whole world! They will always look good as new."

"Or bad as new," muttered Uncle Freddy under his breath, turning away, climbing the porch stairs, abandoning the leaf-raking job for the day.

"Oh, Fred," called Miss Prawn, getting up to her full height, waving her weeding fork at him, "have you noticed the moon? Take a look at the moon. It's full again. Don't say I didn't warn you. Take care."

Uncle Freddy looked over his shoulder at the great pale orb of the full moon rising to the east over the meadow. "Yes, yes, of course. Thank you, Madeline. Thank you for your concern." Actually it irritated Uncle Freddy to have his nosy neighbor tell him how to take care of his own little stepdaughter. But he would never say so out loud. After all—one had to face up to it—Miss Prawn's warning had been correct before. Hideously, horribly, precisely correct.

Inside the house Aunt Alex was throwing supper together in the dark kitchen, setting the table, turning out the meat loaf on a platter.

"My dear, how can you see?" Uncle Freddy flicked the light switch, and the lamp dropped a cone of brilliance óver the table. Instantly the dull china glistened with a blue stripe and the lettuce turned a vivid green and the meat loaf a succulent steaming brown. High over the hanging lamp the tops of the cupboards disappeared in the shadowy gloom of the high kitchen ceiling.

Aunt Alex poured milk, foaming white, into the glasses, and shook her head. "I hate turning on the light," she said. "It feels like winter, to turn the light on at suppertime. And tomorrow it will be worse. Tonight the time changes. The sun will set a whole hour earlier tomorrow. Oh, it's too bad. It's too soon."

"Well, at least we'll all get an extra hour of sleep," said Uncle Freddy brightly. "Think of it! A twenty-five-hour day, a whole hour tucked in before tomorrow begins, an hour plucked from eternity, an hour that doesn't exist, when anything could happen! The dead could arise! The stars and the moon might dance in their courses!"

Talk at suppertime was about Arthur Hathaway. Arthur was the school's worst student, the most hopeless, and the most charming at the same time. Uncle Freddy poked his fork in his salad and groaned. "The boy can talk a blue streak, that's what's so confusing. He can enchant the whole class, including me. But he doesn't read the assignments. He just thinks he does. Oh, yes, Arthur really thinks he's read everything, but he hasn't. Not one single thing."

Eleanor turned her empty milk glass around and around. "You'll have to admit, though, he's really good-looking," she said, glancing up at Aunt Alex.

"Good-looking?" said Aunt Alex. "Arthur Hathaway? Well, yes, I suppose he is good-looking." Aunt Alex got up from the table and went to the stove. "Oh, that Arthur Hathaway!" Hanging over the coffeepot with her face flushed, damp hair clinging to her forehead, Aunt Alex didn't notice Georgie slipping out of the kitchen into the hall in a stream of cats.

Only Eleanor looked up and called after her, "Give Dollabella a big kiss for me, okay, Georgie?"

In the hall Georgie found Eddy coming down the stairs. "Hey, Georgie," said Eddy, "don't you want to see my moon rocket glow in the dark? Look, it's all finished."

"Oh, wow, Eddy," said Georgie, "that's really great." But when Eddy went into the kitchen, Georgie lingered in the hall, gazing up at the twelve stairs to the second floor.

In the kitchen Eddy stood dramatically in the doorway. "Behold!" he said, switching off the light. In the sudden darkness his moon rocket floated, a ghostly green specter, a phosphorescent vision. Eddy spun slowly in one place and the rocket swept eerily over his head in a glowing circle.

"Hey, that's pretty good," said Eleanor.

"Well, now, Eddy, that's really beautiful," said Aunt Alex.

"Why, Eddy," began Uncle Freddy—

And then there was a noise, a thumping in the hall, and a sharp cry.

"Oh, no!" Eleanor jumped to her feet. "Not again! Not Georgie again!" Charging at the door, she collided with Aunt Alex.

"Oh, Georgie *dear*," cried Aunt Alex.

The four of them tumbled out into the hall and

rushed to pick up Georgie. They found her whimpering on the floor at the foot of the stairs.

"Darling *child*," said Uncle Freddy, "are you all right?"

Georgie looked at him, her face screwed up in tears.

"There now," said Aunt Alex. Picking up Georgie, she sat down on the stairs.

Georgie sat up stiffly in Aunt Alex's arms, her legs sprawling. "I'm all right," she said. "I won't try it anymore. I'm too big now, I guess. I'm just too big for flying."

Over Georgie's head Uncle Freddy and Aunt Alex and Eleanor and Eddy exchanged glances of relief. But beside them in the curve of the stairs Henry Thoreau gazed with his marble eyes more solemnly than ever in the direction of Walden Pond. His stony brow was wrinkled with foreboding.

A FAIR EXCHANGE

The Goose Prince pulled himself out of the water and dragged himself up on the shore of Walden Pond. He was worn out. His shoulder muscles ached and he was lame. One of the lead pellets from the shotgun blast that had wounded the child had spent itself deep in the fleshy muscle of his left leg. It was still there, imbedded, festering, giving him pain at every step. Savagely now he pecked at a parasite at the base of his tail, and then, slowly, he began to limp up the steep hill, half lurching on his webbed feet, half flapping upward with his wings. At last he waddled drunkenly into the clearing. He had come for the present.

He must see the little girl again. To say good-bye and give her the present. But how? The Goose Prince hooted softly with worry. The man with the gun was everywhere, and the child was nowhere! Oh, he had seen her once or twice out of doors, and he had rejoiced to observe that she was all right. But she was never alone. Twice he had come floundering down on the porch roof and pecked at the glass, but she had not come to the window. He had peered inside, but he had seen nothing. The room was empty. Perhaps the little girl was afraid.

Sorrowfully, the Goose Prince told himself that

the child had a right to be afraid.

But how was he to give her the present?

Painfully he limped across the clearing, hobbling to spare his throbbing leg, and paused beside one of the granite posts. Lowering his dizzy head to the place where he had buried the present in a cover of leaves, the Goose Prince shuffled with his webbed feet until he found it. The present lay shining in a nest of wizened grass and maple seeds and goldenrod and crumpled bouquets of asters and a clutter of pebbles and acorn caps—gifts from the child.

It was only an exchange he wanted to make, a fair exchange. One present in exchange for the others.

Gently the Goose Prince picked up Georgie's present and carried it away in his beak.

THE CLEVERNESS
OF GEORGIE

She was too big for flying. Georgie knew that.

So she would only say good-bye.

Tonight at midnight it would at last be safe to say good-bye. The hunting season would be over at midnight.

The Goose Prince was not far away. Georgie had caught excited glimpses of him. He was hiding somewhere nearby, hiding and waiting. But now the waiting was nearly over. How could she call to him secretly, silently, at midnight?

Georgie was clever. She had figured out a way.

Now she lay in bed, her head next to Dollabella on the pillow. Eleanor's alarm clock was a lump under the covers. Every now and then Georgie put her head under the covers and looked at the clock. The numbers on the face of the clock glowed in the dark, green like Eddy's moon rocket. The hands moved slowly. Slowly, slowly the minutes turned into quarter hours, and the quarter hours into half hours, and the half hours into hours. Georgie knew the time would pass more quickly if she went to sleep, but she didn't dare. What if she didn't wake up again till morning? Of course she could set the alarm clock to wake her up at midnight, but then

Eleanor would wake up at midnight too. And that would never do.

So she must keep watch, and look at the clock.

It was ten-twenty-two . . .

Ten-forty-seven . . .

Eleven-thirteen . . .

Eleven-thirty-seven . . .

The minute hand was creeping closer and closer to the top of the clock. . . .

There was only a little crack between the minute hand and the hour hand. . . .

Now the crack was gone. The two hands were pointing straight up. It was exactly midnight.

But still Georgie huddled in her bed. Relentlessly she forced herself to wait another five minutes. . . .

Then five minutes more. Because the clock might be fast. You couldn't be sure. And she must be absolutely certain that the last day of the hunting season had come and gone, that it had vanished into yesterday forever.

So it was fifteen minutes after twelve o'clock midnight by Eleanor's alarm clock when Georgie slipped out of bed and pulled on her bathrobe. The bathrobe was too short for her now, and the sleeves felt tight under the arms. Her slippers were too short too. She had to curl her toes to keep them on.

The doorknob mustn't click. Georgie turned the knob slowly until it unlatched, and then she turned it back the other way just as slowly. There. Gently she drew the door inward and padded out into the hall, feeling the large empty darkness expand around her. Softly she crept downstairs. The moon was shining behind the house somewhere, but not a sliver of moonlight shone into the front hall. Georgie had to feel her way, clinging to the stair railing, sliding her hand around the polished skirts of the metal woman on the newel-post, trailing her fingers across the marble nose of Henry Thoreau. But moonlight was pouring through the windows of the kitchen, and when she stepped softly down the back steps, it was flooding the whole outdoors.

The rest was easy. The wet grass made no noise under Georgie's slippered feet. Boldly she walked right through the laundry hanging on the line, smelling the sunshine trapped in her mother's blouse as it slipped over her face. But the yucca hedge was a problem. Its multitudinous sharp points bristled at Georgie in the moonlight. Backing up, she clenched her fists, then ran forward and *jumped*—whee! a tremendous jump—and *thump!* she was down on the other side. Breathing hard, Georgie looked back at the yucca hedge. It had been an ordinary jump. There had been no floating, no lifting and drifting down to the ground—just her new long legs carrying her safely up and over. (Oh well, thought Georgie, at least long legs are good for something.)

In the dim yard of the neighboring house, Miss Prawn's artificial garden was brightly visible. The plastic roses glowed weirdly in the dark—like Eddy's moon rocket, like the phosphorescent numbers on Eleanor's alarm clock—bidding a vulgar

WELCOME TO CONCORD

to any belated tourist who might be sauntering down Walden Street in the middle of the night.

Folding her arms on her chest, Georgie looked at the flower bed. Then she walked firmly to one end of it, reached out her hand, grasped one of the plastic roses, and *jerked* it out of the ground. She jerked out another. Georgie jerked and jerked, plucking one flower at a time, piling the stiff sprays beside her on the ground.

After a while she moved to the other side of the garden and began pulling out more flowers. But then she thought of Miss Prawn. As the new pile of uprooted roses grew bigger, she couldn't help glancing up furtively at the second-story windows of Miss Prawn's house. High and gray and square, the house loomed above the garden. But the windows were empty. There was no horrified face looking down at Georgie, screeching *STOP, STOP.* (Georgie didn't know it, but the indomitable Miss Prawn had abandoned her commitment to watch and wait. She was sleeping at her post. She had failed to *awake her soul! stretch every nerve, And press with vigour on.* She was not standing *firm to the fight.* She was disobedient *behold! to her own command.* But it wasn't her fault. Poor Madeline had risen as usual that morning at the crack of dawn, and by eleven P.M. she simply couldn't keep her eyes peeled a moment longer. She had gone yawning up to bed. She was sleeping the sleep of the just.)

So Georgie went right on pulling the roses out of Miss Prawn's flower bed until only four letters were left out of the sixteen that had so recently proclaimed their *WELCOME TO CONCORD.*

The remaining four letters still spelled a word, a perfectly good word.

COME

said the flowers.

Georgie stood back and looked with satisfaction at the new flowery message in Miss Prawn's garden. Then she picked up all the roses that were lying on the ground, stuffed them under a sprawling bush, leaped back over the sharp dagger points of the barrier between the two houses, and hurried around the side of her own house to the front porch steps.

Solemnly she climbed them—one, two, three— and then she sat down on the top step to wait.

COME

said the flowers in Miss Prawn's garden.

COME
COME
COME

ANOTHER CHANCE
FOR MR. PREEK

Mr. Preek's car was parked across Walden Street beside the Mill Brook meadow. He had been drowsing over the wheel, but now he jerked himself awake and looked at his watch. In glowing red numbers it said

12:28:31.

That meant it was twenty-eight minutes and thirty-one seconds after midnight.

12:28:32 . . .

12:28:33 . . .

Ralph Preek pulled himself upright. Feeling for the button on the side of his watch, he pressed it with his forefinger. Instantly the number 12 changed back to the number 11. The time was now

11:28:58 . . .

11:28:59 . . .

11:29:00

precisely.

Mr. Preek smiled gloomily at his digital watch in the warm shadowy privacy of his car. With a flick of his finger he had extended the hunting season.

Along with every other human being up and down the entire length of the eastern seaboard he had been given another hour to live over again.

And then he had slept through half of it.

Well, what did it matter, anyway? His cause was hopeless. The bird had been too wily for him. Oh, it was still around somewhere, he was sure of that. He had caught sight of it just the other day at Walden Pond. It had been flying low over the trees with something in its beak, and he had fired a wild, crazy shot, but he had missed. He had thought it was his last chance. But then Madeline had written him a letter. She had said something was hanging around the neighboring house. It was an angel, Madeline said. Or a fairy! Well, that was Madeline for you. As a personal secretary the woman was efficiency itself, but in every other way she was as nutty as a fruitcake. The thing wasn't an angel or a fairy. It was the colossal bird he had seen so many times before. And its fiendish purpose was clearer than ever. It was still trying to kidnap the little girl and carry her away to its gruesome nest on some rocky mountaintop, where it would tear at her vitals and crush her fragile bones in its terrible beak. (Mr. Preek was remembering a television show he had once seen about the habits of bald eagles.)

Of course he had reacted at once to Madeline's letter. He had spent the entire day lurking in the neighborhood, keeping an eye on the house, looking for the dangerous creature to show itself. But to no avail. The hunting season was over, and he had failed.

But, no, it wasn't over, not quite yet. Ralph Preek felt for his gun on the seat beside him. The polished wood and oiled steel felt comfortable under his hand. It had taken a lot of careful labor to get the thing back in A1 condition, after he had retrieved it from that swamp at Walden Pond. But he had spared no effort. There was no speck of rust on the barrel. The mechanism was working perfectly. And now there was still another half hour left, thirty minutes more of deadly opportunity. He would make one more foray around the house on foot, just to see what he could see.

Cautiously Mr. Preek opened the door of his car and heaved himself out of the front seat. Softly he walked to the other side of the street and peered through the hedge into the front yard of the tall house with its broad porch and moon-washed tower. Then he gasped.

The bird was standing on the walk.

The girl was sitting on the front porch. She was staring at the bird. She was mesmerized. . . .

FAREWELL

The Goose Prince had appeared from nowhere. One moment he wasn't there, the next moment he was. He was standing stock-still on one foot, his pale breast gleaming. Something lay on the walk in front of him. Something small and round.

Georgie stood up, feeling a smile spread all over her face. She began walking down the porch steps. Then she stopped short, startled, because the Goose Prince had jerked his head back. He was hooting with surprise.

It was because she had grown so tall! Georgie looked down at herself, smiling ruefully at the length of bare white legs gangling below her bathrobe, and whispered, "I'm sorry I got so big."

"It's all right," said the Goose Prince. Then Georgie saw the small bumps beside his beak that meant he was smiling too. "My, my, just look at you. Well, isn't that nice."

"Thank you for coming," whispered Georgie. "I just wanted to say good-bye."

The Goose Prince shifted his weight, wincing dizzily at the ache in his left leg, and then he lowered his head and poked at the thing that lay on the walk in front of him. It rolled a little to one side and came to rest in Uncle Freddy's pile of leaves. "I brought you the present," he said.

"The present?" said Georgie. She had forgotten about the present. "Oh, thank you." She ran down the last step and bent down to the Goose Prince and hugged him, nestling her head in the old place between the beginning of his long neck and the base of his wing. "Good-bye," whispered Georgie. "Will you come back next year?"

"Next year?" Gently the Goose Prince brushed Georgie's sleeve with his wing. "Next year! Well! I'll try. Well, yes, certainly. Next year! I will certainly try." Then he stood back in all his princely dignity and inclined his head. "The present—take good care of it."

Georgie nodded. She couldn't speak. Lifting one hand, she watched the Goose Prince turn away from her and make a limping rush at the night air. Why was he running all to one side? Had he forgotten how to fly? Georgie looked on in dismay as the Goose Prince blundered across the grass, flapping and heaving in a frantic effort to lift his heavy body from the ground. At last he was airborne, and now he was circling over her, looking down. Georgie lifted her face and her two hands in farewell. . . .

The bird was an easy target. Ralph Preek sighted along the barrel and pulled the trigger lightly. There was a deafening report. The bird dropped at the feet of the little girl.

For an instant Mr. Preek thought to his horror that he had wounded the child as well, because she made a tremendous leap into the air. But then he could see that she was all right. She was standing still, staring at the dead bird. Now she was throwing herself down on the tumbled heap of feathers.

Ralph Preek lowered his gun and smiled with grim satisfaction. He walked across the street, got back in his car, and drove away, as the bell in the steeple of the First Parish Church began ringing midnight for the second time.

THE PRESENT DISAPPEARS

Uncle Freddy buried the Goose Prince the next morning at Walden Pond. He didn't ask anyone's permission. He just did it.

Georgie chose the place. Walking stiffly from the car, she led Uncle Freddy to the clearing where the granite posts stood upright around the old house site, and then she stopped and said, "Here."

The place seemed right to Uncle Freddy. It had been his own private opinion that the Goose Prince was Henry Thoreau come back to life, reincarnated, back in the world as a noble bird! So it seemed altogether proper to bury him at the place where Henry had lived at Walden Pond.

The present had disappeared. Georgie looked for it everywhere. She was frantic. Over and over again she remembered the last words of the Goose Prince—*Take good care of it.* And yet she had lost it! She must find it, she *must*!

"Oh, poor Georgie, what *is* she doing?" Aunt Alex watched through the window as Georgie picked up handfuls of leaves and scrabbled frantically with her fingers in the grass and tossed more leaves from one side of the walk to the other.

"She must be looking for something," said

Eddy, and he went outdoors to help.

But Georgie couldn't explain what she was looking for.

"A present?" said Eddy. "Well, what kind of present was it? What did it look like?"

"I think it was round," said Georgie. Her face was pinched. She poked along the fence among the drooping flowers. "It was little, I think, and round. Sort of round."

But the present from the Goose Prince was nowhere to be found. Eddy and Georgie looked for it all over the front yard and the backyard. They looked for it in the street and in the grass on the other side of the road. They looked beneath the porch and under hedges and behind bushes, until the first snowflakes of the season began to fall, and then Eddy persuaded Georgie to come inside.

It was only a light flurry. For an hour or two the snow lay thinly on the ground, with brown leaves and green blades of grass pricking up through it, and then the afternoon sun melted it away. But Georgie didn't go outdoors again to look for the present. She had given up.

Uncle Freddy was in the kitchen when the terrible scraping and thumping began over his head. Running upstairs, he found Georgie trying desperately to wedge the head of her bed through the door of Eleanor's room.

"Dear *child*," said Uncle Freddy, "let me help you. You have to take the bed apart." Heaving at the

mattress, he unhooked the pieces of Georgie's bed
and carried them across the hall and set them up
again in her old room. Aunt Alex made the bed up
nicely, with clean sheets and pillowcases and fresh
blankets and good old Dollabella, while Uncle
Freddy stalked over to Georgie's window and
yanked out the nails with the claw of his hammer.

And then Georgie climbed into her bed and
pulled up the covers and lay down flat on her back
as if she would never get up again.

On Monday morning she didn't come downstairs. Aunt Alex brought Georgie her breakfast in
bed. She didn't make her go to school. Nor did she
ask Georgie to get up the next day—or the next. Day
after day Georgie lay in bed silently, her arms rigid
at her sides, staring at the ceiling. Aunt Alex sat
quietly nearby, sewing or correcting papers. Georgie didn't talk. She didn't read. She ate almost nothing. And she didn't cry. That is, she didn't cry in the
daytime.

But she cried at night. Across the hall Eleanor
would hear small strangled sobs and the murmur of
Aunt Alex's voice or tender noises from Uncle
Freddy. After a while the sobbing would stop, and
Aunt Alex or Uncle Freddy would stumble back to
bed, and in the morning they would be hollow-eyed
and anxious and pale. And in the morning Georgie
would stay home from school again and spend another day in bed.

She stayed in bed for a week. But on Monday

morning of the second week Georgie got out of bed and came down to breakfast. Standing in the door-way of the kitchen, she announced solemnly, "I'm all right now."

"Well, Georgie!" Uncle Freddy jumped out of his chair and patted her arm and fixed her a big bowl of cereal and poured too much milk into the bowl. The milk washed over the brim onto the table.

"Oh, you're so clumsy, Uncle Freddy!" Eleanor rushed happily for the sponge to clean up the table.

"Wow," shouted Eddy, "it's all over the floor." Dropping to his knees, he mopped it up with a paper napkin.

"Would you like some fruit on your cereal, Georgie dear?" Aunt Alex snatched up a banana from the sideboard.

They were all trying hard. Georgie was trying hardest of all. She said thank you and swallowed her breakfast and tried to smile.

And then at last she went to school. And at school she opened her notebook and copied her spelling paper and did her arithmetic neatly and came home with her papers marked *100* and *GOOD* and *A*, just as usual.

And after school there was a lot of cheery talk and things to do, all calculated to help Georgie feel like herself again. From the parlor came the buzzing whine of the sewing machine, where Eleanor was making Georgie a new dress. From the cellar rose the noisy banging of hammers, where Uncle Freddy and Eddy were building a bookcase for Georgie's room. From the kitchen drifted the soft murmur of Aunt Alex's voice, reading aloud to Georgie. Everyone was trying to bolster Georgie's courage. What if it faltered? What if she went back to bed and didn't get up in the morning?

But she did. On Tuesday morning Georgie went off to school just as usual, just as if nothing had ever happened. Everything seemed to be back to normal.

Eleanor knew it was a shaky normalcy. Georgie was putting on a good show, but you could tell she was still miserable inside. The poor little kid, she always took things so hard. She *felt* things so. She was quiet, that was the reason. Still waters ran deep, that was what everybody said. And that was Georgie for you.

On Tuesday afternoon Eleanor came home from school with Georgie heavily on her mind. Opening the front door, stepping into the hall, she called, "Georgie? Georgie, where are you?"

The house was warm. Coming in from the cold Eleanor was immediately engulfed by the dark comfort of the front hall. Her nose quivered. The furnace had been turned on, and every day the hot air from the radiators sank deeper into the spongy interiors of the sofas and chairs. And now there was a fragrance of coats and sweaters shaken out of windowseats, of blankets unfolded and tossed out, ballooning, over beds. Eleanor pulled off her coat, suddenly remembering the time last March when she had stayed at home with a cold, when she had lain comfortably on the sofa in the parlor with three pillows under her head and a heavy down puff on her knees and mugs of cocoa and plates of cinnamon toast on the table beside her. The mixed perfume of heavy sweaters and woolen blankets and boiling radiators brought it all back to Eleanor, the comfortable feeling of the house in the wintertime.

Where was Georgie? The kitchen door burst open. Aunt Alex's students were pouring out into the hall, carrying stacks of cups and saucers, heading for an afternoon class in the parlor. They were laughing and talking and clashing crockery down on the parlor table.

"Well, if it isn't young Eleanor," said Arthur Hathaway gallantly. "*Hello there*, Eleanor." Arthur was carrying the heavy coffee urn. He stared after Eleanor as she hurried past him into the kitchen to look for Georgie.

Eleanor could feel the back of her head being looked at. Ordinarily it would have felt nice, being looked at by Arthur Hathaway. But today all she could think about was Georgie.

Aunt Alex was pouring milk into a pitcher, putting the pitcher on a tray with a bowl of sugar. She glanced up quickly at Eleanor. "She's upstairs," said Aunt Alex. "In her room."

"In her room?" said Eleanor. "Oh, no, she hasn't gone to bed again?"

"I don't think so. She's all right. See if you can find something for her to do."

Eleanor ran upstairs, calling brightly for Georgie. She knocked on Georgie's bedroom door. "Georgie, are you in there? May I come in?"

There was a pause, then the creaky spring of Georgie's bed. Then Georgie opened her door and smiled bravely at Eleanor.

"Well, Georgie!" Eleanor breezed into Georgie's room and darted a glance at the bed. It was a little rumpled, as if someone had been lying on top of the spread. The window was open. "Oh, brrrr," said Eleanor, shivering. She went to the window and closed it smartly, with a *bang.* "Well, now, Georgie, what would you like to do this afternoon?"

Georgie looked out the window. A flurry of small birds darted across her view and disappeared. She tried to think. "Shall we play outdoors?"

"Outdoors?" said Eleanor. "Oh, well, okay. I mean, it's cold out there, but never mind. Do you want to wear my turquoise sweater?"

Georgie nodded and smiled. Eleanor brought the sweater from her dresser across the hall and pulled it down over Georgie's head. "What shall we do outdoors?" said Eleanor.

Georgie's head poked through the sweater. "Shall we have another tea party?" she said.

"Well, why not?" said Eleanor valiantly. (Oh,

brrrr, a tea party out of doors in November. Well, anything to please Georgie.)

No longer did the bush house feel like a secret place. The leaves that had covered it like a spreading parasol had fallen to the ground, and now the bare branches of forsythia dropped cold bolts of wintry sunshine on the tea party within.

Eleanor and Georgie settled themselves luxuriously on comfortable cushions of drifted leaves. "Oh, look, Georgie," said Eleanor, "there's an acorn. And there's another one. They've just fallen from the oak trees. We can make Dollabella a whole new set of dishes."

"Oh, good," said Georgie, and together they began poking in the leaves, looking for more.

But it was Georgie who found something better than acorns.

"Why, Georgie," said Eleanor, "where did that come from? It looks brand-new."

"It is," said Georgie. Joyfully she held it up in both hands. "It's the present. It's the one I was looking for."

THE PRESENT AT LAST

It was a rubber ball. A small rubber ball with blue and white streaks. After the shotgun blast that had killed the Goose Prince, during the tumult and confusion and despair and the rush of people all over the front yard, the ball had been kicked into the bush house. It had buried itself in the drifted leaves.

"The present?" said Eleanor. "Well, well, so that's what the present is." Privately Eleanor didn't think a small rubber ball was much of a present, but she didn't say so. Georgie seemed to be happy with it. "Why don't we play catch in the driveway?"

"All right," said Georgie eagerly. Together they rustled out of the bush house on hands and knees, and then they stood up in the gravel driveway and tossed the ball back and forth between them.

It was a good ball for throwing, hard and firm enough to fly straight and true, making perfect, easy flights, and light enough to drop gently into the waiting hand. "Oh, good catch, Georgie," said Eleanor.

Eddy too was a little disappointed in the present. Georgie showed it to him in the kitchen at suppertime. "So that's it," he said, and then he tossed it playfully at the ceiling once or twice. "It's a pretty good ball, I guess. Here, Georgie, catch."

Georgie caught the ball in both hands and giggled at Eddy. Uncle Freddy nudged Aunt Alex, and Aunt Alex caught Eleanor's eye. Georgie's smile was real and broad and proud. The discovery of the missing present seemed to be all that was needed to bring her back to herself altogether. And if it would do that for Georgie, it was a very fine present indeed.

But it was Georgie herself who discovered the best thing about the present from the Goose Prince.

She had just said good night, and Aunt Alex and Uncle Freddy had looked up from the papers they were grading and Eddy had looked up from the TV and Eleanor had looked up from her homework, and they had all said, "Good night, Georgie." She had walked to the stairs and put her foot on the bottom step. And then she had held up her rubber ball to show it to Henry Thoreau, standing so quietly on his marble stand in the curve of the stairs.

"Look," Georgie whispered, "it's the present. I found it. It was safe in the leaves out there in the yard all the time. I didn't lose it after all."

Dreamily Henry gazed at the ball in Georgie's hand. And then to her surprise, something strange began to happen.

In the half-dark of the front hall the ball was glowing dimly. Georgie was reminded of the way Eddy's plastic rocket ship had glimmered in the dark. Instead of climbing the stairs, she opened the door of the coat closet, pushed through the heavy coats, and pulled the door shut behind her. Then in the absolute blackness at the back of the coat closet, she held up the ball that was her present from the Goose Prince and looked at it.

It was glowing brightly in the dark! It was! Like the moon rocket! But with a radiance very different from the weird green phosphorescence of Eddy's rocket ship. The streaks on the surface of the glowing blue ball were luminous with a pure white light.

And then Georgie gasped. The ball was lifting from her fingers, rising into the air. It was poising lightly above her hand. It was growing larger. The close, muffled space in the back of the coat closet was opening out. The walls and the coats were falling away, becoming a vast darkness, empty but for Georgie and the great gleaming ball that hung before her, turning slowly and majestically in the immense and impalpable night. The blue surface of the ball was streaked with clouds, and below the clouds Georgie could catch glimpses of great land masses, of dark continents and snow-covered ice caps and deep jungles and blue oceans and lofty mountain ranges—the Andes, the Alps, the Himalayas.

"Oh," breathed Georgie. "It's the world. It's the whole world."

It was true. The gift from the Goose Prince was an image of the earth itself, shining and turning in the stupendous immensity of the coat closet under the stairs in the front hall of the big house at No. 40

Walden Street in Concord, Massachusetts.

Take good care of it, the Goose Prince had said.

"Oh, yes," whispered Georgie, renewing her promise with all her heart. "I will. Oh, yes, I will."

Slowly the ball stopped turning and began to grow smaller once again. In a moment it looked like an ordinary rubber ball. It was hardly glowing at all. Georgie held her hand under it, and the ball dropped lightly into her palm. She took it upstairs, showed it proudly to Dollabella, tucked it safely under her pillow, hopped into bed, put her head down on the pillow, and went to sleep.

And nothing woke her until morning, not even the racket in the sky just after she fell asleep, as a last tardy flock of wild geese flew over the house, cleaving the air in a battering plunge, heading for Walden Pond, eager to break the fragile ice with the fury of their clamorous descent. Low over the peaked roof and domed tower of Georgie's house they were shouting at each other, *Go DOWN! go DOWN! follow ME! follow WHERE? right THERE? over THERE? no, HERE! come HERE! come HERE! HERE! HERE! right HERE! come DOWN! right HERE!*

THE MANUAL

THE MANUAL

TRIVIA

TESTOSTERONE

TALES OF
  BADASSERY

RAW MEAT

FINE WHISKEY

COLD TRUTH

KEITH RIEGERT
SAM KAPLAN

 Ulysses Press

Published by:
ULYSSES PRESS
P.O. Box 3440
Berkeley, CA 94703
www.ulyssespress.com

ISBN: 978-1-61243-183-3
Library of Congress Control Number: 2013931795

Printed in the United States by Bang Printing

10 9 8 7 6 5 4 4 3 2 1

Acquisitions Editor: Keith Riegert
Managing Editor: Claire Chun
Editor: Jessica Benner
Proofreader: Elyce Berrigan-Dunlop
Design and layout: Jake Flaherty
Interior ilustrations: see page 258
Cover illustration by Robert Emil Schulz is from the collection of Richard Oberg and is used with the permission of Mr. Oberg and the artist's son, Robert Schulz

Distributed by Publishers Group West

CONTENTS

Introduction

"Damn fine day to be wearing bear skins."

"A man who lives fully is prepared to die at any time."
–Mark Twain

Take pride in your manliness. On average, you are taller (around six inches) bigger (by about fifteen percent), stronger and significantly more hairy than our counterpart sex. Societal norms allow you to forgo painting your face with makeup (save for bowl games), shaving your forest-like legs and chin and refraining from unleashing the full volume of your flatulence.

But achieving this level of masculinity is no walk in the park. It takes years of study, practice and broken bones. But for us mushy twenty-first century lads living in the Western World, we've managed to sign up for a pretty sweet progression from pimply boyhood into the respectful post of the gentleman.

Chances are, as you stumbled awkwardly through puberty, there weren't many hardcore rites of passage you had to endure. Maybe you had to get your braces tightened at the orthodontist. Perhaps your mom yelled at you while you were learning to drive. You probably got rejected and it really hurt. Boo-shut-the-hell-up-hoo.

In other parts of the world, the transition from boyhood to man-dom is really physically painful. For the Satere-Mawe Tribe of the Amazon, becoming a man means sticking your hands in gloves filled with bullet ants, a tropical insect aptly named for stings that feel like you're being shot with a gun, and smiling as your flesh burns.

The soon-to-be men of Pentecost Island in the South Pacific shed their childish fears by bungee jumping off a rickety platform using rigid vines instead of synthetic chords. The closer to the ground they get, the more respect. A cracked skull is basically the mark of the alpha male.

Speaking of cracking your brain open, if you were raised with the Algonquin Indians of Canada, your journey into manhood would have entailed being left in the northern forest alone after taking a hallucinogen 100 times stronger than LSD. The point of which was to help you find your inner man by forgetting your childhood and, occasionally, who you were altogether.

We're not going to tell you to do any of that. Although, if you do, we'd love to hear about it. Instead, all you have to do is read this book and put some deep thought into your own masculinity.

Sit back on your porcelain throne, relax and expand your knowledge of everything. Whether you're heading to into the boxing ring, the frontlines of battle or the Glenlivet distillery, there are topics you should be able to speak to and questions you should be able to answer.

- How do I properly grill a steak?
- Can I survive a hand grenade attack?
- What's the difference between a KO and TKO?
- How do I choose a proper cigar?
- What's the difference between "neat" and "straight up"?

The answers await, brother. Let's stop wasting time. Welcome to *The MANual*. Good luck and we'll see you on the other side.

Blood, Sweat, and Tyranny

WARRIORS, EMPIRES, AND DEATH

TEN WARRIORS WHO PUT THE "AWE" IN AWESOME

Since the beginning of history, men have sought out eternal glory on the field of battle. And their names actually do live on in eternal glory: from Achilles, Genghis Khan, and Scipio Africanus to Washington, Grant, and Nimitz, these men are never forgotten. Here are some warriors that should appear in more textbooks, movies, and your nightmares.

Mad Jack and His Bagpipes

When Lt. Colonel "Mad" Jack Churchill marched on his first Nazi garrison in 1941, he carried just two weapons: a longbow and a broadsword. A couple years later, he led a commando charge in Yugoslavia playing bagpipes the entire time. Of the forty commandos that made the charge, Mad Jack and his bagpipes were the only survivors. For his years of valor and for being a huge badass and the only soldier in all of WWII to kill an enemy fighter with a longbow, he was awarded the Distinguished Service Order.

So Much Depends on the White Feather in the Green Forest

Ninety-three. That was the staggering confirmed body count that Marine scout sniper Carlos Hathcock managed to rack up during the Vietnam War. Not only was Hathcock a crack shot and ridiculously good at hiding, he also had the unbelievable balls to always wear an unmistakable white feather in his bush hat during combat, which for a jungle sniper seems the equivalent of wearing a flashing neon target on the side of his head. His trademark look earned him the name White Feather from the Viet Cong and a bounty on the head behind the feather that today would be worth about $200,000.

Hathcock was such a thorn in the Viet Cong's side (and head, heart, and various vital organs) that entire squads of enemy snipers were sent out to track him. In one torn-from-a-Hollywood-script account, Hathcock went mano a mano in a jungle gully with a highly talented North Vietnamese sniper. With both snipers quietly stalking one another from either end of the ravine, Hathcock caught sight of an unnatural glint of light and, gambling, took a shot right at it. The glint turned out to be the scope of the Vietnamese rifle, which, coincidentally had been zeroed in on Hathcock's face. Unfor-

WHITE DEATH

While Carlos Hathcock was one hell of a sniper, almost nobody compares to the little-known Finnish sharpshooter, Simo Häyhä. Nicknamed White Death by the opposing Russian forces during the Winter War of 1939–1940, Häyhä managed an amazing feat unmatched to this day: he killed 505 enemy combatants, the most sniper kills in history. And he did it in less than 100 days. In the dead of winter. Using a rifle with no telescopic sight.

Rome's Colosseum set the stage for the slaughter of
500,000 people and over 1,000,000 animals.

tunately for the guy behind the scope, Hathcock's shot was
clean and true—perfectly passing through the glass scope and
coming to rest in the man's brain.

A Viking with a Bone to Pick

Descended from a long line of Viking warlord badasses (even
his dad's name is intimidating: Ragnar Lodbrok), Ivar the
Boneless was a Viking to be reckoned with. Ivar's reign of
supreme asswhoopery began in 865 when he and his brothers led an army of Norse berserkers against East Anglia in
England to avenge their father's capture and assassination.
The East Anglians were so petrified of Ivar and his ragtag
team of rabid Viking warmongers that, instead of fighting,
they gave them horses and shelter for the winter. The next
year, Ivar led his army north, where they sacked York and
installed a puppet king.

For perhaps his most dangerous feat, Ivar the Boneless became
the first invader in the history of ever to successfully capture
the fortress of Dumbarton in the Kingdom of Strathclyde.
Sure, it sounds like something out of a bad fantasy novel,
but the fortress was one of England's most secure territorial
strongholds at the time.

What's clear is about Ivar the Boneless is that he was an incredible warrior and savvy commander. What's not clear is why he had such a strange nickname. Ivar's fans say it was because of an almost inhuman physical flexibility, while detractors claim he was impotent or infertile. Our favorite theory, however, is that the man had a brilliant mind but brittle, useless bones, and commanded his armies while riding atop a shield carried by his troops.

A Thousand Ways to Kill

There are countless ways to kill, and Yue Fei wanted to master them all. A Renaissance man of the Chinese military arts, Yui Fei is considered one of the greatest military minds of all

ALL THE MAGICAL COLORS OF BLOOD

The term "berserk" can be traced back to a fabled group of fearless Norse warriors called berserkers, who would work themselves into a nearly uncontrollable, rage-filled frenzy just before battle. So intense was their mania that they were apparently immune to pain. Impaled by spear? A splinter. Sliced by scion? A paper cut. Burned by fire? It'll turn into a tan.

Theorists offer various explanations of how berserkers achieved such heightened levels of savagery, but the best regarded theory is that they were hardcore tweakers who would prepare for battle by getting high out of their minds on one of the world's most potent natural hallucinogens: psilocybin "magic" mushrooms.

time. Strong as an ox, Yue Fei could wield the biggest bows with either hand, he could spar with a spear, and he invented several combat styles, including Eagle Claw and Xingyi boxing. And as if those talents weren't enough? Fei could also bore you to death with his poetry.

Fei's is a rags-to-riches underdog story about loyalty, revenge, and creative bloodshed. He rose through the ranks of the Song army when China was split into three feuding factions, the most powerful of which were Fei's Song and the back-stabbing nomadic Jin to the north. Around 1125, the Jin broke an alliance with the Song, and Fei went absolutely nuts, storming up north leading a ragtag army of 800 against a massive Jin force 50,000 strong. Eventually Fei's overmatched crew was forced to retreat.

But Fei redoubled his efforts and began dreaming of various ways to destroy his sworn enemy. He began an intense and bloody campaign to consolidate the massive Song army, killing any traitor, rebel, or rabble-rouser he deemed worthy of death. Once he had control of all militia within Song strongholds, he proceeded once again up north, winning bloody battle after bloody battle and recapturing Song territory from those meddlesome Jin punks. Fei had momentum, military brilliance, and a fiercely loyal army: he was poised to expand the Song Empire ever northward.

Unfortunately, there was a growing faction of peace-loving hippies in the Song government who not only wanted to end the war, but who thought the best way to create peace was to kill their former enemy's biggest enemy. They sarcastically thanked Fei for all his help, shoved him in a prison, and in 1142 executed their most celebrated and beloved military general.

The Accidental Warrior

For some brave soldiers who fought in World War II, the war metaphorically and emotionally never ended. For Lt. Hiroo Onoda, it literally almost didn't. In 1942, young Onoda joined the Imperial Army of Japan and by 1944 was tasked with waging covert guerilla warfare on the remote Philippine island of Lubang. Onoda and a very small cell of operatives ended up left behind in the high jungles as the island was overrun by Allied forces shortly before the war came to a dramatic end with the unconditional surrender of Japan.

Unfortunately, Onoda never got that final, important message. Despite numerous leaflets dropped by American planes proclaiming the end of combat, Onoda wouldn't buy that Japan had lost. So he continued to hide in the jungle, subsisting primarily on coconuts and tropical fruit, still waging war on the Allied forces…for twenty-nine years. Finally, on March 9, 1974, the Japanese government was forced to send his orig-

Britain owns the distinction of having fought in both history's shortest war (thirty-eight minutes vs. Zanzibar) and its longest (116 years vs. France).

inal commanding officer to Lubang to officially request his surrender, which he reluctantly gave.

Save the Worm for Ingacio

For many twenty-first-century American gringos, Cinco de Mayo conjures up images of guacamole, empty Corona bottles, tequila, puking in a Chevy's sombrero, and some vague connection to Mexico's independence. But in 1862, the date stood for one of the most awe-inspiring underdog victories of all time. That's because on the original Cinco de Mayo, the French Army, being owed a crap-load of money by the government of Mexico, found out just how hard it can be to collect on a loan. On their way to sack Mexico City, the French arrived in the town of Puebla where they met a scrappy Mexican force led by the brilliant commander Ignacio Zaragoza Seguín.

Most of Seguín's troops, whose numbers amounted to about half those of the French, were armed with nothing more than rusty machetes and the steely reserve of men raised on fermented cactus. The French laughed, loaded their pristine rifles and muskets, and were brutally slaughtered by the knife-wielding Mexicans. Having your army's ass kicked by a bunch of guys hacking at you with tetanus-laden machetes

> "They couldn't hit an elephant from this distance."
>
> —*The unfortunate last words of General John Sedgwick, killed by a Confederate sniper during the American Civil War*

did not inspire a lot of confidence from the French homeland and that particular fifth of May helped, eventually, in convincing the French to abandon their colonial ambitions and head home.

An Economy of Blood

The history of New Zealand is coated in guts, gore, face tattoos, severed heads, and intense tribal warfare. Until Europeans introduced potatoes and muskets to the Maori, however, men were too busy farming and doing other domestic chores to do what they really wanted to do, which was, apparently, kill each other all the time. Potatoes, you see, were so easy to farm that the men entrusted their women and slaves to do the job, freeing the Maori men to take their talents to the battlefield.

But this story is not just about potatoes, it's also about guns. Despite 150 years of contact with Europeans, Maoris continued to engage in battle using traditional weapons, including staffs, clubs, and bladed weapons made of wood or whalebone. But one day in 1807, a visionary named Hongi Hika, an emerging war leader of the Ngāpuhi iwi (tribe), had an epiphany that muskets were the weapon of the future. He helped lead his iwi in a battle against their rivals, the Ngāti Whātua iwi, but the Ngāpuhi were besieged as they reloaded their muskets.

Hika was not to be discouraged; he understood the raw, awesome power of the musket and just knew that they were superior to wooden clubs and blades. So in a landmark deal, he traded some prime New Zealand real estate to an adventurer named Charles de Thierry in exchange for no fewer than 500 muskets. He promptly raised an army and between 1806 and 1828 he laid brutal, deadly waste to most of northern New Zealand and basically made himself overlord of the Maori. These skirmishes are now known as the Musket Wars.

But Hika wasn't entirely westernized. He was married to a clairvoyant blind lady and her sister and he still enjoyed chopping off the heads of his slain enemies. Around this time, dried human noggins were a popular novelty item throughout Europe, and Hika realized the lucrative potential of warfare. Thus began a sort of ironic cycle of bloodshed and capitalism: he lopped off more heads in order to buy more weapons, and he bought more weapons in order to acquire more heads.

By the mid-1820s, however, the other Maori tribes had realized the devastating power of the musket and began to procure some for themselves. A bullet pierced Hika's chest in 1827 and, in one of the most badass deaths on record, he encouraged his men to gather around and listen to the poetic whispers of the wind as it whistled in and then out of his lungs.

The Ungentlemanly Gentleman

One of the Second World War's greatest guerilla warriors was the French Count Robert Jean Marie de La Rochefoucauld. Young Robert began his passionate Nazi-killing crusade at the tender age of sixteen after the Germans abducted and killed his father, Olivier de La Rochefoucauld. In seeking vengeance, Robert joined the French resistance movement, which quickly got him put on the Germans' this-guy-needs-to-die list, forcing him to flee first to Paris and then to Spain.

It was here that Rochefoucauld performed his first brilliant act of deceit when, after being sent to a Spanish prison camp, he dropped his French accent and convinced his captors that he was actually a limey Brit, affording him a trip to the British Embassy to get everything straightened out.

The Brits at the embassy were so thoroughly impressed with his acting skills they enlisted him in the most notorious WWII espionage outfit, the British Special Operations Executive, otherwise known as the Ministry of Ungentlemanly Warfare.

After a few months of intensive training in London, he was parachuted into France, where he proceeded to wreak havoc—by doing things like blowing up a factory using explosive-laden loaves of bread. His Nazi-killing did not go unnoticed. Despite being captured and sentenced to death

> "In my dreams I hear again the crash of guns, the rattle of musketry, the strange, mournful mutter of the battlefield. But in the evening of my memory always I come back to West Point. Always there echoes and re-echoes: Duty, Honor, Country."
>
> —US General (and general badass) Douglas MacArthur

twice by the Nazis, Rochefoucald used his intense bloodlust and natural skills to escape. The first time, he jumped out of the back of the truck transporting him to his execution, dodged some machine gun fire, stole a Nazi limo, and made his way back to Paris. The second time, he faked a seizure while in prison and dispatched the responding guard with the jagged leg he had snapped off a table. He then walked around the detention center, shooting Nazi guards before stealing a nun's habit and making his escape.

Good Morning, Vietnam

You know that one savage firefight sequence in every amazing action movie that you absolutely love but think is so far from reality? Well, let Master Sergeant Roy P. Benavidez restore your faith in all that is awesome and explosive.

On the morning of May 2, 1968, Sgt. Benavidez found himself monitoring the combat radio at Forward Operating Base Loc Ninh, just north of Saigon. A Special Forces unit of twelve men, tasked with gathering intelligence on a possible nearby buildup of North Vietnamese Army troops, had just been dropped into the jungle a little ways from the sarge. Well, uncover a slight buildup they did, and the twelve-man

The first recorded use of chemical warfare dates back to the fifth century BC, when the Spartans used sulfur bombs to suffocate the Athenians during the Peloponnesian War.

unit found themselves pinned down by about 1,000 well-armed North Vietnamese.

After listening in horror as three helicopters failed to reach the pinned team, Sgt. Benavidez took action. He hopped on a returning chopper and headed toward the landing zone, which was now awash in a sea of hot lead. Trying to avoid the firefight, the helicopter dropped Sgt. Benavidez 75 yards from the Special Forces team. During his 250-foot dash, Sgt. Benavidez (who had conveniently forgotten his rifle in the confusion of the moment) was shot four times. But he never stopped running. When he reached the crippled team, he immediately set about carrying and dragging all the living soldiers back to the waiting chopper.

With all the soldiers accounted for, and being a thorough military man with little regard for his own personal safety, Sgt. Benavidez then ran the 250 bullet-laced feet back to the dead body of the team leader in order to retrieve any classified documents that might be laying around. At which point he was shot in the stomach, had a grenade blow up next to his back, and then watched the helicopter with all the soldiers he'd just rescued crash back to earth.

Did he cry? No. Where any normal superhuman being would have given up, Sgt. Benavidez was just getting started. The sarge got up, tucked his organs back into his shirt, ran back to the downed chopper, gathered up whatever souls in the wreckage were still breathing, and positioned them in a defensive perimeter until another helicopter could arrive. He then cranked up the radio, called in some air strikes, and ran around handing out water and ammo to the wounded soldiers (what, no moist towelettes?). Oh, and then he got shot again.

When the extraction helicopter finally arrived, Sgt. Benavidez dispatched a couple final North Vietnamese soldiers, was pulled on board, and promptly blacked out. But not before spitting in the face of a doctor who mistakenly declared him dead. By the time he was rescued, Sgt. Benavidez had acquired thirty-seven new holes in his body and had saved the lives of eight men. For his actions, he was awarded the Medal of Honor and two ounces of brand new blood.

Cold, Naked Revenge

During the 1700s, the Catawba Indians (of present day North and South Carolina) were in a near-constant state of warfare with their neighbors, the Iroquois Seneca. The blood feud between the tribes ran deep and fierce. So fierce, in fact, that when a Seneca raiding party happened upon a lone Catawba warrior, a mini war broke out on the spot.

During the skirmish, the remarkably skilled Catawba warrior managed to slaughter seven Seneca before being captured, viciously stripped, and tortured. With their captive now secure, the Seneca went about exacting revenge for their seven

---

"It's better to die on your feet than live on your knees."

—*Emiliano Zapata, Mexican revolutionary
and epic mustache-haver*

fallen friends, marching the naked Catawba warrior back to their village to be burned alive. It's just about here that things went all wrong for the Seneca.

As they paraded the naked warrior around their camp and down to the adjacent river to be toasted and roasted, the Catawba warrior broke free, dove into the river and skinny-dipped across in just one breath. When he reached the other side of the river, the warrior taunted the Seneca by slapping his bare ass (in the midst of rifle fire) before taking off on foot at breakneck speeds presumably only possible when running ass-naked to save your life. The Catawba warrior ran so fast and so far that he ended up with a huge lead over his pissed-off pursuers.

After two days, a group of five Seneca unknowingly caught up to the hiding nude warrior. Unaware of his proximity, the Seneca made camp and fell into a dreamy sleep, at which point the Catawba warrior stole one of their tomahawks and quietly hacked to death the entire pursuing party—still completely naked, of course. Though he was done with his tomahawking, the Catawba warrior was not quite finished with revenge. He threw on some dead man's blood-soaked clothes, grabbed the nicest rifle he could find, and hiked all the way back to the site of his initial capture, where the seven other dead Seneca still lay. There, he scalped each of the corpses and triumphantly returned home to his loving family and presumably peaceful day job.

A BRIEF HISTORY
OF THE BAYONET

Of all the weapons consistently employed by the military, none are as storied, feared, and damned old as the bayonet. The bayonet's story starts way back in Europe during the 1600s. As primitive firearms began to replace trusty bows for the hunting of wild animals, hunters discovered a troubling problem—if you missed the wild boar with your highly inaccurate, slow-loading musket, you were suddenly stuck holding a five-foot piece of iron and wood with a pissed-off, tusked boar ten yards away from you. Enter the bayonet.

After missing the bear, the last thing Jebediah remembered was where he'd left his bayonet.

By the 1700s, bayonets were in use by the majority of gun-toting armies around the world. But they were never very trustworthy. Armies originally adopted "plug" bayonets—so named because they fit into the barrel of the gun and plugged up the musket, preventing it from being fired again—an innovation about as short-lived as the travel fax machine. But soon the bayonet evolved into an effective and deadly secondary weapon. With armies still drawing battle lines at close range, an imminent bayonet charge became a psychologically fierce assault tactic.

By the dawn of trench warfare, however, everything had changed. Nobody wanted to be fighting in a four-foot wide trench with a two-foot bayonet attached to a five-foot rifle. It was a great way to get yourself killed. So, bayonets began to take the shape we know today—medium-sized, multipurpose combat knives that gave soldiers a last-ditch chance at self-preservation.

Today, the standard-issue M9 (Army) and OKC-3S (Marine Corps) bayonets are about as far removed as possible from the spike bayonet of the 1800s. These modern incarnations are compact, ultra lightweight, and versatile as hell—they're designed to be used for everything from piercing body armor and cutting sheet metal to clipping wire and even opening bottles.

> "Only the dead have seen the end of war."
> —Damn true words from the Spanish poet George Santayana

CUTTING YOUR WRITING
CHOPS IN THE TRENCHES

J.R.R. Tolkien

John Ronald Reuel Tolkien, author of *The Lord of the Rings*, didn't experience the same success in war as he did in writing about it. For starters, he delayed enlisting to finish school, and this was before hippies made draft evasion fashionable. Then, when he finally made it to the front lines in France as a member of the British Army, he managed to develop debilitating cases of both trench fever, a disease carried by lice, and trench foot from the constantly soggy conditions. He ended the war early, emaciated and in and out of hospitals.

Ernest Hemingway

Just four weeks on the front in World War I made a man of young Ernest Hemingway. He joined the war as an ambulance driver in 1918 and was deployed to Italy. Within a month of arriving, he was seriously injured by an exploding mortar shell. It was here that Hemingway's education really began. During his six-month hospital stay, he ogled, flirted with, and eventually successfully wooed a sexy Red Cross nurse named Agnes von Kurowsky.

The next year, Hemingway headed home with plans to marry his beloved nurse, only to get jilted when his betrothed fell for an Italian general and broke off their engagement. The turbulent experience became the inspiration for his first bestseller, *A Farewell to Arms*, as well as his lifelong phobia of long-term commitments.

C.S. Lewis

The Chronicles of Narnia author had some very real experiences to draw upon for his classic children's fantasy series. During WWI, the Englishman was deployed to France and saw combat the very day he turned nineteen. After successfully surviving several bloody skirmishes in the trenches, catastrophe struck and Lewis was badly injured by friendly fire when a British shell misfired, killing two of his friends.

A NATION'S
GREATEST HONOR

In 1861, the senator from Iowa, James Grimes, introduced a bill to the Senate to establish a medal of honor for gallantry in the Navy. President Lincoln was all for it. Within two months, bills for Medals of Honor in both the Navy and the Army were signed into federal law. The Medal of Honor stands as the nation's highest military achievement, handed out for incredible bravery to individuals who have gone above and beyond their call of duty. In just over 150 years, 3,465 Medals of Honor have been handed out.

1. Since the beginning of World War II, the majority of the Medal of Honor recipients have received the honor posthumously. During World War II, 57 percent of the 464 Medals of Honor awarded were done so posthumously. In Vietnam, that percentage jumped to 62 percent. Of eleven military personnel awarded the medal in the most recent conflicts in Afghanistan and Iraq, only four have been alive to receive it.

> During his epic seventy-two-year reign, French King Louis XIV never lost an argument or a war, possibly in part because he inscribed the words Ultima Ratio Regum (The Final Argument of Kings) on every one of his country's cannons.

IMPORTANT SURVIVAL SKILL 1

How to Evade a Sniper in the Jungle

1. ZIG The minute you realize you are under fire, zig. Make an erratic lateral movement, removing yourself from the line of fire.

2. ZAG After your initial zig, it's time to zag. Snipers easily track steady linear movement, so before its too late, abruptly shift toward the opposite direction. Make sure your zigging and zagging don't fit any pattern.

3. FLIP The more random your movements, the better your chances of survival. As you zig and zag, be sure to vary your body position. The sniper will be targeting your head or your chest, so make sure these vital body parts are changing position. Stop, drop, roll, do cartwheels or flips. This is when all those parkour lessons you never took would have come in handy.

4. HIDE As with most attacks, your long-term survival depends on your ability to find adequate cover. In the forest, this means looking for the biggest, healthiest tree and flinging yourself behind its loving woody trunk. Move from tree to tree until you find more permanent shelter, preferably a cushy building with concrete walls.

> "A prisoner of war is a man who tries to kill you
> and fails, and then asks you not to kill him."
>
> —British Prime Minister Winston Churchill

2. Theodore Roosevelt is the only American president to ever have been awarded the Medal of Honor. He received it posthumously (in 2001) for heroically leading his regiment of Rough Riders in the bloody assault of San Juan Ridge, Cuba, during the Spanish-American War.

3. Fully qualified children of Medal of Honor recipients are given entry to any military academy of their choice. No questions asked.

4. The Army, Air Force, and Navy each have their own version of the medal. Recipients from the Marines and Coast Guard both receive the Navy's medal.

5. Former Hawaii Senator Daniel K. Inouye received his medal in 2000, joining an astonishing twenty other Japanese American Medal of Honor recipients from his unit, the 442nd Regimental Combat Team. The 442nd, made up almost entirely of US citizens of Japanese descent, stands as the most decorated unit in American history.

6. Two sets of fathers and sons have been awarded the Medal of Honor: Lt. Arthur MacArthur (Civil War) and his son General Douglas MacArthur (WWII), and Theodore Roosevelt (Spanish-American War) and his son Theodore Roosevelt Jr. (WWII). Like his father, Theodore Roosevelt Jr. did not survive to receive his medal.

7. During the Civil War, Medals of Honor were handed out like party favors. At the time, the medal was only a couple years old and proper guidelines had not been set for handing it out. In 1863 alone, 864 medals were handed out to soldiers just for reenlisting in the US Army (they were rescinded fifty-four years later).

8. The youngest recipient of the Medal of Honor was eleven-year-old Willie Johnston, a Civil War drummer boy who gallantly held on to his drum while the rest of his grown-ass unit dropped everything they were carrying and retreated.

9. Recipients of the Medal of Honor are extended invitations to every presidential inauguration and inaugural ball for the rest of their lives.

10. Only one member of the US Coast Guard has ever received the Medal of Honor. Signalman First Class Douglas Munro personally led five Higgins boats in the rescue of a battalion of Marines pinned down by Japanese fire at Point Cruz, Guadalcanal. Signalman Munro positioned his own boat directly in the line of fire so the Marines could be evacuated to the other crafts. His final words were, "Did they get off?"

"War is hell."

—Full-time General (and part-time crazy) William Tecumseh Sherman

---

FIVE REASONS TO
RESPECT THE SAMURAI

A group of samurai chillaxing on a Friday night (c. 1865).

1. Divine Wind

Just as the samurai were gaining prominence in feudal Japan, the Mongol Empire, led by Genghis Khan's grandson Kublai, was busy building the largest, most savage empire Asia has ever known. They'd recently laid waste to Korea and now had their sights set on China, so in 1266 Khan sent a few minions to Japan to demand they send military assistance and accept him as their patriarch or accept the brutal consequences.

The prideful Japanese refused, and the Mongols never forgot. After they'd captured China, the Mongols turned their attentions across the Sea of Japan. Not one for half-assing an attack, Kublai sent an immense fleet of highly trained soldiers to lay siege to the Japanese coast. During the monsoon season of 1274, about 25,000 men landed in Hakata Bay on the island of Kyushu.

The Mongol soldiers were equipped with everything from poisonous arrows and swords to fricking ceramic grenades. But the fearless samurai, as we now know, were not the type to roll over and play obsequious, so they met their enemy on the beach on horseback. The samurai did the best they could, but they were outnumbered, outmatched, and pretty much shit-out-of-luck.

Despite losing the battle, the samurai were relentless enough to deplete their enemy's supply of arrows, and before night fell the Mongols retreated to their ships to avoid attack. That night, as if by divine providence, a great storm came and by morning the Mongol fleet had lost about 200 ships and perhaps 13,000 men.

KUBLAI KAN'T

The Mongol's massive defeat during the Battle of Koan had a larger historical significance: it ended the previously unchecked spread of the Mongol Empire. Who knows, if it hadn't been for a little divine wind, we might all be Khans now.

Seven years later, Kublai's army returned, this time with two massive fleets (one Chinese and one Korean) totaling as many as 4,500 ships and 140,000 men, the largest seaborne military invasion the world would see until D-Day during WWII. The samurai, however, had built walls on several beaches and were better prepared for large-scale warfare.

The samurai's preparations and vigorous counterattacks (collectively referred to as the Battle of Koan or the Second Battle of Hakata Bay) forestalled the Mongolian fleet just long enough to let the gods take over. In June of 1281, a great typhoon, or kamikaze (divine wind), swept across land and water; massive, swarming waves pelted the ill-suited Mongolian ships and torrents of windswept raindrops the size of boulders beat down from above, sending as many as 100,000 Chinese, Koreans, and Mongolians to their watery graves and saving Japan from their would-be-captors.

2. Don't Bring a Long Sword to a Samurai Sword Fight

The samurai warriors had a remarkable arsenal of weapons at their disposal: kama (dual-purpose farming sickles), tessen (fake folding paper fans made of solid steel), daikyu (power-

> "One who is samurai must before all things, keep constantly in mind, by day and by night … that he has to die."
> —*Daidoji Yuzan*

ful longbows), and kabuto wari (helmet-splitting clubs). But no weapon is as well known and respected as the katana, the samurai sword.

DELICATE MAYHEM

For such a formidable weapon, the katana is notoriously finicky. The swords must be stored blade up, or they quickly lose their edge. They also require constant maintenance—they must be kept well oiled to prevent the blade from rusting.

During the Middle Ages, when Europeans were bludgeoning each other to death with brittle long swords, the samurai had perfected the art of bladesmithing by folding together both high- and low-carbon steels to allow for both elastic durability and razor sharpness. Beside the gut-piercing tip, the blade of the katana was slightly curved, greatly increasing the efficacy of each strike by reducing the contact area. This meant that each blow with a katana was a blow with a perfect edge so sharp and powerful it could literally slice an English long sword in half.

But, just in case the katana wasn't ass-kicking enough, the samurai also carried a smaller version, the ritualistic wakizashi sword, that was used solely to allow the warrior to easily commit ritualistic suicide, presumably for embarrassing his finely crafted katana.

3. The Honorable Exit

The samurai had rituals for everything from preparing for battle to pouring tea, so there's really nothing weird about the fact that life's big events, like dying, were done strictly by the book. For the samurai, seppuku, which means "self disembowelment," was the preferred method for exiting the planet.

The technique went something like this: if a samurai was shamed in battle, dishonored his master, or was facing imminent capture, he would draw his short sword, plunge it into the left side of his abdomen, and draw it quickly across his stomach and then upward. For those intent on showing true courage, they would follow this gut-spilling cut with a second violent incision from the top of the abdomen downward.

This method of suicide was neither painless nor at all quick and the samurai normally bled to death slowly.

Eventually, the powers-that-were in Japan started using seppuku as the preferred method of execution as well. In order to allow a condemned prisoner the honor of taking his own life, the man was asked to kneel on a tatami mat where he was presented a small table with a short sword and given the opportunity to perform his own execution. Immediately upon

A NOT-SO-INSTANTANEOUS EXIT

After being severed from the body, the human head remains conscious for up to eight seconds.

committing the act, a friend or relative of the condemned would raise a katana and decapitate the dying prisoner, thus ending the suffering but keeping his honor intact.

Ritualistic seppuku ceremony in Kobe, Japan (1868).

4. The Way of the Warrior

During the Second World War, the insular island nation of Japan, a fledgling world power with just 100 million people, was able to wage war on an overwhelmingly stronger United States (as well as Britain, Australia, Canada, the Republic of China, and Russia simultaneously) for more than 1,000 blood-soaked days. How did the Japanese accomplish such a tremendous feat? One word: Bushido.

Literally translated as "The Way of the Warrior," the Bushido code evolved slowly—over nearly a millennium of feudal warfare—from a combination of Confucianism, Zen Buddhism, Shintoism, and the militaristic teachings of Japan's noble warrior class, the samurai. Bushido was composed of very simple, yet powerful tenets: loyalty, courage, mastering the crap out of martial arts, self-control, mercy (albeit limited), and, above all, honor to your family, ruler, and country until death.

The code originally rose to prominence starting in the 1400s when Japan was a very fractured set of islands. Shoguns and warlords rose and fell faster than stalks of rice and the samurai had to abide by the strict set of morals just to keep total anarchy from sweeping over the land. Over the centuries to come, the rules of conduct solidified and, during the long, stable Tokugawa Shogunate (1603–1868), the Bushido code went from an unspoken set of ideals to the actual law of the land.

By the time Pearl Harbor rolled around, Japan's entire military had been steeped in the Bushido code. For the Japanese, the mindset helped create a hardened force to be reckoned with in the Pacific, but also led to tragic consequences—from banzai suicide charges and kamikaze air raids to the abhorrent treatment of enemy prisoners of war and foreign civilians.

5. Miyamoto Musashi

In samurai culture, the term rōnin was designated for wandering samurai warriors who had become masterless. Some arrived at this bastard state upon the death of their master;

others had simply been disowned. Miyamoto Musashi, on the other hand, seems to have simply inherited the position from the gods themselves. Why? Because Miyamoto Musashi may have been the greatest sword fighter in history.

Musashi's early life is as mysterious as it damn ought to be. He might as well have been forged from the discarded steel at the Kyoto Katanaworks or crawled out of a dragon's recently disemboweled intestines, because the fury he brought to Japan was magical. Rumor had it that he was born in the Harima Province on the island of Honshu, the son of a famous swordsman named Shinmen Munisai, who had placed a katana in the hands of young Miyamoto while he was still nursing.

Regardless of his early years, Musashi burst onto the samurai scene out of nowhere right around the time his body slipped stealthily into puberty. At the age of thirteen, Musashi answered a written call for dueling partners posted by a (fully grown) traveling samurai by the name of Arima Kihei. Kihei, apparently unfazed with having to fight a mere child, attacked Musashi with a short sword only to have the thirteen-year-old Musashi beat him to death with a wooden staff.

After his first duel, Musashi hung around home for a couple years waiting for his voice to drop. Then he hit the road to tour the countryside in what is called a *musha shogyu*, basically the most terrifying coming-of-age imaginable where young samurais wander the countryside looking to hone their skills.

As coming-of-age stories are wont to do, Musashi's took a weird and unexpected turn when he somehow found himself fighting as a paid warrior in some ill-fated battles. Whatever happened during this time, it's around then that he decides to focus on fighting duels with only a wooden sword.

A couple years later, around the time he was legally allowed to drink sake, Musashi wandered into the renowned Yoshioka Martial Arts School and challenged the school's master and namesake, Yoshioka Seijuro, to a duel. Seijuro happily accepted, only to become enraged when Musashi showed up to the duel super late and carrying nothing but his wooden replica of a sword. When Seijuro attacked him, Musashi brutally smacked him in the arm with his fake sword, crippling the master martial artist for life.

When Seijuro's brother challenged Musashi for revenge, Musashi dispatched him in the same brutal manner. Taking out the two star martial arts masters of one of the best martial arts schools in Japan did not go over well with the people around town and, before he knew it, Musashi was facing off against a whole clan of swordsmen. At this point, Musashi realized he was in a bind and gave up the fake sword, drawing both his katana *and* ritualistic wakizashi short sword (which nobody ever fought with) and went about slicing and dicing his way through the whole crowd, inventing his own brand new duel-sword fighting style along the way.

Once he'd killed the head of the clan, he moseyed on out of town and up to Hozoin where he had heard there were

IMPORTANT SURVIVAL SKILL 2

FIVE EASY STEPS TO SURVIVING A HAND GRENADE ATTACK

1. DIVE Don't run. If the grenade explodes while you're running, surprise, you'll get a back full of shrapnel. Instead, hit the floor face first and with your head as far away from the grenade as possible.

2. FEET TOWARD THE GRENADE Position the soles of your feet toward the grenade and, for your children's sake, close your damn legs. This way, the soles of your shoes (and feet) will absorb most of the oncoming shrapnel.

3. COVER Pull your elbows into your ribs to protect your vital organs and cover your ears and head. It's about to get loud.

4. CLOSE YOUR EYES AND SAY AHHHHH There's going to be a shock-blast, so close your eyes and open your mouth to keep your lungs from exploding.

some monks he could fight who were masters of the lance. Mushashi kept this lifestyle up for another couple years, alternating between fighting duels, meditating, and working in the fields with the Japanese peasants. During one duel, Musashi's opponent, a master martial artist named Muso, was so inspired by Musashi's fighting style he crafted a new school of staff fighting around the experience.

Finally, at the ripe old age of 30, Musashi packed up his dueling trophies and retired. He spent the remaining thirty-one years of his life perfecting his two-handed sword fighting technique and teaching students who were just glad they didn't really have to fight him.

GATLING'S GOOD INTENTIONS

In the 1860s, Dr. Richard Gatling set about inventing a rapid-fire, "automatic" gun. The purpose? To reduce the future casualties of war. How would more bullets flying at the same time help reduce war dead? Well, at the time, wars were fought by lining up entire armies within shouting distance of one another and yelling "fire," so Gatling believed that if you could replace all those rifle-wielding foot soldiers with one guy cranking out rounds, a lot less souls would be lost. It was a great thought, but the tactics of warfare were not about to keep up with his newfangled technology; the sizes of armies grew and the result was the bloodiest century in world history—thanks in part to Gatling's highly effective invention.

FIVE BLOODY POWERS

Cracker Jacks, Here, Get Your Cracker Jacks

The violent 500-year reign of the Roman Empire can be summed up in one monumental edifice: the Colosseum.

THE HOUSE THAT VESPASIAN BUILT

The Colosseum could seat just over 50,000 spectators, about the same as Yankee Stadium. But the Yankees still suck.

Where today we watch men in tight pants chase little balls in places like Petco Park and Tropicana Field, citizens of Rome filed into the Amphitheatrum Flavium to watch blood sports, including detailed battle reenactments, exotic animal hunts, and gladiator-on-gladiator death matches.

Gladiators fought one another with spears, swords, and bows. Sometimes, during halftime, patrons could watch men pitted against wild rhinos, hippos, elephants, lions, tigers, panthers, and crocodiles.

Nine thousand animals were slaughtered during its inaugural games alone and, by the time Rome collapsed, nearly half a million people had fought and died on arena's hallowed floor.

Bred into Empire

By the time it reached its peak, the Mongol Empire covered 16 percent of the earth's surface. It was the largest contiguous empire in history. But its most lasting legacy isn't on the ground; it may be in your blood.

When Genghis Khan was just a young man, a rival tribe kidnapped his wife and something inside of him snapped. He unified several Mongol-Turkic tribes, annihilated his enemy, and rescued his wife. But he didn't stop. He proceeded to sweep across the Eurasian continent, swallowing village after village.

It turns out Genghis Khan wasn't just a fighter; he was a lover, and apparently a prolific one at that. As he sacked villages throughout Asia, he would have every man and pregnant woman killed before bringing in the surviving fertile women to spread his seed. Genghis Khan had a lot of seed. Though his empire no longer exists, his legacy lives on in today's world population—as many as one out of every 200 people alive today are blood relations to Genghis Khan.

"In peace, sons bury their fathers. In war, fathers bury their sons."

—*Greek philosopher Herodotus*

The Empire on Which the Sun Never Sets

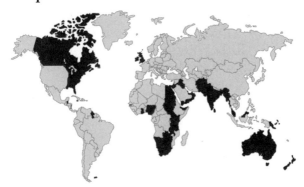

Portion of the world previously forced to play cricket
(British Empire).

Why are the proper, crumpet-sampling Brits on a list of the bloodiest powers in history? Because they were most likely the bloodiest. During more than 400 years of global rule, the British Empire engaged in over 100 individual wars, killing as many as 100,000,000 of the planet's inhabitants through violence, disease, and famine.

Before its rapid decline after WWII, the British Empire had earned the nickname "the Empire on which the sun never sets," so large that the sun was always shining on it somewhere.

Back to the Farm

Sometimes violent takeovers aren't ignited abroad; they burn from within. That's what happened in the 1970s in Cambodia when, at the height of Communism's sweep over Southeast Asia, the Communist Party of Kamphuchea grabbed power.

THE NEW GREAT EMPIRE?

At its height, the British Empire, the most expansive in history, commanded over 20 percent of the planet's population. Today, the People's Republic of China rules over 1.35 billion people, or 19 percent of the world's population.

Little was strange about the rise of the Communist Party in a country next door to Vietnam and China, but what happened in Cambodia is one of the most bizarre and disturbing episodes in modern history. The Khmer Rouge, as the Communist Party became known, were obsessed with farming. The party dreamt of a completely self-sufficient agrarian society for the Cambodia of tomorrow. So they went about building it.

The Khmer Rouge forcibly moved everyone living in Cambodia's cities to the countryside. Citizens with no farming experience in their entire lives were forced to adapt to their new situation or starve. Those who disobeyed were simply killed. By the end of their short, drastic social experiment, the Khmer Rouge had managed to murder nearly two million of their own citizens; another estimated two million Cambodians died from starvation and disease. In the end, the population of Cambodia was cut in half.

Shrinky Dink

You may have never heard of the Shuar people, a semino-madic, semi-terrifying Amazonian tribe from modern-day Ecuador and Peru, but you're surely familiar with their work: shrunken heads.

The Shuar, who were constantly feuding with neighboring factions, are a spiritual people who believed that a dead enemy was still a dangerous enemy. Thus, a successful skirmish was measured not by a count of bodies left on the battlefield, but by the number of shrunken enemy's heads, called *tsantsa*, in the victorious Shuar's trophy case. (The purpose of the shrinking was superstition—they believed shrinking the head would trap the person's soul and prevent it from seeking revenge.)

But the Shuar aren't just famous for their head collection. Fiercely prideful of their homeland and their freedom, the Shuar repeatedly beat back every invading people who approached—first fending off the Inca and then the Spanish. Who knows, maybe some superstitions work. They remain an independent tribe to this day.

REVENGE IS A DISH BEST SERVED GOLD

When the Spanish came in to the Shuar lands looking for riches, the Shuar fought back and captured the governor of the Spanish-held Logrono region. They gave him one of the most symbolically apt executions ever—pouring scalding-hot molten gold down the man's throat.

W IS FOR WAR...ELEPHANT

Elephants are one of earth's most intelligent, trainable, and deadly animals. They weigh in at about five tons, have inch-thick skin, and can move at almost 20 miles per hour. They are essentially living, breathing, crapping tanks. And man has known it for centuries. Unlike a horse, which will neigh and whinny and carefully step over an enemy body in battle, elephants just go ahead and trample them to death, which made them history's fiercest cavalry.

Death by Dumbo

If you thought death by electric chair was inhumane, imagine living in a world where a condemned criminal was executed by an elephant stepping on their head. As recently as the nineteenth century, rulers living in India and Southeast Asia used highly trained Asian elephants to do just that—one of the most horrific methods of capital punishment ever invented.

MORTE ELEPHANTUM

Execution by elephant made it all the way to the Roman Empire, where the preferred method of execution was decapitation, or *capitalis*. From the Latin word caput, meaning "head," it is the root of our modern term, "capital punishment."

But head crushing was just the beginning, and the powerful royals who administered these barbaric punishments were always eager to employ a new method of elephant-induced agony. They had their pachyderm executioners taught to use their trunks to toy with prisoners before ripping their limbs from their bodies. They even attached sword-like contraptions to their tusks to allow the elephants to slash up the condemned.

The Alps Are But Snowy Hills

> *"I swear so soon as age will permit…I will use*
> *fire and steel to arrest the destiny of Rome."*
> —*A pimple-faced teenage Hannibal to his father Hamilcar Barca*

Choosing to go to war against Rome in the 200s BC is like you offering to jump into the ring with Mike Tyson circa 1985. But that's exactly what Hannibal Barca did when he led a Carthaginian Army over the Italian Alps and directly into the heart of the Roman Republic. While most Mediterranean powers were happy just to maintain a scrap of autonomy, Hannibal wanted an empire.

Hannibal's illustrious career as one of history's greatest military minds began around 221 BC when he took control of his father's army in modern-day Spain. After consolidating his power on the Iberian Peninsula, Hannibal was popular, cocky, and immensely powerful. And when Rome tried to crash his party by allying themselves with the city of Saguntum (south of Barcelona), Hannibal sacked it and started a war with the most powerful empire on earth.

Not to half-ass his first real war, in 218 Hannibal began one of the most epic and fabled journeys in military history: crossing the Italian Alps with nearly 38,000 foot soldiers, 8,000 horsemen, and, brazenly, thirty-seven war elephants.

The war elephants, probably a now-extinct subspecies of the African elephant known as Atlas elephants, were ill-suited to make the arduous journey across the snow-plastered Alps. Not only did they require a lot of food, but their large size made narrow passages across the icy cliffs a nightmare. Some elephants starved to death; others fell to their deaths. Still, at least one elephant survived the journey: the one Hannibal most often rode.

Despite the loss of most of their elephantry and perhaps as much as half the infantry, Hannibal's arrival from the Alps took Rome by total surprise. He swiftly won two battles in Trebia and Lake Trasimene, liberating tribes that quickly allied with him. Thus the war raged on, with Hannibal outsmarting the Romans at every turn. Hannibal was so successful, in fact, that he spent the next fifteen years tearing up the Italian Peninsula. By the end of his campaign, Hannibal had amassed an army large enough to sack Rome. But Carthage's government stalled on the decision.

Then around 212 BC, the Romans realized the best tactic against Hannibal was simply to ignore him completely. They turned their attentions across the Mediterranean Sea and attacked Carthage's Sicilian territories, and Hannibal's threat to Rome began to weaken. Though he held on in the Italian Peninsula for another decade, his victories were diminishing. Eventually, with the Roman armies approaching their homeland, Carthage recalled Hannibal to Africa, ending the campaign completely and ushering in an unsteady peace.

For a time, Hannibal tried politics on for size, and in 200 BC he became the chief magistrate of Carthage, restoring some of the kingdom's luster. Hannibal's renewed power frightened Rome and they demanded his surrender. Instead, he went into exile, voluntarily of course, and for a time lived a life on the road. When the Romans finally tracked him down and ordered his execution, he still disobeyed, choosing instead to take some poison and leave behind a letter that, roughly translated, read: "Let us relieve the Romans from the anxiety they have so long experienced, since they think it tries their patience too much to wait for an old man's death."

Not Your Average Joust

"My brother, why do you hide yourself in the canopy shadows? Let us fight the elephant battle for our own honors. No future kings will do what we are going to do."

—Siamese King Naresuan to Minchit Sra, the Crown Prince of Burma

Truer words have rarely been spoken: no two monarchs would ever fight to the death atop elephants again. Which is unfortunate because elephant-mounted death matches are pretty much the tits when it comes to working out differences.

> The Kingdom of Siam employed war elephants as late as the Franco-Siamese War at the end of the nineteenth century.

At the height of the Burma-Siam war in 1591, King Naresuan challenged the crown prince of Burma to a joust to the death atop war elephants. The battle ended quickly, when Naresuan managed to deliver a decisive deathblow to Sra with his lance. The Elephant Battle victory essentially ended the war, and today is still celebrated in Thailand.

THREE TECHNOLOGICAL INNOVATIONS THAT CAME OUT OF BEING SUPER PARANOID ABOUT THE SOVIETS

The Interwebs

During the 1960s, the skittish US government commissioned several agencies to research ways to remotely connect sensitive data networks in different corners of the country into nationally connected super networks. The goal was to provide an information system broad enough to survive the localized nuclear attacks they believed were imminent.

By the early 1990s, the now-global networks were opened to the public for commercial use and became known colloquially as the Internet, the World Wide Web, the web, and someday simply as the AWWWWW, Cats!

GPS

In 1960, the world's first Global Positioning System, named "Transit," could give an accurate location anywhere in the world once every sixty minutes using five satellites to triangulate the position. Its purpose was to stop nuclear attacks from the USSR by developing a real-time method for tracking bombers, subs, and even Intercontinental Ballistic Missiles (ICBMs). Although, in a world where ICBMs traveled at 13,000 mph, it's hard to see how a once-an-hour GPS system was quite up to snuff (since Washington D.C. and Moscow are only 4,800 miles apart).

No, you are not using traditional GPS to precisely guide your way to the bar with your iPhone. But you are using something similar. During WWII, the military used the LORAN system that fixed ship position using ground-based radio receivers, a system very similar to today's cell triangulation using cell towers and Wi-Fi hotspots. But don't fret, you are still more tech savvy than your grandparents: current smartphones are also assisted by satellite-based GPS to help get that extra-precise distance between you and your next pint.

Digital Photography

Before digital photography, spy satellites still relied on good old-fashioned film to take top secret recon photos. The only problem was that the image was stuck in the film canister, the film canister was stuck in satellite, and the satellite was stuck in space. So every top secret roll of film had to be ejected through the atmosphere and allowed to float down to earth with a tiny parachute. During one disastrous spy mission, a broken parachute lead to a canister plummeting 16,000 feet into the Pacific Ocean. It took the Navy three deep-sea search missions to find it.

Things finally improved in the 1960s with the Kennan-11, a digital imaging system that could relay real-time photos to the Navy.

Today digital photography has all but replaced its tangible predecessor and allowed for the myriad drinking photos posted on social media that help us document this important era in post–Cold War history.

Seven World War II Military Innovations You See Every Day

The Jumbo jet

Today's Boeing and Airbus fleets owe their beginnings to Nazi Germany's revolutionary Messerschmitt Me 262, the world's first operational jet fighter. Although there were never enough produced to swing the tide of World War II, the Messerschmitt terrifyingly outperformed all Allied fighters at the time and helped usher in the age of the jet engine.

Walkie-talkies

A Canadian invention, the walkie-talkie, known more boringly as "the handheld receiver," was originally used for two-way communication between military personnel during the war.

> Random Terrifying Fact: At least fifty active nuclear weapons, most of them Russian, are currently designated "lost at sea."

Today most militaries use far superior communication technologies, but walkie-talkies are still extremely popular among both children and rent-a-cops.

Duct tape

During WWII, the US military joined forces with Johnson & Johnson to create an adhesive tape that could be torn by hand and used to create a waterproof seal for ammunition cases.

Called duck tape by soldiers, the impressive tape was so effective that soldiers were soon using it for MacGyver-esque stopgap repairs on everything from dungarees to guns and Jeeps to fighter planes.

The microwave oven

The microwave oven actually has its origins in a completely different technology: radar. Britain's Royal Air Force was first in successfully tracking enemy aircrafts approaching British shores using radio waves, technology they termed "Chain Home" and that later became known as RADAR (Radio Detection and Ranging).

As the technology advanced, scientists discovered the microwave, a wavelength that resonates at the same frequency as water molecules, thus producing heat and revolutionizing leftovers.

Silly Putty

The happiest accident of the war was undoubtedly the invention of Silly Putty, a bizarre substance discovered by scientists

IMPORTANT SURVIVAL SKILL 3

HOW TO SURVIVE A NUCLEAR ATTACK

1. FIND SHELTER Caves are a good choice, as are deep rivulets and crevasses in the terrain. If you have none, dig as fast as possible. As a last result, go indoors and hope for the best.

2. LOOK AWAY FROM THE BLAST An atomic bomb explodes with the same brightness as the sun and this is not the time to go blind.

3. AVOID THE FALLOUT No, the black water falling from the sky is not potable. After the explosion, scalding hot chunks of radiated dust clouds known as black rain will plummet back down to earth. This black rain is almost as deadly as the initial blast.

4. STAY INDOORS Stay in your shelter for at least eight days to allow the atmospheric radiation to clear.

5. FIND SUSTENANCE Water: Groundwater is contaminated—do not drink it. Instead, seek well water. Always boil and filter. Building water is also safe: In the likely event that the water isn't running, you may extract the water trapped in piping.

Food: Puncture-free cans of food are good to go. Animals are edible, however, remember to skin the carcass and toss the heart, liver, and kidneys, which have by now absorbed deadly levels of radioactive toxins. Avoid meat close to the now radioactive bones. Eschew aboveground fruits and vegetables in favor of root vegetables like potatoes and carrots.

6. FORAGE IN THICK CLOTHING Wear goggles, gloves, hats, and long-sleeved shirts or jackets. You don't need to worry about looking cool; there's nobody left.

struggling to invent a replacement silicone-based synthetic rubber. Grown children all over the world can thank Japan for occupying most of the world's rubber-producing regions, forcing America to think outside the egg.

The Jeep

Suburban soccer moms and gas-guzzling off-road enthusiasts everywhere are forever indebted to the United States Army, who commissioned Ford and Wyllis-Overland to build the world's most famous sport utility vehicle, the GPW, which was quickly nicknamed the Jeep. There were about 640,000 Jeeps in operation during the war, including one failed amphibious model that royally sucked on both land and water.

Hot pink fishnets

Nylon was originally invented in 1940 as a cheap replacement for the costly silk and hemp used in parachute chords. Today it lives the glamorous life, making up everything from guitar strings and pantyhose to car engine parts and tires.

> "Certainly there is no hunting like the hunting of man and those who have hunted armed men long enough and liked it, never really care for anything else thereafter."
>
> —*Ernest Hemingway*

Meat

HISTORY IN THE FLESH

In 1976, America had a great year. We celebrated the bicentennial of the Declaration of Independence. We landed spacecraft on Mars. *Rocky* roared into movie theatres from Los Angeles to Philadelphia. The VCR was invented. But what eclipsed all of those unparalleled causes for celebration was that 1976 was the beefiest year in our country's glorious history. During that year, Americans consumed an average of 89 pounds of beef *per person*. That's a quarter-pounder every day.

Since then, it's hard to say that meat hasn't lost a little bit of its *je ne sais quoi*. More people are eating veggie burgers. Even the manliest of men are concerned about terms like "cholesterol," "heart disease," and "death." But the glory of meat will live on as it has lived for 50,000 years. Meat has helped craft our history, our biology, and our cultures. It will live on in our hearts (literally) and in our colons (very literally. Seriously, it takes forever to clean it out of your colon. John Wayne was full of meat when he died). Sorry, we digress. We dedicate this section to the glory that is edible flesh.

THE ORIGINAL ERA OF
BIG-GAME HUNTING

When you think of big-game hunting, the first thing that comes to mind is the bygone era of the early 1900s, when "going on safari" meant shooting animals, not photographing them. But the truth is that the real era of big-game hunting wasn't in this century. Or this millennium. The biggest and most impressive hunting feats happened way back about 13,000 years ago. And the animals our human ancestors hunted, and eventually killed off, were so much more massive, dangerous, and exotic than what we know today, we can only begin to imagine what it was like.

By the time the Europeans arrived in the New World, the landscape looked a lot different than it had when the continent's first human inhabitants arrived. While bears, buffalo, and mountain lions still roamed the vast wilderness, many spectacular species of megafauna had long since been wiped out by skilled hunters and the changing climate.

American mastodon: Believe it or not, North America once had thriving elephant populations of its own—the elephant's relative, the forest-dwelling mastodon. Spread across the country from Alaska to the Rio Grande and from California to Florida, the American mastodon was a formidable presence. Bull mastodons grew to over nine feet tall, weighing in at four tons.

Mammoth: Almost everyone knows the woolly species of this now-extinct genus. But at one point, mammoths roamed Europe, Asia, North America, and Central America, with species as different from one another as a wolf is from a shih tzu. In Siberia, the massive steppe mammoth stood 15 feet tall, the same height as a one-story house. But it was the woolly mammoth of Europe and North America that played a vital role in human hunting and survival for almost 30,000 years. In the cave paintings found throughout Europe, woolly mammoths were among the most popular animals. Early man had an almost spiritual relationship with the woolly mammoth; they built their homes from mammoth bones, buried their dead alongside mammoth tusks, and, in some brutally cold winters, eked out survival only thanks to the mammoth's meat. When the Bering Land Bridge opened between Asia and North America, early man followed the mammoth migration from Alaska to Kansas.

In case you were wondering, the Biggest Bear in the Woods title now belongs to the polar bear. Males can weigh as much as 1,500 pounds.

Ground sloth: While the modern sloth has a reputation as a benign, lazy species, the giant ground sloth of yore was anything but. Growing as long as 20 feet from head to tail and with massive, powerful frames, the now-extinct ground sloths hold a place among the largest land animals of all time. Thanks to their thick, protective hides, massive size, and long, sharp claws, the ground sloths were a difficult prey to take down. Early human hunters in both North and South America had to get precariously close to the sloths to kill them, making the animals one of the most dangerous big game.

Smilodon (saber-toothed tiger): Although not technically tigers, the Smilodon certainly earned the "saber-toothed" portion of its well-known nickname. With giant, spear-like canines that could grow to nearly a foot long, powerful, compact, 800-pound bodies, and strong forearms, the Smilodon was an adept killer. Surprisingly, the Smilodon's jaw was significantly weaker compared to that of other carnivorous cats, so researchers postulate that instead of trying to quickly snap their prey's windpipe, the Smilodon would use its giant, knife-like teeth to pierce its pinned prey's jugular, resulting in a swift death from blood loss. The Smilodon lived throughout North and South America until as recently as 8000 BC, when the changing climate and competition from human hunters dwindled its population.

American lion: It may sound even more out there than a forest-dwelling North American elephant, but this continent was once patrolled by giant, fierce lions. What's perhaps even more frightening is that these cats were about 25 percent larger than today's African lions, possibly making them the largest felines ever. A fully grown male lion stood about eight feet long and weighed over 900 pounds. Using keen intelligence, brute strength, and group hunting skills, these extremely savvy predators fed on pretty much any meaty thing they could sink their teeth into, including deer, bison, camels, and even mammoths. Making matters worse for the first humans to arrive in North America, these lions were fairly awesome at hide-and-seek when they cozied up in grass-lined caves during cold winters.

Short-faced bear: An abundant genus of bear hunted voraciously throughout western North America up until about 11,000 years ago, subsisting on about 35 pounds of fresh flesh every single day. Weighing in at over 2,000 pounds and able to stand to 15 feet, the short-faced bear was the largest bear in history. In fact, they may have been the largest land-roaming, carnivorous mammal ever.

It's a Bird-Eat-Bird World: Haast's Eagle

Not only did New Zealand have the largest flightless bird, it also had the world's largest eagle. Though their ten-foot wingspans were rather stubby for their 25-pound bodies, the Haast's Eagle's were incredible hunters, swooping down on their favorite food, the flightless moa, at speeds exceeding 50 miles per hour. Europeans visiting the islands for the first time were told tales of the eagles carrying off people as well.

Megalania: Possibly the most terrifying animal ever, the megalania was as close to Godzilla as nature has ever come. Growing to an estimated size of 25 feet and perhaps as large as 4,000 pounds, the megalania was a supersized version of the equally vicious Komodo dragon. Being the largest lizard ever to crawl out of the ocean was apparently not enough for the megalania; it also carried a lethal cocktail of venom and infectious bacteria.

Giant moa: If you have a phobia of *Sesame Street*'s Big Bird, stop reading now. Because the giant moa put that big yellow chicken to shame. Growing to a freakish 12 feet tall and weighing perhaps as much as 600 pounds, moas were the largest bird-like things since the dinosaurs. Unfortunately for their existence, the moa couldn't fly, which made them particularly easy prey for the Polynesians who settled New Zealand. The Maori finally prepared their last giant moa meal sometime around the start of the fifteenth century.

A TASTING GUIDE TO EXOTIC ANIMALS

Of course, you don't have to go back in time to sink your teeth into some strange creatures. Here's a brief tasting guide to today's more exotic dishes.

Crocodile
- *Found in:* Egypt, Kenya, Tanzania
- *Tastes like:* fishy turkey
- *Typical dishes:* tail fillets are pan-fried, deep-fried, or barbecued

Alligator
- *Found in:* Australia, Thailand, South Africa, Cuba
- *Tastes like:* crabby chicken
- *Typical dishes:* tail fillets are fried, barbecued, or used in soup

Turtle
- *Found in:* Cayman Islands, southern United States, China, Korea
- *Tastes like:* gamey veal
- *Typical dish:* soup

Bison

- *Found in:* North America
- *Tastes like:* lean, flavorful beef
- *Typical dishes:* steaks, roasts, or burgers

Cockroach

- *Found in:* Thailand
- *Tastes like:* flavorless (absorbs the flavor of the oil in which it's prepared)
- *Typical dishes:* boiled or deep-fried

Grasshopper

- *Found in:* Mexico, China, Uganda
- *Tastes like:* light, crunchy, and earthy
- *Typical dish:* fried with salt and lime

Camel

- *Found in:* Saudi Arabia, Kenya, Libya, Kazakhstan
- *Tastes like:* very coarse, loose beef; very tough
- *Typical dish:* lightly fried with salt and pepper

Ox Testicle

- *Found in:* western United States, western Canada
- *Tastes like:* chewy liver
- *Typical dish:* deep-fried with a tasty dippin' sauce

Yak

- *Found in:* Himalayan regions of Tibet and Nepal, Mongolia, Russia
- *Tastes like:* rich, very lean red meat
- *Typical dishes:* steak, fillet, or ground into patties

Caribou (reindeer)

- *Found in:* Canada, Alaska, Sweden, Russia
- *Tastes like:* chewy lamb/beef hybrid with a strong livery aftertaste
- *Typical dishes:* steak, casserole

Zebra

- *Found in:* Namibia
- *Tastes like:* sweet, lean, juicy beef
- *Typical dish:* steak (medium rare recommended)

Guinea pig

- *Found in:* Peru, Bolivia, the Democratic Republic of Congo
- *Tastes like:* rabbit with a crispy, delicious skin
- *Typical dish:* slow-roasted whole

Kangaroo

- *Found in:* Australia
- *Tastes like:* tender, wild, and intense meat flavor
- *Typical dish:* steak or ground into patties

DIET DOWN UNDER: KANGATARIANISM

One of the hottest lifestyle diets in Australia is kangatarianism, the forgoing of all other meats except for the occasional kangaroo steak. Australians claim that eating wild kangaroo is much more ethical than eating farm-raised animals, kangaroos aren't harmful to the environment, and they aren't butchered in inhumane slaughterhouses.

Nutria (river rat)
- *Found in:* southern United States
- *Tastes like:* light chicken
- *Typical dish:* gumbo

Rattlesnake
- *Found in:* United States, Nicaragua, Peru
- *Tastes like:* mix between chicken, frog, and turtle
- *Typical dish:* fried in bite-sized pieces

HOW TO KILL AND COOK
A POISONOUS SNAKE

There are over 3,000 species of snake on the planet and fewer than 400 of them are poisonous. Snakes are naturally shy animals, so don't go out killing them for sport. But if you end up winning a mano-y-serpiente battle with a venomous serpent, you might as well not let it go to waste. Here are the five steps to cooking a snake.

Cut Off the Head

Most snakes' sack-like venom glands lie above the mouth behind the eyes, so make sure to cut an ample amount of distance down the body to ensure the elimination of any toxins. In addition, you'll need to make sure the snake hasn't recently poisoned and consumed any other animal. A poisoned and consumed rodent will retain its toxicity until fully digested by the snake.

Strip the Skin

Next you'll need to cut the skin off the same way you would a fish. Depending on the size of the snake, the thick skin should tear off the body fluidly.

Remove the Guts

Make a long incision along the snake's belly. This will open up the abdominal cavity, allowing you to pull out the guts.

Rinse and Soak the Meat

Snake meat looks like a cross between chicken and fish. But it tastes little like either. Snake meat is naturally tough, gamey, and a bit messy. Rinse the meat thoroughly, fillet the snake into four-inch chunks at the same angle as the ribs, and, if you have the time, allow it to soak in salt water for a full day to remove the gamey taste and texture.

Bread and Fry

Unlike a nice steak, snake meat needs a bit of help in the taste department. Bread the fillets with egg, flour, black pepper, and salt. Heat up either vegetable or canola oil and fry the snake fillets until golden brown.

The antivenin for the African black mamba's deadly bite is created by injecting the snake's diluted toxin into a sheep and then harvesting the antibodies for human use?

BEEF

Origin of the Steak: The Aurochs

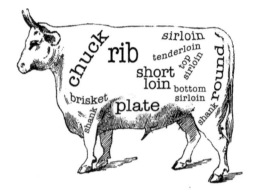

Imagine an angry bull charging you at full speed. Now imagine that same bull faster, angrier, more athletic, and with larger horns. Now you've got a good picture of the wild cows our ancestors had to deal with.

More than two million years ago, the world's climate became seasonal, cool, and dry, very similar to our world today, and vast expanses of grassland opened up throughout Europe and the Indian subcontinent. The explosion of grassland opened a new world to large grazing animals like the antelope, bison, and one particular animal whose descendants would one day inhabit every continent on the planet: the aurochs.

> Contrary to popular belief, bulls are not enraged by the color red.
> In fact, they can't even see it; they're red–green colorblind.

The aurochs had a lot more in common with a bull bred to fight in the Spanish bullring than with the modern cow. They were calm, fairly docile herders, but only until they were provoked. And provocation didn't require a spear in the back; these animals hated just being teased, striking their tormentors with three-foot horns before chucking them effortlessly with 1,500 pounds of muscle.

But despite a mercurial temperament, there were few animals on the grasslands as easy to get close to. And around 10,000 years ago, the early settlers of Mesopotamia roped them up and began to domesticate them. Over the millennia to come, the aurochs became one of the foundations of modern civilizations, as well as one of man's first experiments with Mendelian genetics. In Europe and India, the aurochs were actually bred right out of existence, giving way instead to the common taurine cattle of Europe and the zebu of India.

THE ANATOMY OF FIVE DIFFERENT CUTS OF BEEF

Filet mignon: The "dainty fillet" as it's known in French is one of the butcher's most prized cuts. Filet mignon is actually just the front end of a larger piece, the tenderloin, a small, snaking strip of muscle on either rear hip of the cow. Because the cut is from a seldom-used muscle, it's one of the most tender pieces of meat on the animal; due to its limited size, it's also one of the most expensive.

T-bone and porterhouse: Can't decide on just one cut? Try a T-bone or a porterhouse. These expensive, large, and delicious steaks contain meat from two of the tastiest cuts of beef: the tenderloin and the strip steak. Both the T-bone and porterhouse come from the short loin and have that recognizable T-shaped bone dividing the two delicious meats. Porterhouses are cut farther back and have larger servings of tenderloin.

Rib eye: Juicy, fatty, and dripping with flavor, the rib eye is a boneless cut from the cow's rib section. Rib eyes contain no eyes; they were traditionally called that to indicate meat from the "eye" or center of the rib. A slice of beef with a rib or two is simply called rib steak.

Popeseye: A Brit butchering of "Pope's eye," these steaks are tender, thin, fast-cooking cuts from the rump—essentially the cow's massive derriere. The cut originated in Scotland and is delicious when pan-fried to a nice buttery brown.

Sirloin: These tasty cuts come from just behind the short loin, from the part of the back just near the rump. Always ask for a *top sirloin*, the choicest part of the sirloin. Compared to the bottom sirloin, deceptively called "sirloin steak," the top sirloin is leaner, smaller, more tender, and more expensive.

MEDIUM RARE A steak is defined as medium rare when the center of the cut reaches between 130 and 135 degrees Fahrenheit.

MEDIUM The ideal doneness for marinated, less expensive steaks is medium. The center of the meat should reach between 140 and 150 degrees Fahrenheit.

Grilled

Chomping into that perfectly charred steak fresh from the grill is one of the greatest feelings known to modern man. The trick to grilling the perfect steak begins with choosing the perfect cut. And marble cuts, such as the rib eye, are among the best for grilling.

Just before putting your steak on the grill, flavor it with a thin coat of olive oil (to give it that perfectly charred appearance) and liberally sprinkle it with salt and pepper. For a perfectly seared, tender steak, the grill should be hotter than hell but with no licking flames. Cook the steak to your desire, remove it from the grill, and let it sit for a couple of minutes to allow the inside juices to open. Then devour. **Preferred cuts:** rib eye, round, top sirloin, filet mignon.

Dry-Marinated

If you don't want to spend a day's earnings on a single meal but you still want to cook an impressive steak, try marinating a cheap cut like skirt steak. You can soak your steak in a favorite marinade, but an increasingly popular method is to dry-marinate the steaks in salt.

To prepare, simply coat both sides of the steak in an avalanche of salt. Seriously, a lot of salt. Let it sit for an hour for every inch of the steak's thickness, at which point the salt will have brought the steak's internal juices to the surface. Now simply rinse the salt off the steak, pat thoroughly dry with a paper towel, and either grill or pan-cook it. **Preferred cuts:** skirt steak, sirloin, flank.

Pan-Seared

The trick to a perfectly seared steak? Quick and hot. Cooking the steak on the highest heat possible will allow the surfaces to get nice and crispy while the interior remains juicy and pink. You can use a good grill, but many top chefs actually prefer to pan-sear a nice cut of meat since the flat pan helps create an even, crispy crust that traps in the flavor.

For the ultimate pan-seared steak, begin by placing your favorite cast iron pan (sans the steak) in the oven and heating

HOW TO PROPERLY COOK A STEAK

FOUR INCREDIBLE METHODS FOR PREPARING BEEF

As descendants of skilled, savage hunters, we have a biological need to sink our teeth into a sizzling-hot hunk of fresh meat. Even if you don't spend a lot of time cooking, manning the grill is a man's rite of passage. But what's the correct way to prepare a steak? Should you season it? And how cooked should it be? Well, that all depends on several factors, including your personal taste, the cut of meat you choose, and whether or not you have a grill.

TWO RULES OF COOKING STEAK

Never cook it cold. Always let the steak warm up to room temperature. A steak straight from the fridge simply won't cook evenly.

Rare, medium rare, or well done, it's up to you. Unlike other meats like pork or chicken, beef is pretty safe to eat raw as long as the exterior has been cooked. As a rule of thumb, the rarer the center of the steak, the juicier, more tender, and more flavorful it will be.

it to 500 degrees Fahrenheit. Transfer that super-heated pan to the stovetop (use an oven mitt) and turn the heat up to the maximum. Lay your steak in the sizzling-hot pan and sear each side until you get a nice, golden-brown crust (about thirty seconds per side). Turn off the stove and return the pan (this time with the steak) to the 500-degree oven to let the inside cook, around two minutes for medium rare and three minutes for medium. **Preferred cuts:** rib eye, strip, tenderloin.

Broiled

Broiled steaks are a great option…if you have a great broiler. Professional steakhouses use really hot broilers—some can get as hot as 1,800 degrees. Chances are your broiler doesn't do that. Still, a home-broiled steak can be delicious, especially if you have a nice porterhouse or T-bone.

Begin by brushing a fine coat of olive oil onto the cut and then preheating the broiler to the highest setting. Place the steak in a cast iron pan (or, for that barbecue look, a roasting rack) and toss it in the oven, about four inches from the broiler. After about four minutes, remove the steak, throw on some salt and pepper, flip it, and return it to the broiler for another four minutes or so. Done. **Preferred cuts:** porterhouse, T-bone, top sirloin.

TAKING THE ANIMAL OUT OF THE MEAT

When the French Normans conquered England in the eleventh century, they put the English-speaking Anglo-Saxons to work in the fields to oversee their livestock while the French simply *ate* the meat. Today, we still refer to living animals by their English herdsman names while using words of French origin to speak about edible meat. For those who need a quick primer, here's a breakdown of several animals and their corresponding culinary names:

Cow/Beef (French *bœuf*)
Pig/Pork (French *porc*)
Young cattle or calf/Veal (French *veau*)
Sheep/Mutton (French *mouton*)
Chicken/Poultry (French *poulet*)
Deer/Venison (French *venaison*)

The word "venison" originally came from the Latin word *vēnor* ("to hunt") and was used for the meat of any hunted animal, including deer, hare, and boar.

One of the main reasons the French began naming their meat differently from their animals was that it removed the guilt and unpleasantness of consuming once-living flesh. We've continued this tradition in English with terms like Rocky Mountain oysters (deep-fried calf testicles) and sweetbread (cow pancreas or throat). *Bon appétit!*

PORK

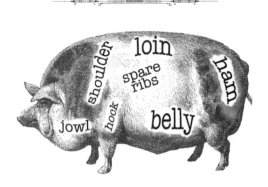

Incredibly, dogs are the only animal in the world to have been domesticated before the pig. Intelligent, sociable, and delicious, Eurasian wild boars were a natural choice to be brought into the fold of human civilization. Like the dog, the exact story of the domestication of pigs is lost to the fact that nobody bothered to take notes during prehistory, but what we do know is that settlers throughout Eurasia began effectively herding and keeping wild boars more than 9,000 years ago.

As voracious omnivores (literally eating just about anything), pigs proved particularly easy to keep. They would feed as happily on roots and grasses as they would discarded meat and fruit. Before long, the domestication of pigs spread throughout Asia, Europe, Polynesia, and Australia, arriving in the Americas in the 1500s alongside the Conquistadors. A testament to their immense popularity, the pig, whose ancestors' population was once limited to a small region of the world, has become one of the most common mammals on earth with an estimated population of over 990 million.

BEWARE THE PORK CURRY

Think septic tanks are foul? They have nothing on the **pig toilet**. An efficient and common form of latrine used in China and India for nearly 2,000 years, the pig toilet is pretty much exactly what it sounds like: an outhouse that funneled waste directly into a pig trough. Hungry pigs will apparently eat just about anything. And considering what those pigs were used for, apparently so will people.

CHICKEN

From Junglefowl to Yardbird

It sounds odd, but the story of the average country chicken starts way out in the hot jungles of southern Asia. That's where the red junglefowl, the domestic chicken's direct ancestor, had made its home for thousands of years when humankind wandered into the Asian subcontinent. The birds lived a quiet existence in their native habitat, feeding on insects, seeds, and fruit. They hardly flew in the dense jungles, taking to the air only in order to roost in the trees or escape momentarily from ground-based predators.

Then, at least 5,000 years ago, the early inhabitants of southern Asia started snapping up the junglefowl and keeping them close by. A beautiful, savory relationship began. The junglefowl would provide humans with eggs, meat, and entertainment in the form of cockfighting; in return, human settlements provided an ample supply of seeds and insects, as well as protection from predators.

By the fifth century BC, the domesticated junglefowl had spread throughout the Mediterranean, from Egypt to Greece and from Mount Zion to the Iberian Peninsula. Which means people have been cursing crowing roosters at dawn for a very long time.

LORDS OF THE FLIES

The Hawaiian island of Kauai is overrun by what appears to be red junglefowl. But, while the ancient Polynesians carried domesticated birds across the Pacific, today's wild brood is actually just modern chickens gone feral. After Hurricane Iniki slammed into the island in 1992, hundreds of chickens broke free of their coops and spread out over the island.

Drinking with Hemingway

BOOZE AND BOXING

Ernest Hemingway was a man. He hunted wild game in Africa, drank absinthe in Paris, and ran with the bulls in Pamplona. He wore a respectable mustache. Enjoyed a well-fought boxing match. When he was seventeen, Hemingway adopted the writing style of the first newspaper he worked at and then never gave it up. For that steadfast dedication to clean, crisp writing, he was awarded the Nobel Prize for Literature. In the sixty-one short years before he shot himself, Hemingway had four wives. Yes, Ernest Hemingway was a man.

Ernest Hemingway served in World War I even though the United States was not yet a belligerent. He took jobs as a war correspondent first during the Spanish Civil War and then throughout WWII. At the Liberation of Paris, he was awarded the Bronze Star just for showing up. Yes, Ernest Hemingway was a man. And that should be celebrated. Here are two of his favorite subjects: booze and boxing.

EVERYMAN'S DRINK: BEER

"Beer is proof that God loves us and wants us to be happy."
—*Benjamin Franklin*

Birth of the Brewski

Around the advent of agriculture, we humans discovered one very important lesson: pretty much any starchy substance with sugar, when exposed to natural yeasts found in the air, will start to gloriously ferment. And that happened a long time ago. In the Fertile Crescent of Mesopotamia, there's evidence that a beerish drink was produced and consumed as far back as 6,000 years ago.

In his book, *The Complete Guide to World Beer*, author Roger Protz echoes numerous anthropologists when he says, "When people of the ancient world realised they could make bread and beer from grain, they stopped roaming and settled down to cultivate cereals in recognisable communities." In other words, not only is beer as old as civilization itself, it helped create the frickin' thing.

Beer then spread to any society that was growing any cereals at all—the ancient Greeks taught the Romans, and the Gauls, Barbarians, and Egyptians were all drinking homemade brews as well. And, like the great modern culture of microbrewing, every taste was different.

By the time 1000 AD rolled around, one big advancement had been made—the addition of hops, a flower growing on the Humulus vine. Hops helped to add flavor and aroma to beer in addition to helping preserve it for future consumption.

Then, at the end of the fifteenth century, man made one giant leap for beerkind: beer-making was taken out of the home and put in the hands of budding professionals. (Considering the number of DIY beer kits now available, apparently we've regressed.) A lot of these newfangled microbreweries were housed in monasteries, where monks worked tirelessly to perfect the art of brewing in order to keep the monasteries in diamonds, furs, and cloaks. So the breweries grew and a golden era of beer innovation began.

The Surprisingly Limited Origins of Beer

Rest, my Precious

The term "lager" (from the German *lagern*) means "storehouse" and comes from the frigid breweries of southeast Germany where brewers were forced to store barrels of fermenting beer for up to a month—instead of the normal week—because the low temperatures hindered yeast growth. Fortunately for the brewers, the wait was worth it as the slow-fermenting beer turned out (arguably) better brews.

Getting pissed on the Thames

Porters, England's stout ales, were named for London's river porters among whom the high-alcohol brown ales were especially popular.

Guinness actually is good for you

All the way up until the Industrial Revolution, beer was one of the primary sources of vital nutrients and vitamins for the underclass in Europe.

> "A fine beer may be judged with only one sip,
> but it's better to be thoroughly sure."
>
> —*Czech saying*

It's the water

In the rough-and-tumble cities of medieval Europe, drinking groundwater was a sketchy proposition (i.e., you could easily get cholera and die). Instead, parched citizens of all ages relied on clean, refreshing ale to stay hydrated.

The battle for the manliest beer

Samuel Adams Utopias is a consistently produced ale so strong (54 proof or 27 percent alcohol by volume) that thirteen states consider it too manly for sale. Where it is sold, patrons can purchase a bottle for a mere $150.

However, a Scottish artisanal brewery called BrewDog absolutely demolished Utopias' paltry accomplishment with their limited edition brew called The End of History. Served in taxidermy roadkill and coming in at a whopping 110 proof, The End of History is by far the most epic beverage ever manufactured. The twelve furry bottles (seven were stuffed into weasels, four into squirrels, and one into a rabbit) sold for $765 each.

RAUCOUS BACCHUS: WINE

Considering the ease with which the sugars in fruit will ferment, the real history of wine probably goes back to our prehistoric ancestors who most likely got hammered on fruit mush in their caves after long days of hitting mammoths with sticks. But even wine as we know it today dates back an impressive 8,000 years. Back in the day, before humankind had even discovered writing, we discovered grapes.

The greatest thing about grapes is that they're basically their own naturally pre-packaged alcohol factories. Not only is the grape easily pressed, but it has a lovely thin skin that carries around its own yeast for fermentation. So even in the earliest grape-blessed civilizations, all you had to do was walk out of your hut, grab a couple bunches from the field, mash them up in a pot, and let nature work its magic.

The only issue was that grapes are notoriously hard to grow. The same thin skin that made them so mashable also made them extremely vulnerable to changes in climate—grapes were killed by heat, frost, mold, insects, and even sunburns. Cultivating grapes became an art form limited to a couple regions around the Mediterranean and, thus, wine became some seriously upper-class drank. Interestingly, very little has changed between ancient Greece and Rome and modern day America; back then beer was considered the beverage of choice for the masses while wine was a bit snobbier.

EVEN THE GODS COULDN'T HANDLE THEIR WINE

The Ancient Egyptian god of red wine, Shezmu, was also the god of slaughter, execution, blood, and oil. (Also, inexplicably, perfume.)

If You're Going to San Francisco...Bring Me a Bottle of Pinot

When Spanish monks started establishing Catholic missions up the California Coast, they brought their grapevine clippings with them. Wine was an important part of the Catholic sacrament and getting shipments from Europe to the West Coast of North America was not going to happen. Fortunately for them, it turned out that the coast of California conveniently had the same climate as the best wine-growing regions in the Mediterranean. Unfortunately for the monks, their wine varietals kind of sucked and California's famed wine production didn't begin in earnest until vintners like Robert Mondavi started producing the good stuff in the late 1960s. Today the wine craze has swept over America: You can find wineries in surprising locations from Washington State to New Jersey.

Nine Wine Descriptions You Should Know

Reds

Pinot noir: Native to the Burgundy region of France, pinot noir is a finicky, hard-to-grow grape grown mostly in cooler regions. It is considered one of the finest wine-producing grapes, with a wide variety of flavors and aromas.

Merlot: Originally from France but now grown in Northern California, Chile, and Australia, merlot is a medium-bodied grape with strong hints of cherry and plum.

Cabernet: One of the world's easiest grapes to grow, cabernet sauvignon is a hybrid of cabernet franc and sauvignon blanc. It is dense and peppery.

Zinfandel: Zinfandel, which made its way to the states from Croatia, has flavors ranging from raspberry to pepper.

Chianti: A wine particular to a region rather than a grape, Chianti wine comes from the Chianti region of Italy in central Tuscany. It can be made from a variety of Chianti grapes and is generally aged for at least seven months in oak.

THE FOUNTAIN OF YOUTH?

Red wine contains a compound called resveratrol that has been proven to increase the lifespan of some animals by up to 50 percent. Sadly, in order to achieve the same longevity benefits and live to 150, you'd have to drink about 1,000 bottles every day.

Whites

Sauvignon blanc: With origins in France's Bordeaux region, sauvignon blanc is crisp and refreshing, with flavors ranging from vegetal to tropical.

Chardonnay: Originally from France's Burgundy wine region, chardonnay's flavors range from oaky and lean to sweet and fruity. It is easy to make and is used in many sparkling wines.

Pinot grigio: Also originally from Burgundy, pinot gris or pinot grigio is subtle and crisp. It's basically a white replica of pinot noir.

Riesling: A high-sugar wine from cold-ass Germany, Riesling has a strong, flowery scent.

The World's Most Expensive Wine

The most expensive bottle of wine ever sold, a 1787 Chateau Lafite, auctioned in 1985 for $156,000, which translates today to around $315,000. The winning bidder, billionaire

A WINE FIT FOR A CARTEL

The Corsican wine Vin Mariani had all the characteristics of a truly remarkable beverage. Namely, it contained both wine and cocaine. While everyone else in the 1800s was jazzing up their wines with brandies and bubbles, Signor Mariani spiced his with coca leaves, marketing the invention as the ultimate pick-me-up (which we're pretty sure it really truly was).

Malcolm Forbes (yes, *that* Forbes), was under the still uncon-
firmed impression that the bottle had once been part of President Thomas Jefferson's personal cellar (the initials T.J. are
etched into the side of the bottle). Whether the bottle ever
truly belonged to Thomas Jefferson is of no consequence, as
Forbes bought the bottle for bragging rights rather than a
desire to imbibe: the 200-year-old Bordeaux probably turned
to undrinkable sludgy, vinegary crap sometime in the early
nineteenth century.

The World's Most Expensive Drinkable Wine

A 1997 Dom Romane Conti consistently sells for about
$1,540, making it the world's most expensive drinkable
wine. With suggestions of berries and leather and tantalizing
undertones of soy sauce, licorice, and flowers, this French red
Burgundy is apparently the perfect complement to a good
burger.

OPEN A BOTTLE OF THE BUBBLY

CHAMPAGNE

The accidental innovation that is champagne can be summed up in one phrase: "*Merde*, it's cold!" The Champagne region happens to be in the coldest, dreariest corner of northern France (the annual mean temperature is just 50 degrees Fahrenheit). But that didn't stop the freezing citizens of Champagne from growing wine grapes, as difficult as it was. In fact, the chardonnays and pinots they managed to produce were prized around the country, so wine was big business for these northerners.

The biggest problem they faced was that in order to properly activate the yeast, they needed the warmer temperatures of their cousins to the south. But that didn't stop them from trying. And as they attempted to ferment the wines in the cold, they discovered an unfortunate side effect of chilly yeast—it produces a lot of carbon dioxide. So much CO_2, in fact, that their bottles started busting and every time they opened one up, the wine fizzed and bubbled. It took a while for this new carbonated wine to catch on, but eventually it did, and with serious style.

> Careful, on average, twenty-five people accidentally
> die each year from flying champagne corks.

Mr. Bubbles

Mr. Dom Perignon, the name synonymous with extravagantly priced bubbly (a magnum of Dom sold for a record $1,000,000 in 2010), was a chubby Benedictine monk from northern France. He is credited with revolutionizing the production of the region's unique white wine, which we know today as champagne.

Leave the Champagne to Your Wife

The "Veuve" in the beloved Veuve Cliquot champagne means "widow" and is named after Barbe-Nicole Cliquot, whose husband died and left her his champagne-producing estate (which she in turn made into an empire).

The Most Expensive Bottle of Liquid Ever Sold

$1,946,417 was the final auctioned purchase price of a bottle of Henri IV Dudognon Heritage Cognac Grande Champagne.

THE FASCINATING HISTORY OF SPIRITS

If the liquor aisle is any indication, it would appear that man can distill just about anything. Vodka is made from potatoes or grain; gin from berries; tequila from succulents; rum from sugar; whiskey from barley; bourbon from corn, and soju from rice. This human ingenuity—actually more of a parched thirst for something boozy—has led to some lip-smacking drinks, hair-burning shots, and downright fascinating events in history.

> *"I should never have switched from scotch to martinis."*
> —*Purported last words of Mr. Humphrey Bogart*

Bartending Terms You Should Know

Call drink: A two-ingredient beverage like Jack and Coke (the term "cocktail" refers to a drink with three or more ingredients).

Neat: Served alone in a glass with no ice.

Nip: One quarter of a liquor bottle.

On the rocks (or over): Served over ice.

Shooter: A straight shot (neat).

Straight up (or up): Shaken (or stirred) with ice and then strained into a glass.

Tot: A small serving of liquor.

Twist: A lemon peel.

Virgin: Something you should never order.

Well drink: A drink made with an unspecified brand of liquor, usually the cheapest swill and normally pretty crappy.

The Green Fairy

Like all respectable liquors, absinthe was originally peddled as medicine. Toward the end of the eighteenth century, Dr. Pierre Ordinaire concocted a "healthy" digestive aid made from three garden herbs—grand wormwood, green anise, and sweet fennel—distilled to a powerful proof, giving absinthe its traditional kick. Dr. Ordinaire then sold his recipe to two sisters in Couvet, Switzerland, who continued to sell small batches of absinthe as medicine.

When a man named Major Daniel Henri Dubied approached the sisters with interest in buying the recipe, absinthe was once again passed along. It was with Major Dubied and his son-in-law Henri-Louis Pernod that absinthe first started really flowing. They built two large-scale distilleries, starting two linked brands of liquor: Dubied Pere et Fils of Switzerland and, the more famous French brand, Maison Pernod Fils.

In the 1840s, France invaded Algeria and the French troops were issued bottles of absinthe as a malaria preventative. When they returned to Paris, they brought a developed palate for the distinctive drink, nicknamed the Green Fairy, and absinthe quickly became the beverage of choice at Parisian bistros and cafés.

Absinthism

By the end of the nineteenth century, absinthe had been vilified. The reason given by quack scientists was the wormwood. Though wormwood had been used since antiquity as a medicinal herb, the presence of a powerful chemical compound known as thujone quickly gave it a false reputation as a highly addictive hallucinogen (it's not). Enjoyers of absinthe quickly found themselves labeled with "absinthism," a condition ten times worse than alcoholism. And by the 1910s absinthe was being banned in countries from Europe to North and South America.

Today, absinthe is once again legal throughout the world, although the recipe no longer reflects that of Dr. Ordinaire.

While very high proof, several of absinthe's herbal ingredients have stimulant properties that counter the depressant effects of alcohol, leading the drinker to a mentally clear, balanced intoxication experience.

The correct way to enjoy the Green Fairy

Pour one jigger shot of absinthe into a glass. Lay a grated absinthe spoon on top of the glass. Place one sugar cube on the spoon. Pour up to four jigger shots of cold water (to taste) over the sugar cube to dissolve it into the absinthe.

Yo Ho, Yo Ho, a Rum and Coke for Me

Kill-devil be the name, but "rum" got the fame. It was a wicked, blindingly strong drink that put the sailors of the Caribbean in a stupor, earned the name kill-devil, and later became the drink known the world over as rum.

Sugarcane was native to just two places on earth: India and Papua New Guinea. But once the Chinese got ahold of its unique sweetness, sugarcane became one of the most heavily sought-after crops in the world thanks to mankind's natural sweet tooth. It spread everywhere fast. So fast that almost as soon as Christopher Columbus and his crew had set foot on the islands of the Caribbean, they had planted the first sugarcane. Eventually some ingenious European immigrant to the Caribbean started fermenting and distilling molasses—a useless, sugary, nasty-looking byproduct of granulated sugar production—and rum was born.

The image of the rum-guzzling pirate is anything but a myth. In the early days of maritime exploration, stored drinking water would become a slimy, algae-infested mess, so sailors had to devise methods of masking the disgustingness. As first they added wine or beer, but it became unfeasible to meet the thirsty seamen's needs on longer voyages, so it was replaced with rum.

Rum has been the sailor's drink of choice since 1655, when Britain conquered Jamaica. Rum in its delicious, undiluted form, however, proved problematic, as sailors would often forgo their ration for days on end, opting instead to swill the spirit in excess in one drunken sitting. Among other obvious problems, this tendency caused unacceptable dehydration.

Grog was the solution. Originally referring to watered-down rum (and now a variety of rum-based drinks), this lower proof intoxicant was hydrating as well as enjoyable, and became the beverage of choice for sailors the world over. By the mid-1700s, some admirals and captains tossed lime juice into the mix, and the boost of vitamin C could ward off scurvy (although it usually became oxidized and therefore ineffective). By 1756, grog was deemed so *healthy* that Britain's Royal Navy actually mandated that their sailors drink grog twice daily, and this awesome grog-drinking requirement was practiced all the way up to 1970. So next time you head out on a cruise, make the healthy choice by drinking rum with every meal.

CAP'N RUM

The liquor business has demoted Sir Henry Morgan. Better known as Captain Morgan, Henry Morgan actually retired from Jamaica-based privateering a full admiral in the English Royal Navy.

The Beautiful Blue Agave

> *"One tequila, two tequila, three tequila, floor."*
> —George Carlin

It's hard to fathom just how far men will go for a glass of booze until you know the story of tequila. The farther into Mexico the Spanish Conquistadors got, the lighter their casks of brandy became, until one day their Central American party dried up altogether. Desperate for anything they could ferment and shove down their throats in the middle of the desert, the Spaniards turned to a harsh, booze-like drink that the native inhabitants imbibed, called *pulque*, made from the heart of the blue agave plant. Not caring to waste their time on the low-alcohol content of *pulque*, the Spaniards began distilling the fermented juice into the New World's first native spirit.

WHISKEY 101

By the end of the fifteenth century AD, the process of distilling fermented grain had arrived in Britain, Scotland, and Ireland. Undoubtedly the islands erupted in celebration. And Scotch whiskey in its earliest form was a pretty simple no-brainer—Scotland already had plenty of barley fields being used for bread and ale production, so the only piece of equipment needed was a still.

Whiskey production ramped up in Scotland throughout the Renaissance, with small distilleries opening up in nearly every village from Edinburgh to Elgin. When the British government took control of its northerly neighbor in 1707 and saw how profitable the liquor had become in Scotland, they decided they wanted in and started taxing the crap out of it. But if we've learned anything from William Wallace, it's that the Scots take orders from nobody. Instead of paying taxes on the booze, they simply took it underground and started

Uisge Beatha

In Gaelic, whiskey is called *uisge beatha*, or the "water of life." The name comes from the early medicinal form of the beverage and Latin name *aqua vitae*. The funny thing is, *uisge beatha* deserves the title: recent studies have shown a shot of Scotch has more life-preserving antioxidants than a glass of wine.

smuggling moonshine from one end of the country to the next in such quantities it nearly put the few remaining legal distilleries out of business.

Across the Atlantic to Add an "E"

America has always been seen as the Land of Opportunity, and for Scottish and Irish distillers struggling to make money in a sea of native whiskey (or "whisky," as it is spelled in Scotland and Canada), the New World colonies looked like a great place to ply their trade. When they arrived across the Atlantic, the distillers made straight for the hills and ran into a monumental problem: Barley doesn't grow well in the harsher North American climes. Not to be deterred, the distillers simply switched from a mash made of barley to one made of rye and American rye whiskey was born.

The House of Bourbon

By the end of the eighteenth century, distillers had made it out to the newly declared state of Kentucky, a wild and rural stretch of land that had, until the Revolutionary War, been Indian territory. In order to honor France's help in the recent revolution, a large portion of northern Kentucky was named Bourbon County after Louis XVI's Royal House of Bourbon. Somewhat ironically, what the whiskey makers discovered in Bourbon County was a very similar soil to the best French wine-producing regions and one of the holy grails of alcohol production—pure alkaline waters filtering through the limestone rocks of the Blue Hills.

Because native corn grew so well west of the Allegheny Mountains, it quickly surpassed rye for the production of mash in the recipe, and charred oak barrels were introduced to give the corn whiskey a smooth, woody flavor and its distinctive amber color. Shortly after, the whiskey producers of Bourbon County started shipping vast quantities of the drink down the Mississippi to New Orleans in barrels emblazoned with the point of origin, giving birth to the world-famous name.

Anatomy of a Bourbon

No, it does not need to come from Kentucky to be called bourbon. Actually, carrying that hallowed title only takes the following characteristics:

- At least 51 percent corn mash
- Aged in a new, American, charred white-oak barrel
- Entered that barrel at no more than 125 proof
- Bottled above 80 proof
- Made in America

The term "sour mash" refers to the process of transferring the yeast from one batch of whiskey to the next when fermenting the liquor in order to keep the taste consistent from barrel to barrel.

Between the Rocks and a Hard Taste: The Correct Way to Drink Whiskey

Drinking whiskey on the rocks dulls the taste, but taking it neat dulls the taste *buds*. The proper way to imbibe whiskey is with just a splash of pure mineral water. (Drinking it with Coke just makes you look ridiculous.)

The Holy Ghost

The alcohol content in whiskey is so high that it quickly loses volume to evaporation. This significant loss, known as "the angel's share," makes an old batch of whiskey extremely rare.

A Costly Scotch

In 2005, a bottle of Dalmore 62 Single Highland Malt Scotch Whisky that had been bottled in 1943 and made from a blend of aged single malts sold at an auction for the ridiculous price of $58,000. The jubilant new owner was in a good mood—he promptly opened the rare scotch and enjoyed it with his companions.

A Whiskey Worth its Weight in Gold

Macallan Fine and Rare Collection: no diamonds, no fluff. Just a bottle of good, rare whiskey. It sold for $38,000 in 2005.

ETHANOL MISCELLANEA

Regional vs. Generic

Generic

Mezcal: Fermented blue agave

Regional

Tequila: Mezcal from slopes of the Tequila Volcano in Jalisco, Mexico

Generic

Brandy: Distilled wine

Regional

Cognac: Brandy from the Cognac region of western France

Generic

Whiskey/whisky: Fermented barley, corn, or rye

Regional

Scotch: Malt barley whiskey (peat smoke optional) from Scotland

Regional

Bourbon: Corn mash whiskey from the United States

WHISKY OR WHISKEY?

Without the "e," "whisky" refers only to the Scotch and Canadian varieties. "Whiskey" refers to the Irish and American drinks.

The London Gin Plague

Here's something ironic: The juniper berry, the key ingredient in gin, was originally used to ward off the bubonic plague, but it was the fermented version of the berry that ended up being the real epidemic. During the mid-eighteenth century, cheap gin flowed through London like soiled rain water in the gutters, turning huge swaths of Britons into fall-down drunks. The alcoholism in London got so bad that the city's birth rate actually dropped below the death rate and an entire city began to drink itself to death.

The World's Hardest Drinkers

The Republic of Moldova is a very impoverished Eastern European country that, according to a recent study, is home to the world's heaviest drinkers. The study found that, on average, adult Moldovans consume the equivalent of 18.2 liters of pure ethanol every year, the equivalent of 900 beers or roughly three a day. A good chunk of that consumption comes from bootleg liquor: homemade wine and vodka. Eastern Europe in general accounted for most of the drunkest countries, with the Czech Republic, Hungary, Russia, Ukraine,

Estonia, Andorra, Romania, Slovenia, and Belarus rounding out the top ten. For those keeping score at home, America isn't even in the top fifty. Drinking around 9 liters per year, we have a lower annual drinking average than Korea (a surprising fourteenth on list with 14.80 liters consumed annually).

"Only Irish coffee provides in a single glass all four essential food groups: alcohol, caffeine, sugar, and fat."
—Alex Levine

"It takes only one drink to get me drunk. The trouble is, I can't remember if it's the thirteenth or the fourteenth."
—George Burns

"I only take a drink on two occasions— when I'm thirsty and when I'm not."
—Brendan Behan

"Alcohol may be man's worst enemy, but the bible says love your enemy."
—Frank Sinatra

ALL MIXED UP: COCKTAILS

Until Prohibition made liquor illegal, the popularity of cocktails was pretty low. But as soon as the Eighteenth Amendment was ratified, speakeasies everywhere started crafting up new ways of illicitly getting drunk. The main reason for the fancy cocktails? The illegal liquor flowing in America was of somewhat questionable quality, so it was best to hide the booze in a blend of other ingredients. Although many cocktails originated in illegal saloons in America, the drinks became very popular in Europe as they were introduced by expatriate American bartenders who flocked to London and Paris.

The Oldest Cocktail in the United States

America's oldest cocktail is widely regarded as the Sazerac. Invented in New Orleans well before the Civil War by a man named Antoine Peychaud, the drink was named after his favorite brand of cognac, Sazerac-de-Forge et Fils. The Sazerac earned its true popularity when, in 1870, a popular bartender by the name of Leon Lamothe tweaked the recipe to include rye whiskey and absinthe. When absinthe became illegal, additional bitters were substituted to mimic the taste.

But now that you can once again enjoy absinthe, we highly recommend the original recipe: one shot of American rye whiskey, a half shot of absinthe, two dashes Peychaud bitters, sugar cube, and a twist of lemon. Serve straight up (shaken over ice and strained) in a highball glass.

Two Drinks Courtesy of Ernest Hemingway

"Always do sober what you said you'd do drunk.
That will teach you to keep your mouth shut."
—*Ernest Hemingway*

Death in the Afternoon

Hemingway could drink. If you need any proof of that, savor three to five of these absinthe-infused cocktails in one sitting (per his instructions) and see how you hold up. It's like a mimosa on steroids and it'll knock you clear off your seat.

Pour one shot of absinthe in a champagne glass; fill the rest with champagne.

Death in the Gulf Stream

Once you've had your near-death in the afternoon experience, revive yourself with Hemingway's patented pick-me-up from his absinthe days in Paris.

Ingredients: three dashes of Angostura Bitters, one shot of lime juice, one lime peel, two shots of gin. Serve straight up.

> In Russian, vodka means "little water."
> For that, Russia, we salute you.

AND YOU THOUGHT GREY GOOSE WAS EXPENSIVE

At $10,000, the Algonquin Hotel martini is one of the most expensive cocktails in the world. The reason it's so expensive? It's served on the rocks. Or, rather, a single big, fat, 1.52-carat diamond rock. The patron has to place the order at least 72 hours in advance to allow a hotel minion time to run around New York City and track down the diamond.

If $10,000 isn't boss enough for you, there's a beverage sold at London's Movida nightclub for $71,000 (35,000 British pounds). It's made with Louis XII cognac, Cristal Rose champagne, and a garnish of edible flakes of twenty-four-carat gold leaf. Like the Algonquin Hotel martini, this beverage is also served on ice: a blinged-out eleven-carat white diamond ring, to be precise.

Two Other Drinks Thanks to the Lost Generation

The Sidecar

As the story goes, a WWI US Army captain with a penchant for drink frequented a small bistro in Paris, arriving there daily in the sidecar of his military-issued motorcycle. When the captain fell ill with a cold, the bartender whipped up this new drink to give him a boost. Come on, it's not that far-fetched. It does have a lot of vitamin C.

DEATH BY LIQUOR

As fun as drinking is, it is more dangerous than either AIDS or malaria. Drinking causes 2.5 million deaths per year.

Ingredients: one shot cognac, one half shot Grand Marnier, one half shot fresh lemon, lime, or orange juice. Stir and imbibe.

French 75

The first Howitzers were impressive guns and the French 75mm field gun from WWI was a jaw-dropping anti-personnel weapon worthy of a raised glass or two. Or three.

Mix one shot gin with one half shot fresh lemon juice in a champagne glass. Fill the rest with champagne.

SOMETHING TO GO WITH YOUR DRINK?

The Proper Way to Smoke a Cigar

Let's get one thing clear: smoking does not make you manly. Cigarettes dampen your sex drive and your athletic prowess, shorten your already too-short life, and even accelerate male-pattern baldness. We can all agree that there's nothing manly about being an impotent, bald, dead fatty. But there are times in a man's life where he is expected to smoke a cigar and he is expected to enjoy it. These times include:

1. Before his wedding day
2. At the birth of his children
3. At the birth of his grandchildren
4. On his deathbed (because why the hell not?)

El Puro Nace

Two things of note were discovered in 1492: the New World and cigars. When Christopher Columbus and company arrived in the West Indies, one of the first islands they happened upon was Cuba.

As the story goes, a couple of intrepid crewmembers were sent ashore to make contact with the local inhabitants and found a group of Indians smoking a fragrant leaf rolled up in a cornhusk. One of the sailors named Rodrigo de Jerez gave the cornhusk cigar a try, thus introducing greater Europe to mouth, throat, and lung cancer.

By the early seventeenth century, Cuba was already producing tobacco for export back to Europe and by the turn of the nineteenth century, it had become the island's most lucrative cash crop.

Cigar Terms

Anatomy

Bouquet: The scent of the unlit cigar.

Aroma: The scent of the cigar after you've sparked it.

Barrel: The body of the cigar.

Foot: The smoking end of the cigar.

Cap: The round piece of tobacco at the top of the cigar that holds the wrapper together.

Cuban orgins

Clear Havana: A cigar made purely in Havana, Cuba.

Habanos S.A.: The chief Cuban cigar manufacturer.

Cohiba: The Taíno Indian word for cigar and the name of Cuba's most famous brand (and Fidel Castro's favorite).

Vuelta Abajo: Cuba's premier tobacco-growing region. Cigars from this region are widely considered the best in the world.

Accessories

Guillotine: A cigar cutter with a single or double blade.

Bullet punch: A cigar cutter that punches a round incision in the cap of the cigar.

Humidor: A climate-controlled box that maintains cigar freshness. The ideal settings for a humidor are 70 degrees Fahrenheit with 70 percent humidity.

Choosing a Proper Cigar

There are three general types of cigars: machine-rolled, hand-rolled, and handmade. Talk to any experienced cigar aficionado and they'll tell you the same thing: the only acceptable cigar choice is handmade.

But what's the difference between handmade and hand-rolled? Handmade cigars are crafted entirely by hand by a master

DID YOU KNOW?

A properly humidified cigar can stay fresh for more than half a century.

cigar roller (the whole "rolled on a virgin's thigh" type deal). A hand-rolled cigar has its filler tobacco made by machine and is then assembled into its wrapper by hand. There's very little difference between hand-rolled and machine-rolled, so don't get duped.

Finally, if you're going to buy a cigar, do it right and purchase it from a tobacconist, not a bodega.

The Five Steps of Smoking a Cigar

Enjoy the bouquet

When you first unwrap your cigar, it's important to enjoy the smell of the unlit cigar. Hold it up to your nose and smell along the entire barrel. Then say something poetic, preferably in Spanish, such as, *"Ah, el primer olor de la tierra fértil después de seis meses en el mar"* (Ah, the first scent of the fertile earth after six months at sea).

Cut the cap

In order to draw smoke from the cigar, you need to open the cap. Don't cut too much or the wrapper will start to fray; cleanly clip just enough of the wrapper to draw smoke. The larger the opening, the more smoke you'll take with each draw.

Don't inhale

Smoking a cigar is not about sucking the smoke into your lungs (you'll cough one up). It's about holding the smoke in your mouth and enjoying the taste.

Take your time

You need to leave enough time between your draws to allow the cigar to cool. If you burn it too fast, the heat will ruin the taste. Take one puff every sixty seconds or so. But don't count out loud.

Put it out

You never smoke a cigar all the way to the end. The last two inches or so will taste like crap, becoming more bitter as it nears the end. When you're done, don't mash it into the ash-tray; lay it on the side of the tray and let it burn itself out.

Boxing

A HISTORY OF ORGANIZED FISTICUFFS

> *"If you ever dream of beating me you'd better wake up and apologize."*
>
> —*Muhammad Ali*

Boxing in Antiquity

> *"Do not challenge me too far with show of fist, or you may rouse my rage; and old as I am, I still might stain your breast and lips with blood."*
>
> —*The Odyssey*

Boxing wasn't always the sissy sport it is today; back in Ancient Greece, boxers weren't confined by things like rings, rounds, and time limits. They would fight until one boxer gave up, was knocked out, or, in many instances, died. Boxers were (and still are) a prideful breed, so fights could last for hours—even days—before anybody admitted defeat. If a match started to drag, both boxers could agree to trade blow for blow, eliminating such superfluities as defense, movement, and strategy.

Boxing was introduced as an Olympic sport in 688 BC. As with most events of the ancient Greek Olympics, contestants were pretty much naked, though boxers did wear leather thongs wrapped around their knuckles for protection.

As Rome rose to power, boxing continued to be popular both as a sport and in gladiatorial matches. Bouts between slaves or criminals were immensely popular, at least in part because of the insanely high stakes: they were often fought to the death, while the winner might be granted freedom. For the extra-special wow factor, and to expedite the death process, Romans began to affix razor-sharp metal spikes to the boxer's hand thongs. One variation was the myrmex, which translates beautifully to "limb-piercer."

THE DEATH OF BOXING IN ROME

By the late fourth century, Rome's Emperor Theodosius the Great was intent on spreading Christianity throughout the Roman Empire and erasing paganism from the face of the earth. In 391 AD, he issued an edict that forced the closure of all pagan temples, including Olympia, where the ancient Olympics were held. By 394 AD, the Olympic Games in Greece were a relic of the pagan past.

Around 500 AD, Theoderic the Great forbade boxing because of the unchristian damage it inflicted upon boxers' precious faces, which were made in God's image.

Russian Fist Fighting

Russians have been organizing fistfights for centuries. Known simply as Russian fist fighting, the sport has existed at least since the thirteenth century and fights were traditionally held for large congregations—often on ice—during holiday times;

children fought first, followed by teenagers and progressively older contestants. It's unclear if the elderly participated in the title bouts.

While Russian fist fighting included standard one-on-one bouts, it also had a variation known as wall-on-wall fighting, which was fought between teams and could include hundreds of fighters. Each side was governed by a resident badass who was not only their best fighter but also their commander and primary tactician. Teams would fight using "walls" of people, while leaders would hold back until the perfect moment, when they'd rush forward and fire a flurry of heavy punches. Wall-on-wall fighting was like tug-of-war, except the objective was to beat the crap out of your opponent until you forced them out of the designated fighting area.

Prizefighting: Bare-Knuckle Badassery

Modern boxing's predecessor emerged in England in the early sixteenth century in a gruesome, gloveless form known as bare-knuckle boxing, prizefighting, or fisticuffs. As the name might suggest, boxers wore no gloves, which significantly changed the tactics required of a good fighter. A misplaced punch that struck skull instead of face could result in a shattered fist. Parries were more difficult as well, for the same reason. Overall, bare-knuckle boxers were *more* careful and less likely to unleash wild power punches.

Although the unspoken guidelines of gentlemanly fighting etiquette (no pulling hair, scratching, biting, hitting below the belt, etc.) were generally observed, early bare-knuckle boxing had no written rules whatsoever. Rounds had no time limit and only ended when a fighter fell, got knocked down, or simply gave up. More importantly, bouts had no round limit, and fights would often last for hours on end. The longest official fight on record lasted six hours and fifteen minutes.

The first official bare-knuckle champion was James Figg, who reigned as champion from 1719 to around 1730, when he voluntarily stepped down. Figg was a multitalented fighter who could open up a bottle of 100-proof whoop-ass with everything from fists to backswords (according to some sources, boxing emerged as practice for fencers). He opened an amphitheater and apparently amassed an unbelievable record of 269 and 1 (although he did tally several of those wins by beating his employees). He is considered the father of modern boxing.

As with most things savage and badass, bare-knuckle boxing was not without its dangers. In one of bare-knuckle's earlier manifestations, bands of giant bruisers would roam England trying to gather crowds and cajole the largest locals into fighting them. Because pugilism had no rules, rings, or time limits, death was not an unlikely outcome. Fighters could die from brain injury, exhaustion, or even by hitting their head on stones or other nearby debris.

THE REBIRTH OF BARE-KNUCKLE

In 2011, bare-knuckle boxing enjoyed its first sanctioned bout since 1889. Bobby Gunn was crowned bare-knuckle champion of the world after his third round knockout over Richard Stewart.

No Sissy Footing, Boys

The Irish, apparently only interested in the blood and guts of pugilism, created a variation of bare-knuckle boxing known as the Irish Stand Down in which fighters were forbade from maneuvering around the ring. In other words, all they could do was stand still and punch the crap out of each other. It was popular in Irish ghettos throughout the UK and US.

In the USSR, in the early twentieth century, there was a sport known as face slapping, which unsurprisingly consisted of men slapping each other across the face. In 1931, two professional face slappers set a record by slapping one another silly for thirty straight hours. The audience, growing weary and bored, demanded the bloodied slappers finally stop.

Modern Boxing

A document called the Queensberry Rules for the Sport of Boxing, written by a Welshman named John Graham Chambers in 1867, revolutionized the sport by instilling more structure through a set of officially mandated rules and regulations. Now known as the Marquess of Queensberry Rules, the document was the first in boxing to require gloves. It also standardized the parameters to include a 24-foot ring, a three-minute round length, and a fifteen-round limit (reduced to twelve in the 1980s), and introduced the concept of points and developed a clear definition of the term "knockout."

KO vs. TKO

A **knockout (KO)** is called when a fighter, grounded down by a punch (not a trip or a fall), cannot rise to his feet for a count of ten seconds.

A **technical knockout (TKO)** is subjectively called by a referee who determines a fighter to be too injured, delirious, or wimpy to continue the fight.

Death in Boxing

Despite important innovations such as rules and referees and gloves, boxing is still deadly, surprising exactly nobody. When the strongest people in the world are punching each other in the head as hard as they can, accidents will happen. A strong punch or a hard fall can result in brain damage or neck injury, and even when a boxer is able to leave the ring, a bad injury can linger and result in delayed death. To get technical about it, the scientific term for the most common fatal brain injury is acute subdural hematoma.

THE IRONY OF BOXING GLOVES

Boxing gloves were originally designed to protect the puncher's hands from breaking. Unfortunately, their remarkable efficacy in protecting the hands allowed boxers to fire punches with more power and reckless abandon, ironically making boxing *more* dangerous by increasing the chance of a fatal blow.

Even if you manage to make it through every fight without a death-inducing injury, you may still be screwed. In about twelve to sixteen years, boxing's ghosts could rear their ugly heads in the form of dementia pugilistic, a variation of dementia caused by repeated concussions that afflicts about 15 to 20 percent of professional boxers.

According to a study on deaths of boxers, perhaps as many as 1,355 boxers have died due to injuries since 1890. Of these, head and neck injuries accounted for about 80 percent, though a surprisingly large percentage of these injuries came from falls or what the study labels as "misadventure," which means nobody knows where the hell the brain injury came from. Other deaths occurred from heart failure, infected injuries, a ruptured spleen, and once, according to the study, too much ice water.

Boxing is so dangerous that several health organizations, including the American Medical Association and the medical associations of Britain, Canada, and Australia, have called for a worldwide boxing ban.

A Round Too Many

In 1982, Duk Koo Kim, a South Korean boxer, died four days after suffering a coma-inducing subdural hematoma in a boxing match against fellow lightweight Ray Mancini. Kim's mom, who flew out to see her son while in a coma, took her own life later that year. The referee of the fight also took his own life less than a year after the tragic fight.

According to reports, Kim suffered his hematoma in the fourteenth round from a single punch. Until that point, the match had been incredibly even and well fought.

Kim's death spurred several changes aimed at helping protect the boxer's safety, including reducing matches from fifteen rounds to twelve. Pre-fight medical checks were also vamped up to include brain and lung tests, among other precautionary examinations.

THE ANATOMY OF A JAB

The jab, the most common punch in boxing, is the most important tool in your boxing tool shed. While it's kind of wimpy compared to other blows, it's safe, simple, and effective. You can use it defensively, either to keep an opponent at a distance or parry his punches, or in an offensive combo by following it with a more powerful punch such as a hook or a cross.

Stand

To fire a jab, begin by getting in your natural boxing stance. Your legs should be about shoulder width apart, with one leading foot, and your elbows should be tucked in. Remember! Lead with your off foot (i.e., your left, if you're right-handed).

Extend

Extend your leading arm towards your target, be it a nose, chin, gut, or, if you just found out your girlfriend's been cheating on you, a car window. Chances are you're not going to knock your opponent out with a jab, so concentrate more on speed, balance, and recovery than pure power. Keep your weight centered so that you can quickly fire another punch or defend against your opponent's counterattack.

Twist

As you're extending, your arm should be twisting inward, towards your body, so that when you strike your palm is facing downward. Simultaneously, try to raise your punching shoulder a bit up and in. This will not only provide punching power, but it will have the added bonus of protecting your chin.

Clench

Counterintuitive but true for almost every punch, keep your fist relaxed until just before contact.

THE ANATOMY
OF A LEFT HOOK

The hook can be a powerful weapon, but is also relatively hard to perfect. And while you can fire a hook with either fist, the basic hook is thrown using the leading hand (i.e., your wimpy, weaker hand). A well-delivered hook can result in a knockout. For the purposes of these instructions, we're assuming you're not a southpaw.

The Dipsy-Doo

The hook is sort of like a dance move. It requires dipping, swiveling, and bouncing. From your normal boxing stance, begin with an elegant yet manly dipsy-doo: bend your knees slightly and drop your fist and head a bit to the left.

The Swivel-Bounce-Punch

Bounce back towards the right, swiveling your body as you do so. To increase the power of the punch, lift onto your left toes while digging your right heel into the ground. Remember, this is a manly endeavor: lift onto the ball of your foot, not your tippy toes like some womanly ballerina.

The Punch

Don't forget to punch! If it wasn't already obvious, you should also be firing your punch while swiveling your body. Remember, as always, to keep your fist loose and relaxed until contact. Aim for the jaw or temple—a proper left hook can easily result in a knockout.

The Finish

If you've executed the punch properly, you will only be able to see your stunned opponent out of the corner of your left eye; the rest of your body should be facing to the right.

THE ANATOMY
OF AN UPPERCUT

The uppercut, if properly executed, can be among the most devastating blows in boxing or bar fights. A powerful uppercut to an opponent's chin (known to boxers as "the sweet spot") can rattle his soft brain against its rock-hard chamber, making it one of the more effective knockout punches along with the hook and the cross. However, the uppercut is also risky as it takes time to unleash and the mechanics will leave you momentarily exposed to a counterattack.

Get Close

The best uppercuts are those that take your opponent by surprise. Crowd your opponent's body and distract him, perhaps with a flurry of jabs and body blows, or by having your hot girlfriend wink at him from the first row.

Crouch Down

The power of the uppercut comes more from your legs, hips, and torso than from your arms. Bend your knees and get ready to explode into the attack.

Stay Grounded

Contrary to instinct, the most powerful uppercuts are those delivered from a grounded position. Keep your hips low and resist the temptation to jump into the punch.

Twist and Shout

The uncoiling, or torquing of your hips, is the most important part of an effective uppercut. For right-handed uppercuts, lift with your right calf while planting your left heel into the ground. This will naturally cause your hips and shoulders to uncoil, sending a springy force up through your body, through your arm, into your fist, and out through your opponent's cranium. Many boxers find it helpful to release a shout or a grunt to increase passion and power.

Fire the Punch

The trick to a good uppercut punch is to let your arm follow the natural uncoiling of your hips and shoulders. Keep your entire arm and fist relaxed until *just* before impact, tightening at the last possible moment. Remember to aim for the chin. The nose and mouth are decent second choices. A punch to the solar plexus or gut will do in a pinch.

Don't Stop to Admire Your Work

Because of the twisting and torquing required, the uppercut is a *huge* risk. If you landed it properly, chances are your opponent's lying in puddle of his own drool and blood. But if you somehow missed your target or are a noodly-armed weakling, you've left yourself dangerously exposed to a vicious counter-attack. To ensure you have enough time to recover, don't let your fist soar into the rafters. Snap your arm back towards your own chin as soon as possible after impact.

MASTER OF THE UPPERCUT

Michael Gerard Tyson was born in Brooklyn, New York, during the summer of 1966. Three days before his twenty-second birthday, he became the undisputed heavyweight champion of the world. Despite a career that was marred by in- and out-of-the-ring antics, Mike Tyson truly earned his nickname, The Baddest Man on the Planet. Out of fifty-eight career fights, Tyson won fifty times, forty-four of them by obliterating knockout. His secret was a combo body-shot right-hook and right uppercut that turned the lights out on numerous opponents and earned him the title of "hardest hitter in heavyweight history."

FIVE BOXERS YOU
SHOULD HAVE HEARD OF

The Galveston Giant

Jack "The Galveston Giant" Johnson was the world's first African American heavyweight champion of the world. In addition to amassing an incredible eighty wins and forty-five knockouts in 114 official career fights, plus about forty or fifty unofficial wins, he was also one of the world's first celebrity athletes and was probably the most famous African American of the early twentieth century.

Johnson was considered a crafty and patient boxer and was famous for teasing and punishing his opponents. He began matches slowly and, in a brazen show of vanity, often chatted up friends and audience members *during* the fights. As the bouts wore on, he actually bothered giving a crap and fought progressively harder with each subsequent round. At the time, white audience members wanted a show, especially from black fighters, and Johnson was more than willing to give them one. He ensured that fights were sufficient in length by carefully eschewing knockout blows until the later rounds. He also held up weakened opponents when the may have otherwise collapsed so he could deliver flurries of painful punches.

Johnson became the world colored heavyweight champion in 1903 when he beat Denver Ed Martin. He held the title for

2,151 days and only relinquished it because he wanted to beat up whites as well as blacks.

During the peak of Johnson's career, African Americans were barred from fighting in the world heavyweight championship bout. But Johnson refused to let racial barriers hold him back: He followed Tommy Burns, the champion at the time, around the globe, purchasing ringside tickets to each of the man's bouts. From this strategic perch, Johnson would hurl taunts and insults at the frazzled champ and, in 1908, Burns succumbed and agreed to fight. On December 26, 1908, Johnson fought Burns in the first-ever biracial world heavyweight title bout. Johnson won the bout after fourteen rounds by referee's decision.

Johnson's title absolutely enraged the white masses, who began rioting across the United States. African Americans rejoiced, viewing the victory as social progress. Time and time again, a new "Great White Hope" emerged from the shadows only to be defeated by Johnson. The animosity towards Johnson ran so deep that James J. Jeffries, a former heavyweight champ who'd retired six years earlier, came out of retirement for what was labeled The Fight of the Century. Though the fight lasted fifteen rounds, it was an easy victory for Johnson, who felled Jeffries twice, forcing him to throw in the proverbial towel.

Johnson lived a colorful out-of-the-ring life, dabbling in amateur automobile racing, and he often bought himself stylish hand-tailored clothing. Johnson also broke the racial barrier in his personal life; in addition to marrying three white women, he showed as much stamina out of the ring as in it, as evidenced by the parade of women that sometimes came in and out of his hotel rooms.

The Real McCoy

"The Kid McCoy," also known less glamorously as Norman Selby, is considered by most the greatest light heavyweight boxer in the history of history. He used an infamous, cat-like "corkscrew" punch (and rough tape around his fists) to slice open his opponent's faces, and used a keen, "scientific" style to accrue a career record of eighty-one wins—fifty-five by knockout—in ninety-six matches.

McCoy was an undersized scrawnster—he probably weighed no more than 160 pounds after a typhoon—but fearlessly fought men twice his weight. He was crowned middleweight champion of the world, but apparently found no joy in the wimpy title, for he never defended it. Instead, the noodly-armed boxer tried his luck against the best heavyweights of the time. Though he never captured the world heavyweight crown, he beat several very good, very large boxers.

But McCoy owes his legacy equally to his wily antics, both in and out of the ring. His boxing arsenal was filled with devious trickery, and he's credited for inventing the "oh-snap-dude-your-shoe's-untied-oh-wait-lookout-I-just-punched-the-crap-out-of-you" trick, which is a mainstay in modern schoolyard tomfoolery. He also beat the reigning welterweight champion by coating his face in flour to give himself a sickly, pallid appearance, thus luring his opponent into a false sense of security. A more cruel version of trickery, perhaps known as the "watch-out-for-those-nails" ruse, was quite literal: Before a bout against a barefoot brawler, McCoy would toss a handful of nails into the ring, and as his opponent hobbled around to avoid possible impalement or tetanus, McCoy would besiege the sap with his signature corkscrew punch.

Outside of the ring, McCoy was known to stir up the occasional ounce of trouble. He was once was ridiculed in a bar because he was so slight that the patrons refused to believe he was truly McCoy. Challenged to a fight by a drunken scoundrel, McCoy easily silenced the rabble-rouser with a swift knockout punch. The snake, upon waking, reportedly muttered, "Oh my god, that was the Real McCoy."

McCoy's acting talents were so good that he took them to Hollywood, appeared in some movies, and befriended some funny guy named Charlie Chaplin. But by the 1920s he was a drunken, horny, impoverished mess.

Always the ladies man (he had ten wives over the course of his life), McCoy wooed a married woman named Teresa Mors. But during her divorce, chaos ensued and tragedy struck when Mors was fatally shot in McCoy's apartment. The subsequent legal proceeding was the OJ Simpson murder case of the 1920s, and the "if the glove don't fit" moment occurred when McCoy and his attorney enacted Mors' last moments by wresting on the courtroom floor. In a split jury decision, he was found guilty of manslaughter.

Battling Siki

Born Baye Fall in Senegal in 1897, Battling Siki was an incredible boxer who briefly reigned as the light heavyweight champion of the world and, for one incredible stretch between 1919 and 1922, amassed forty-three wins in forty-six bouts. But throughout Siki's life, racism and hatred overshadowed his in-the-ring success. Critics and media painted him in wild, savage colors, and racist epithets like "gorilla," "chimpanzee," and "child of the jungle" clearly upset Siki. Siki's career was derailed by partying and wild antics and he eventually met tragedy on the streets of New York City.

Siki was only eight when a French dancer saw him sitting by a dock, staring longingly at the boats and ocean. She offered to take him to France and he agreed, though sadly he didn't risk saying goodbye to his family for fear that his patron would change her mind. Under her tutelage, he moved to France, and by the time he was a teenager he was already boxing professionally, though the beginning of his career was unremarkable. During WWI he joined the French forces and for bravery he was awarded the Medal of Honor.

He returned from war a man and quickly rose to the top of the French boxing scene with the abovementioned winning streak. The streak culminated in 1922 in an epic bout against Georges Carpentier, the reigning light heavyweight champion of the world. The classic match (which was incidentally attended by none other than Ernest Hemingway himself) was apparently rigged, but after Carpentier attacked Siki with an unclassy amount of violence, Siki returned in a rage, and in the sixth round landed a ferocious right windmill that knocked Carpentier out cold. However, the ref, perhaps under the influence of bribery as well, claimed Siki had tripped Carpentier and disqualified the Senegalese boxer. Luckily, the three ringside judges overturned the call and Siki was crowned light heavyweight champion of the world.

The success and accompanying media attention, however, proved too much for Siki, whose reign and boxing success was to be short-lived. He embarked upon an epic and very expensive journey of partying, carousing, and world-class tomfoolery. He devoured champagne and absinthe like they were Evian and was regularly seen gallivanting up and down the streets of Paris in a tuxedo and top hat, walking his lion cubs. Yup. Lion cubs. And if those shenanigans aren't convincingly wild enough, he also had two Great Danes, which he trained to perform tricks whenever he fired his revolvers into the Parisian sky.

Siki's partying took its toll and his life quickly spiraled out of control. On St. Paddy's Day of 1922, just a few months after earning the title, he relinquished it to an Irishman named Mike McTigue. Soon thereafter he moved to Manhattan where, despite the existence of Prohibition, he trained while plastered. There are accounts of him brawling his way to freedom after refusing to pay the tab at speakeasies, and others of him sneaking out of taxicabs after long, meandering rides. Siki was teetering on the dangerous edge of revelry, and it caught up to him one night in 1925 when he was found dead with two bullets in his back.

The Black Terror

William "The Black Terror" Richmond, born a slave in Staten Island, gained his freedom during the Revolutionary War when Britain gained control of New York. Lord Percy, the Duke of Northumberland, got to know the fourteen-year-old Richmond, who was charming, quick-witted, and had an amusing knack for mimicry. The Duke asked the young Richmond to be his servant and in 1777 the two of them went to England.

Richmond lived a relatively peaceful and sheltered life in the Duke's household and began working as a carpenter's apprentice. Richmond's fists turned out to be as quick as his wit, though he may have never discovered his talent had racism not run rampant on the streets of London in the late eighteenth century. One day a gutterpunk hurled a racist comment in Richmond's direction, and Richmond responding by hurling a flurry of lightning-fast punches that absolutely demolished the bigot—by some accounts leaving him totally blind.

There were more racists, more derisive comments, and more patented Richmond-style beatdowns. Richmond began to realize that his hands could make more money throwing punches than shaping wood, and so in 1804 the undersized Richmond entered London's pugilistic underground. Despite losing his first bout, he captured the English-speaking world's attention as The Black Terror. At about 140 pounds, Richmond was a welterweight by today's weight classes, but he often fought—and beat—boxers who were more than 60 pounds heavier than him. Oh yeah, and Richmond never received a single boxing lesson.

Richmond's strength was his defense; he was quick and in early rounds would consistently parry or dodge every punch by ducking, slipping, sliding, and countering. In his most famous fight, one for the crown of English bare-knuckle boxing, Richmond went *sixty rounds* against the future world champion Tom Cribb, who was unable to land a single punch in the early rounds. Richmond was technically superior, but after several rounds Cribb's massive size and dominant strength wore Richmond down and he eventually lost.

Unlike most stories in this pervasively tragic list, Richmond's ends happily; at age fifty-two he retired from boxing and used his money to buy a club and start a boxing academy.

Your Body Is Your Temple of Doom

DISEASES, DISORDERS, AND
DEFORMITIES THAT'LL MAKE YOU
FEEL BETTER ABOUT YOUR LIFE

YOU ARE A FILTHY, FILTHY HUMAN BEING

Let's talk about you. By the looks of it, you are a disgusting creature.

During your lifetime, you will produce enough mucus to fill a backyard swimming pool. And you'll produce enough saliva to fill two.

Your tongue is a regular melting pot of life; it can be home to as many as 1,000 unique types of bacteria. That white film on the top of your tongue? That's New York City. Only your tongue's metropolis is made up of tens of millions of living bacteria and dead skin cells. Pride yourself on your oral hygiene? Good for you; your mouth is still dirtier than your toilet seat. Now, don't forget to floss.

Let's talk a little more about oral hygiene. In your mouth, bacteria grow like microscopic weeds. Spend a couple of days not brushing and the 100,000 individual bacteria on each tooth can bloom to ten million. And while most of these bacteria are harmless, plenty of them aren't. Some bacteria found in the mouth are responsible for a ridiculous number of issues that, by all logic, shouldn't be affected by stuff crawling around in your kisser, like heart disease, osteoporosis, and even dementia. All thanks to the warm bacteria that make your mouth smell like a dirty diaper in the morning.

Your mouth is dirty, but what about the rest of your body? Glad you asked. You've basically got an entire universe of life in your stomach and intestines, where fifty million bacteria per square inch call home. In fact, the leading danger of the unpleasant intestinal disorder ulcerative colitis is that the plethora of bacteria in your colon might accidentally get released through bleeding ulcers into your normally sterile internal organs.

But don't think that all your bacteria is safely locked up inside your body. Each square inch of your skin also contains over thirty-two million bacteria. It's this bacteria that causes your body to stink when you sweat. And you sweat a lot…up to a pint a day. So, maybe you're using the wrong soap?

Let's back up to thirty-two million bacteria per square inch of skin. You've got a lot of inches of skin on your body. After all, the skin is the largest human organ. And it creates some other headaches. For one, do you think that's dust you're sweeping up every couple of weeks in your apartment? It's not. It's you. Every day you shed 600,000 skin cells. So a lot of that dust covering your floor is actually your former body.

Now that you're sufficiently comfortable with your body, let's spend a quick minute talking about what comes out of it. I'm talking mounting the ivory throne. Heading to the gentleman's office. Clearing some excess inventory. Poop.

Let's start with the fact that you fart an average of fourteen times every day, with some days being more audible than others. Farts are actually harmful to the environment; cows collectively release up to 100 million tons of methane per year through excessive farting, making them the one of the worst emitters of greenhouse gases.

What's more, you are your own little food factory. Of all the food and drink you take into your body, you process only a small percentage into energy (depending on how much fiber you're eating). The rest of it, on average about 400 pounds per year, gets flushed out of your body and into the toilet.

Of course, as it turns out, you're not necessarily the only one getting fed...

WORMS. WOOOOORMS. WOOOOOORRRRMMMS.

The Tapeworm: The *Other* Other White Meat

You need to respect tapeworms. They've been around for at least 250 million years and they're not going anywhere. Also, they're huge and hermaphroditic and should rightfully creep you out.

The tapeworm's life cycle is like an odyssey of horrors. It goes something like this: the adult tapeworms drop their ladyboy eggs into the intestine of their host (normally a nice bulky mammalian farm animal) who deposits the eggs through their poop into the same field where all their friends are munching on grass. The baby tapeworms then enter the new host, latching onto whatever fleshy thing they can—muscles, fat, etc. And when that farm animal eventually ends up on your plate

> The longest tapeworm in the world makes its home in the intestines of sperm whales. The whale tapeworm, *Polygonoporus giganticus,* can grow up to 100 feet long.

as a 12-ounce, partially cooked steak, you enjoy every last bite, tapeworms included.

A couple of months later, the tapeworm has latched onto the side of your intestine, sucking vital nutrients from your diet and growing stronger and larger, hoping to one day have some children of its own. When it finally dislodges from your intestinal wall, the tapeworm ends up cruising down your intestinal tract with the rest of your unwanted materials. If you're lucky, you flush it down without noticing. If you're not lucky, you end up giving birth to a three-foot long tapeworm in the middle of what was supposed to be a romantic bath. But, you know, water births are supposed to be really, like, spiritual.

The Pinworm: Check Your Underpants

The pinworm, like its larger, hungrier tapeworm cousin, enjoys a particularly adventurous odyssey through your intestinal tract. The start of the pinworm's story begins when you unwittingly consume it as a wee little egg along with a couple dozen of his sisters and brothers, normally as part of some sort of undercooked meat dish. The eggs are tiny and colorless, so unless you're scanning your meal with a telescope, chances are you're going to be none the wiser.

After your accidental dinner of worm babies, you get to play the role of nurturing incubator while a colony of pinworms blossoms in your small intestine. Here, they hang out, play pinworm games, and grow stronger and larger, eventually feeling bold enough to venture down your gastrointestinal tract.

When they reach your ileum, the last stop in your intestines before the colon, the traveling pinworm colony pauses for a raucous sex party, impregnating all the womenfolk and exhausting all the male pinworms to the point of death.

Finally, in the middle of the night, the pregnant females wriggle their way through the rectum and out your anus, where they drop off their eggs and die. But not before all their wriggling around itches the crap out of you, forcing you to unconsciously scratch your behind, spreading the eggs from your butt to your hand and, eventually, from your hand to your mouth—thus starting the beautiful circle of life all over again.

The Guinea Worm: Let's Hang Out

Of all the parasitic worms in the world, the guinea worm has to be the most panic-inducing. The water- and flea-borne worm is not particularly harmful—the victim's symptoms are normally limited to nausea and mild fever—but when the guinea worm is fully grown—and we're talking three-feet-long fully grown—it decides it wants out of your body and starts painfully pushing its way to one of your feet or arms. When it gets there, the guinea worm starts knocking on your skin, eventually creating an itchy, burning blister that it knows you just can't help but pick at.

When you finally open the blister, the worm sticks its head out, waiting for you to plunge your infected arm into some soothing water, where it will take the opportunity to reproduce. Now you've got the head of three-foot long worm sticking out of your arm. What to do? This is where the situation gets thoroughly suicide-inducing. You can't just pull a guinea worm out of your body; its head will break off, the worm will die, and then its carcass will begin to rot inside your arm. Instead, you have to wrap the head of the worm around a stick and slooowly roll the worm out over a span of up to three months.

GOD-AWFUL PARASITES

Chagas Disease: The Kiss of Death

In the middle of the night, the beetle-like triatomine bug emerges from a crack in the wall of your Cancún hotel room, drops down onto your body, and begins sucking your blood. It's preferred feeding location? Your face. The tendency to face-suck its victims has earned the triatomine the romantic nickname of the kissing bug. But really, it's less like a kiss and more like a Hot Karl, because once its done making out with your cheek it inexplicably takes a crap on your face.

After it's eaten and defecated, the bug moves on, but its poop doesn't. Through all your tossing and turning, the fecal matter eventually finds its way into either the bloody wound or your eye. Unfortunately for you, inside that poop is a really messed-up parasite called *Trypanosoma cruzi* that enters your bloodstream and sets up camp all over the place. Then, nothing happens. For thirty years. You show no weird symptoms (beyond maybe some mild fatigue, body aches, and nausea) and live your life normally until one day, you simply drop dead when your parasite-enlarged heart explodes.

The scariest thing about this disease? A lot of people have it. Chagas disease, as it is called, is endemic to Central and South America and the Center for Disease Control estimates that between eight and eleven million people are living with the disease right now. They just don't know it yet.

Candiru: Worst Frickin' Catfish in the World

Catfish are not the most majestic creatures on planet Earth. They're slimy. They bite. They're freakish bottom-feeders. But none are as savage as the *Vandellia cirrhosa*, the dreaded candiru. This miniscule, parasitic, bloodsucking catfish has a propensity for hiding…in the urethra of human men. You read that right. Do a little skinny-dipping in the Amazon River and you may end up with a miniature catfish in your pee hole. But wait, wait, it gets worse. This devilish little catfish has spiny barbs on its gills that allow the fish to anchor itself in place. And you thought your gonorrhea was bad.

OLD-TIMEY DISEASES THAT STILL WANT TO KILL YOU

Bubonic Plague

It starts with swelling in the worst place imaginable: your groin. Next, painful blisters pop up on your neck and under your armpits. The chills set in and your temperature runs to 103 degrees Fahrenheit. You vomit uncontrollably. And then, when you couldn't imagine the experience getting worse, it does. Gangrene takes over your hands, arms, and feet and your skin begins to painfully rot off while you're still alive. If you're lucky, four days after you noticed your swollen groin, you slip into a coma and die. If you survive, your good looks will have literally fallen off your face.

That was what it was like to contract the flea-borne bubonic plague. And in the Late Middle Ages, the so-called black death swept across the globe with devastating force, wiping out between seventy-five million and 200 million people, nearly a quarter of the world's population and half of Europe.

But the bubonic plague never disappeared; people still contract the plague every year. Most of the time it happens in the far reaches of the world like India or Peru, but in 2012, cases were reported as close by as Colorado and Oregon. Fortunately, the bubonic plague isn't as deadly when treated quickly, killing only a small percentage of those infected.

The Spanish Influenza

While every school child learns about the bubonic plague, the 1918 flu pandemic is one of history's best-kept secrets. Perhaps it's too scary to teach children that something as simple as the flu, in the twentieth century no less, killed as many as 100 million people worldwide in just two years. Whatever the reason, the "forgotten pandemic" was particularly catastrophic since it easily dispatched young, able-bodied men and women in their teens and twenties, a demographic that usually doesn't succumb to the flu.

Symptoms of the flu were god-awful. In addition to the normal fever and body aches associated with the flu, Spanish influenza caused extreme internal hemorrhaging. Blood would pour out of every single one of the victim's orifices—ears, nose, mouth, anus, and even eyes. While the infected often died from secondary infections such as pneumonia, hemorrhaging in vital organs like the lungs could also kill quickly. About one in three people living on earth became infected with the Spanish flu, and between 10 and 20 percent of them died.

How does this affect you in the twenty-first century? Well, the Spanish flu is believed to have been a mutated strain of H1N1—the same form of influenza, better known as swine flu, that killed an estimated 17,000 people worldwide in 2009.

Scurvy

Scurvy isn't just for pirates. The devastating effects of vitamin C deficiency can hit anyone at any time. Aside from unsightly lesions that appear on your arms and legs, the most visible sign of scurvy is that your gums dissolve into a thin, spongy mess and your teeth start to feel looser and looser until they begin falling out. As scurvy progresses, your skin turns a sickly, jaundiced yellow and becomes pocked with oozing wounds that bleed uncontrollably. At the very end, your body becomes wracked with fever and, if left untreated, you die. All because you didn't drink your orange juice.

The problem with vitamin C is that foods chock-full of it—oranges, broccoli, strawberries, etc.—go bad fairly quickly, making them exceptionally difficult to transport, say, on a ship from the Caribbean to the South Pacific. This dilemma left seafarers back in the day with nothing to eat but cured meats, basic grains, and hardtack. Entire crews would often come down with scurvy on long journeys out at sea, only to have to fight to replenish their bodies the moment they hit dry land.

One of the primary groups in danger of developing scurvy today: college students. Close to broke and on their own for the first time in their lives, these poor souls can fall into pathetic vitamin-free eating patterns, just one step away from becoming potheads with dentures.

THE MANual

Sleepy Sickness

Encephalitis lethargica, aka sleepy sickness (aka, "Aahh, zombies!!"), raged around the globe right after everyone had just gotten over the Spanish flu. The sweetly named disease came on gently, typically with a run-of-the-mill sore throat, before paralyzing the afflicted person in a completely motionless state; physically frozen, eyes peeled open, and unable to speak. But completely conscious. After recovering (if they did), the patient would display horrific personality defects ranging from psychosis and intense sexual aggression to uncontrollable bouts of shouting.

Although new cases of the disease abruptly stopped appearing in 1928, doctors never figured out what caused sleepy sickness. Or if it would ever come back.

Cholera

For most of us, cholera is something that people died of on the Oregon Trail right after they lost three oxen trying to ford a river. But the disease is actually alive and well. It still affects an average of four million people each year, killing about 100,000 victims annually. The disease, which is caused by the lovely bacterium *Vibrio cholerae*, is transmitted the same way as most other forms of gastroenteritis—via food or water contaminated with the feces of someone who has cholera. Which is scary considering how quickly and viciously cholera epidemics spread. Apparently, it's very easy to eat fecal matter.

Unlike your traditional stomach flu, cholera is unbelievably powerful. As the bacteria enters your digestive system, it triggers your intestines to drain all of the liquid in your body through your colon, causing gallons of fishy-smelling "rice water" to shoot from your butt. During particularly severe epidemics, victims are lined up in hospital beds covered in plastic with a simple hole and bucket to catch the prolific amount of wastewater. Although cholera is now rarely deadly if treated quickly with fluid and antibiotics, some virulent strains can kill within two hours of the first appearance of symptoms.

NOT YOUR ORDINARY AIRSICK BAG

Some forms of cholera come on so quickly that commercial aircrafts making long-haul flights are still required to carry IV bags in case someone begins showing symptoms mid-flight. Without the emergency fluids, the stricken person could die from dehydration before the plane is able to land.

Syphilis

It did what all the G-men in the country couldn't: took out the notorious gangster Al Capone. No, it's no free-shooting, Thompson-toting, rogue agent; it's the slow and steady sexually transmitted disease syphilis. First noticed at the end of the fifteenth century, syphilis destroys the body in three distinct stages.

First, within a couple days to a few months after one particularly wild night, a few painful lesions appear at the point of contact with the infected host. In case you didn't guess, this is normally somewhere around your private parts. Next, a particularly nasty (but painless) rash spreads over your body. Unfortunately, those are just the overtures. Because somewhere between three and fifteen years after your initial infection, it finally spreads to your central nervous system and your brain, causing violent seizures, tremors, depression, and eventually blindness and dementia.

But don't be fooled into thinking syphilis is a relic of some bygone era. In 2011 alone, the Center for Disease Control estimates there were over 46,000 new cases of syphilis in the United States, nearly the same as the number of new cases of HIV.

Awww, Poor Baby Has the Stomach Flu?

Nope. There's no such thing as the "stomach influenza." The persistent vomiting and diarrhea you are experiencing in front of your girlfriend is caused by a variety of infectious viruses and bacteria conveniently lumped together under the term *gastroenteritis*. In layman's speak, it simply means that you consumed food or water contaminated with infected fecal matter. You ate poop, dude.

Scabies

Latin may be a dead language, but its word for "to scratch" lives on in the miniature, eight-legged mite known to scientists as *Sarcoptes scabiei* and to you as scabies. The parasitic mites spread by hot and heavy skin-to-skin contact, but you won't notice for another month or two. First, the female will find a nice location on your skin for a permanent baby-dropping burrow. After digging a warm little hole, she'll begin popping out two or three eggs a day for the rest of her life. These eggs will grow up to be nasty little buggers who love nothing more than devouring human flesh.

While the females spend most of their time relaxing in their cavernous apartments in your skin, the males are out wandering around your body, digging holes and hoping to meet a nice fertile female to settle down with and have more flesh-devouring offspring.

You can actually see the mites' homes: The burrows they've drilled through your skin appear as little pimples. But what's worse is that your body is actually allergic to the mites themselves and, as your immune system tries to attack the scabies, it causes you to itch uncontrollably.

In people with compromised immune systems, the infection can be ten times worse. Mite populations explode and lead to infestations called crusted scabies—covering the entire body in a layer of scabies-encrusted skin.

Smallpox

Here's a scary statistic: Smallpox killed between 300 million and half a billion people in the twentieth century *alone*. If you were to count the infectious disease as a natural disaster alongside earthquakes, tsunamis, and floods, smallpox would be the number-one deadliest natural disaster in history.

One of the most dreaded airborne diseases, the smallpox virus multiplies quickly, spreading through your mouth, throat, and lymph nodes and into your bloodstream about ten days after infection. Eventually it even infiltrates your bone marrow. And the symptoms are swift and brutal. At first you think you've come down with a common cold, but within two weeks your throat and mouth are covered with virus-filled lesions. Once the lesions burst, they fill your saliva with vast quantities of the virus, turning you into a biological weapon.

A couple days after your mouth starts spewing smallpox, it spreads to your face, arms, stomach, and then legs (this is where the *pox*, or "spots," part of the disease comes in) until pretty much every inch of your skin is covered in small, disgusting pimples. While the mortality rate for the impressively deadly disease has only ever been about 30 percent, it left entire populations reeling. And those who survived were often scarred for life by the festering rash.

Although the World Health Organization proudly proclaimed smallpox officially eradicated in 1971, both Russia and the United States kept living samples of the disease. It's just a bad movie script waiting to strike.

YOUR BODY HAS A
MIND OF ITS OWN

Exploding Head Syndrome: You Know What? Actually Not as Bad as It Sounds

Despite its utterly terrifying name, exploding head syndrome is entirely mental. It can start up at any point in your life, but usually occurs during times of extreme stress. Just as you're about to enter that nice deep sleep...*BANG!*...you're startled awake by what could only be someone playing the clash cymbals by your head. Only its actually just you hallucinating someone playing clash cymbals, possibly the most annoying hallucination to have right before you fall asleep. Immediately after the head explosion, your heart races, you sweat and curse, and you probably have a pretty tough time getting back to sleep. While the occurrence for most people is rare, some unfortunate dreamers have chronic exploding head syndrome, often leading to an intense phobia of going to sleep. The cure? Relax. Take a vacation.

Alopecia Areata: Hair Today, Gone Tomorrow

Most men curse genetics for their normal bout with male-pattern baldness. But those who suffer from the rare alopecia areata have the real frustration. That's because alopecia areata is totally random. Instead of a handsome horseshoe of hair loss, it happens in clumps, patches, or, in the case of alopecia areata universalis, it happens *everywhere* (eyebrows, eyelashes, chest hair, leg hair: all gone). While the hair can grow back eventually, its reemergence is as random as the hair loss itself.

Acromegaly: Growing and Growing and Growing

As you pass oh-so-gracefully through puberty, your pituitary gland works overtime, secreting the necessary human growth hormone (HGH) to turn you from a four-foot child to a six-foot pimple factory. And at the end of puberty, your pituitary gland shuts down production of HGH and congratulates itself on turning you into a man. But sometimes it starts back up again.

Acromegaly, a form of adult-onset gigantism is one terrifying prospect. It can happen to anyone. Normally caused by tumors on the pituitary gland, the disorder restarts HGH production in your body with a vengeance. And almost overnight you start growing again (and growing and growing). Your hands and face swell and before you know it you have an uncanny resemblance to Andre the Giant. That's what happened to Tanya Angus, a five-foot-eight college student who, at the age of twenty-one, began to transform during a single semester away at school. By the time she died from related heart failure after battling the disorder for over a decade, Tanya's uncontrollable gigantism had taken her from a slender frame to an enormous seven feet and 400 pounds.

Life's Hard for the Big Guy

John Middleton was an impoverished, nine-foot English giant who, as the story goes, lived in a house so small he had to sleep with his feet sticking out the window.

Lewandowsky-Lutz Dysplasia: Growing Roots

So rare that it's normally referred to by its Latin name, *Epidermodysplasia verruciformis*, this hereditary disease is one of the strangest in the world. The disease, which is caused by the common *human papillomavirus* (HPV), is characterized by the uncontrollable growth of massive warts all over the body. One Javanese man named Dede Koswara developed such an intense form of the disease that his skin and limbs began to resemble the bark and branches of a tree, earning him the nickname Tree Man. The wart growths were so massive that Dede lost use of his hands beneath multiple pounds oversized warts. When Dede finally had an operation to remove the growths, doctors cut off a full 13 pounds of wart-covered flesh. Unfortunately, within a couple of years the growths had returned.

Permanent Insomnia: Sleep When You're Dead

Almost everyone deals with short bouts of insomnia from time to time. Stress, anxiety, upset stomach, and hormonal shifts can all cause restless nights. But, for a very unlucky few, insomnia can become so persistent it becomes permanent.

That's the story of Thai Ngoc, a Vietnamese farmer who, in 1973, came down with a bad fever and reportedly lost the ability to sleep. Despite desperate attempts to get some shut-eye with home remedies, pills, and alcohol, nothing worked for the insomniac. When doctors observed Thai in 2006, a full three decades since the last time he successfully slept, he was miraculously in excellent health. Although he was a little grumpier than your average farmer and had reduced liver function, he showed remarkable energy for a man who hadn't slept in over 10,000 nights. In the ultimate test of a rested man, he could still carry a 100-pound sack of rice for over two miles.

REM Behavior Disorder: Go Live Your Dreams

At the other end of the spectrum from permanent insomniacs, you have the particularly troubling rapid eye movement behavior disorder. This adventurous sleep disorder causes people to act out their dreams as they're happening. For most sleepers, entering the REM cycle of sleep is pleasant, quiet, and full of wild, action-packed dreams. And for most people, the REM cycle comes with REM atonia, the off switch that paralyzes the body so it can't act out the Olympic ski jump happening in a dream. But people lacking that off switch do act out their dreams, turning what was a quiet night into a sleepy ambulance ride to the hospital.

SPOOKY FREAK
SHOW DISORDERS

Siamese Nightmare

Conjoined twins are identical twins who joined forces in the embryo, and they can be connected pretty much anywhere—at the pelvis, back, chest, face, or even skull. Most conjoined twins share at least some internal organs, including the heart, making separation a precarious—and often impossible—undertaking.

As you might imagine, conjoined twins have it pretty tough. Only about 25 percent of them survive past infancy, and those who do face a lifelong struggle. Besides the obvious obstacles ("Which way are you walking?" "Can you please make love more quietly?"), conjoined twins suffer much worse burdens that are often particular to the locale and nature of

THE ORIGINAL SIAMESE TWINS

Chang and Eng Bunker, the conjoined brothers born in Siam (now Thailand) in 1811 were the basis for the term "Siamese twins." Connected at their midsection, the brothers each had a full set of arms and legs. They married a pair of sisters who bore twenty-one of Chang and Eng's children between them. Logistics? We want to know too.

their attachment. Parasitic twins—twins whose relationship is asymmetrical—are perhaps the least fortunate, as one is usually smaller, weaker, and completely dependent on their more able twin.

The Elephant Man: Elephantiasis

Elephantiasis, or *lymphatic filariasis* as it's properly known, is spread by a cooperative combination of two unsavory characters: parasitic worms and the mosquitoes that carry them. The worm uses the mosquito as a mail service, getting its thread-like larvae deposited into your skin. From there, the roundworms wriggle through your body, working their way into your lymphatic vessels, where they can thrive for the better part of a decade.

Although the worm is unpleasant, it's not actually what causes your limbs to balloon to the size of an elephant's. The worm is teeming with heavy-duty bacteria that your body tries to attack, causing localized inflammation. As the inflammation builds and backs up, it causes swelling under the skin, creating grotesquely sized body parts—normally around the legs and feet.

For such a disturbingly deformative disease, elephantiasis is remarkably common; it afflicts about 120 million people, primarily in Africa and Southeast Asia.

HOLD ON, IT GETS WORSE

One particular form of elephantiasis, known as scrotal elephantiasis, targets the scrotum alone, leaving the victim to suffer with testicles swollen to the size of a watermelon.

Children of the Night: Xeroderma Pigmentosum

Of all the things you can be allergic to—peanuts, cats, your own semen (it happens)—the sun has got to be one of the worst. But that's what afflicts about one in every 250,000 people around the world. Known as xeroderma pigmentosum, this genetic disorder causes its victims to develop severe sunburns after just a few minutes exposed to sunlight. The disorder also causes the eyes to burn red after any exposure to ultraviolet light, often forcing the victims to live their lives entirely after the sun has gone down, hence the term "children of the night."

A SHORT GUIDE TO LITTLE PEOPLE

Dwarves: Dwarfism can be caused by over 200 conditions, including basic growth-hormone deficiency, which results in a proportionally smaller person, and achondroplasia, which causes disproportionately short limbs and an abnormally large head.

Primordial dwarves: Primordial dwarves can be even smaller than normal dwarves because they grow at a stunted rate during every single phase of development. At a mere one foot nine, the seventy-three-year-old Mr. Chandra Bahadur Dangi is the shortest adult ever measured.

Midgets: Don't call a little person a midget—it's actually offensive. It means something close to "sand fly" and was used mockingly by side-show promoters. For a long time it was used to describe proportional dwarves, but today it's essentially a slur.

Little people: People who are abnormally small-bodied prefer to be called little people. Little people are often defined as people under four foot ten.

Pygmies: Although the term "pygmy" is most closely associated with the small hunter-gatherer tribes of central Africa, it actually refers to ethnic groups all around the world, including in Indonesia, the Philippines, Bolivia, and Brazil. In fact, the term refers to ethnic groups where adult males' average height is less than four foot eleven.

Hobbits: Hobbits are fictional, moron. *Never* call a little person a hobbit.

THE REAL HOBBITS

However...about 18,000 years ago, on the island of Flores in Indonesia, a group of very little people flourished. These so-called hobbit people were about three and a half feet tall and shared the island with giant rats, huge lizards, and a species of tiny dwarf elephants called Stegodon.

Nature's Werewolf: Hypertrichosis

Sometimes our body's hair-producing hormones start working overtime, resulting in humans covered in thick coats of fur-like hair. Hypertrichosis can strike in utero, giving infants those classic, adorable full-body beards.

Also known as the werewolf syndrome, the condition has two basic forms; general hypertrichosis results in a monkey-like, full-body coat, while localized hypertrichosis is limited to hairiness in a specific region like, say, the elbow.

Lionel the Lion-faced Man is one of the most famous real-life werewolves. During his heyday in the early twentieth century, the sideshow performer had eight-inch hair dangling from his face and four inches of hair sprouting from pretty much everywhere else.

An Earie Record

Hair in weird places is an unfortunate drawback of virility. Men have more hair than women do on their chests, stomachs, backs, arms, feet, hands, noses, and ears because they naturally have higher levels of a male hormone called androgen.

Under the androgenic hair rubric of manliness, an Indian grocer named Radhakant Baijpai is the manliest of all men. Despite his wife's incessant pleading, Mr. Hadhakant refuses to chop off his gnarly, record-holding 5.19-inch ear hair.

The Sea

SASHIMI, BOATS,
UNCOMPROMISING WATERS

"The cure for anything is saltwater—sweat, tears, or the sea."
—*Isak Dinesen*

No, "Isak." From the beach, the sea may *seem* like a cure-all. But once you enter those waters—those deep, rolling waters—the sea is a lot more like a beautiful psychotic woman. She'll woo you, kiss you, and tussle your hair with salt before she starves you, drowns you, and feeds you to the fish. Survival in the depths of the sea is brutal and filthy and short-lived. And on the surface, it's even harder. There are 139 million square miles of open ocean on the planet, each one more unforgiving than the last. But the wide blue is like that beautiful psychotic woman. Who among us can help but pine for her?

PARTS OF A BOAT EVERY MAN SHOULD KNOW

masthead

mast

headstay

backstay

main sail

jib sail

jib sheet

boom

main sheet

waterline
bow pulpit

keel

hull

rudder

bow (front) - stern (back) - starboard (right) - port (left)

NINE BOATS THAT
CHANGED HISTORY

The Raft

Man and beast have used the raft, nature's seagoing vessel of choice, since life first crawled out of the sea. Flat, hull-less, and made of any organic material that floats, rafts became a primary way that life spread across the planet.

After the breakup of the Pangaea supercontinent, biological nonanthropogenic (not man-made) rafts of clumped vegetation enabled flightless animals to populate distant continents and islands.

Until the nineteenth century, man-made rafts were employed primarily as primitive barges, transporting logs downriver. Today they are most commonly used for white-water rafting, an outdoor adventure sport enjoyed by families and drunken teenagers around the world.

The Dugout and the Canoe

The earliest known engineered water vessels were basic boats made from the hollowed trunk of a single tree. Known as the dugout, logboat, or monoxylon, these simple boats ranged dramatically in size, from single-person vessels to massive army ships, and ancient specimens have been found on nearly every continent. The world's oldest, known as the Pesse canoe, dates all the way back to 8000 BC.

Early northern European models were relatively small and only suitable for tranquil waters. But the Slavs made enormous dugouts, which they sold to the Vikings, who employed the dugouts as the first warships. And halfway around the world, the early Pacific Islanders used giant logboats to begin their epic spread through the world's largest ocean.

While the hulls of the first dugouts rarely strayed from the natural shape of the tree from which they were formed, early boat builders soon discovered the advantages of boats with sharp, pointed edges and formed hulls, leading them to fashion sleek lightweight canoes. Soon wood was scrapped for lighter materials and the canoes evolved to include canvas exteriors built around strong wooden frames.

The canoe is perhaps most commonly associated with Native Americans, who built bark-skinned canoes that were light, durable, and excellent for voyages across rivers, whose shallow waters often necessitated a boat that could be portaged. Northwestern coastal Native American tribes adapted canoes for rivers, lakes, and oceans and for purposes ranging from travel and river fishing to seal and even whale hunting.

When Europeans discovered the Americas, they adapted the canoe for inland exploration. Canoes were utilized by early voyagers such as Alexander Mackenzie, who used a canoe to cross North America in its entirety, and Lewis and Clark, the first Americans to accomplish the same.

The Kayak

The first thing you should know is that "kayak" translates to "man's boat" or "hunter's boat." The second thing you should know is that the early Inuit and Eskimo tribes, who invented the kayak at least 4,000 years ago, were apparently awesome.

The world's first water vessel designed with a covered, water-tight deck, known as the skirt or spraydeck, the kayak was a hearty traveling boat. Even the material was impressive: the earliest Inuit kayaks were built with frames of whalebone and skirts made from stretched, stitched sealskin. These watertight skirts allowed the hunters to roll the kayak back upright when it capsized, a necessary innovation considering the Inuit never bothered to learn how to swim (the waters were simply too damn cold for doggie-paddling lessons). In addition, they were hunting huge sea life—seals, whales, and walruses—all of which could knock a kayak end over end.

The Galley

Named for the small sharks that swam the Mediterranean, the galley (from the Middle Greek *galea*) kick-started the future of boat design. Powered primarily by hordes of toiling rowers, the galley was the dugout canoe on steroids, allowing men and materials to travel longer distances and ushering in maritime trade. Virtually all Mediterranean powers quickly adopted the ships, with the Greeks, Romans, Carthaginians, Assyrians, Phoenicians, and Byzantines all using galleys for trade and war.

In its earliest version, the galley could accommodate two sets of fifteen to thirty oarsmen, but a race to develop larger, better galleys for purposes of raiding and warfare led to double-decker banks of rowers on either side. An additional outrigger hull was later added to apply a third bank of manpower.

The largest galleys could accommodate up to 170 rowers in addition to the scores of marines, archers, and even cavalry on the deck above.

The first naval engagement on record, the Battle of the Delta, was fought around 1175 BC between the Egyptians and some group righteously known only as the Sea Peoples. Early galley warfare was limited to pulling up next to one another and attempting to board the other vessel while pelting it with

THE VIKING LONGSHIP

Between the ninth and thirteenth centuries, Vikings used their own versions of the galley, the Viking longship, to raid, trade, pillage, and plunder throughout northern Europe. Like the Mediterranean galley, the Viking longship, was powered by a swarm of rowers. But, unlike their southern contemporaries, the Vikings built their sleek ships so lightweight that the crew could carry them, allowing the marauding Vikings to beach their ships and begin a raid before their unlucky foe had time to prepare.

rocks. But by the eighth century BC, the Greeks had turned the ship itself into a weapon, adding sharp bronze rams beneath the bow's waterline to sink their unsuspecting foes.

In a glimpse of the cannon-driven warfare that would one day dominate the sea, in 672 AD the Byzantine Navy began to attack ships using what became known as Greek fire, an incendiary mixture that would burn on water.

The Sailboat

The sail stands at the top of man's most important innovations. There's only so far we as a species could have gotten with sweat and oars; it was the sailboat that turned the world's oceans and seas into passages for exploration. As early as 3200 BC, the Egyptians and Sumerians had developed square-rigged boats for trading with other civilizations. The ancient Polynesians equipped their double-hulled outriggers with simple cloth sails that helped push their boats from the South Pacific to the islands of Hawaii. The Chinese traveled up and down the Asian continent, trading under sail.

But in the late fifteenth century, sailing boats went from simple means of trade to vessels of global exploration. The change happened with one simple alteration to sail design. While traditional sailboats of the Middle Ages were powered by square-rigged sails that allowed the craft to travel in one direction only, a new style of fore and aft sail design took a couple of the sails and turned them almost 90 degrees. The innovation allowed European ships to sail against the prevailing winds for the first time, freeing captains from the constraints of sailing within known wind patterns. The ocean was about to open up.

By the sixteenth century, the Age of Discovery had become the age of sail. Vast fleets of massive, sail-powered ships took to the sea and any country that wanted to be worth a damn started shipbuilding like crazy. England, Spain, France, Portugal, and Holland suddenly became locked in a race for the globe, vying for control of resource-rich regions in Africa, Australia, Asia, and the New World. And it was the sail-powered ship that enabled the rapid expansion.

THE COMPASS

The Age of Discovery would not have been possible had Europeans not figured out how to pinpoint magnetic north. The compass, the first device capable of determining cardinal directions during cloudy travel days, helped open up the world of navigation. Interestingly, while Europeans probably didn't start making their own compasses until the late twelfth century, the Chinese had been using them since as far back as 206 BC.

The Clipper Ship

The age of sail reached its soaring heights with the advent of the three-masted clipper ship. Introduced at the end of the 1700s, these incredibly fast tall ships became the go-to vessel for speedy trans-ocean crossings. In the Far East, clippers were used to transport lucrative balls of opium throughout Asia and to America and Europe. In the United States, decades before the Panama Canal would revolutionize sea travel, clippers were a primary method of voyaging between New York and gold-rich San Francisco, sailing the length of the two continents, rounding South America's treacherous Cape Horn, and arriving in San Francisco Bay just 100 days later. Even in storms the ships were spectacular. Seasick passengers on slower ships rocked by waves and wind often reported seeing clippers pass them by at full speed as though passing through calm, easy waters.

These majestic ships' glory days were short-lived. In order to achieve their remarkable speeds through narrow hulls, they gave up excessive amounts of cargo space, and when the Suez and Panama Canals opened up and the steam-powered ship came along, their fate was sealed.

THE ROARING FORTIES AND FURIOUS FIFTIES

The fastest way to sail around the globe is to catch a ride on the Roaring Forties, a very strong westerly wind that blows in the Southern Hemisphere just above Antarctica at latitudes ranging roughly from 40 to 50 degrees (thus the name!). The Roaring Forties howl around the globe almost entirely interrupted, allowing sailing vessels to cruise east with remarkable speed.

The most dangerous portion of the journey dips brave captains even farther south into winds known as the Furious Fifties (between 50 and 60 degrees south latitude) as they round Cape Horn. If anyone ever doubted the remarkable capabilities of the clipper ship, this route put the question to rest. It was the favored way for the ships to circumnavigate the globe, taking them from Europe to Africa, Asia, Australia, and back again in as little as seventy-two days. To this day it is known as the Clipper Route.

The Steamer

In 1819 the SS *Savannah*, a hybrid steam and sailing ship, crossed the Atlantic and effectively put an end to the age of sail. The age of the drunken cruise had begun. By 1838 the SS *Great Western* was making scheduled transatlantic journeys between Bristol and New York. A decade later, trading steamers from the California coast were arriving in ports throughout China and Japan.

Though they were unburdened by the fickleness of the wind, nineteenth-century steamboats were no grand solution; they required copious amounts of wood or fuel, leading to pollution and massive deforestation unseen at any other time in history. At one point, so many trees were chopped down along the middle Mississippi that the soil eroded and huge tracts of land flooded.

ONE BIG WRECK

The RMS *Titanic* may be known best for its tragic icy fate, but at the time of its maiden voyage it was known simply as the largest steamship ever built.

KNOTS

Ever wonder why the speeds of boats are measured in knots rather than miles per hour? The answer lies in actual physical knots. Out of sight of land, sailors could only estimate their speed by casting a rope with evenly spaced knots attached to a piece of wood called a chip log. One sailor would drop the line in the water, letting the knots slip through his fingers while another sailor would time out thirty seconds. The standardized distance between knots (47 feet, three inches) and time (28 seconds), allowed sailors to calculate the ship's speed.

The other main issue was reliability. Early steamboats along the Mississippi were hard to manage and tricky to control; scores were destroyed by collision, fire, or boiler explosions, several of which caused massive losses of life. In 1858, a single boiler explosion on the *Pennsylvania* killed 250 passengers, including Mark Twain's younger brother, Henry Clemens.

Submersibles and Submarines

There's one big difference between submersibles and submarines. Submersibles are boats that rely on external help to function underwater; submarines can head out under the waves on their own. But both have been pined over since antiquity. While subaquatic vessels were initially envisioned

KNOW YOUR SHIP PREFIXES

USS: United States Ship

USAV: United States Army Vessel

HMS: His/Her Majesty's Ship (UK)

RMS: Royal Mail Ship/Steamer (UK)

FV: Fishing Vessel

HSC: High Speed Craft

MS: Motor Ship

NS: Nuclear Ship

PS: Paddle Steamer

SS: Steamship (screw-propelled)

SY: Sailing Yacht

as a means of exploring our underwater worlds, the military quickly blew up that romantic notion and nailed the true potential for an undetectable underwater boat.

The *Turtle* got the age of underwater exploration started, albeit very crudely. The rebel Americans used the one-man, hand-powered, acorn-shaped submarine during the Revolutionary War in an unsuccessful attempt to sink a British warship. Despite its unsuccessful attempt at overly complicated sabotage, it was the first boat ever to utilize screw propulsion.

Though both the Union and Confederacy used subs during the Civil War, the technology was not useful until the Russians and Japanese went at it during the Russo-Japanese War. These early U-boats ranged in size from about 67 to 84 feet and could carry fifteen sailors.

Then, during WWI, the Germans began to perfect the art of underwater warfare, using massive fleets of U-Boats to terrorize British and American ships crossing the Atlantic.

Nuclear Ships

In one radioactively charming twist of fate, ship propulsion has come almost full circle to where it began. Where our ancestors 5,000 years ago learned to harness the boundless energy of the wind, we have developed the power to stay at sea indefinitely, without the drawbacks of coal- and diesel-fired engines and without having to rely on the wind. These suckers are nuclear.

In 1954 the United States Navy launched the USS *Nautilus*, the world's first operational nuclear-powered submarine. Today, nuclear reactors power eighty vessels in the Navy's fleet, including submarines, cruisers, destroyers, and huge aircraft carriers. The Nimitz-class aircraft carriers, which sailed all over the world between 1968 and 2006, could stay at sea for an astonishing twenty straight years without refueling. Of course, the bill for these nuclear behemoths is equally staggering—each one cost an estimated $4.5 billion dollars.

Throwing a nuclear power plant on a floating ship might be a little bit dangerous, right? Yes, especially when you consider that in the past half century at least five nuclear-powered subs (three Russian and two American) have been lost at sea. Let's all go scuba diving!

BOSSES OF THE PACIFIC

THE POLYNESIANS

Across the Pacific with a Pig

Around the time Europeans were discovering that there might be a world beyond the Mediterranean Sea, the Polynesians had already spread out across the vastest ocean on the planet. Somehow, in the 64 million square miles of open water in the Pacific, they had found the few specs of islands out there. By 1000 BC, tribes from Taiwan had arrived by boat to the Mariana, Marshall, and Caroline Islands. Within a few centuries they had made it to Tonga and Samoa. From there, the great expansion of the Polynesian societies took off, with large families making perilous voyages south, east, and north, all the way to New Zealand, the remote Easter Island, and Hawaii.

In search of dry land for months on end, the Polynesian navigators brought live pigs, fruits, and vegetables aboard their large, double-hulled canoes. Scores of seafarers died during the journeys, but the venturesome explorers continued to make the voyages for centuries. Researchers believe that Polynesians regularly traveled between Hawaii and Tahiti, despite the 2,700 miles of open ocean separating the island chains, and perhaps even established steady trade routes.

The Polynesian Triangle represents the known areas of exploration and settlement by the ancient Polynesians. In additional to their thriving settlements, the intrepid Polynesian explorers may have even established contact with the inhabitants of South America long before Columbus arrived. Even Antarctica may not have been beyond their reach, as indicated by shards of pottery found on islands just north of the icy continent.

Navigating by the Skin of Their Balls

As every good sailor lost at sea should know, there are plenty of telltale signs of land you can look for (besides actual land). Seagulls, frigates, and other pelagic birds that call land home are a sure sign of dry soil close at hand. In some regions of the world like Tahiti, sailors say you can actually smell the fragrant earth long before you can see the mountains.

But the explorers who first found Hawaii used navigation techniques that make those sight-based methods look like amateur hour at the kiddie pool. While the Tahitian sailors were adept at navigating by the stars, they often used tactical methods to *feel* distant lands. More conservative Tahitian sailors would dip their hands in the water to assess subtle changes in ocean currents as they redirected around islands. The ballsier Tahitians would stand naked at the prow of their boats to detect tiny waves bouncing off land...all with their pendulum-like testicles.

Man Seeks Wooden Raft to Sail Across Pacific

History has had its share of ridiculous theories, but none so outlandish as Thor Heyerdahl's theory of Polynesian origins. A Norwegian student of zoology and geography and an amateur expert in all things tiki, Heyerdahl developed a fierce love of Polynesia and a pretty-far-frickin'-out-there theory that the original inhabitants of the idyllic Tahitian, Easter, and Hawaiian islands were not from Asia but were actually Incan settlers from modern-day Peru. Rather than backing up his theory from a desk in Oslo, Heyerdahl set out to prove it himself.

Heyerdahl moved to Peru and built a 45-foot balsa wood raft he called *Kon-Tiki* using only materials that would have been found in ancient Peru. He then found five other Norsemen insane enough to join him and in 1947 launched *Kon-Tiki* into the Pacific Ocean's swift-moving Humboldt Current.

Not long into the journey, as the crew sailed due west across the largest ocean on the planet, a giant beard of algae and seaweed took root on the underside of the raft. Small fish then showed up, hitching a ride on what was quickly becoming a mobile buffet. With all those tasty little swimmers around, bigger fish joined the party. That, naturally, attracted hundreds of sharks. True to their adventurous nature, the crew of the *Kon-Tiki* invented the sport of open-ocean barehanded shark fishing, which they claimed was "precautionary, should anyone fall overboard."

Miraculously, after just 101 days at sea, *Kon-Tiki* crashed directly into the outer reefs of the Tuamotu Archipelago, breaking up on the sharp reefs. Thor Heyerdahl had proven that it was, after all, possible to sail from Peru to Polynesia way back in the day. Unfortunately, his theory never held up; it was debunked less than a decade later.

IT'S EASIER THAN YOU THINK TO GET LOST AT SEA

Thar She Blows (a Hole in the Side of Your Ship): The Real Moby Dick

Today, Herman Melville's epic sea story, *Moby Dick*, is universally familiar, (even if you haven't read it). Captain Ahab seeks maniacal revenge on the great white sperm whale that lost him his leg. Man is locked in eternal battle with nature. Ahab spots whale, whale sinks ship, and everyone dies save Ishmael, who narrates the tale. Tragic.

Only thing is that old Herman borrowed that story from the true and much, much more horrific saga of the whaleship *Essex*. In 1820, the crew of the 90-foot whaler *Essex* was cruising smack dab in the middle of the vast, 64-million square mile Pacific Ocean, looking to harpoon them some sperm whales and have them a time, when tragedy struck in the form of a giant, torpedo-like sperm whale.

After more than a year of arduous, omen-filled travel, tensions were already high onboard the *Essex* when they spotted their first whale spouts. All hands hit the harpooning boats and left the mother ship behind with a couple sailors to man the controls. Things were going fine until one enormous bull sperm whale, looking as scarred and grizzled as an aquatic Danny Trejo, decided to exact revenge for 5,000 years of whale murder. The bull whale zeroed in on the *Essex* from nearly a quarter mile out and rammed the ship's bow head-on, splintering the hull into toothpicks before disappearing into the depths below. The boat followed shortly thereafter.

The crew looked back at what was left of the *Essex* in horror, immediately realizing they were thousands of miles from salvation with nothing but tiny whaling boats and a couple floating turtles. They salvaged whatever supplies they could and debated their next move. The Marquesas Islands were a mere 1,300 miles upwind, but the sea-wrecked boatmen became convinced that the island was populated by savage cannibals, so they voted to sail east instead. The Marquesas, as sailors around the world soon learned, were inhabited less by cannibals and more by scores of free-loving Polynesian women.

The crew used spare cloth to rig some makeshift sales and chose a rugged, 4,000-mile route all the way back to Chile. With inadequate supplies, twelve of the twenty sailors died along the journey, succumbing to starvation and thirst while surrounded by the largest body of water known to man. And in tragic irony, the eight who survived did so only by eating seven of their deceased comrades. When he was rescued, four months after the *Essex* sank, the captain was found on the floor of his boat, delirious with exhaustion and gnawing on a human bone.

THE MOMENTARY JOY OF WHALING

A Nantucket sleighride was the exhilarating thrill whalers experienced after harpooning a whale. Attempting to escape its fate, the harpooned whale would drag the whaleboat behind it at speeds up to 25 mph. For many of the whalers, this thrill was likely their last, as their boats were carried over the horizon and lost to the endless ocean.

The Real Robinson Crusoe: Alexander Selkirk

Alexander Selkirk was a grade-A, fist fighting, rabble-rousing a-hole, so naturally he became a pirate. In 1704, at the age of twenty-seven, Selkirk found himself on an English privateering galley named *Cinque Ports* on its way to terrorize Spanish ships off the Pacific coast of South America.

But when the ship rounded Cape Horn and started taking on water, Selkirk freaked out, claiming that the *Cinque Ports* was bound to sink. When the ship reached the remote, barren Juan Fernandez Islands, 370 miles off the coast of Chile, Selkirk could take no more and begged to be left on shore. The captain obliged, dropped off his personal belongings, bid him good luck and sailed north without him. Alexander Selkirk was marooned alone.

Despite the survivalist romance of it, being marooned on a desert island pretty much sucks. It's lonely and, in Selkirk's case, damp and *cold*, with windy, frigid winters dipping into the 30s. But what's worse was that this isolated archipelago had no native animals, which meant any creature accidentally introduced by passing ships thrived. And this meant rats. Thousands of them. Scurrying over the island and devouring anything they could sink their teeth in.

During his first few weeks on the island, the rats attacked Selkirk like he was 150 pounds of prime rib. He stayed as close to the shoreline as possible, hoping in desperation to spot a passing ship, but ended up fleeing inland when scores of hormonal sea lions stormed the beaches to mate.

In the middle of the island Selkirk found the two animal species that would be his salvation: cats and goats. He milked and hunted the feral goats and later sewed himself new rags using their skin. He quickly ingratiated himself to a litter of feral kittens, letting them sleep in his makeshift hut so they could keep the insatiable rats at bay.

Wracked with hunger and loneliness, Selkirk then turned to the goats living on the island for both sustenance and companionship. When he wasn't hunting them, Selkirk would read the bible aloud to the roaming herds of goats. Eventually Selkirk became so adept at goat-catching that when he ran out of ammunition for his only gun, he started running them down and killing the goats by hand.

Despite the less than idyllic life, a Scottish pirate could find himself in worse situations than being marooned on an island. One alternative was being captured by the archenemy Spanish. And on two separate occasions, Spanish ships docked on Selkirk's island, forcing the castaway to play a game of hide-and-go-seek for his life.

Finally, after four years and four months of complete isolation, another British privateering ship named the *Duke* came to his long-awaited rescue. Selkirk quickly repaid the men for rescuing him by employing his new goat-catching skills, feeding the scurvy-ridden sailors their first nutritious meal in months. The captain of the rescue ship was so taken with Selkirk's vitality, ingenuity, and peaceful demeanor that he made him second mate of the *Duke* for the long journey home.

Five Months of Fish and Rainwater

Chinese sailor Poon Lim holds the record for longest survival at sea on a life raft. After the British merchant ship he was sailing on was torpedoed by a German U-Boat in 1942, Lim spent 133 days adrift at sea, the ship's only survivor. After nearly five months alone in the Atlantic, Lim finally made landfall in Brazil.

The Great Wide Pacific: A Record Survival at Sea

In October 2005, five Mexican fishermen set out on what was supposed to be a three-day shark hunt in the Pacific in a 27-foot motorized boat. When they accidentally ran out of fuel, the five men began drifting westward away from the coast of Mexico. Two of the men succumbed to starvation within the first few months, but the other three survivors managed to survive on anything they could find—seagulls, turtles, fish, and shark.

After a record-setting nine and a half months lost at sea, the survivors were spotted by a Taiwanese fishing trawler. When they were rescued, the men were informed they were a mere 200 miles from Australia. They had drifted 5,500 miles, crossing the Pacific Ocean in its entirety.

Frigid Winds and Dogs for Dinner

By the end of the nineteenth century, most of the globe had been "discovered." There was no more sailing to some tropical paradise, dropping anchor, and naming the newfound island and its natives after you. So those men seeking to make a name for themselves turned to the more inhospitable, remote, and uncharted corners of the world. Expeditions set out for the deepest jungles of the Amazon and Congo. Men traversed the dark, cold northern latitudes. And still others headed south to brave the ball-shrinking, freezing hellscape of the last unexplored continent: Antarctica. In just twenty short years between 1897 and 1917, known as the Heroic Age of Antarctic Exploration, seventeen expeditions lost nineteen grizzled men along the way. Those who survived the expeditions returned with remarkable tales and stirring stories of how they managed to escape the frozen wastelands of Antarctica.

One of the most remarkable tales belonged to geologist Douglas Mawson, who led the Australasian Antarctic Expedition of 1911. The expedition, which consisted of thirty men, set out to explore, chart, and bring back specimens from the Great White Continent. After wintering at their base camp near Commonwealth Bay, Mawson split the party into groups, and in 1912 he and two other members, Lieutenant Belgrave Ninnis and skier Xavier Mertz, set out to chart Antarctica's far eastern regions. It was on this journey that his adventure turned into one of the worst nightmares of survival ever documented.

Mawson's Far Eastern Party had made amazing time, traveling over 300 miles from base camp in a month with two teams of sled dogs. Then, on December 14, 1912, seven days before the Southern Hemisphere's summer solstice, disaster struck. One of the expedition's members, Lieutenant Belgrave Ninnis, unwittingly took his sled over a covered crevasse. Thawed by the summer sun and unable to take the weight of the man, sled, and team of huskies, the ground beneath Ninnis opened up and he, the sled, and the dogs vanished into the frozen abyss below. Mawson and Mertz desperately searched in vain for any sign of the lost Ninnis and his sled, which had been carrying their stockpile of food and the party's only tent.

Bereft of the most basic essentials and a third of their party, the two remaining explorers had little chance of surviving the blustery, snow-swept journey that lay ahead. They returned to the previous night's camp and Mawson managed to improvise a tent using some spare canvas and poles by disassembling the remaining sled. With the sled disabled and knowing they would soon run out of food, Mawson began to slaughter the sled dogs for survival, boiling everything from their gamey flesh to their tough feet and livers.

For days Mawson and Mertz struggled on toward base camp, navigating through icy winds that whipped at their weakened frames with relentless force, at times exceeding speeds of 200 miles per hour. Beaten by weather, hunger, and cold, Mertz soon became listless and despondent, insisting on spending a full day doing nothing but recuperating in the relative warmth of his sleeping bag.

Still 100 miles from base camp, Mertz's condition deteriorated further. Periods of lethargic hopelessness were interspersed with violent fits of mania. His skin and hair began to slough off and he was overcome by diarrhea. Mertz died in his sleeping bag on January 8, 1913. Later it was determined that eating the dog's livers probably caused his demise, as dog livers contain *too* much vitamin A and can cause the weakening affliction hypervitaminosis.

After burying his friend, Mawson set off again, when he discovered that the skin on the bottom of his feet was falling off and crippling sores on his soles were soaking his socks with blood. After resting a full day, he continued, only to find himself facing a fate similar to that of Ninnis when he stumbled into a crevasse himself. He would have disappeared into the white depths had his mangled sled not stuck in the ledge. Dangling inside the crevasse, Mawson used all of his remaining strength to haul his body out.

A few days later, and three months after the party had left on their expedition, Mawson finally made it back to base camp. Skinny, weak, and nearly hairless, he arrived just in time to see his expedition's ship disappear over the horizon. Luckily, several of his party had bravely remained behind and Mawson spent the next winter recovering with his friends on the frozen coast of the Antarctic.

Around the World in...Never Mind

In 1968, the UK newspaper *The Sunday Times* hosted a thrilling solo, nonstop sailing race around the world. One of the competitors was an unknown businessman and (very) amateur sailor named Donald Crowhurst. Down on his luck and hell-bent on making a name for himself, Crowhurst ignored the naysayers and launched his ill-equipped boat into the Atlantic on a quest for fame and fortune.

Everything went terribly from the start and, by the time Crowhurst reached the waters off South America, his hopes for making it around the world alive were finished. But would ol' Don give up? Bollocks no! Crowhurst fabricated a complicated logbook and gave untruthful radio reports that showed him on a rip-roaring pace around the globe, and in an era prior to GPS and other location technologies, how the hell was anybody going to prove him wrong? With his web of lies in place, all Crowhurst had to do was wait (completely alone) off the coast of Brazil until the other contestants rounded Cape Horn and passed him on the home stretch. Then, he could simply slip in behind them and finish a respectable, unscrutinized anything-but-first.

Astoundingly, his plan almost worked. That is, right up to the point where the leader of the race abruptly forfeited and the new lead boat suddenly sank. Facing the terrible possibility of winning and having his lie exposed, Crowhurst finally gave up the dream. He cut off his radio and disappeared into the ocean. His ship was found drifting and abandoned but the logbook entries found on board reveal an increasingly tormented mental state. Crowhurst was never seen again.

THERE'S A STORM A BREWIN'

HOW TO TELL THE WEATHER WITHOUT THE DAMN WEATHERMAN

Heading out for a sail? Want to know if you've got a chance to get lost at sea in a storm? You don't need the Weather Channel to know what's coming. The weather is all about pressure. Barometric pressure to be exact. For the sake of simplicity, let's reduce this discussion to two types of pressure: high and low.

High pressure

A high-pressure system means that a bunch of air has been compressed in the upper atmosphere and then descended down to sit somewhere above some godforsaken place like Lubbock, Texas, that hasn't seen rain in a generation. The high-pressure air column is an ornery, solitary piece of sky that forces any weather near it to head in the opposite direction. The predominant winds blow out from the center of the high-pressure system, creating clear skies and, in the summer, hot-as-hell temperatures.

DID YOU KNOW?

Barometric high pressure will cause the bubbles that form at the surface of your coffee to move to the sides of your cup.

Low pressure

Low-pressure systems are, unsurprisingly, just the opposite of high-pressure systems. The air in the upper atmosphere becomes less dense and begins to rise, creating a vacuum underneath. The newly formed vacuum, an insatiably needy bastard, sucks in all the air around it, including cold air from the north and wet air from the south. And what do those two make when they meet up? Storms.

DID YOU KNOW?

Because the air in a low-pressure system is less dense than normal, birds have difficulty flying through it, causing them to cruise lower than they normally would. So if you see thousands of birds flying west at breakneck speeds six feet above your head, you might want to batten down the hatches.

Rain's a comin'

On land, the best way to predict rain on your own is through your nose, by sniffing for that earthy, vegetal scent. Before the rainstorm comes, the lower air pressure allows gases in the soil to expand, giving the air an earthy fragrance. The leaves of trees react by opening their stomata, the plant equivalent of pores, to breathe in more carbon dioxide. This planty musk mixes with the earthy fumes to give the sky its rich pre-rain fragrance.

But on the water, things are more difficult to tell. Before the obvious storm clouds approach, you'll be able to spot an oncoming storm by looking at wind direction, cloud type, and wave patterns. In the Northern Hemisphere, weather systems typically move to the east, causing normal westward winds, so a stiff breeze blowing in the opposite direction can indicate a storm on its way. Clouds are a bit trickier. Look for the tell-tale formation of banded cirrus clouds—wispy, high-forming clouds that string together like cloth—as these indicate an approaching patch of inclement weather.

As the humidity rises ahead of a storm, haze hangs over the sun. True rain experts can observe subtle shifts in wind for insight. A counterclockwise (i.e., north to west) shift means a storm is approaching from the direction the wind is blowing *toward*, as wind moves from high-pressure systems toward areas of stormy low pressure. A clockwise shift in wind (i.e., from north to east or east to south) means good weather is on the way. Why? It's the same thing that makes a hurricane spin.

This Is Why Hurricanes Spin

We can all thank the magical Coriolis effect for the awe-inspiring radar pictures of approaching hurricanes. What is the Coriolis effect? It goes a little something like this: the earth rotates on its axis *fast*. And thanks to the large distance the equator has to travel, the relative speed at the equator is incredible (a blazing 1,038 mph to be exact), whereas at the North Pole, which hardly has any distance to go in a given rotation, the rotation is nice and slow.

This difference in relative rotation speed causes anything, even air, traveling between the pole and equator to curve. Throw a ball hard enough north from the equator and it'll curve westward. Throw that same ball from the North Pole south and it'll curve to the east. Throw a massive amount of air, water, and thunderheads and they'll do the same. As the low-pressure system draws in more and more air from north and south, the curve becomes more pronounced and more visible, eventually forming the characteristic eye and sweeping bands of clouds.

GIANT WAVES

Not only does wind help feed storms and hurricanes, it also creates ocean waves. Whether it's beneath massive storms, or a cloudless, breezy day, wind pressing down on thousands of square miles of ocean begins to generate waves that travel out in all directions across the globe. We normally only come in contact with the waves at the tail end of their journey—on the beach. Though the contact is brief, it can be impressive.

Mavericks, Jaws, Teahupo'o, Ghost Tree, and Cortes Bank are some of the names synonymous with the world's biggest waves. But just why do these waves get so damn big? One word: topography.

The majority of big waves form because of one distinctive feature: an oddly placed seamount. As the wave approaches the shore, the seamount slope causes the wave's center to grow upward and slow down, which bends the faster-moving outer sections of the wave inward toward the building crest. This works to magnify the wave energy at one central peak, turning what would normally have been an impressive 20-foot wave into a monster 80-foot giant.

A Shipper's Nightmare Is a Surfer's Wet Dream: Cortes Bank

When the captain of the steamship *Cortes* spotted a mass of giant, violent waves breaking in the middle of the open ocean, his first thought was that he'd discovered an underwater volcano. It turns out that he'd stumbled upon an uncharted seamount. Located 100 miles west of San Diego, California, Cortes Bank is capped at its highest point by Bishop Rock, which lies just six feet under water. Aside from being capable of producing the astounding 100-foot waves sought after by big-wave surfers around the world, Cortes Bank is one of the Pacific's most treacherous shipping obstacles.

THE LARGEST WAVE EVER SURFED (SO FAR)

In November 2011 Garrett McNamara broke the all-time world record for largest wave ever surfed by riding a 90-foot wave in Nazare, Portugal. To give city-dwellers some perspective, the ride was the equivalent of sliding down the face of a nine-story building.

Rogue Waves

Of all the ocean's impressive phenomena, none have terrified sailors over the centuries as much as rogue waves. The craziest thing about these freak waves is that, until 1995, they were considered by scientists to be as mythical as sea monsters; not one had ever been recorded. That all changed when, on

New Year's Day in 1995, a single 84-foot wave was recorded cruising by the Draupner research platform off the coast of Norway.

But what scientists had, until then, doubted for centuries, seafaring captains had always feared. In one of the most famous accounts, in 1942, the famous steamer RMS *Queen Mary*, loaded with American soldiers headed for England, was broadsided by a rogue wave estimated at 90 feet, forcing the ship to list just a few degrees shy of capsizing.

Rogue waves differ from the monster surfing waves in that they occur in the middle of the open water, where there should be no dramatic shift in wave height. Because these freak waves are so rare, science has yet to get definitive answers on how they form. Most likely they are formed from multiple smaller waves traveling in the same direction that combine energy into one enormous force.

TSUNAMIS

It has been known for centuries in Japan as the village-crushing "harbor wave," called *tsunami* in the native tongue. Hundreds of feet above sea level in the coastal hillside villages of Japan, it's still possible to find ancient rock tablets emblazoned with tsunami warnings, encouraging citizens not to build their homes any closer to the sea. And throughout history, these tsunamis have proven to be the sea's most ferociously destructive force.

Unlike the wind-borne rogue waves that terrorize oceangoing ships or the giant breakers that pound shorelines in Hawaii, California, South Africa, and Portugal, tsunamis are formed from the cold, dark seafloor itself. When the tectonic plates that make up the earth's crust thrust upward or separate, they can displace tremendous amounts of seawater, creating enormous, fast-moving walls of water hundreds of feet tall and a hundred miles wide. Here are five tsunamis that shook the world.

THE WEAPONIZED TSUNAMI

During WWII, Allied forces experimented with creating man-made tsunamis to attack coastal cities and towns of Japan. The idea was to substitute the earth's natural tectonic movement with one huge underwater explosion. Small-scale experiments were carried out with mixed results, but it was too difficult to control the power (and direction) of the killer waves, so the weaponized tsunami was eventually scrapped.

The Original Atlantis: Helike

In the dead of winter in 373 BC, the bustling port city of Helike, Greece, disappeared along with all its inhabitants in the middle of the night. An earthquake in the Mediterranean liquefied the ground underneath the city, dropping it below sea level, and was followed almost immediately by a massive tsunami that left it inundated for all time. For centuries after, visitors to the site claimed that the submerged ruins of the former city could be seen in the waters just offshore. And many scholars believe it was the tragic real-life story of Helike that inspired the story of another city mysteriously lost to the sea: Atlantis.

The Day Portugal Burned and Drowned Simultaneously: The Lisbon Tsunami of 1755

Talk about one-two punches. The 1755 earthquake south of Lisbon was a complete knockout. When the estimated 8.5

magnitude earthquake struck the Atlantic, it shook the Kingdom of Portugal's wealthy capital city for up to five long minutes. Huge scores of elegantly designed stone buildings, built as high as five stories, collapsed, igniting fires that raged around the city.

To escape the growing inferno, many citizens made for the open harbor and crowded onto boats along the waterfront. It was here that they were greeted by a quickly receding sea

THE DEADLIEST OF THE DEADLY: THE 1931 CENTRAL CHINA FLOODS

While hurricanes and typhoons can cause widespread death and destruction, floods have historically been among the world's deadliest natural phenomena. Of these, the 1931 Central China floods took between one and four million lives due to drowning and waterborne diseases, easily topping the charts of the worst disasters in history.

The floods occurred due to a disastrous series of weather events. A two-year drought ended dramatically with a slew of snowstorms and, just as the snow began to melt, China was struck by seven cyclones and prolonged downpours of heavy rain. The flooding destroyed the regions surrounding the Yellow and Yangtze Rivers, some of the most densely populated regions in the world at the time. The catastrophic flooding inundated the valleys with waters 50 feet above normal. Those who didn't die from drowning, cholera, or typhus struggled to survive the economic collapse that followed.

followed by a succession of violent waves ranging in height from 20 feet to over 90 feet that capsized the moored boats and drowned everyone on board. The earthquake and ensuing tsunami killed almost a quarter of Lisbon's 270,000 inhabitants and instilled in the Portuguese king a lifelong fear of living indoors.

The Great Japanese Earthquake of 2011

The tsunami that hit Japan on March 11, 2011, stands as the single most well-documented natural disaster in history. The tsunami, generated by a powerful 9.0 earthquake off the Pacific coast of Japan, overtopped 40-foot defensive tsunami walls, destroying over 400,000 buildings and killing over 15,000 people.

Japan is no stranger to tsunamis; its islands, of course, sit atop the Pacific Ring of Fire in a zone known for megathrust earthquakes. On average, the country is hit by one tsunami every seven years.

The Indian Ocean Tsunami of 2004

The day after Christmas in 2004, a catastrophic undersea earthquake off the Sumatran coast created an 80-foot tsunami that spread out in all directions across the Indian Ocean. The tsunami hit the world's most crowded oceanic coastline, stretching from Africa to India to Indonesia, displacing almost two million coastal inhabitants and killing an estimated 230,000 people.

While the tsunami-prone Pacific Ocean is littered with tsunami tracking buoys, and coastal cities from Tokyo to Honolulu to San Francisco all have tsunami warning systems, until the 2004 tsunami, the coastal population of the Indian Ocean had no early warning system whatsoever. Residents and tourists were still on the beaches when the tsunami hit.

WHAT THE SEA WASHED IN

The power of the 2004 tsunami is still on display in Banda Aceh, Indonesia, where visitors can climb aboard the *Apung 1*, a 2,600-ton ship that broke free of its moorings during the tsunami and was carried nearly two miles inland, coming to rest the middle of the flooded city. The grounds around the wreck have become a touching memorial to the losses suffered on December 26, 2004.

MEGATSUNAMIS

Just in case you thought tsunamis were panic-inducing, they've got nothing on their larger, deadlier cousins: megatsunamis. These unearthly waves are created by massive landslides, giant meteors, or the collapse of entire mountains. The power generated creates wave tops that can be as high as 3,000 feet (two Empire State Buildings stacked one on top of the other). Fortunately, they're exceedingly rare. But that doesn't mean they don't happen.

Lituya Bay, Alaska

In 1958, a steep mountainside along the narrow inlet of Lituya Bay, Alaska, suddenly collapsed. The resulting landslide sent an estimated 90 million cubic feet of dirt, trees, and debris splashing down, displacing so much water it created a single wave almost 2,000 feet high. Somehow it killed only five people.

The Looming Disaster: Canary Islands

One of the most worrisome potential sites for disaster is in the Canary Islands off the Atlantic coast of Africa. One particular island in the chain, La Palma, has seen volcanic eruptions on and off for centuries. But after the last large eruption in 1949, the western side of the island actually separated from the eastern side and began slipping into the Atlantic below it.

Although the slide stopped shortly after the volcano did, one trillion tons of volcanic rock currently sits rather precariously above water. If the island collapsed into the water, a megatsunami hundreds of feet high would wash across the Atlantic, devastating the East Coast of the United States from Miami to New York. The good news? Scientists predict the event will most likely happen, but not for another 10,000 years.

THE SEA'S MOST DANGEROUS ANIMALS

Puffer Fish: Get High or Die Trying

The first sign you've ingested a fatal dose of puffer fish, the world's second deadliest vertebrate, is when your lips go numb. Then, after throwing up for a bit, it's your whole body's turn. Finally, in addition to the onset of paralysis, your heart rate skyrockets, your blood pressure plummets, your lungs stop working, and then you slip painfully into a coma and probably die.

Yet, despite the possibility of incurable death, the toxic puffer fish is a highly sought-after delicacy in Japan, Korea, and China, where experienced chefs prepare tasty meals ranging from puffer fish sashimi to puffer fish soup. If the chef uses *just* the right amount of poisonous meat, the patron will

A RECIPE FOR ZOMBIEISM

Sushi chefs aren't the only ones who prepare meals using puffer fish. There is ample evidence that Haitian witch doctors once fed their victims a mixture containing several toxins, including the puffer's tetrodotoxin, causing the consumer to enter a death-like trance and become what is known in Creole as a *zonbi*.

become pleasantly intoxicated, but a bit too much of the fish's toxin and it's the diner's last supper.

Box Jellyfish: The Invisible Killer

These notorious little box jellyfish, found in the waters near Australia, are impressive killers. The "sea wasps," as they're kindly called, have hundreds of thousands of miniature venom-injecting javelins in each of their tentacles, capable of killing a full-grown man in as little as five minutes. The danger the box jellyfish poses to humans is compounded by its near invisibility. The jellyfish is translucent and, unfortunately, tends to hang out near beaches. Although it is rarely deadly if treated quickly, jellyfish stings kill around thirty people per year in the Philippines alone, where the antivenin is rare.

Stonefish: Camouflaged Agony

As its name implies, the stonefish looks a whole lot like a rock or coral, making it dangerously difficult to spot and easy to step on. Unlike other fish that just swim away, these jerks stay still and raise their spike-lined dorsal fin like a mohawk, injecting its oh-so-deadly venom into any bumbling surfer who wades too close. The pain of a stonefish sting is so horrifically unbearably that victims regularly beg to have the afflicted region amputated.

The Red Sea Fire Urchin: The A-Hole

The only thing worse than getting stung by the deadly Red Sea Fire Urchin is getting stung *and* bit by the deadly Red

Sea Fire Urchin. If this colorful urchin fails to kill you by piercing you with its venomous shell, it also has the ability to inject your foot with venom from its anus-like mouth. That's just messed up.

Sea Snake: The Moody Murderer

Sea snakes like to hang out in warm, tropical waters and are among the most venomous snakes in the world. Fortunately, they tend to be kind and forgiving of humans and often hold back a bit when they bite, releasing only trace amounts of venom. However, if the snake is in a particularly bad mood when it bites, its victim will go through a miserable series of symptoms, beginning with sweating, headache, and nausea, progressing to a terrible full-body ache, and ending with paralysis, respiratory failure, muscle breakdown, dark reddish-brown urine, and ultimately cardiac arrest.

Stingray: The Scuba Slayer

Any fish deadly enough to kill a man no croc could do in deserves some respect. The stingray, a fish related to sharks, has a tail lined with highly venomous stingers, which it uses exclusively for protection. The fish will whip its stinger into the perceived threat—often leaving the venom-laden spine *in* the victim's wound. A stingray sting rarely causes death, but can be fatal if the sting slices open an artery or occurs near a vital organ.

Blue-Ringed Octopus: Murder by Kisses

The blue-ringed octopus's bite is so soft its victims often don't know they've been bitten until they find themselves unable to breath or move. The venom of this octopus is a cocktail of deadly neurotoxin chemicals similar to that in the puffer fish. Death feels the same too: victims are fully aware of the fact that they've been rendered totally helpless and are unable to move or cry for help. If the bitten victim doesn't receive artificial respiration quickly, there's a darn good chance that they'll suffocate to death.

Killer Whale: The Sadistic Pack Hunter

Although we almost excluded killer whales from this compendium of seaborne death-harbingers because they aren't inherently dangerous to humans AND because of their back-asswards matrilineal social system (pods of killer whales are led by females), we ultimately felt obliged to include them because they engage some of the most gloriously badass hunting techniques anywhere on earth. They definitely deserve to have "killer" in their name.

Hunting alone, the 30-foot killer whales use their superior size and strength to kill or immobilize prey, such as large fish, seals, sea lions, and even smaller sharks, by either whipping them with their powerful tails or by ramming them at full speed with their giant noggins. These head butts can be particularly gruesome, as a well-located orca ram can cause a prey's internal organs to explode upon contact.

But when hunting for larger prey in groups, killer whales get all strategical. They'll take out dolphins, sharks, mink whales, grey whales, and, on occasion, the blue whale (the largest animal to ever exist). Hunting these giants takes incredible patience and cooperation, which has earned the killer whales the title "wolves of the sea." Groups will target a weak-looking prey and, after successfully separating the weakling from its group, take their time to kill it. Instead of attacking their prey, they drown it, either by enclosing it from above to prevent surfacing or by physically holding it underwater—sometimes upside down—until it suffocates.

Saltwater Crocodile: The True Man Eater

What's a crocodile doing at sea? It's crushing your bones in the warm, salty sand. It's also the only true man hunter on this list and holy crap is it terrifying. Saltwater crocodiles are massive and, when they get hungry, they'll feed on anything. That includes birds, monkeys, kangaroos, wild boar, water buffalo, tigers, lions, sharks, and humans.

In addition to their size (up to 20 feet long and 2,000 pounds), saltwater crocodiles are quick, immensely strong, and highly territorial, treating intrusive humans—on land or even in boats—like an enemy worth tasting. While no reliable data exists, experts estimate that saltwater crocodiles fatally attack around fifteen people per year.

THE BATTLE OF RAMREE ISLAND

During WWII, the Allied forces drove about 1,000 Japanese soldiers into the murky, crocodile-infested swamps of Ramree Island, off the coast of Burma, trapping the soldiers in the waters. As many as 400 Japanese soldiers may have been killed by saltwater crocs.

Great White Shark: Yeah, Just Plain Terrifying

Great whites are infamous killers, suspected each year of attacking swimmers, surfers, and boaters with their powerful jaws and razor-sharp teeth. These predatory fish are *huge*, reaching lengths of up to 20 feet and weights exceeding 4,000 pounds. The good news for swimmers and surfers is that these sharks enjoy meals high in fat, like seals, sea lions, dolphins, tuna, whales, and, you know, other sharks.

Unfortunately, great whites don't know exactly how scrawny you are, so they tend to take *test bites*, after which the shark might determine that you would, in fact, be a pretty awful meal. But a shark's nibble is a bit more powerful than need be—it can sever your arm, leg, or torso. Of the 129 victims of shark attacks in the last twenty-five years, at least twenty-nine have bled to death.

SOME RELIEVING FACTS ABOUT SHARK ATTACKS

You Have a Better Chance of Being Killed by a Bee

There are a lot of things statistically more dangerous than sharks: freak fireworks accidents, being struck by lightning inside your house, undercooked sausage attack, walking down the street. So, really, don't worry about it.

There Aren't Many Great Whites in the World

Taking a dip in the ocean? Worried you may immediately be eaten by a great white à la *Jaws*? Fear not: great whites are considered an endangered species with a worldwide population estimate of just a few thousand. You should feel free to go in past your ankles.

Just Stop Peeing

Sure, it's one of the greatest feelings in the world. The cool ocean enveloping your body, the warm urine dissipating all around you. You're adding your own salty water to the ocean. But do you know what else pees in the ocean? Dying seals. And do you know what loves dying seals? Sharks.

You Can Fend off a Shark

If you do happen to find yourself mid–shark attack, it is possible to fend off the fish. Experts suggest punching, poking, or grabbing at the eyes and gills—pretty much the only sensitive areas on the sharp-toothed fish.

WHAT'S IN MY SUSHI?

Real men love sushi, and that is not a euphemism. The Japanese delicacies of *sashimi* and *nare-zushi* (sushi) offer everyday landlubbers an authentic taste of the sea. And chances are you, my friend, are a landlubber. So, before you take to the open ocean or your local sushi bar, let's learn you something about the creatures of the sea/delicious rolls on your plate.

The Two Most Popular Rolls

Tuna rolls (Maguro/Tekka)

Aside from sharks, *Thunnus* are the most ubiquitous apex predators in the world's oceans. These behemoths of the deep can grow up to 15 feet long and 1,000 pounds. In addition to their staggering size, tunas use massive, oxygen-rich muscles to reach speeds nearing 50 miles per hour while hunting. Unfortunately, overfishing has severely depleted the numbers of fish worldwide, resulting in some insane prices for sashimi. Currently, the record amount of money paid for a single, 600-pound tuna is over $730,000 at Tokyo's Tsukiji Fish Market.

California rolls

Even the poor saps among us that failed to develop a taste for raw fish can usually enjoy a California roll or two. The essence of Americanized sushi, the California roll consists of rice (on the outside), seaweed, avocado, cucumber, *tobiko* (flying fish roe) or sesame seeds, and imitation crabmeat. What is imitation crabmeat, you ask? It's much more complicated than you think.

This oddly flavorless, shapeless seafood filling is actually a hugely popular product in Japan called *kamaboko*, which is made from pulverized white fish meat (usually haddock or pollack) that is minced to a fine white paste and mixed with a bunch of random ingredients, like MSG and egg whites, to give it that "authentic" crustacean texture. Add a layer of red food coloring and voilà, you've got some authentic, grade-A *krab* meat.

Melanogrammus aeglefinus, *or the common crab-wannabe.*

THE MAGIC OF KELP

Don't care for seaweed? You might like it more than you know. Carrageenan, a compound found in red kelp, is used as a thickening agent in everyday products, including toothpaste, shampoo, sunscreen, peanut butter, ice cream, soy milk, processed ham, and even beer.

A Japanese Sushi Menu (Before It Hits Your Plate)

Squid (Ika)

The "giant" version of these cephalopods can grow up to 45 feet long.

Puffer fish (Fugu)

Very little of this Japanese delicacy is edible; the rest of it carries a powerful neurotoxin called tetrodotoxin.

Eel (Unagi/Anago)

Consider the Japanese eel a salmon in reverse: it leaves its freshwater home to spawn hundreds of miles away in the middle of the ocean.

Mackerel (Saba)

Mackerel, macrill, mackarell, macquerel, mackril, not only does the name "mackerel" stand for dozens of different small coastal fish, there have been at least nineteen different ways of spelling it.

Salmon (Sake)

After traveling through the ocean their whole adolescent lives, salmon always manage to make a beeline for the same river they were born in when it's time to mate.

Flying fish roe (Tobiko)

You're probably used to this fish's delicious eggs, but the non-embryonic adult version can "fly" out of the water for up to 650 feet while getting 19 feet above the surface of the sea.

Octopus (Tako)

Octopuses are so intelligent that experts theorize they have a level of problem-solving skills similar to that of a three-year-old human child.

Sea urchin (Uni)

The spiny, hedgehog-like sea urchin is actually a close relation to the sand dollar. The gonads and roe are the most popular edible parts.

Masculaneous

HEROES, VILLAINS, ADVENTURE,
AND INTRIGUE

THE FASCINATINGLY DISHONEST ORIGINS OF EVERYDAY PLACES

Everything has its own intriguing story of creation. Plastic was invented as a substitute for ivory billiard balls and New York City was founded as a fur trading post. Some innovations come about from moments of human genius, others from the tragedy of war or by total accident. But some are the intentional or inadvertent creations of the more dishonorable peoples of the world: the thieves, brigands, drug dealers, and unsavory characters who have, in their own weird way, shaped history. Here are a couple of their stories.

How the Highwaymen Lit Up London

By the seventeenth century, London was among the world's largest cities. But with just 225,000 citizens in 1605, it resembled more a large town than a thriving metropolis. In fact, the areas immediately surrounding the city were still wooded countryside where unlit dirt roads wound from the country's capital to towns like Bath, Exeter, and Dover. It was on these roads that a new form of criminal was born: the highway robber. Highwaymen, as they were called, would set up shop on isolated, well-covered stretches of road, lying in wait for unprotected stagecoaches carrying wealthy travelers. Though they were armed with pistols, they were ever the gentlemen, avoiding violence whenever possible by making a dashing escape on horseback.

Their exploits quickly reached folk-hero status in the eyes of England's impoverished masses, who dubbed them "the Gentlemen of the Road," either because they robbed only the rich or because they employed an eccentric, gentlemanly flare while doing it. Each one was a character. Captain James Hind, for example, refused to rob anybody but the wealthy members of England's parliament. The well-dressed Claude Duvall was exceedingly polite to the people he held up.

Highway robbery became so fashionable that it even spilled into London proper. During 1690, robberies were so com-

A COLORFUL EXECUTION: THE HANGING OF JOHN "SIXTEEN STRING JACK" RANN

One of the most famous highwaymen was John "Sixteen String Jack" Rann, a thief whose wit and flamboyant robbing attire made him an extremely popular figure. While on the job, Rann always wore wild outfits, such as breeches decorated with sixteen colorful silk strings. He once showed up to his own trial wearing flowers in his suit and bright blue ribbons cascading from his iron shackles. Even at his own execution, in 1774, the twenty-four-year-old Rann maintained his charming, happy-go-lucky demeanor. Wearing a lovely, newly tailored pea-green suit, he bantered playfully with the crowd, joked with the executioner, and performed a little jig before he was hanged.

mon in Hyde Park, the city's largest public commons, that King William III was forced to commission the construction of Rotten Row, a wide road passing through the southern stretch of the park illuminated by over 300 oil lamps, the first streetlights in London.

The Island Bought with Opium

A Chinese opium den circa 1860.

If you think our current trade deficit with China is bad, it's nothing compared to what Britain faced back in the late 1600s. Four hundred years ago, just about everything European citizens wanted was made in China. Tea, porcelain, silk: The land was like one bourgeois warehouse and people from Italy to Britain couldn't get enough.

Before long, Britain's state-sponsored corporation in the region, the British East India Company, was creeping in on the action. British merchant ships landed in the Chinese ports of Macau and Guangzhou eager to fill their holds with all the exotic valuables they could without capsizing.

Problem was, there wasn't much the Chinese wanted from the Europeans. A primarily agrarian culture, the Chinese were proudly self-sufficient and looked down upon most of the European-made goods the merchant ships were trying to barter. Who could blame them? Nobody wants Scottish wool underpants when they could get a cheaper version in silk.

Pretty much the only thing the Chinese would take for their tea, cloth, and plate ware was silver. And, surprise surprise, silver was expensive. Pretty soon the British ran out of the metal entirely and had to start buying it from other European powers just so they could shuttle it off to China. The British government wasn't having it.

So what did the British do? What any slightly evil empire would: They organized a massive, state-sponsored drug cartel, run by none other than the world-famous East India Company. What the British Empire lacked in sensual underwear they more than made up for in opium. Two of their colonies, India and Bengal, were chock-full of poppy fields. The Chinese people had no idea what was in store for them.

By the time the eighteenth century rolled around, thousands of Chinese villagers were partying on copious amounts of opium like it was, well, 1699. Impressive quantities of the drug, rolled up into enormous, sticky poppy balls, were entering the Chinese ports and you could hardly find a single merchant that remembered what silver looked like.

What's really astounding is that Britain's drug pushing in China doesn't just subsist for a couple decades; it goes on for hundreds of years, right up to the Communist Revolution. But way back at the time that the Chinese Qing Empire began earnestly cracking down on opium use, the damage had been done. Thousands upon thousands of Chinese were full-blown addicts and opium was flowing in through the country's border like it was a sieve.

Finally, the Chinese government came down hard on the Anglo dealers. They closed rivers to commercial trading, raided ports, confiscated 11,000 pounds of opium, and made 1,600 arrests. The sweeping drug bust in China was massive. (To put it in perspective, the Drug Enforcement Agency's famous 1991 heroin bust, the largest of all time, netted just 1,000 pounds of heroin with a street value of around $4 billion.)

And what did the Chinese get for it? A big, fat war. Two of them actually. Being cut off from their lucrative customer base royally pissed off the British government and they retaliated in 1839 by sending in Her Majesty's Royal Navy. By 1843, everything had fallen apart for China. The British had taken control of the mouth of the Yangtze River, laid siege to Guangzhou, and decimated China's Navy.

The Chinese sued for peace. And in return the British were granted Treaty Ports in what became Canton, Shanghai, and Fuzhou. But one of the biggest concessions came when the Chinese government officially ceded control of the island of Hong Kong to the British government. The island that opium bought was finally returned to the Chinese government in 1997.

Hoover's Sin City

For all its modern debauchery and notorious reputation, Las Vegas, Nevada, was left out of the Wild West completely. Billy the Kid, the O.K. Corral, the Lincoln County War, Wyatt Earp: They were all elsewhere. When a small fort finally sprang up in Vegas, it was abandoned. The Mormons moved in for a while…and then left. For over a century Las Vegas remained a dusty outpost, a stop on a route to a better place. Even right up to 1930, as Americans flooded west, Las Vegas only managed to attract a couple thousand residents.

That all changed with a river and one of the most ambitious engineering projects in US history: the Hoover Dam. At the start of the 1930s, with the country in the throes of the Great Depression, new forms of employment were desperately needed. The United States, recently electrified, was also starting to demand electricity. The Colorado River could provide both. Desperate to do something to help get the nation on the right track, President Herbert Hoover agreed to the construction of a massive damn across the river's Black Canyon.

As soon as construction started, Las Vegas ballooned four-fold in population with tens of thousands of down-on-their-luck, unattached men wandering into the dusty outpost, hoping for work at the dam. Now, where there are tens of thousands of single men, there are needs. By 1931, with the dam still five years from completion, the first gambling license had been issued to the Northern Club (the current site of La Bayou Casino) and later that year The New Frontier Hotel and Casino broke ground on what would eventually become the world-famous Las Vegas Strip. All thanks to a president's dam.

THE ORIGINAL SIN CITY

In the 1850s, when Las Vegas was still a dusty outpost, it was New York City that owned the title City of Sin. On the island of Manhattan alone, there were hundreds of saloons, opium parlors, and gambling halls, and over 30,000 prostitutes working at any given time, one for every sixty-six people living in the city.

Cocaine City

"I'm a decent man who exports flowers."
—*Pablo Escobar*

Yes, and Miami was built with sweat, orange juice, and honest hard work. In the 1960s, Miami was about as far from its current incarnation as a glamorous metropolis as it could have been. The city of just 250,000 people was sleepy and quiet, with a shadow of a downtown, citrus groves throughout the suburbs, and family-friendly resorts dotting the beaches. All that was going to change thanks to a white powder from South America.

The Florida peninsula, the continental United States' southernmost point, juts into the Atlantic and Caribbean like one large, inviting landing strip. And during the 1970s and 1980s, that was exactly how it was used. In the early 1970s, cocaine, previously a scarce drug in the United States, began to trickle in from South America. Then, in 1975, an enterprising gangster named Pablo Escobar took control of the cocaine trade in Medellín, Colombia, and the spigots into the United States opened.

Escobar picked Miami as the top destination for his drug shipments. The wide-open seaports, rural suburbs, and proximity to the Caribbean Islands and South and Central America made it the easiest place to bring drugs into the country. The shipments, which soon topped out around half a billion dollars each day, required a brand-new cottage industry in America. Thousands of people were employed to transport, store, and move the cocaine from Miami to the rest of the country. The industry generated billions of untaxed, dirty dollars that needed to be spent somewhere. What better place than a tropical paradise?

Before the Federal Government had fully wised to the extent of the cocaine trade, the entire economy of the city of Miami was skyrocketing thanks to it. The previously subdued downtown grew upward with dozens of skyscrapers financed in cash. High-end stores moved into previously vacant lots all over the city. And within twenty years, Miami had nearly doubled in size.

Today, the city's sordid past has largely been forgotten. Instead, its glittering downtown, glamorous beach resorts, and seaside boutiques have turned Miami into one of the nation's top tourist destinations. But it was all made possible by a little criminal ingenuity and a whole lot of coke.

The Brief Life of Pablo Escobar

Pablo Escobar's life is a rags-to-riches story, where the riches are billions of dollar bills, each of which contains trace amounts of cocaine.

As a young boy, Pablo Escobar set himself the lofty goal of becoming a millionaire before his twenty-second birthday. He started by trying every criminal enterprise he could, dabbling in selling fake lotto tickets and stolen cigarettes, auto theft, and kidnapping. Eventually Escobar landed on one lucrative business: drug trafficking.

With a single plane, Escobar began transporting cocaine through Panama and into the United States. By the 1980s, Escobar was the king of cocaine, controlling an estimated 80 percent of the world's entire freaking market. Daily flights were moving an astounding estimated 15 tons of coke across the US border, earning Escobar a net worth between three and thirty billion dollars. Based on those figures alone, if he were alive today, he would be the seventh richest person in the world.

Escobar's drug-fueled rise to the top was short-lived. In 1991 he was arrested and imprisoned in a Colombian jail called La Catedral, widely referred to as Hotel Escobar. Like all good criminals with an eye on the future, Escobar had helped design the prison himself. Hotel Escobar was less of a prison and more of a, well, hotel; it was equipped with a soccer field, a bar, a Jacuzzi, a decorative waterfall, and, for some reason, an oversized dollhouse.

How the Fall of a Kingdom Gave Birth to the Mafia

Sicily has always been a troubled island. It's wracked with oppressive heat blowing off of Africa and it has volcanoes, tsunamis, and earthquakes. But more than anything, its strategic position, smack dab in the middle of the most fought-over sea, has gotten it nothing but trouble, politically. In little more than 2,700 years since the Greeks first founded the southern city of Syracuse, the island of Sicily has changed hands to no fewer than eight foreign powers, ranging from the Romans, Vandals, and Arabs to the Normans, Swabians, and Spanish.

So it was no wonder that, when Italy finally annexed the island kingdom in 1860, they found that the Sicilian citizens wanted very little to do with their brand new stable government. And no sooner had the yoke of feudalism been thrown off than the first taste of the mafia had begun. After the dissolution of the feudal kingdom, with little government protection from mainland Italy and virtually no police, scores of desperate peasants had turned to petty banditry to survive and were swarming through the farms of western Sicily.

For the farm owners, the *mafiosi*, a butchering of the Arabic word for "bravado," was the answer. The newly minted landowners, most of them former peasants, began hiring whatever able-bodied men they could, many of them former thieves and violent bandits themselves, to protect their valuable citrus orchards from outside criminals. Now, if it sounds like a potentially bad idea to have criminals hired to go after criminals, it was. More often than not, the newly formed patrols began colluding with the thieves on the other side and before long each town's independent militia had become its own little crime organization.

By the waning years of the 1800s, the Mafia was fully entrenched in Sicily. The small village bands had coalesced into larger crime syndicates. Eight separate clans (*cosche*) operated in the suburbs around Palermo alone. They bought politicians, planned kidnappings, forged money, and murdered witnesses. Elaborate initiation ceremonies created lifelong members in what they called *cosa nostra* ("our thing"). And in return for a lifelong commitment, any member sent to jail had both his family and his legal fees taken care of.

GANGSTER WITH A HEART OF GOLD

Alphonse Gabriel Capone, America's most famous mobster, amassed an incredible $100 million fortune (worth over $1 billion today) from bootlegging liquor during Prohibition. Capone was vilified for his powerful criminal organization as well as his excessive acts of violence like the Saint Valentine's Day Massacre. Yet Capone always stayed true to his Sicilian Mafia roots; like the earliest members of the Mafia, he made sure he took care of his own. As his gang's prominence grew, Capone paid for daily milk to be delivered to Chicago's schoolchildren and opened soup kitchens to help combat the pain of the Depression among the area's Italian immigrants.

AWESOME ADVENTURES
THAT WERE PROBABLY
A TERRIBLE IDEA

Neil Armstrong's Life Insurance

On July 16, 1969, Apollo 11 lifted off from the Kennedy Space Center in Florida and headed toward the moon. Four days later, after traveling 238,900 miles, Neil Armstrong, Buzz Aldrin, and Michael Collins touched down on the lunar surface. The grainy black-and-white shots beamed back to the rest of us earthlings were amazing. But while America celebrated a great triumph, all of NASA was secretly holding their breath. That's because voyaging to the moon during the 1960s was about the most dangerous thing you could do.

Before the Apollo 11 moon landing, NASA had sent kamikaze crafts to practice. Each one of the Ranger spacecrafts crashed spectacularly into the surface of the moon while relaying thousands of images of the lunar surface back to Earth. The first mission, Ranger 4, just seven years before Armstrong's first steps, managed to send back a whopping zero images before its demise. Considering the plan was to land a man on the moon within the decade, things were not off to a good start.

If that wasn't enough to make the astronauts nervous, there was more. When the healthy, athletic thirty-eight-year-old

Neil Armstrong tried to acquire life insurance before his flight, the estimated annual dues came in at roughly three times his yearly salary. Not one to give up on mankind, Armstrong and the rest of the crew took matters into their own hands and went about ensuring their families' future comfort by signing hundreds of photographs that were to be sold should Apollo 11's voyage turn into a one-way trip.

The Accidental Invention of the Road Trip

In 1903, fifty-three long years before the Interstate Highway System was even conceived, Horatio Nelson Jackson invented the cross-country road trip. On a stopover in San Francisco, California, Jackson was talked into a $50 bet that said ain't nobody could drive an automobile from the Pacific Ocean to the Atlantic. Despite being a crappy driver, Jackson took the bet, bought himself a brand new (whopping) twenty-horse-power Winton, enlisted a twenty-two-year-old mechanic as a driving partner, and set out to drive across the continent.

Understandably, things went terribly. In 1903 the western United States was still, well, the Wild West. Most dusty towns they passed had never seen a paved road, let alone an *auto-mo-bile*. At times, the Winton, which Jackson named the *Vermont*, broke down every few miles, blowing tires like they were party balloons. Finally, sixty-three days after leaving San Francisco, the *Vermont* sputtered into New York City, becoming the first automobile to drive from sea to shining sea. As for the $50 bet, Jackson never managed to collect it.

From Cape Town to Cairo, All for a Fine Piece of Tail

How far will a man go for a fine woman? In 1898, British adventurer Ewart Grogan took the question literally and answered: 6,000 miles. In an effort to convince his crush's wealthy stepfather that he was worthy of his stepdaughter's hand in marriage, Grogan walked nearly 6,000 miles from Cape Town, South Africa, to Cairo, Egypt. During the trek he was stalked by lions and headhunters and had a number of his party die from malaria. But, by the time he arrived in Cairo, he'd managed to win the woman's hand and became a folk hero for being the first European to walk the length of the African Continent.

How Smallpox Misplaced a City

When the first Spanish and Portuguese explorers arrived in South America and ventured into the dense jungles of the Amazon, they came across the incredible ruins of an abandoned city. They took detailed notes about grand archways, planned-out city streets, and neatly rowed gardens. The only thing they couldn't record, in the middle of the vast forest, was the location of the mysterious city. And for the next 175 years, men tried in vain to find it.

One of those men was Percy Fawcett. In 1925 the former British officer and experienced adventurer was fifty-seven years old. He had fought in the trenches of WWI, climbed mountains, and led some of the most extraordinary expeditions of discovery through Peru and the most remote sections of the Brazilian Amazon, disappearing into the forbidding jungle only to return years later, healthy, unscathed, and leading his brutally depleted parties.

But despite his lifetime of success and bravery, one thing consumed Fawcett: what he called the Lost City of Z. It was those first reports from the Conquistador explorers that gripped his interest. The idea that there was once a thriving city somewhere in the richest, most uninhabitable jungle on earth was enough to drive him mad.

And so, on April 20, 1925, Fawcett led his small expedition party, including his own son, into the heart of the Amazon rainforest near the Xingu River and only a couple dozen miles from the most remote place on earth.

Neither he nor anyone from his party was ever heard from again.

Most people assumed he had been killed by the uncontacted tribes of the upper Xingu River. Others thought he had simply been lost in the jungle.

What's incredible is that not only were the original stories of the "lost city" true, but that Fawcett was possibly standing on top of it as he made his way up the Xingu. In 2008, an anthropologist from the University of Florida uncovered a massive settlement covering nearly 8,000 square miles at the headwaters of the Xingu River. The area was once home to as many as 50,000 inhabitants living in twenty-eight separate "towns," each with an enormous wooden plaza at the center. From the town plazas, long, maintained roads stretched out, some lined with carved canals for trade via canoe.

For more than a thousand years, the people of this vast Amazonian civilization flourished. But when the first Europeans landed in South America, the diseases they brought with them, like smallpox, traveled faster than they could. Frightened, diseased citizens wandered from town to town in search of help and the illnesses spread throughout the entire Amazon so quickly that, by the time the Spanish caught up with the diseases they'd brought, there was nobody left.

Unfortunately for Percy Fawcett and the explorers that followed him into the Amazon in the decades to come, there was no physical city packed with riches to find. The inhabitants of the so-called lost city built their thriving metropolis with wood instead of stone. By the time Fawcett reached the Xingu, the voracious jungle had swallowed up every last sign of its former inhabitants. All that was left were subtle outlines of the city in the landscape and a rich history of culture buried just beneath the soil.

FIVE SUPERHUMAN POWERS NOW WITHIN YOUR GRASP

We thought we would end *The MANual* with a brief look toward the future. Here are a few exciting innovations that may one day revolutionize your life.

Mr. Insomniac

For centuries, common man has been encumbered by one crippling, time-sucking daily need: sleep. And countless souls have strived to limit its incessant necessity. Thomas Edison, Winston Churchill, and Nikola Tesla all lived by a polyphasic sleep schedule that broke daily sleeping into two or more brief catnaps, adding up to a total of about three hours of sleep per day.

Finally, all that sleep scheduling became obsolete at the dawn of the twenty-first century with a magical drug called Modafinil. Originally designed to keep narcoleptics from randomly falling asleep mid-sentence, the true genius of the drug was soon brought to light (by who other than the US military?). On Modafinil, you can stay awake forever. And unlike with caffeine, cocaine, or methamphetamines, the wakefulness you feel on this magical pill is as steady and normal as though you just woke up.

Of course, what's a superpower without a crippling side effect? Modafinil's Kryptonite turns out to be its tendency to cause toxic epidermal necrolysis, a disorder in which the top layer of your skin sheds off like a snake's. Except, instead of emerging from your layer of dead, old skin even more awesome and powerful, in the case of Modafinil, you just have a very good chance of giving in to that proverbial eternal sleep.

The Incredible Ant

For decades scientists have pursued a miracle: building an Iron Man–like mechanical exoskeleton suit that would allow people with crippling disabilities like paralysis to walk again. And for decades it seemed a pipe dream of the future.

Welcome to the future. Well, almost. As quickly as the human race adopted smartphones, we may also soon be using helpful exoskeletons in our day-to-day lives. Beyond full-body contraptions to give the disabled the power to walk again, the US military's current project is called the Human Universal Load

Carrier (HULC). A lightweight support system that attaches to the legs, feet, and back, the hydraulic system would help soldiers in the field carry packs up to 200 pounds for hours with the same effort they'd use to carry a fanny pack.

The suit technology has advanced so quickly that components that weighed hundreds of pounds less than a decade ago now come in at a total of just 30 pounds. The only huge hurdle still facing the quest to become a real life Iron Man is, of course, energy. Using a full-body exoskeleton to move hundreds of pounds of gear takes a lot of power and so far there haven't been small batteries capable of the task. One early prototype even failed because it had to be plugged into the wall to be used.

Okay, so maybe this technology is a little less like an Iron Man suit and more like a giant ant suit, but we're definitely getting there.

Spidey Hands

Ever dream about effortlessly scaling the Empire State Building to save a dangling damsel in distress à la Peter Parker?

EDISON V. TESLA

Thomas Edison and his one-time-mentee-turned-nemesis, Nikola Tesla, had an ongoing feud over who could sleep less. Tesla often made fun of Edison for being excessively lazy for dozing more than four hours a day.

Well, hold onto your Spiderman action figure. What if we were to tell you that today you could do just that...only very slowly and while making a lot of noise?

Engineering students from Utah State University accepted a challenge posed by the US Army to create a device that could get four Special Forces soldiers over the wall of a building without the use of grappling hooks. Their solution was a set of vacuum-powered suction cups that can scale just about any building surface. The only problem? The suit literally had two vacuum cleaners attached to the back, making a covert operation possible only if you were assaulting a building filled with working janitors.

It's a Bird, It's a Plane, It's a...Man-Plane Hybrid

Jetpacks have been around since WWII (the Nazis built one called the *Himmelstürmer*, or "sky stormer") and since the day the first one was tested they have pretty much always sucked.

The main problem with the jetpack is that it requires a phenomenal amount of energy (usually highly flammable fuel mounted on your ass) to produce an extremely hard-to-control flight. You really might as well light yourself on fire and jump off a building.

But like so many technological black sheep, this too has its golden sibling: the jet-powered wing suit. This particular best-invention-ever combines a pair of small, kerosene-fueled jet engines with a pair of manageably sized carbon fiber wings worn on the back like the coolest JanSport backpack in the schoolyard. And man, can the sucker fly (well, actually more like fall slowly).

Pilot Yves "Jetman" Rossy has proven the incredible maneuverability of the jet-powered wing suit. He has successfully crossed the Strait of Gibraltar and the English Channel and flown through the Grand Canyon. The suit he uses doesn't have any steering controls, so he drops his shoulders to initiate dives, raises his head to climb, and uses his hands and feet to roll and yaw. Oh, and he can reach a top speed of 190 mph. Unfortunately, you can't just say, "up, up, and away," and launch off the ground; you still need to jump out of an airplane to begin the flight.

Naturally, the wing suit has not gone unnoticed by the military. Germany is developing the Gryphon Glider, a (currently unpowered) six-foot carbon-fiber wing worn by Special Forces paratroopers. With the Gryphon, paratroopers can safely jump out of a transport plane at 30,000 feet in friendly territory and then glide at 130 miles per hour, penetrating enemy lines by up to 120 miles and completely undetected by radar.

Spidergoat Armor

Pound for pound, spider silk is the strongest material in the natural world. Even the smallest spiders can spin webs to catch insects 100 times their size. Some spiders even routinely feed on bats and birds that get caught in their elastic webs. But recently scientists have discovered that the Darwin's bark spider is capable of spinning a web so strong that, when woven together into a lightweight, flexible armor, it would be ten times stronger than Kevlar.

The only issue? When was the last time you heard of a spider farm? Unlike silkworms, arachnids are notoriously difficult to farm, so scientists are attempting to think outside the web…by transferring the spider's silk-producing gene to a universally known domesticated animal: goats. It sounds like something out of a bad science fiction story, but, if successful, newly engineered spidergoats could begin producing super-strong body armor from their udders.

Appendix

SELECTED BIBLIOGRAPHY

Ash, Russell. *Discovering Highwaymen*. New York: Shire, 2011.

Bowden, Mark. *Killing Pablo: The Hunt for the World's Greatest Outlaw*. New York: Grove Atlantic, 2001.

Craughwell, Thomas J. *The Rise and Fall of the Second Largest Empire in History: How Genghis Khan's Mongols Almost Conquered the World*. Beverly, MA: Fair Winds, 2010.

Daniels, Jared. *How to Cook Steak: The 5-Step Formula for the Perfect Steak*. Amazon Kindle.

Diamond, Jared M. *Guns, Germs and Steel: The Fates of Human Societies*. New York: Norton, 1999.

Gorn, Elliott J. *The Manly Art: Bare-Knuckle Prize Fighting in America*. Ithaca, NY: Cornell University, 1951.

Grann, David. *The Lost City of Z: A Tale of Deadly Obsession in the Amazon*. New York: Double Day, 2005.

Hays, J.N. *Epidemics and Pandemics: Their Impacts on Human History*. Santa Barbara, CA: ABC-CLIO, 2005.

Henderson, Charles. *Marine Sniper: 93 Confirmed Kills*. New York: Penguin, 1986.

Heyerdahl, Thor. *Kon-Tiki: Across the Pacific in a Raft*. New York: Simon & Schuster, 1950.

Lendler, Ian. *Alcoholica Esoterica: A Collection of Useful and Useless Information As It Relates to the History and Consumption of All Manner of Booze*. New York: Penguin, 2005.

Martin, Paul S. and Richard G. Klein. *Quaternary Extinctions: A Prehistoric Revolution*. Tucson, AZ: University of Arizona, 1989.

Musashi, Miyamoto and Kenji Tokitsu. *The Complete Book of Five Rings*. Boston: Shambhala, 2000.

Philbrick, Nathaniel. *In the Heart of the Sea: The Tragedy of the Whaleship Essex*. New York: Penguin, 2000.

Protz, Richard. *The Complete Guide to World Beer*. London, U.K.: Carlton, 2004.

Standage, Tom. *A History of the World in 6 Glasses*. New York: Walker, 2005.

Strauss, Darin. *Chang and Eng*. New York: Plume, 2001.

Zacks, Richard. *Island of Vice: Theodore Roosevelt's Quest to Clean Up Sin-Loving New York*. New York: First Anchor, 2012.

IMAGE CREDITS

All images sourced from shutterstock.com

Introduction
man with rifle © Antonio Abrigiani

Blood, Sweat, and Tyranny
Roman warrior © Antonio Abrigiani
Bear hunting © Antonio Abrigiani
Sniper rifle © igorlale
Samurai © Antonio Abrigiani
Seppuku © Antonio Abrigiani
Grenade © SS1001
World map © Volina
Nuke symbol © gigibgm

Meat
Moose © Hein Nouwens
Mammoth © Denis Barbulat
Snake head © Morphart Creation
Parts of a cow © Morphart Creation
Steak logo © Squarelogo
Parts of a pig © Antonio Abrigiani
Parts of a chicken © Antonio Abrigiani

Drinking with Hemingway
Bourbon bottle © RetroClipArt

Map of beer © Aleksandar Mijatovic
Cigar © AKaiser

Boxing

Boxing © Antonio Abrigiani

Your Body Is Your Temple of Doom

Skull © Anteromite
Tapeworm © Morphart Creation
Scabies © Morphart Creation
Wolfman © Antonio Abrigiani

The Sea

Squid and whale © Pika
Parts of a boat © Aleksei Makarov
Raft © Antonio Abrigiani
Canoe © Nicku
Kayak © Denis Barbulat
Galley © Antonio Abrigiani
Viking ship © Denis Barbulat
Clipper ship © Regien Paassen
Steamboat © Hein Nouwens
Submarine © Tshooter
Polynesia triangle © Stasys Eidiejus
Tuna © Morphart Creation
Haddock © Hein Nouwens
Ika © Pika
Fugu © Pio3
Unagi © Hein Nouwens
Saba © Morphart Creation

Sake © Morphart Creation
Tobiko © Hein Nouwens
Tako © Morphart Creation
Uni © Hein Nouwens

Masculaneous

Masked man © Antonio Abrigiani
Opium den © Antonio Abrigiani
Map of Sicily © Antonio Abrigiani
Bat man © Hein Nouwens

Appendix

Original photo of authors © Margo Harrison
  Skull on wall © Corepics VOF
  Dinosaur © Linda Bucklin
  Plaque behind dinoasur © RaidenV
  Ram head © Joppo
  Background edge © Euroshot

ABOUT THE AUTHORS

Keith Riegert lives in Brooklyn, New York.

Sam Kaplan resides in Oakland, California.

Each man enjoys a fine glass of whiskey and the company of an intelligent woman.